OUT OF
TOUCH

MICHAEL SARAIS

CLOUDY DAY
PUBLISHING

OUT OF
TOUCH

MICHAEL SARAIS

A CIP catalogue record for this book is available from the British Library

ISBN: 978-1-8380160-7-4 (Hard Cover)

ISBN: 978-1-8380160-5-0 (Paperback)

ISBN: 978-1-8380160-6-7 (E-book)

Cover Artwork by Hidayatul Azmi

michaelsarais.com

CLOUDY DAY
PUBLISHING

To Jack. A real-life superhero with a heart of gold.
And to Amy Jane. A brilliant mind and a wonderful friend.

PART ONE

2008-2009

CHAPTER ONE

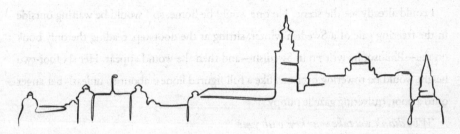

VINCENT

2008

'**V**incent? VINCENT?'

The bloody teacher's voice was still echoing in my head. I couldn't believe I fell asleep in the middle of a philosophy lecture. Well, I couldn't believe I fell asleep in class. Philosophy, though? That was soporific on the best of days. The days that weren't so damn dusky so early in the afternoon. My mind was not yet accustomed to the veil of darkness that enveloped the country in the middle of the day. I couldn't quite cope with seeing the sun rising and setting just by looking out the window. Not that a December in the UK would be particularly luminous, but Stockholm was truly remarkable at condensing daylight and displaying it for a few short hours.

I was down to the last five steps before the main door to the house. It was a quaint, wooden, burgundy cottage-style home with white accents. A normal person would have walked at a steadier pace, rushing home to take their shoes off, lie on the heated bathroom floor, while staring at the ceiling and contemplating life choices. Instead, I was standing immobile in front of the main door, my poor old Converse soaked from the snow.

Hi, pneumonia.

I checked the time. Half past three in the afternoon. Good, excellent even. I calculated that would give me a solid hour and a half—two, with traffic—to just exist, without the constant disappointed look my host mother would give me at any given time. I tapped every single pocket of my jeans, my puffer jacket, and even the tiny one on my flannel shirt, but it was pretty obvious I didn't have the house keys on me.

Fuck.

I could already see the scene. No one would be home, so I would be waiting outside in the freezing gale of a Swedish winter, sitting at the doorstep, reading the only book on me—Philosophy written in Swedish—and then she would appear. Her six-foot-two height would be towering over me, like a full-figured lioness about to unleash her anger onto a poor, quivering gazelle puppy.

'Why didn't you take your keys with you?'

'Why are you so ditzy?'

'Why haven't you made any Swedish friends yet?'

'Why is your hair like that?'

'Why do you wear those clothes?'

And my personal favourite,

'Why don't you spend your time doing something useful, instead of hanging out with those exchange student friends of yours?'

I sighed, resigned to my inevitable fate when a passing thought hit me like a single bolt of lightning.

The spare key. The spare key was hidden outside, under a frog-shaped stone sculpture. It was put there by my host father because his daughter would lose her keys on a daily basis. But she was fine. She didn't get the level of bollocking I would receive, because I was the "stranger in their house"; the evil, brown-haired English monster leeching off them for food and shelter, always a source of disappointment and never—ever— being able to measure up to the *wonderful* Oscar, the gorgeous, perfect-in-every-way Brazilian exchange student they had the year before.

Well, fuck them. I had found the key to open the back door and I would finally be able to take my shoes off and bolt upstairs as quickly as possible, to hide in my room and listen to Paramore until my ears would bleed.

I opened the back door of the house and entered the laundry room. The dryer was on, which made the room nice and toasty. I took my wet shoes off, placed them exactly where *she* wanted. Not one centimetre off, or my head would roll. I took my coat off and leaned against the dryer for a few seconds, trying to get my body temperature to steer away from frozen corpse as much as I could.

The dryer was on.

Oh no, no, no, no, no.

'Amanda, *är du hem?*' Ingrid shouted from the other side of the house.

Well, fuck. Goodbye, time with myself. Goodbye doing the moonwalk across the corridor out of sheer happiness of being alone without the host mother.

I took a deep breath, told that churning feeling in my stomach to shut the hell up, stretched my arms as if I were about to enter a match of arm wrestling with the evil, giant witch with short platinum hair. Kind of like Ursula from *The Little Mermaid*. I really should have known I was living with a Disney villain. That was her giveaway.

I didn't say anything. I didn't want her to go "ah" in disappointment, after finding out I was the one home. I walked as quietly as I could, trying my best not to be spotted and shot on sight, and as soon as I left the laundry room, I could hear her speaking to my host dad, Jonas.

Truth be told, my Swedish wasn't that great. I had only been in the country for three months and, well, it would have taken longer than that to learn a spanking new language I'd only heard in a *Catherine Tate* sketch. But I could pick up a few things if people didn't speak too quickly.

I wish I didn't though. Ingrid, the sea monster, was going on a tirade, expressing in detail, the many, many ways I had managed to disappoint her throughout my stay there.

'He doesn't clean often enough.'

'He should get a haircut.'

'He should stop hanging out with those other exchange students.'

'He should stop speaking English and finally speak Swedish.'

'He should stop spending so much time in his room and do something useful.'

She was probably also about to mention how I was the anti-Christ, but I thought that was my cue to walk in.

'I'm home!' I sang, popping my head into the living room.

'Hey Vincent,' said Jonas, with a big smile.

Unlike the rest of the clan, Jonas Lindberg was an absolute pleasure to be around. He always told the best stories and he often seemed genuinely interested in knowing how my life was going. He had bright blue eyes—like the rest of the family—greying brown hair and would usually be seen wearing denim dungarees around the house.

My host mother stared into my soul, as if my rosy cheeks from the cold outside also pissed her off.

'How was your day?' I asked, with glee.

'Good,' she said. 'Are we still not ready to switch to Swedish yet?'

I was incredibly conscious of speaking it in front of her—or anyone—but especially her. I wasn't going to mispronounce words for her entertainment. If we spoke English, I would have the upper hand.

'You're home from work early,' I said, stating the goddamn obvious.

'Yes, I took the afternoon off. How was school?' she asked.

Could I tempt fate with an honest answer? Or was I going to pretend I loved spending dark afternoons surrounded by dusty old books and weird theories about the origin of the human mind?

'It was alright,' I said with caution.

'Did you make any Swedish friends yet?'

Ugh.

'I haven't been asked such a question since primary school,' I said with a shy smile.

'Well, you know, it's part of integrating into Swedish life. And it would also help you with the language, if that is something you faintly care about.'

'I think they all like speaking English a little bit too much.'

'Then you should tell them not to. Otherwise, you're just wasting precious time.'

I continued to look at her and kept smiling. I wanted to roll my eyes, but I couldn't escape her direct eye contact. I could only nod and hope she'd pick a different victim.

They were sitting around the coffee table, having tea and some form of dark bread slices with liver pâté. Jonas was reading his paper, while she was just preparing her laser eyes to incinerate me.

'How was *filosofi*, Vincent?' she asked. She was obviously not done grilling me yet.

'Oh, yes!' Jonas exclaimed. 'Is that going well?'

'Uhm, actually...'

'What is it?' she asked, sensing my unease.

'...I have been considering dropping it.'

Her eyes squinted. Confused, or perhaps she was just exhilarated at the idea that she now had something she could use to insult me and my "work ethic".

'I have to say, when I first signed up, I thought it was going to be about understanding people's emotions and why they do certain things. I can't say I have a deep interest learning about the ins-and-outs of the origins of the world, told through the eyes of ancient old white men spouting what really sounds like nonsense.'

Boy, was that forward of me. May my memory be a blessing. Tell my real mother I loved her.

'But it would still be useful for you to learn about it,' she insisted.

'I mean...' I stuttered, trying to avoid her deadly stare. '...Not really.'

'What do you mean? I thought you wanted to be a part of that world. That's what you said in your application. You want to make films; you want to shoot documentaries about people.'

'I just...don't think it's all that relevant. And it's a facultative subject, so I can easily drop it without much trouble.'

Jonas was silent. His cheeks were filled with food, completely devoid of willingness to take part in such trite conflict.

'...and what would you be doing instead?' she asked.

'I am not sure. I could do with the extra time off in the afternoon.'

'To go out with those "English" friends of yours?'

I didn't need to engage. I didn't need to start something. I just needed to let her know that I ultimately decided what I liked and what I didn't like doing. Fuck her judgemental diatribe. She could save that for her own child.

'I just thought I could either spend more time with my camera—and sunlight—or read more, possibly Swedish books, even. Finesse the language, potentially.'

'I told you weeks ago to go register at the library. Did you do it?'

'Not yet.'

'Well, that would have been a good start. I can't say I'm confident I'll be seeing you back and forth with books. I think it's a terrible idea to leave the class.'

I took a deep breath, trying to find my mental happy place. My left fist was clenching. I would have loved to shy away from a squabble, but I had to mark my territory.

'I have thought about it for quite some time. I gave it a fair chance, I reckon.'

'I can't force you, of course,' she said. '...I just didn't think you'd be such a quitter.'

Ooh. Tell me how you really feel now, would you Ingrid?

'My mother taught me to concentrate on things I actually enjoy doing. That's been my *philosophy* growing up.'

See what I did there?

'Has that helped? Have you ever finished a project?' she asked, looking at me squinting her eyes and curling her lips in what I could only assume was literal disgust.

'The ones that mattered.'

'Look,' she said, while putting down her cutlery. 'You have a very limited amount of time in this country. You can do what you always do, or you could do something outside your comfort zone and learn something new. It's completely up to you.'

'I will find something,' I stated firmly.

'Here is hoping!' she said, dismissively.

Choke on that.

'Okay,' Jonas intervened. 'Vincent, why don't you go take a warm shower? You must be freezing! We'll be having meatballs for dinner,' he said, in his adorable Scandinavian accent.

'Yes, I should go,' I said.

'And please, give that bathroom a clean,' she added. 'I shouldn't have to chase you to do it every time.'

'Yes ma'am,' I said while grinding my teeth and squashing my better judgment to stick a fork into her neck. 'Actually, there's something I left at school.'

'Of course you did,' she said, twirling her moustache and petting the crow sitting on her shoulder.

'I'll be back soon,' I announced, heading straight back out, trying my hardest not to scream while still being in the house.

I put my jacket and my gross shoes back on and ran outside.

The cold hit me like a cricket bat to the face.

I needed time away. I needed some quiet time to myself, where no one would harass me, or judge me for not measuring up to their ever-changing expectations.

The house stood at the top of a hilly road, which had become more of a nuisance with every passing day. The ice I'd encounter in the early mornings was surely going to become my demise at some point. A good old banana peel slip gag and I'd be falling onto my head with my feet in the air and a severe concussion.

I lived on *Lidingö*—a small island just outside Stockholm—which was very leafy and residential. Some of the richest people and celebrities lived there. Mainly because it was so bloody quiet, yet only half an hour away from the city centre. I walked—slipped—down the hill and took a right turn. Fresh snow was on the ground, so every step left a footprint. I knew where I wanted to go, somewhere I could find a moment of reprieve to myself.

Just ten minutes later, I went past a little harbour with numerous little boats belonging to people living in the area. The moon was already shining into the water, and the silence made the place feel like it was only available to me.

A couple of minutes later, my eyes were graced with a lovely scene. A tiny sandy beach with pine trees all around it. The waves were lightly crashing into the cold sand. I found a rock overlooking the water and I sat there, staring at the horizon in front of me.

I had a tiny urge to give into my emotions and let it all flow. No one would hear me. No one *could* hear me. It was just me and this magical place which embodied every reason why I decided to do this exchange program. I wanted to breathe the clean fresh air, to be surrounded by the most beautiful landscapes and to feel the freedom of being away from the home I grew up in.

So I didn't get sad. I decided to focus on being happy.

I rummaged through my backpack and pulled out my video camera. A gift from my friend Claire back home. She had taught me everything she knew about cinematography. We used to film around Bath, trying new techniques. Now I was alone, feeling homesick and stuck in a new life that felt so foreign at times.

I turned the camera on, opened the display and checked the footage I had taken so far. It was me going through the motions at Heathrow airport, saying goodbye to friends and family I wouldn't see for a year, flying to another country for the first time, and my arrival to the camp, where all exchange students gathered at during their first few days in Sweden.

I turned the volume up and watched myself being someone completely different for the first time in my life. I watched that seventeen-year-old kid being spontaneous and making friends with people in an easy, natural way. I didn't think I had it in me.

'This is, what? Day two of Swedish camp?' my voice narrated, while zooming into the nature and the late-night light sky. 'It's around eleven at night and the sky is awake. All of us are awake. No one warned us we'd need an eye mask.'

'Vincent, what are you doing?' a female voice could be heard in the background of the video.

'This is Hazel. My brand-new friend from New Zealand. Girl has been travelling for twenty-six hours to get here.'

'I'm so flipping jet-lagged.'

'Wait, let me hold the camera,' said another voice, in a thick German accent.

The frame moved to our faces, and we danced stupidly together.

'We have been awake for two days. The three of us will probably fall asleep right before we get to meet our new host families!' I said, extremely excited.

'This is Vincent Stewart,' said Daniel, pointing the camera at me. 'Memorise this face. He's going to become a film director, win all the Oscars and make all the money!'

'As if!' I shouted.

'And because Hazel and I are his best of friends, we shall bask in his bright future, and we will all be rich and living in a mansion together!'

'I don't think I want to live with you two!' said Hazel.

The screen suddenly turned itself off due to low battery, and my eyes were glossy. The footage was from only three months earlier, but I felt further than ever from that happy boy who just couldn't wait to shoot his *Year in the Life* documentary.

My legs were starting to feel frozen. The wind was howling, and little snowflakes started dropping onto my cold, red nose. I put my camera back into my backpack and made my way home, hopefully to an apologetic Ingrid and not round two of her *Let's shit on Vincent* parade.

A little over an hour later, I stood near the dining table, after setting it up for dinner. Jonas was making his specialty, macaroni and meatballs; a horrific concoction designed by Swedish people to pour gasoline all over centuries of perfectly curated Italian cuisine.

'Dinner's ready!' said Jonas, pouring the macaroni into one bowl, while the meatballs were placed into a separate one. 'Is the ketchup on the dinner table?'

Yup. Ketchup.

'I'll grab some,' I said while opening the double-doored fridge. Swedes loved their condiments, and naturally, we would have a whole shelf designated to them.

We sat at the table. I was famished. I had to be very careful about the way I ate, as one time she told me off in front of guests for having bad optimal posture. I somehow had to pretend I was having dinner with the Queen.

We all drenched our macaroni and meatballs with ketchup and dug into this so-called "comfort food". It wasn't bad. It just felt wrong.

I made it my mission not to piss her off in any way, shape or form that evening, but I knew it would be hard to contain an angry tiger.

'Did you find the thing you went back to school for?' Jonas asked, trying to start a conversation.

'Yeah, I did,' I said.

'I received a phone call from Daniel's host mother,' said Ingrid. 'She told me you'll be spending the night over next week?'

'Yes, sorry. I should have mentioned it. It completely slipped my mind.'

'It would also seem we are the only family still speaking English,' she added.

Christ. Let me swallow my balls in peace, woman.

'I'm still not comfortable with the language. I struggle to remember sounds. It's my fault. It's just me trying to cope with it.'

'I just can't see you working hard enough. Is it just me demanding too much from you?'

'Maybe,' I said, snappily.

'You know, you always have the option to change families, if you don't feel like we are on the same page.'

'Ingrid,' Jonas said.

My stomach closed, I felt like everything I had eaten until then was about to come back up.

'I just think—'

'Excuse me,' I said, moving my chair away from the table. 'I just need to use the bathroom real quick.'

I made my way upstairs, passed the bathroom and entered my room. I closed the door behind me and sat against it. I started sobbing and trembling, I put my hands on my face and let out an exasperated cry. But really, my only thoughts were,

Why does she hate me?

Why can't I do anything right?

Why can't I meet her expectations?

WHAT'S WRONG WITH ME.

I took the suitcase out of under my bed and slapped it onto my mattress. I started throwing my clothes in it, one after the other. I didn't care about folding them, I didn't care about doing it properly. I just knew I wanted to be gone. I wanted to leave the house, even if I'd be transferred to another part of Sweden. Even if that meant being away from Hazel and Daniel, even if that meant I'd be forever alone. I was done. Decision made.

And then I thought.

What are you doing?

That's how she wins. Why does she get to send you away?

I wiped the tears off my face and took a deep breath. I needed a few seconds to gather my thoughts. I needed to perhaps talk about it with my friends. I needed advice. I couldn't succumb to the overwhelming desire of getting away from her. I needed to think better. I needed to think about my future.

This is not who I am, I thought.

I couldn't be impulsive. I couldn't make such an important decision without calculating all the pros and cons. I needed to relax and reassess my plans.

I sat down in front of my laptop; silently savoured the pleasant draft wafting in from the slightly cracked window above.

'*How was your day?*' popped up a message in the corner of my screen. It was my sweet mother, instant messaging through MSN. I wanted to describe what had happened, in detail, but it was late, and I didn't want her to worry. She still wasn't used to my absence. A three-hour flight separated us. If I told her my host mother was an angry, wicked sorceress whose mission was to make me miserable daily, she'd ask me to come straight home.

Eyes on the prize, Vincent.

I was about to type a vague answer, when Facebook beeped with a new notification. A friend request.

How I liked those. I thought it would probably be another exchange student, late to the Facebook party, but it wasn't anyone I knew.

"Teddy Clarke," I quietly muttered to myself, wondering if we'd ever crossed paths before.

CHAPTER TWO

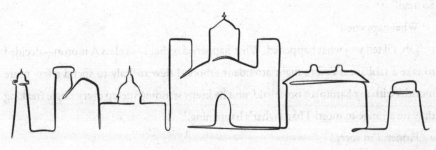

TEDDY

2008

I wanted to scream. I got into my car and slammed the door as hard as I could. I turned on the engine and then the heating on full blast. I dialled his number on my Sidekick for one last time, before I begrudgingly went home. A solid eight rings later, I'd left him a colourful voice message.

'Francesco! This is the third time you've stood me up. I've had it! This time you didn't even bother calling to cancel, which is a fucking travesty. I'm looking forward to an explanation. Have a nice evening, you dipshit.'

I closed my phone and threw it on the passenger's seat. I drove away from the piazza where we were supposed to meet forty-five minutes earlier and made my way home.

I drove around the wet roads of Cagliari, struggling to see ahead. Traffic in Italy was an outrageous beast. When driving around *Tassie*, I'd often been the only car on the road, and it was generally a pleasing experience.

Though even on the greyest of days, Cagliari still felt picturesque. The cobbled roads, the waves crashing into the harbour, the people sitting at bars drinking coffee—it all felt like home to me. I had missed this. This feeling of belonging, the fun bickering with my host sister Laura and, of course, the *carb*-licious food.

I was just about to make a left when my phone started ringing.

'Fucking finally!' I shouted, straight after picking up.

'Jesus, is that how you greet your mother?' she said.

I turned to the phone, confused. 'Mum! Sorry, I thought you were Francesco. I'm mad. So mad!'

'What happened?'

'Oh, I'll tell you what happened. What happened is that I—a class A moron—decided to take a sabbatical before flight attendant school; I flew to Italy to spend a few more months with my Sardinian boyfriend, and he keeps standing me up every single freaking time we arrange to meet! That's what's happening.'

'Honey, I'm sorry.'

'It's my fault, really. I should have forgotten all about him and moved on with my existence. Fuck knows if I'm able to start school later now! What if deferring was a huge mistake?'

'You can't think like that. Sure, Francesco was a big reason for you to go back to Italy, but there are plenty of other lovely people you get to spend extra time with!'

'So, you don't believe I made a mistake?' I asked, calming myself down, slightly.

'I think you should enjoy these few months with your host family. After you do end up becoming a flight attendant, God knows when you'll see them again!'

I sighed. 'I just feel tossed aside, you know?'

'I know, no one likes that, trust me.'

'It's not just that. I had this amazing year-long experience in Italy as an exchange student. I was everyone's favourite Australian gay best friend. I had a wonderful family that considered me as one of their own, an amazing tan, and a hot Italian boyfriend who used to take me around the city on his Vespa, parading me like a trophy boy. And now? I'm the loser who came back to a grey city, where everyone has moved on without me and all I do is cry and pine over a boy who doesn't even have the decency to call me back. God, I'm mad again!' I said, slamming my hands onto the wheel, repeatedly.

'You just have to live these few months as a completely different experience, Teddy. Just live one day at a time. I'm kind of jealous I didn't get a sabbatical before university.'

'What stopped you?' I asked.

'I had your brother!'

'Ah, lovely. Speaking of my idiot brother, have you heard from him recently?' I asked, knowing I hadn't spoken to him in months.

'No, not at all,' she said, sounding hurt.

'Mum, are you okay?'

'I'm just tired. It is like four in the morning here in *Tassie*.'

'You should go to sleep! What are you doing up so late?'

'I have a headache. I've been marking some papers and lost track of time. Besides, I have a doctor's appointment early in the morning.'

'You'd tell me if there was something wrong, right?' I said, slightly worried.

'Of course. It's just...I'm having trouble concentrating. I probably need to take a multivitamin or something. Now go have fun. Have some wonderful Italian pizza with Laura. Don't think about Francesco.'

'I love you, mum. Goodnight.'

'Goodnight, Teddy bear.'

I smiled and drove home. My rage had finally quietened. For a little while, at least.

'I'm hooome!' I sang, while entering the house.

'Teddy, Teddy, Teddy!' Laura shouted, running and sliding across the corridor to meet me.

She was getting ready to go to dance class. Lugging a massive duffle bag across her shoulder, she dropped it heavily to the floor, and a pair of pointe shoes fell out.

'What do you want me to do with this?'

'Excellent question,' she said, tying her dark blond hair into a tight, ballet-like bun. Her big bright green eyes staring at mine, like a child begging for another marshmallow. We often said our matching eye colour made us real siblings, which always made me feel somewhat special. I couldn't imagine a life without my second family.

'Can you—hey. Actually. What are you doing here? I thought you were going to meet up with Francesco?'

I gave her a look, trying to convey just how much I was dead inside and how much I wanted to murder that poor little *coglione*.

'Didn't show up again? Wow. Did he call at least?'

'Nope.'

'I'm sorry,' she said, touching my shoulder. 'But! Does that mean you can drive me to dance class? I'm so late.'

'Sure, why the hell not.'

'Great. Let me put shoes on and then we can go,' she said, flying back into her room.

My room was just next to the living room. I stood outside, by the door, looking at it with sweet nostalgia. It was exactly how I had left it at the end of my exchange year, half a year before. All the photos I took with all my friends were still hanging on the wall. There was even a big Australian flag my host family had gotten me to hang over my wardrobe. Now that I was back, everything felt different, like a lifetime had passed.

'Shall we go?' Laura asked from the corridor.

'Coming.'

We jumped into the car, which was still toasty from my angry trip home earlier, and made our way to dance class, which just so happened to be stupidly close to Francesco's house.

'The fuck is up with this rain?' I asked, squinting my eyes trying to see the road ahead.

'Now you know why I didn't want to walk,' she said, while looking down at her phone.

'This is not the weather I left a few months ago!'

'You're the dumb one for wanting to get back to this hell hole.'

'Gee, thanks. And here I thought you missed me,' I said, poking her side.

'I wanted to come see you. It was your turn to host me and feed me.'

'Oh, you'd love the Australian gourmet experience, coming from Italy.'

I drove for another ten minutes, and finally got to Laura's dance studio. Torrential rain continued to fall over the city, and I longed for those late spring days I would spend at the beach, instead of going to school. Francesco would drive us around the city. I'd hug him tight and trust him to take me to gorgeous, hidden spots. Cagliari wasn't the most gay-friendly place on Earth, but we never cared. We'd kiss in front of horrified families and hold hands. I missed that...I missed having a boyfriend to call mine.

'Is everything okay?' Laura asked, her light green eyes piercing into my soul.

'Why are you asking?'

'Well, you have been stood up once again. I wouldn't want you to feel miserable. I happen to very much enjoy your company. It's nice to have my Aussie brother around again.'

'It gives you cool points with your ballerina gang?'

'Yeah, there's at least five of them who want to have sex with you. Gay and not.'

I smiled. I really enjoyed the attention I got. It was almost like being a local celebrity. If only they could understand me when I opened my mouth, trying to mutter a decent sentence in Italian.

'You could dye your hair a crazy colour, a mid-life crisis platinum.'

'I'm eighteen-years-old, *stronza*.'

'Fine, it's a break-up platinum. I will see you later,' she said while laughing. 'We should have pizza for dinner when I'm finished.'

'What about your diet?'

'I'll have a small one, and you can scoff down a giant one.'

'Yeah, that sounds about right,' I smiled. 'Enjoy your pirouettes.'

'Piss off,' she said while getting out of the car.

'I am so proud of all the phrases I taught you!' I shouted, before she closed the door. I was about to depart, when Laura knocked on the window.

'What's up?' I asked.

'Isn't that Francesco, over there?' she asked, pointing at a guy under an orange umbrella surrounded by a group of four other people.

'It most certainly fucking is,' I said, as I ground my teeth.

'Don't run him over! Jail in this country isn't exactly gay-friendly.'

He ditched our plans to meet friends. Friends that he could have met any other day. Was it steam coming out of my ears or...?

'I'm going to go home and put on a pair of fluffy Christmas socks and then watch *Gossip Girl*, thank you very much,' I declared.

'Have fun!' she shouted, running into the building.

I looked at Francesco in the distance and I nearly ripped the wheel off.

Fuck him.

I came home to an empty house. Laura's parents were on the mainland, visiting relatives in Tuscany. Since I had a few hours to kill before Laura would be finished with her dance class, I popped a cold bottle of prosecco open and took a sip, straight from the bottle.

I went into the study, where we kept a desktop computer. I opened MSN and waited for messages to come through. I missed my Australian friends, but I knew I was so privileged to have another family on the other side of the world, always looking forward to having me stay with them.

I still couldn't shake the disappointment and the slight homicidal rage I felt knowing Francesco was just flat out ignoring me. I checked my phone again. Zero messages from him. It's like I didn't exist anymore. All I wanted to do was to make him feel as insignificant as I was feeling.

I opened Facebook, to see if anyone had "poked me" or sent me dumb stuff, but my main goal was to get myself out there. I needed to flirt with a new, hot boy and stop feeling so expendable. If Francesco wanted nothing to do with me, that was his loss.

I was about to delete him from my friends when something else caught my eye. I couldn't recall Facebook suggesting friends, or "people you may know" before, but it was certainly the first time I had noticed. Mainly because there was a particularly hot guy who was suggested to me.

Vincent Stewart.

Medium length dark brown hair, big grey eyes, plump lips and a cute smile. I couldn't take my eyes off him.

Was this my gift? Did I accidentally pray and have my wish granted?

Of course, it would take a person with zero shame to befriend a complete stranger on the internet. As far as I knew, it could have been a decoy photo of an overweight, seventy-five-year-old bald woman living in Tennessee, but I did it anyways.

What did I have to lose, really?

Friends in common? One. *Amanda Lindberg.*

Amanda. I couldn't quite remember who she was, but I was more than happy to find out who *he* was. I drank a mouthful of bubbles and clicked on "add friend" without much regret. I mainly wanted to see more photos—hopefully a few shirtless ones—but it was not necessary. His giant grey eyes were more than enough for the moment.

Shirtless would be a bonus, though.

Pizza with Laura was a glorious idea. Not only was it delicious, as per usual, but we also finished the prosecco, which made me merry.

After dinner we both went into the study to watch some TV. Laura was such a lightweight, she'd usually fall asleep a few seconds after starting any film. I, however, was in a much better mood. If I were still in Australia, I'd go out with some mates and dance it out, but Cagliari wasn't exactly party central mid-week in December.

'What are you doing?' she asked, lying on the sofa, wrapping herself in a fluffy blanket.

'Will you actually watch a movie?'

'We'll see how long I'll last.'

'Our 85-year-old neighbour, Giuseppina, will probably be up for another four hours. Shame on you.'

'Every muscle in my body hurts. Giuseppina wasn't jumping around in pointe shoes all evening.'

'My Giuseppina can do *everything*. Don't you dare,' I said, giggling.

'Has she seen you yet? I swear she'd have a heart attack if you knocked at her door. She was obsessed with your face!' she said, rolling her eyes.

'What can I say? I'm just a ray of sunshine!' I said, with a big squinty eye smile. Then the image of a beautiful face blasted through my brain. '...speaking of ray of sunshine.'

'What?' she asked.

'I have just added this beautiful guy on Facebook, and he just accepted my request,' I said while raising both my eyebrows.

'A random guy?'

'We have a grand total of *one* friend in common. I say it's enough.'

'Enough for what?'

'Not to be considered a creeper.'

'It's definitely within creeper territory,' she said while tying her wavy hair into a pony-tail.

'You reckon?' I asked, disappointed.

She yawned. 'Will you be speaking to him?'

'I feel like *that*'d be kind of weird.'

'Eh. Isn't that the point of Facebook? Just say hi. I'll be here taking a quick power-nap.' She flipped to the side and closed her eyes. She fell asleep within seconds.

I wished I could do that.

I wasn't sleepy at all. My blood was still boiling from earlier in the day. I checked my phone and noticed there was a single missed call from Francesco and no messages. It was probably a pity call to tell me he had just forgotten we had plans together. *Again.*

Fucker. My hand was shaking so much, I thought I'd pulverise my phone. I put it down, took a deep breath and sought happy thoughts. I sat in front of the desktop computer and held my head with a fist against my cheek. I was tipsy and angry, a bad combo when you're on Facebook, ready to put someone on blast through a relatively "vague" status message.

I was just about to type something when the little chat window opened up.

'Hello.'

Holy shit!

I nearly fell off my chair. Vincent had accepted my stupid photo stalking request and now he said hi to me. I nervously tapped my fingers onto the mouse. I didn't know what to do.

Should I answer?

What if he asks why I added him?

What if he's one of those extremely homophobic straight guys and asks someone to bash me in the street?

I was feeling a little lame for befriending a random guy. Did the whole debacle with Francesco really turn me into a desperate idiot?

Deffo.

But he messaged me first.

'Hi you!' I typed with trepidation.

'Do we know each other?' he sent. No smiley face.

I quickly stalked his photos to see if we even lived in the same country, but that was, sadly, not the case. From what I could gather, he was also an exchange student. He seemed to hang out with a lot of people from IESP—the International Exchange Student Program—the company that had helped us travel around the world and find host families that weren't absolute psychos.

Who the fuck was Amanda Lindberg, though? She was the only connection we had together, and I had zero memories of ever seeing the girl. Her face didn't help either. Her mousy face just looked like any white girl with blonde hair and blue eyes.

Oh.

Of course.

The answer was in front of me. *IESP Campout.*

A couple of times a year during the exchange, all the students would meet at one specific spot to have a campout. It was incredibly fun—mainly because we'd sneak alcohol in—but also because we would get to discuss issues we encountered throughout the year, and no one would understand more than another exchange student.

Amanda came from Sweden and was sent to Tuscany. I didn't get to see many exchange students outside the campout as I didn't live on the mainland.

'Not yet,' I typed. 'My name is Teddy; I was also an IESP exchange student last year.'

'Oh, fun! Where from?'

'Australia. I come from a little town in Tasmania.'

'That's far! Isn't it...tomorrow there already?'

'It would be! I'm actually back in Italy to spend some time with my host family again. I couldn't stay away for long.'

'Couldn't imagine doing the same...'

'You don't get along with yours?'

'It isn't the friendliest, I'd say. I am Vincent, by the way.'

'That rhymed,' I typed, sending a smiley face.

I turned around to check on Laura; she was snoring ever so slightly. Her tolerance for alcohol wasn't particularly great.

I couldn't imagine not getting along with the family. The Marini family had always treated me like their second child. I even called them *mamma* and *papa*, after all.

Vincent stopped replying for a bit. I took the extra time to have a look at his photos. He appeared to love his city very much. Stockholm looked beautiful. Lots of photos with other exchange students. I suppose living in the capital of a country would allow for more fun activities. Most of the photos were taken with two friends. A blue-eyed-curly-haired kid named Daniel, who looked about fifteen, and a pale, tall girl named Hazel. There were no hot Swedish boyfriends in sight.

'Where are you from, by the way?' I asked.

'A small city named Bath, in the UK.'

'I have always wanted to visit England! My host sister and I were thinking of going on a week-end trip at some point, to see London.'

'London is cool. I will probably move there to start uni.'

'So jel.'

'What are your plans after you finish your Italian holiday?' he asked.

'I want to be a flight attendant.'

'You do? That's cool. Travel the world and everything.'

'That's the plan! What does Vincent Stewart want to be when he grows up?'

There was a pause. I saw him typing for a bit, then it stopped. I just stared at the screen giving him a chance to answer, but no response.

'I don't really know,' he wrote. 'Hey, Teddy.'

'Yes?'

'How was going back home, after the end of your program?'

I sighed. I didn't want to lie to him. I was sad, I cried, I was depressed. It wasn't really a fun story. It was brutal. That's why I went back.

'It was tough. I had made a lot of friends here. I really didn't want to go back to the other side of the world, where everything is so damn far. I just wanted to be Italian for a little bit longer.'

'That's what I'm afraid of. Yes, I don't particularly get along with the host mother, but I really enjoy living in Stockholm and doing whatever I want with my friends.'

'You could always change your family if it becomes too unbearable. IESP will take care of it if you ask.'

'It's just...I could get sent anywhere in the country. What if my next host family lives in the Arctic Circle?'

'That's a risk, alright.'

'Maybe I can deal with her. Just for the location alone, it's worth being on the receiving end of her passive-aggressive comments.'

'Haha, give me an example.'

'She told me I looked homeless, just a few days ago. But useless, lazy, complacent, clumsy and entitled are also thrown around like confetti.'

'Jesus.'

'She doesn't like me much. Today was one of those days where her comments were a little more cutting than usual.'

'I'd say!' I said. 'I'm sorry. But you have *me* now! A veteran! I know all the intricacies of being an exchange student. I could be your shoulder to cry on!'

'I'd like that,' he wrote.

I smiled. In a fuzzy and warm kind of fashion. He was cute. Very cute. Fucking distance, man. 'How's the language learning going? I know nothing about Swedish.'

'It's uhm...a process. Everyone speaks English, so it's very easy for me to be lazy and rely on that.'

'You couldn't do that in Italy. But everyone is so lovely. Imagine getting something for free each time you enter any sort of food establishment.'

'Nice!' he typed.

I was about to type a response, when Laura woke up.

'Hey, what are you doing?' she said, with her eyes still half-closed.

'Nothing!' I said, while closing the Facebook window.

'Don't tell me you're doing what I think you're doing,' she said while getting up.

'I'll have you know I am not pining.'

'What *are* you doing then? Let me see,' she said while standing next to me. I opened Vincent's profile photo for her to see.

'Oh yeah,' she said. 'Is that the guy you were talking about earlier?'

'Yeah, lives in fucking Sweden, though,' I said.

'Why are you chatting then?'

'I don't know. He just seems nice, I guess. And I'm lonely! My host sister is narcoleptic.'

'Okay. Well. You know what? I was going to help you flirt, but now I am going to bed and I'm leaving you with your awkwardness,' she said while squeezing my shoulder.

'Thanks for that. *Buonanotte*,' I said.

She gave me a pat on the back and left the study. I opened the Facebook window once again. It was getting late, but I wasn't yet ready to go to bed.

'I had a look at your photos,' he said. 'It looks like you had an amazing time in Italy. Lots of friends, too.'

'I did, yeah. As I said, I was devastated when it was all over.'

'Did you date as well?'

Oh! Someone was being curious. Interesting.

'Some,' I said. 'What about you?'

'Not really...'

'No one cute?'

'Oh no, everyone is super attractive here. I just have trouble connecting with the girls.'

Oh.

'The girls?' I asked.

'Yeah, why?'

'Nothing! I'm sorry? You didn't strike me as a...uhm...straight dude,' I typed.

'Oh! Is that right?'

I wasn't sure what to say. My gaydar had hardly been wrong in the past. Was I just poking the closeted Brit with a stick?

'Yeah, I shouldn't have assumed.'

'So, what were your other impressions, if I may ask?'

I tapped my fingers onto the table and took a second to come out with a sentence that wouldn't make me sound as if I had been salivating onto my keyboard as soon as I saw his bright grey eyes.

'I think you're very aware of how good looking you are, and that this isn't the first time another guy noticed you.'

'That's a fascinating theory, Teddy.'

'Am I wrong?'

'No one really sees me, to be honest.'

'I don't believe that to be true.'

'Does Teddy Clarke really think he knows me better than I do? In the few minutes we got to interact?' he typed. Another smiley face.

'Minutes? I have nothing but time on my hands, Vincent.'

'You're going to prove me wrong, then?'

I liked playing. I liked his banter.

'I think people are blind, if they're not seeing you.'

I took a deep breath and stretched my arms. I knew nothing could happen between us, but at the same time I couldn't stop talking to him.

'Well, aren't you a charmer, Clarke.'

And just like that, I said goodbye to a night of sleep, in favour of getting to know the grey-eyed Disney prince.

Zero regrets.

CHAPTER THREE

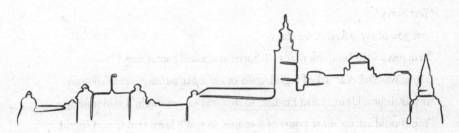

VINCENT
2008

A week had passed since I threw my own pity party in my room, planning to pack my things and tell *Bitchgrid* to get out of my life for good. Since then, my suitcase had made its way back under my bed, I hadn't shed a single tear and I legitimately looked forward to coming home. It wasn't, of course, because she had decided to be nice to me, *au contraire*, she just became more cunning with every passing day.

Her latest critique? I allegedly didn't use cutlery correctly, my posture was wrong, and the one *second* I accidentally had my elbow on the table, I may as well have told her I was a serial killer. But I didn't care. I was eating as quickly as I could, hoping I'd be excused from the table, so I could lock myself in the bedroom and not have to see her stupid, round face. It wasn't looking likely, as the whole family was together.

However, a silver lining. Since Amanda was home, she monopolised the entire dinner time talking about school, her part-time job or whatever after-school bullshit she had going on. She was telling some dreadful customer tale in Swedish, which often sounded like murmur at the end of a long day. And because I was too tired to handle Ingrid's daggers, I didn't bother to participate. As I used my fork to search for bones in the salmon on my plate, I felt Ingrid's eyes on me, as if I were a lunatic for trying to avoid suffocation. But I didn't make eye contact, I just sat there quietly, chomping on my boiled potatoes, and hoping I wasn't next in line for the guillotine.

'How was school, Vincent?' Jonas asked with a smile.

I was still staring at my plate, completely absorbed with my own thoughts.

'Vincent?' Ingrid asked, with a slight raised tone.

'Yes? Sorry.'

'Are you okay?' asked Amanda.

'I am just a little bit tired, that's all. Sorry, you asked something?'

'How. Was. School?' asked Ingrid again *in not a patronising way whatsoever.*

'It was alright. Uhm...I had English, so that was easy enough,' I said smiling.

'You should ask for more hours of Swedish, so you'll learn faster,' said Ingrid.

'...sure, why not.'

She didn't look satisfied. She looked like she wanted to take another dig at me, but she was probably put off by my defeated tone. I was too tired to enjoy the evening sparring.

'Hey,' I said, suddenly. 'Amanda?'

'Yes?' she turned to me.

'Did you know a guy named Teddy during your exchange year?'

'Teddy?'

'Yes. From Australia.'

'It sounds familiar...' she scratched her cheek, trying to think. 'Was he a little...?'

'...what?'

'...gay?'

'Maybe,' I said, concerned that was the only qualifier she had for him.

From our long chats every night that week, it was easy to see that Teddy was funny, spontaneous, cheeky, smart, and...well, not at all ugly.

'I think I remember him from camp. He was sent somewhere south?'

'Yeah, Sardinia. That's him.'

'Oh, yes. He was a cool guy. Very funny. Very cute, too. Why are you asking?'

'Uhm...he added me on Facebook, we started talking this week. I was just wondering if you knew him personally.'

'Yeah, he was very nice. I remember everyone loved him. We had lots of fun every time us exchange students were all reunited,' she said with a smile. 'Sometimes I wish I got to hang out with the others more. I was so focused on making Italian friends, I missed out on being closer to people like him.'

I smirked at Ingrid. 'Yeah, I'm glad I have a group of people who understand exactly how it feels to be an outsider.'

'Maybe you wouldn't feel as much as an outsider if you spent less time chatting on your laptop,' Ingrid said.

So close.

I took a deep breath and didn't say anything else. After all, I was *dying* to get back to chatting on my laptop. We would usually have dessert upstairs, in the TV room, while watching a film or some crazy Swedish programme about food or home makeovers. I was expected to spend at least an hour there. It was part of the "bonding experience". It also used to be one of my favourite activities to do with the family since *she* wouldn't get the chance to attack me, not when we were watching something on TV. Despite that, my daily evening chat with Teddy was what I was really looking forward to.

I faked a yawn, said *god natt*, and I sprinted inside my bedroom. I sat on my reclining chair, put my feet on my grey fluffy stool and placed my laptop on my legs. I silently savoured the pleasant draft wafting in from the window above.

'I'm so sorry I'm late!' I wrote to Teddy.

He was online already; I liked to think he was waiting eagerly to talk to me. Even though he had plenty of other friends he could speak to, or actually see.

'Ciao Vince!' popped up on my screen. I smiled. Was I really that excited to receive a message from Teddy?

'*Are we doing nicknames now?*'

'*I'm Aussie. We shorten every word.*'

'*Can I call you Ted then?*'

'Don't you dare,' he typed. 'How was your day?'

'*Didn't do anything special, just hung out with my friend Hazel, from New Zealand.*'

'*Ah, good ol' neighbours. Does she sound ridiculous when she speaks?*'

'No more ridiculous than what I assume you'd sound like...' I said, with a smiley.

'*Watch it you. What's with the sass tonight?*'

'It's probably due to how little sleep I got this week, wouldn't you agree, mister-let's-chat-every-night-until-4am?'

Enter my schoolgirl giggle. The hell was wrong with me?

'I slept heaps. I don't know what you're talking about!'

'Some of us had to go to school!'

'Did you *actually* go?' he asked.

'Rude. I'll have you know I am a very diligent student.'

'So, it's a no?'

'It's a no.'

'I'm turning you into a bad boy already and I'm loving every second of it.'

'Speaking of bad boys...' I teased.

'...Yes?'

'Who is the guy in so many of your photos?'

'Have you been looking at my photos? How come?'

I wasn't sure if he was feeling flattered or somewhat offended.

'Just quickly.'

'Aww.'

Flattered.

'I believe you're talking about my ex, Francesco,' he said.

'Ex-boyfriend?' I asked.

'Yeah!'

'What happened, then?'

'I went back to Australia. I thought we loved each other, I missed him. I missed my Italian life, I was miserable.'

'Is that why you went back to Italy? To see him again?'

Was I *actually* being jealous? What on earth? *Why?*

'It was a big part of it. I thought I was in love, after all.'

I couldn't imagine being so upfront about being gay. I hadn't even seen guys holding hands before.

'What happened when you came back?' I inquired, oddly curious. Way more curious than I expected to be.

'*Well, he acted as if I didn't exist. I wanted to catch up, but he won't return my calls or meet me. He stood me up three times this month.*'

'*The hell with him. You deserve better.*'

'*What's "better", Vincent?*'

I laughed out loud. Mainly because I didn't know how to respond. It was almost like I enjoyed being put in difficult situations where I could say the wrong thing at any given time. It had to be the gayest thing I had ever written.

'*Someone who will treat you like a prince.*'

Correction. This was.

He didn't reply straight away. I wondered if it was because he was pissing himself laughing at me being the cringiest boy in the world.

'Any volunteers there?' he asked.

'*Maybe you should come and see for yourself.*'

Vincent, what the fuck are you saying?!

'I'm joking,' I started typing. I blushed, then deleted it. I guess I wanted to see his reaction. I could always say I was kidding afterwards.

My mind was running wild. *Wild.* What if Teddy *did* come over? What would I say to the family? I could tell them he was an old friend. He could sleep in the guest room. We could go out together and I could introduce him to Hazel and Daniel. How fun would that be? All this anxiety-inducing chat, but in real life. No, he couldn't. We couldn't.

'Oh, is that an invitation or...?'

No, no, no, no, no, it's not. Abort. Jokes. Just jokes. Aaah. Kill me. Kill me now.

I panicked, looked around my room. I needed to change the subject. Any subject.

My brain? Was giving me nothing. An empty car park located in the post-apocalyptic ghost town of Why-am-I-like-this. I'm your mayor, Vincent Stewart.

'I'm joking, relax. I'm broke as fuck at the moment,' he typed. 'Did you blush?'

How do you know?

'*No, why would I? Nope. I'm cool. The coolest. I don't blush.*'

But the blotchy English boy did indeed blush.

'You know I'm playing, right?' he typed.

'Yeah, yeah,' I said.

'*Where would you take me?*'

'I'd give you the city tour. I know all the good places.'

'Could we go for a dance?'

'Well, I can't go out dancing until I'm 18, but I will be very soon.'

'Who said anything about going to a club?' he asked. 'I want a ball.'

'You're a strange boy.'

'Are you saying you wouldn't dance with me?'

I furrowed my eyebrows. 'I can't dance.'

'I'd lead. And...pick the song.'

'What's the song?' I asked, curious.

'Love Story. Taylor Swift.'

I quickly minimised our conversation window and googled. I had no idea who Taylor Swift was. I didn't want to seem clueless, so I immediately checked her MySpace to see if I could listen to her songs.

The lyrics. Jesus.

I would listen to *Fall Out Boy, Paramore,* or *Linkin Park.* This was a cute pretty girl singing about Romeo.

'Are you Googling?' he asked.

'No, no, no. I have absolutely heard the song before! It's sweet.'

'You'll be the prince and I'll be—'

'...the prince?'

'Yeah!'

I smiled, and I wondered if he was smiling with me. The night passed in a blur of stories from back home, little secrets and lessons in Aussie slang, dotted with flirty comments that made my stomach swoop with every word. I couldn't stop myself and I didn't understand why. Teddy had become important to me.

The morning after I couldn't stop yawning. My eyes were dry and red, and the thought of skipping school once again seemed like a nifty idea. It was, after all, a sunny day in December; a rare sight in Stockholm, and the very idea of being stuck behind my school walls, spending another day trying to keep up with the rest of my peers in my broken

Swedish seemed futile. I also wasn't in the mood to intrude on conversations to make those goddamn Swedish friends Ingrid would so often bang on about. I was curious how a tiny, insignificant part of me almost wanted to make her happy, even if she was an absolute dick to me. Perhaps it was just a bizarre form of Stockholm syndrome.

Ha!

I walked through *Kungsgatan,* from Old Town. It was a long, clean, pedestrian road, filled with stores on either side. I had my camera on me and I was taking a few shots, which I would speed up into a time-lapse later. I'd often forget to take filler shots, so being by myself for a bit was the perfect occasion to obtain some extra footage.

I was heading to a coffee shop named *Wayne's Coffee,* a chain exclusive to Sweden, and I couldn't stop thinking about Teddy. We both stayed up extremely late, again, just talking and laughing at each other's stories. His exchange experience was so interesting, and I found it was useful to think about what my life would look like six months down the line, when I would be back home in Bath, with my old friends, my old lunch spots, my old life. Gone would be the smell of cinnamon I'd encounter with every step. Gone would be the hot dog sellers, with their big upside-down tubs of mustard and ketchup I'd have to squeeze like a cow's udder. Gone would be my best friends; the ones I couldn't imagine my life without.

I finally reached the café, just past the stone lion sculptures, where all the tourists would take photos of themselves riding them. I sat down outside, with a warm fluffy blanket—a custom across most places in Stockholm—and watched people walking up and down, nobody rushing to go anywhere. The bright blue sky put a smile on everyone's face, another rarity I didn't get to experience often. Funny how much in common Swedes and Brits had with regards to weather affecting moods and yet, so many differences.

'I'm here!' Hazel said in her slightly diluted Kiwi accent. Hazel was late as usual. She had woken up late and missed her first few classes, which was another reason why we both figured today was a good day to avoid school entirely.

'About bloody time,' I said, sending her an air kiss.

Hazel was smiling big. The sun was touching her porcelain skin and her thick straight hair, making it look more auburn than her usual dark chestnut.

'You ordered anything?' she asked.

'No, was just waiting for you.'

'I'll get the drinks. Mocha?'

'Yes, please.'

She entered the café and queued for our order. I really needed a strong coffee. I didn't know what came over me, why I thought it was acceptable for me to speak to a stranger over the internet until four in the morning. Especially when I had to leave the house early to go to school, or, more precisely, give the impression of going to school. I couldn't imagine the shit storm I'd have to face if Ingrid found out I wasn't at school. She would probably have enough ammunition to kick me out and fulfil her ultimate goal to relinquish me somewhere else, so I could be somebody else's problem.

'Here,' Hazel said, while placing a gigantic cup of coffee in front of me.

'Thanks. Come under the blanket,' I said, while lifting the lime green blanket to share between the two of us.

'So, what's up? I'm gonna let you know I had to skip a long day of maths to meet you.'

'Whatever will you do?'

'Shut up,' she smiled while blowing her drink, as if it wouldn't get cold within seconds in the winter air. 'Did you spend another night chatting to your Australian lover?'

'My lover?'

'Yep. The one I keep seeing leave you hundreds of messages on your Facebook wall!'

'...it's not that many,' I said, awkwardly.

She grabbed my camera and pointed it at me.

'Introducing Vincent Stewart's face!' she said, while recording. 'The gorgeous, talented director of...what are you calling this?'

'I don't know yet! Give it back!' I said, trying to take the camera from her, unsuccessfully.

'Nope! I'm not done! Vincent, what's Sweden like?'

'Fucking cold! And filled with arseholes like my former best friend Hazel.'

'Hazel! She sounds divine! What is *she* like?'

'Dead! She was killed because she touched something she shouldn't have!'

'Mister Stewart. We hear there's a green-eyed boy in Italy who wants to see you naked, what do you have to say about that?'

'Oh my god!' I said, finally snatching the camera from her.

She couldn't stop laughing her head off. 'Okay, okay! I'm sorry! It's just too funny.'

'I really don't think that's what's happening, thank you very much.'

'What if it was, though?' she teased.

I stuttered for a second. I wasn't quite sure what to say.

'I'm not gay.'

'I didn't say anything of the sort.'

'Good.'

We remained in silence for a few seconds. 'Because I'm not,' I added.

'You're not. Got it. Just very happy to avoid sleeping for a week just to talk to a cute Australian. Nothing gay.'

'...nothing gay.'

I took a sip of my coffee. The foam was warm and sweet. My hands were getting warm from holding the mug. It was all so cosy. Stockholm was cosy. I turned to Hazel and she was still staring at me with a big dumb smile, like she knew something I didn't.

'What?' I asked.

'Just know you can always talk to me,' she said. 'About whatever.'

'I know,' I said.

'Good, because you'll have to remember your incredibly wonderful and supportive friend when you're a famous director and I'm stuck in New Zealand photographing weddings between cousins.'

'You could always move to Australia,' I said, taking another sip of now tepid coffee.

'Oh yeah! I could move in with—'

'Don't say it,' I interrupted her.

We remained in silence for a few seconds, both watching the world around us. As people walked up and down in front of me, I caught a glimpse of a jogger with wavy light brown hair. The only one in a sea of Nordic blonde. And then I wondered if Teddy was a fast or a slow walker, I wondered what his hair would look like under the sunlight, I wondered if he was taller or shorter than me, I wondered if I'd be able to rest my chin on his shoulder.

I—

No. I did not like men.

Chapter Four

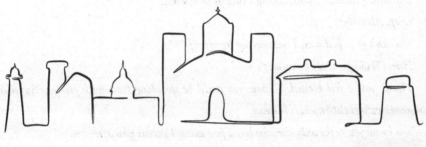

Teddy

2008

Cazzo was my favourite Italian swear word. I said it all the time. It sounded funny and you could pretty much place it anywhere in a sentence. I'll admit my year in Italy didn't necessarily teach me everything there was to know about Italian, as I spent so much time with Laura, who spoke perfect English and Francesco, who wanted to learn it. Yes, I was the obnoxious Aussie who'd order drinks in broken English and would get royally smashed on cheap—albeit delicious—red wine.

I was navigating the house in the dark. It was three in the morning, and it was time for a sandwich with tomato and mozzarella. At least I thought that was what I made. I couldn't see anything, and I didn't really want to turn the lights on and wake everyone up. It wasn't their fault I had turned into a nocturnal animal.

I walked as quietly as I could. My fleecy socks allowed me to glide across the floor without making a sound until I stubbed my pinkie toe onto the door frame.

'*Cazzo!*' I shouted. I couldn't help it. It hurt and it hurt bad. I hobbled my way to the desk as if I had suffered from major foot trauma.

I sat in front of the computer and the light nearly blinded me.

'I'm back!' I typed.

'Did you make sandwiches for the whole neighbourhood?' Vincent asked.

'Oh, I'm sorry. Do you think you'd be faster at assembling food in absolute darkness and trying to be inaudible to the human ear?'

'I'm English. I'd just order a kebab.'

'It's 3am, Vincent,' I said, taking a bite of sandwich.

'Crap. Already?'

'You can't go to bed now. I hate eating by myself!'

'Fine. I'll oblige. Only because it's you.'

'Thank you. I feel blessed. I know you could be spending time with glorious Swedish amazons with giant knockers instead.'

'You know you're the only one who has a full-access Vincent pass after hours.'

'Full-access? Why wasn't I made aware of this before? What does that entail? Is there a meet and greet?'

'How's the sandwich, Teddy?' he said, clearly changing the subject.

'Okay. Don't answer that,' I teased. 'And it's...decent. You know what definitely doesn't go with tomato and mozzarella?'

'What?'

'Vegemite.'

'You eat Vegemite. You *like* Vegemite,' he iterated.

'Yeah? Do I have to show you my passport again? I told you where I'm from.'

'I love your mid-sneeze passport photo, so I'll gladly look at it again. Also, Vegemite is rubbish.'

'Sir, how dare you? You're insulting a staple, a cultural phenomenon, a—'

'You know it's just a Marmite rip-off, right?'

'I don't think I can speak to you anymore. I think we should see different people.'

'And where do you think you're going to find someone as cute as me?'

'Shit,' I typed.

Vincent Stewart, why do you do this to me?

'Do you have any plans for the weekend?' he asked.

'It's a big day for Laura tomorrow. She should find out whether she'll get to go to London for an audition. I'll take her to stuff our faces, whatever the outcome.'

'London, huh? Maybe she and I will meet there next year!'

'You're not allowed to like her more than me.'

'Am I allowed to like *anyone* more than you?' he asked.

'*Nope.*'

'*Understood.*' *Smiley face.*

'*What's Vincent doing this weekend?*'

'*I'm planning on avoiding my host mo*nster*'s jibes by staying over at Daniel's host parents' house in the countryside.*'

'*Daniel is the horny kid that looks like a cabbage patch doll?*'

'*That's the one!*'

'*Wait, countryside? Does that mean no internet?*'

'*I'm afraid so. There's phone signal, though.*'

'*Does that mean you'll still wish me goodnight? By voice? Late night phone call?*'

I lit up.

'Teddy, I think it's time you find out something about me,' he wrote, ominously.

Please say gay.

'I *hate* speaking on the phone. Hate, hate. I get anxious, I sound stupid, I forget words. It's not cute,' he said. He was lying, clearly, because he was always cute.

'You're telling me you'll never grace my ears with your voice and *pommy* accent?' I teased.

'*Yep. And I stand by that.*'

'Can I bribe you?'

'*Nope.*'

'*Are you sure? My mum is pretty rich.*'

'*Nah. I'm terrified. And speaking to you? Are you crazy?*'

'*Why?*'

God, I loved trying to make him feel awkward. I could feel him blushing through the screen.

'*Because! You're so—*'

Hot? Smart? Funny as fuck?

Then I waited. And I waited. And I waited. Did Vincent fall asleep mid-love declaration?

'WHAT?' I typed, tapping as hard as I could.

'I forgot what I was going to say,' he said.

'How convenient!' I replied, let down. I was hoping for an *actual* response. 'Fine. No phone call. Besides, you probably wouldn't understand me and it would be messy.'

'You're from Australia. It's not exactly a foreign language.'

'Do you think Hazel would secretly record you for me?'

'God, I hope not. I wouldn't want you to hear any of that. And before you ask me why, I'll have you know it's finally bedtime.'

'Aww, already?' I asked, pouting, as if he could see me.

'I need a tiny little bit of sleep. I already look like a vampire as is.'

'Who complains about looking like a vampire? Do you not have *Twilight* fever like the rest of the world?' I asked.

'It won't be out for a while here. It takes a while for films to get subtitled.'

'Hey, I'm going to watch it dubbed. In Italian. That's something.'

'I don't think it's for me, anyways. I may pass.'

'What's there not to like? Glittery boys? Dead-eyed main actress? I think you'll miss out!'

'Maybe we could go to the cinema at the same time. Watch the film and then discuss afterwards.'

'Like an international date?'

'I guess.'

'That is the silliest idea I've ever heard. *I love it.* Yes!' I typed, mega excited.

'Okay, perfect. I'm glad. And now, I sleep. Speak tomorrow?'

'Speak tomorrow. Goodnight Vincent.'

'Goodnight Teddy,' he said.

Sweet dreams.

The morning after, the sun was shining bright after what seemed like a whole month of rain. I was leaning on Laura's parents' car waiting for her to come out of dance practice, so we could do some Christmas shopping and perhaps take a drive by the beach. I was wearing my favourite purple sunnies, my tight jeans, and a dark green Pashmina I had stolen from Laura. I felt cute. The reality was I had to wear the sunglasses to cover the roaring eyebags my lovely English pen pal had caused me with his cuteness.

Meanwhile, I was on the phone to my darling mother, whom I bored to death with the details about this very funny guy I had met online.

'It sounds like you're making progress,' she said, after listening to me saying out loud how adorable it would be to have a long-distance cinema date, which was surprisingly subdued. She would normally say to my face if I went a bit over the top with things. Which, really, was my specialty.

'Okay, what's happening. This is not sounding like you? Who are you and what have you done with Veronica Clarke?' I asked.

'I know my child, Teddy. If you're feeling whatever you're feeling that means he must be someone special.'

'I didn't say anything about feeling anything.'

'I can hear it from your tone. Besides, it's been a solid forty minutes of Vincent this, Vincent that.'

'It's Laura's fault for taking forever to get out. I'm hoping it's because it's good news!'

'I'm so excited to find out whether she'll get to go to London! I've always wanted to go.'

'Hey, when I become a flight attendant, I'll put you in first class and we'll go together,' I said with a big smile. 'I'll serve you all the best champagne on board too.'

'God, I'd have to take a hell of a sleeping pill with it too. Don't think my poor head could handle such a long flight.'

'Is everything alright? Have you been to the doctor?'

'I'm doing some blood tests sometime this month. I just read too much and it's hard to cut back on that when you teach English literature.'

'Okay, but let me know as soon as you know anything. I have to go now. Laura's emerged, love you, mum!' I said, hanging up.

Laura's face was droopy, looking as if someone had run over her favourite puppy. The image wasn't all that promising.

I walked towards her doing jazz hands, but she just gave me the worst look.

'Oh boy,' I said. 'What happened? Are we crying?'

Her emerald eyes looked up at me, everything about her face was trying its hardest to look upset, but I wasn't buying it.

'It went well! You're just doing that thing!' I shouted, pointing at her with my index finger.

She tried to keep her sad face together, but she cracked suddenly and burst out laughing.

'I made it!' she said, jumping and putting her arms around my neck.

'I'm so disgustingly proud of you!' I said, giving her a tight hug.

'We need to celebrate. I'm expecting all-you-can-eat kind of celebrations.'

'So, you want to ruin your diet even though you're going to London?'

'Teddy, today I want to eat a gigantic mountain of sushi. I'll hurt you.'

'Fine, fine! Shall we walk, then?'

She threw her duffle bag into the boot and grinned at me.

We walked together under the gentle arch of the colonnade and passed the endless parade of outdoor seats with people drinking coffee or reading the paper. The air smelled of sea and sugar. Bakeries upon bakeries were taking fresh pastries out of the oven and displaying them in their windows, enticing tourist and—let's face it—anyone with a sense of smell, to stuff their faces with them. I was content. I felt like I was in my own picturesque fantasy, with my incredible sister, walking on the shiny cobblestones of my favourite place in the world, looking like a gay male version of Audrey Hepburn, smiling until my cheeks hurt.

I was smiling until my heart sank. I stopped walking and put my arm in front of Laura to halt her.

'What?' she screeched.

I only had to give her a quick look and a head nod for her to understand fucking Francesco was up ahead. As soon as she saw him, I pulled her down behind some unsuspecting people having lunch, and we crab-walked our way behind a news agent's kiosk. *Like the adults we were.*

'Why are we hiding?' she asked.

'Francesco is up ahead!' I blurted. 'What do you think we are doing?'

'Yes, I don't think we should hide though,' she added. 'Who is he with? I can't see from here.'

'Some hoebag homo. He's probably gross and has no taste.'

'I'm only seeing gigantic muscular arms.'

'Alright! Let's not compliment the douchebag, thank you,' I said, while I squinted my eyes at her, as I tried my best to communicate my disdain.

'How long should we hide for? I'm starving,' she asked.

'We will stay here forever. We'll die here.'

We remained in silence for a bit, trying to detect whatever was going on between the two fuckers. And then something magical happened. *Muscle Mary* got up and left the table.

'Do you think he's leaving him or just going to the toilet?' Laura asked.

'This is my chance!' I shouted.

I ran as fast as I could. I bolted my way to the table and sat in front of Francesco. Panting as if I were about to have a heart attack.

'Teddy!' he exclaimed. 'What—'

'Nah huh,' I interrupted. 'Let *me* speak.'

Gasped for air for a few seconds.

'How *dare* you. You piece of crap. You told me you loved me. You told me you couldn't live without me. You were crying at the airport begging me to stay with you.'

I could only assume the veins in my neck were throbbing like a Dragon Ball character, as he avoided eye contact.

'Teddy, *mi dispiace*—' he pleaded.

'I'm not finished!'

In the meantime, his little date came back to the table, probably confused, so I put my hand over his face, without even looking at him.

'Shush, you. I can't believe what a god-awful person you really are. I put everything on hold to come back here and give us another chance and you just flat-out ignored me? I came back for you! For us!'

'It's complicated,' he said. 'I'm sorry.'

'You're not, though. You're selfish and you don't give a shit about me. You only care about yourself and I never, ever want to see you again. I deserve so much better than you. I deserve someone who treats me like...a prince. I deserve a guy who looks forward to speaking to me, every day.'

'Fine. Are you finished?' he asked, with his stupid punch-me face.

I looked at him like the parasite he was, looked down at the plate in front of me, scooped a clump of carbonara with my bare hand and threw it straight at his stupid face.

'Che *cazzo*!' he shouted.

I got up, walked back to Laura, who was ready with wet wipes.

'Good job,' she said.

And I never felt prouder of myself.

It had been quite the day. Throwing pasta at Francesco was a pretty fun development and Laura and I had a blast during lunch. But it was late evening and it was dark, Laura went to bed, and I was staring at my desktop computer aimlessly. Vincent wasn't going to be online. He was going to spend time with his real-life friend. He wasn't worrying about the stupid Aussie guy living on the other side of Europe.

I didn't know why I allowed myself to be so sad. Giving Francesco a piece of mind was needed, but I so wish I didn't feel so alone in the evening.

I typed *goodnight Vincent* and then deleted it letter by letter.

Don't be pathetic, Teddy.

I leaned back on my chair and looked outside. The stars were shining bright in the clear sky. Full moon reflecting on the dark sea, glittering silver. I wondered if we were staring at the same moon.

I took a deep breath and was about to turn the computer off, when he popped up.

'Guess what? Turns out there is a little internet over here!'

I couldn't believe he had messaged me.

'Hey there. I wasn't expecting you tonight!' I typed, trying to mask how glad I was I'd gotten to speak to him. Even for a little.

'Well, surprise then! How are you? How was your day?'

'I don't really feel like talking about it. I was actually heading to bed.'

'Wait, are you upset? What's going on?'

'Don't worry, Vincent. Please go have fun with Daniel.'

'That definitely doesn't sound like you're okay. Can I call you?' he asked.

Call me? What?

'Huh?!' I typed.

'Yes, a phone call. So, I can make sure you're actually okay.'

'You don't need to do that.'

'I'm about to ring the number you have on Facebook!'

'Wait, my number is on Facebook?'

Then my phone started ringing. I looked at it as if I was expecting the "seven days" call from *the Ring*. He was calling me. For real.

'He-llo?' I stuttered.

'Hey there.'

Warm, deep, sophisticated voice. *Swoon.*

'What's...going on?'

'I could ask you the same question. Why are you sad?' he asked.

'Honestly, I can't remember now,' I giggled. 'It's weird to hear your voice.'

'Weird?'

'It's the first time I've heard it. I'm just—I wasn't expecting this. I thought you hated phone calls.'

'I do, but you're sad. What happened today? Did Laura not succeed?'

'Wait,' I said, getting up from my chair, walking to the study door and closing it behind me, so I wouldn't wake up the rest of the family. I lay on the couch and made myself comfortable. 'Laura got her audition.'

'Oh, amazing. She must be so excited.'

'She is. She can't wait to go to London.'

'That's amazing. So why is my Teddy sad?'

Your Teddy?

'Okay. But it's boring. And you could be doing something much more fun than chatting with me. Like being with your friend Daniel, who must be wondering why the hell you locked yourself in the bathroom for so long.

'There is no bathroom here.'

'What? Where do you—?'

'Can we not discuss that now? I'm outside, freezing, hoping a moose doesn't stomp on my neck. So would you just get on with the story so I can proceed to console you?'

'Alright, alright. Jeez. I saw Francesco with another guy, and I freaked out. I gave him a piece of my mind and threw pasta on his face.'

He cackled. For a while.

'I'm sorry, this has to be the most dramatic Italian showdown I've ever heard of. You did good.'

'Thanks.'

'So why are you sad?'

'I'm sad because...I guess I allowed myself to feel a certain way. I'm always the fool falling in love and then always ending up alone.'

'You're not alone. You have people who adore you and...you have me.'

'I don't have you, Vincent.'

'Are you joking? Now that we heard each other's voices...that's it. We are bound.'

I smiled at his silly comments. And his silly accent. What was I sad about, again?

'So, how was your day in the countryside? Did you wear gum boots?' I asked.

'I did indeed. Not a look I intend to replicate in the future.'

'I can't wait to see photos. By the way, are you aware this call is costing you a fortune?'

'Ten minutes with Teddy Clarke? Worth every penny.'

His voice was smooth, intoxicating even. Before I even realised, my hand was inside my pants. Hearing his breathing, so close to my ear...I couldn't control myself.

Teddy, no.

I took a deep breath and slid my hand out again.

'The things you say sometimes...' I said, under my breath.

'What?'

'What?'

'You said something.'

'Nothing. It's dumb. But I'm really happy you called. It's nice to know you're this...real person, I guess.'

'You thought I was a robot?'

'You're so polite, you could easily be one.'

'Piss off!'

I laughed.

'Do you feel any better?' he asked.

'I do. Thank you. I'd feel even better if you were here.'

'Oh,' he said, on an exhale, I could hear the sound of shifting fabric in the background.

'Oh, what?' I asked. Maybe I overstepped. Scared him like a little defenceless *Robin*. A *sexy* Robin.

'You...uhm...make me blush, I guess.'

'I'd like to do more than that.'

His breathing hitched and I would swear I heard a tiny moan.

'Hey. I...have to go now, Teddy. Something just came up. Speak tomorrow, okay?'

'Yeah, sure. Did I say anything—'

'Nope, nope. It's just. It's nothing. Goodnight Teddy.'

'Goodnight—'

And he hung up. So quickly.

I hoped I didn't say anything too forward. Did I?

Crap, did I?

CHAPTER FIVE

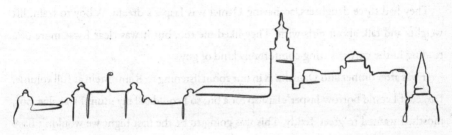

VINCENT

2008

S wedes were a tiny bit bizarre. People in the UK claimed they like the countryside, but
what they really meant is that they enjoyed going to Yorkshire pubs and enjoyed a
pint of beer for half a quid. Swedes? Not so much. They meant heading to their cabin
in the woods. No toilets, no TV, and definitely no Wi-Fi. Instead, they traded all their
comforts for a dip into a partially frozen lake, a naked family sauna, and a piss in the
woods.

Daniel and I were happy to spend time together at his host parents' summer cabin for
the weekend. We had somehow found each other during our orientation camp. I was
drawn to him because his face looked like a porcelain doll, but his vagina-obsessed mouth
came out with the filthiest stuff I had ever heard in my life. And English was this kid's
second language. His host family was way too adorable. I didn't know if I was the only
one being sent to *Miss Trunchbull*, but I for sure felt like I was missing out on having a
decent, pleasant family. His host father, Jasper, was a sport addict. He ran the Stockholm
marathon every year, the New York one twice, and had no issue skinny dipping in front
of us. I had only been at the cabin for a few hours, and I had seen his *peen* far more than
my own.

His wife, Annika, was a freaking genius of cuisine. I wasn't particularly fond of fish, but she'd whip up amazing meals and would not rest until I was filled to the brim with her delicious creations.

They had three daughters, so having Daniel was Jasper's dream. A boy to train, lift weights and talk about girls with. They liked me too, but it was clear I was more of a reading-in-the-corner-sitting-comfortably kind of guy.

It was after dinner and Daniel was in our room listening to Rammstein at full volume. I asked if I could borrow Jasper's laptop for a bit, so I could tell my mum I was alive but, mostly, I wanted to greet Teddy. This was going to be the first night we wouldn't have really talked, so I felt like I owed him at least a teeny salute.

'I'm going outside for a bit!' I announced to Daniel, who removed one of his earphones to hear.

'You're going to take a shit?' he half-shouted.

'You think I'd tell you?'

'Do you want company?' he asked.

'You'd do that?'

'Yeah, of course. You're my bro. I'd do anything for you.'

'Don't call me bro. It's weird.'

'You're my most favourite bro. Now go forth. Shit away.'

'You're a vile, vile human and Switzerland should be ashamed of having you represent it abroad,' I said, with a little smile.

I ran downstairs and managed to walk outside without being spotted. I assumed the parents would be in their room, but there was a fifty percent chance they'd be naked in the sauna, doing it. Daniel walked in on them multiple times. I was hoping that I would be spared from such a view.

I hid behind a tree. The forest was terrifying and cold. I couldn't see anything, but it was basically a zoo out there. Weird animal noises all around. I was scared a bloody polar bear would come out of nowhere like in *Lost* and chew my legs, but hey, at least I'd get to have one last chat with the *Tedster*.

'Ten minutes with Teddy Clarke? Worth every penny,' I said, knowing damn well I was sounding like an overly attached stalker.

'The things you say sometimes...' he murmured. It was as if he was trying to speak in the sexiest way possible.

And it was that exact breathy voice that made my dick hard. Maybe it wasn't his voice. Maybe it was just the fact that I hadn't had my daily wank, and it was my body's way of telling me it was time. Maybe it had nothing to do with Teddy. Why would it, anyways?

I slipped my hand under the waistband of my jeans and I could feel my dick pressing against my zipper.

Oh, man.

I unzipped my jeans and pulled it out of my pants. It was so hard, it hurt. I had to sort myself out. Teddy just so happened to be speaking directly to my ear. The whole stroking-dick-in-the-woods was completely unrelated to boy.

'What?' I asked.

'What?'

'You said something,' I said.

Speak to me more, Teddy. Talk dirty, even.

Wait what?

No. No. No. Brain. Sort yourself out.

And as I was freely choking my dick under the moonlight, he did say something.

'I'd like to do more than that.'

I wasn't sure what he meant, but by that point I would have let him do anything. It wouldn't be gay for him to put his hand on my cock. It was just a body part. It would have been like him touching my forehead. An elbow, even.

Vincent, what the fuck are you saying?

I was getting really close to shooting a load onto the poor, traumatised tree in front of me, when I, for some god forsaken reason, decided to check the world around me. That's when I locked eyes with Daniel, who was staring at me from our bedroom window.

Fuck.

'Hey. I...have to go now, Teddy. Something just came up. Speak tomorrow, okay?' I said, while quickly putting my—still—throbbing hard dick inside my jeans and zipping them back up.

'Yeah, sure. Did I say anything—'

'Nope, nope. It's just. It's nothing. Goodnight Teddy,' I said, and quickly hung up.

Well, shit. Now I had to have such an awkward conversation with Daniel. Great.

I walked as slowly as I could. I was trying to make up a story that would make sense, but nothing was fitting the bill. I was hoping that by the time I'd walk upstairs in our room, Daniel would have the decency to pretend to be fully asleep but, alas, that did not happen.

I opened the door and he was standing there, in front of me, with a huge grin. He caught me. And now he wanted the details.

'Dude, you could have told me you were going outside to shoot some spunk!'

'Please don't say that out loud again.'

'There's nothing to be embarrassed about. I've been needing to do it too. Why do you think I went on such a long run this afternoon?' he said.

'I didn't need to know that,' I said, while walking past him and sitting on my bed.

'Well, I didn't need to see you going at it, but hey, what's done is done. Who were you talking to?' he asked, while sitting on his bed, adjacent to mine.

'No one.'

'You were having phone sex.'

'I was not having phone sex.'

'You were on the phone and jerking off. That's phone sex.'

'No. I was on the phone. And scratching myself for like a second.'

'You were scratching yourself for a while.'

'Oh my god, how long were you spying on me?!'

'There isn't much entertainment around here. It's not my fault you did a full peep show in front of our window. You could have hidden better.'

'I wasn't going to go any further! That forest is creepy as hell.'

'Whatever creature lives in it, just got a full Vincent show!' he cackled. 'Come on, who was it? Is it a secret lover? Oh god. Was it your host sister?'

'I pretty much despise my host sister.'

'Even better. Tell me more.'

'Why? This is so weird.'

'Ha!' he exclaimed, while pointing a finger at me. 'It's that guy.'

'NO!' I said, quickly.

'It so is!' he got up and sat right next to me. 'You can tell me anything. That's what best friends are for.'

'I think Hazel is my best friend,' I teased.

'We are a trio. There isn't a hierarchy.'

'I mean—'

'Vincent!' he interrupted. 'Best friends. End of story.'

I took a deep breath and tried to make peace with the thousands of thoughts that were racing in my head, telling me who I was and who I was supposed to be.

'I don't know, Danny. I don't know what I'm feeling.'

'Do you want to talk about it?'

'There's nothing to talk about really. I can't...I'm not.'

'Okay,' he said, grabbing my face with both of his hands. Then proceeded to slowly move towards me, his lips getting dangerously close to mine.

I slapped his forehead with the palm of my hand and furrowed my eyebrows. '...the fuck are you doing?' I asked.

'Ow. I was going to kiss you, so you'd know if you're gay or not!' he said, while rubbing his forehead. 'Isn't that how it works?'

'That's not how any of it works! I would never be gay for you!'

'Well, that's just rude, Vincent. I'd probably go gay for you.'

We both laughed.

'And your breath smells of onions,' I said. 'Honestly, put some more effort in next time.'

'Not if you're going to hit me again.'

'You deserved it.'

'So you're not gay. Or bi.'

'I...one hundred percent do not wish to kiss you,' I said with a smile.

'Okay. But if you ever wanted to check...'

'I'm good,' I said, putting my hand in front of his face. 'Now get the hell away from my bed.'

And then, out of nowhere, he gave me a hug. I wasn't one for physical contact, but it felt nice. I hugged him back.

'You'll be fine, Vincent,' he said.

And my mind went back to picturing Teddy's face. Again.

Get out of my head.

The weekend hadn't continued to be as quiet as I wanted it to be. I was attempting to jog with Daniel, but it soon became clear we were not at the same level of fitness. My heart was pounding out of my chest, breathing became a chore, and my legs had been cramping for what felt like an hour.

'Jesus. Lord. I can't do this,' I muttered.

'What do you mean you can't? Of course, you can,' he said, enthusiastically like a true personal trainer. On crack.

I slowed down and lay on the grass, trying to catch a breath.

'Does this mean we're done now?' he asked, sitting next to me.

'I did not come to this country so I could kill myself running next to you,' I said. 'Where the hell are you getting this energy from? It's cold and it's Saturday. Why aren't we having a coffee or something?'

'This was your idea!'

'What? Running?'

'To come with me. I would have been happy to meet you at the cabin later.'

'I want to get into shape.'

'You're lying down,' he noted, while running his hand through his light blond curls. He turned to me, his giant ocean blue eyes stared at me then he started laughing.

'Yeah, yeah. I am lazy,' I said sitting up.

'There are other ways to impress him, you know.'

'Not this again.'

'Maybe I meant capital H. I could be a crazy church kid, as far as you know.'

'You may want to tone down the amount of pre-marital sex, then.'

Then my phone started ringing.

'Let me guess,' he said, rolling his eyes out.

'It's my host sister.'

'You know it's not nice to lie! I'll see you later!' he said, while running away from me.

'*Hej*, Amanda,' I said. Confused as this was the absolute first time Amanda had called me. 'Is everything *okej*?'

Check me out, incorporating Swedish into my vocabulary.

'Hejhej. How's the countryside?' she asked, peppily.

'It's...alright, cold and I miss having a bathroom more than anything. What's going on?'

Amanda and I had a bit of a weird relationship. It started off well. She was only a year older than I was and I honestly thought we could get along. She was an exchange student the year before, so we had that in common. We could bond over that, and she usually had extra insight on how to navigate the difficulties of learning a new language, living in a foreign country or dealing with the inevitable home sickness. But she got bored. We didn't share much beyond that and she stopped asking me to hang out with her and her friends. So, speaking to her on the phone was curious to say the least.

'Good, good. So, do you remember that my parents are going away in the last week of January?'

'Yeah, like a few days after my birthday or something.'

'Yes. Yes! So, we'll be home alone for a few days.'

'Okay...?'

'Well, my friends and I are actually thinking of going somewhere too.'

'What are you saying?'

'I'm just wondering if you'd be okay being alone in the house? I know IESP is a bit funny about leaving exchange students by themselves—'

'Gosh. Please. Go.'

Really, never come back.

'Are you sure?' she asked.

'I'll be an adult then. I'm sure I can cope without you guys for a little while.'

'I was thinking you could stay with one of your friends? I could get mum to call their parents and arrange, if that's better.'

'Honestly, I'll be more than fine.'

A few days without the Lindbergs? Yes please. Make it a month.

'Perfect. Well. Have a nice weekend then! I'll see you at home.'

'*Hej då.*'

This was excellent news.

After a weekend spent outdoors with some truly lovely people, I finally arrived home on Sunday evening. The house was empty and silent, just the way I liked it. The family was off to watch the opera and I had politely declined to join them, in favour of having a whole evening to myself without the constant fear of being attacked left, right, and centre. I left the laundry room, took my wet socks off, and walked barefoot into the kitchen. The heated wooden floor felt like a big warm hug for my feet. I opened the fridge, grabbed a carton of orange juice—*apelsin* in Swedish—and poured myself a glass. It was a word I always found confusing as hell as I always thought it sounded like apple.

I walked past the long dining table, Jonas and Ingrid's bedroom, turned right and trotted upstairs, heading to my room to enjoy juice and my stash of English chocolate my mum would send regularly. My little room was toasty, so I dumped my backpack on the floor, stripped to my pants, slightly opened the window above my chair and sat down in front of the laptop.

I chomped on a chocolate orange slice and opened Facebook to see who was online. Well, I wanted to find *someone*, really.

'Look who it is,' popped up on my screen.

I made myself comfortable and couldn't help the smile that appeared. Snacks and a chat with Teddy were what I needed after being *at one with nature* the days prior.

'*Teddy boy. I'm back to our original programming.*'

'*Chat until 4am?*'

'If we're lucky,' I said. Wink face.

'Did you have a nice weekend, then? We didn't get to talk much!'

'It was. I always have fun with Daniel and his family is surprisingly nice to me. Makes a change.'

'Cool, cool, cool. I have to say, I really enjoyed our phone call.'

'You did?'

'Yeah, I'm sad it was so short.'

I could feel my face blushing, the heat of blood rushing to my head made my cheeks blotchy and hot. 'We could always do it again,' I said.

'How about now?'

Now? I'm not mentally ready, Teddy.

'Okay,' I typed, without thinking twice.

My phone started ringing. The +39 prefixes were a dead giveaway it was him. I picked up and moved my laptop onto the floor.

'Hello Vincent,' he said in his warm voice. You could easily tell when he was smiling. It was kind of like when you listened to Belle sing in Beauty and the Beast.

'Hi you.'

'This is weird, isn't it?'

'A little weird. Good weird, like staring at a platypus!'

'Wow. Out of all the majestic animals, Vincent. But that's good to hear. Not freaked out anymore then?'

'No. I'm happier to talk this way. What did you do during your weekend?'

'Bought Chrissie pressies for the Italian family and a few to send back home.'

'To your parents?' I asked, realising I didn't know much about his upbringing.

'My mum. My father died in a car accident before I was born.'

'Teddy, I'm sorry.'

'It's fine. It's not like I've ever met him.'

'Well, still.'

'Honestly, it's okay. I had an older brother growing up. I'm sure it was harder on him.'

'Had?'

'We don't speak anymore really. He's travelling around the world and I'm pretty sure he's forgotten all about us.'

'What's he like?'

He huffed. 'A douchebag.'

I laughed. I left my chair and lay on my bed to be more comfortable. 'I'm a little jealous. I've always wanted siblings.'

'You have Amanda now!' he teased.

'Lucky me.'

'So, what's Christmas like over there? I always thought it was weird to have it in winter.'

'Summer Christmas has to be the most bizarre experience.'

'What? It's amazing! We go to the beach, we get drunk. It's great.'

'Maybe I should spend a Christmas down under, to experience the magic.'

'I'd show you around. We could wear matching speedos too!'

'I would never wear speedos, Teddy.'

'Why are you ruining the fantasy, Vincent?'

'Oh yeah? What fantasy?' I asked. Before I even realised, my hand was inside my pants. Hearing his breathing, so close to my ear...I couldn't control myself.

'Do you want to hear the sweet version or the spicy version?' he asked.

I took a second to reply. Even though I was in the mood for the latter, I decided getting a piece of Teddy's mind was going to be far more rewarding than a moment of "self-care."

'Okay, this may not actually include speedos.'

'You don't say,' I chuckled.

'My fantasy is really simple. I'd like to meet a guy. A sweet, lovely, handsome guy. And we'd love each other. Everyday. We would compliment each other, daily. We would do things together, see the world. We'd dress like Disney princes and dance together.'

'At a ball?'

'At a ball.'

'Where the heck will you find a ball?'

'I don't know, Vincent. It just happens. It's my fantasy.'

'Okay. What else?'

'Then it's the happily ever after. The living together, the waking up next to each other every day, having a kid...all of it.'

'Do you have anyone in mind or...?' I asked, teasing him to tell me what I wanted to hear. An ego boost, really.

'I wouldn't mind having to see *your* face every day.'

'Is that so?'

'Sorry. I know it's wrong for me to say—'

'What else would you like to see?' I asked, just under my breath. Bulging inside my pants, feeling the heat running through my veins, reaching every single corner of my body.

'What are you wearing?' he asked.

I was sure he was trying to tease me. I didn't care whether he meant it or not. My dick was getting hard in my hand. I couldn't control it. It was just happening.

'Oh, I couldn't tell you that,' I said. 'Not a lot.'

'You have to, or my mind will run wild.'

'Well...I'm only wearing my pants, if you really insist on knowing,' I admitted.

'Damn.'

'Are you thinking of me?' I asked, while stroking my cock with my eyes closed. I was trying to imagine Teddy doing the same thing. Naked on his bed, touching himself, losing his breath over me.

'Ye-yes.'

'What would you do if I were there?'

'Vincent don't make me say things. I think you know what I would do...'

'Indulge me,' I said in a cheeky tone.

'Well, first of all, I'd pull you towards me, I'd grab your thigh and then I would run my hand up, under your t-shirt.'

'Go on...'

'I'd look into your gorgeous grey eyes, run my hand through your hair, my nose slightly touching yours...I'd feel your shallow breath on my lips...'

'Okay...'

'What are you doing, Vincent?'

'Just keep going,' I said, taking my pants off, and a heat wave travelled throughout my body, my dick got firmer and firmer, I kept stroking it, imagining Teddy's hand on it.

'I'd kiss you, softly at first, nip at your bottom lip,' he said. '...then run my tongue along the seam of your mouth, pushing in to meet yours.'

'Would you kiss my neck?'

'I'd put my lips on your neck, softly blow on it, my hands trailing down your back, lower and lower. Rub my finger down your cleft, soaked with sweat.'

'Take them off, Teddy.'

'We are naked, legs tangled together. You'll be sitting on my—'

'You'll be sitting on mine,' I quickly interrupted.

I didn't know why I needed to say that.

'I'll sit on your hard cock, wet with precum, while you slowly push your way inside me, stretching me open. My hands on your chest, I moan in pleasure while you thrust...further and further, until you're all inside me, filling me up. Your hand on my cock, the other on my ass, holding on as I roll my hips, feeling you move inside me.'

'I'm about to—' I whispered.

'Not yet, Vincent. Even if you feel like you're about to explode, you'll slow down, kiss me again while your hands caress my back, up and down. Then I ride you, just a little bit faster.'

'Are you near?' I asked. My hand was moving fast and I was fighting a loud moan.

'I am, ready to come all over your chest...'

'I'd grab your arse, ready to shoot my load in you...'

'Fuck...!' he moaned, loudly.

'Teddy...' I shouted, while I came all over myself, some hitting my face. I could barely breathe. That had to be one of the most intense and erotic moments I had ever experienced. Being so far and yet so in sync with a guy living on the other side of Europe felt incredible. I couldn't believe we did that.

'Wow,' he said.

'That was...something...' I muttered, while staring at my ceiling with wide eyes. The whole scene replaying in my head, minus the crazy horny hormones.

'You having post-wank regrets?'

Yes. No. Maybe. Fuck knows.

'No...no...it was just...different.'

'Are...we, okay?'

'Well...I'm knackered now, after all that. It's quite a mess over here,' I said with a little stutter.

'Vincent...'

'Goodnight Teddy.'

I hung up and sighed. I threw my phone onto my bedside table and I grabbed my head with my hands.

What had I done?

CHAPTER SIX

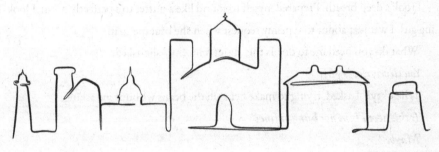

TEDDY

2008

It had been more than two days since I last heard from Vincent. This was the longest we'd went without speaking to each other. It was fine. I was fine. I wasn't freaking out over it whatsoever. I was calm, zen. The portrait of balanced thoughts.

I didn't think for one second Vincent had stopped talking to me because we got frisky on the phone. I wasn't overthinking it at all.

It was half past nine in the evening. I was wearing my trusted ratty Batman pyjamas, with a tartan blanket over my legs; another reminder of Vincent and the hundreds of flannel shirts he'd sport in his pictures.

As I refreshed my Facebook page one more time, hoping he'd pop online, my fingers decided it wasn't his page I would be searching for, and before my brain had completely caught up, I was typing out a message.

Not to Vincent.

To Hazel.

Stalker.

'*Kia ora,*' I typed, feeling polyglot as fuck.

'G'day,' she replied. 'Fancy making your acquaintance Mr. Edward Clarke.'

'Edward? Is it you, grandpa?' I chuckled. 'I hope this isn't too odd. I'm perfectly aware that contacting you has stepped over some sort of sanity line.'

'Not at all, what is it?'

I took a deep breath. Prepared myself to sound like a nutter to a perfectly normal-looking girl. I was just about to type my request when she beat me to it.

'What do you need me to do? Is this about Vincent?' she asked.

You clever, clever girl.

'Is he okay?' I asked, trying to make her spill the beans without me asking.

'Is this about him not being online?'

'Maybe.'

'Have you guys really been chatting every single night?!' she asked. She sounded surprised, as if it wasn't something normal people did. And she was right. Vincent wasn't normal. He was wonderful. Even discounting how he looked (I had dedicated a lot of time to photo research), his dark hair always fell on his face, his gunmetal grey eyes, and his smile that wasn't quite perfect but was perfect on him. He was funny and sarcastic, intelligent and softly spoken. And I was, undoubtedly, smitten as.

'Yes, and it's been wonderful.' Smiley face.

'Look...Vincent may need a moment to think things through. He isn't like you. He is the kind of person who looks at things from a thousand different angles. He likes logic and things that make sense. And currently...not a lot does.'

'So, I should give him space.'

'I think you should give him a little time. To ponder things. It's very clear he has feelings for you. I'm just not sure he knows what they are just yet.'

I couldn't help but feel a little guilty about Vincent having trouble coming to terms with the nature of our relationship and the way it had evolved over the past couple of days. I wished I could be there, with him. That's all I wanted. Just to be near him.

But Hazel was right, being intense was a huge part of me, and I knew I had to calm myself down a bit. Vincent and I had so much in common, but our personalities were vastly different sometimes.

'I can do that,' I said, with a little smile on my face.

'He's busy with a school assignment, anyways. Being the procrastinator he is, he let the deadline loom closer and closer and now he's freaking the hell out in front of a psychology book written in Swedish. He's screwed, basically.'

'I see. Yeah, that sounds like him.'

'I can talk to him, if you want?'

'What would you say to him?'

'I'd tell him his little Aussie Romeo is pining over him!'

'Hey!'

'What?' she sent a cry-laughing smiley face.

'How do you know about Romeo?' I asked, thoroughly entertained.

'Trust me, we are all sick of hearing him hum that song. And Vincent? Very cute guy, but *definitely* not a singer!' she typed.

'Can you record him next time?'

'I'm more of a photography kind of gal!'

'Yes! That's true! Your photos are always so bloody great!'

'Thank you!'

'I mean it. You're so talented. Will you pursue photography when you fly back home?'

'Ugh. I'd like to. I don't know yet, though. I can't think about the future without going a little crazy.'

'Hey, if you decide to come to the dark side, the uni where my mum graduated has an amazing photography course.'

'Oh, seriously? I'll look it up. I can't say I'm all that thrilled to go back to New Zealand.'

'Yeah, must be tough living in a place ruled by Hobbits.'

'Mate. I don't even like *Lord of the Rings*,' she admitted.

'How many sheep do you own?'

'You're getting zero photos.'

'Are you wearing *jandals* right now?' I kept teasing.

'Goodnight, Teddy!'

'Alright, alright. I'm done making fun of you! It's just nice to finally put a voice to the stories,' I typed.

'Wait, what stories?'

'Something about you falling face first into a pile of snow?'

'That was Vincent!!'

'I know, I know. Hey. Can I ask you one more thing?'

'Yes?'

'Do you think I could get his address?' I asked. 'I'm not going to show up at his door or anything. I swear.'

'Aww. Was hoping for you to do just that.'

I was glad she was on board. She was exactly like Vincent described her. Snarky, yet sweet.

'I'm just preparing for Christmas.'

'What are you going to send?' she asked. 'Just to get my facts straight with the police.'

'It's just a bear!'

'A...*Teddy* bear? You are so, so cute,' she said.

'It's dumb. So dumb, oh my god. Forget I asked.'

'No, no. Please. It's an amazing idea. I don't have his address right now, but I will ask for you, okay?'

'Are you sure?'

'It will be our secret,' she typed, with a wink smiley.

I smiled and stretched my arms. It felt like *Operation Suffocate The Cute Boy With Fluffy Earthly Possessions For Christmas* was going to be a success.

Laura was going to be home at any minute, and I really didn't want to look like the loser who stayed at home waiting for his "special pen pal" to go online. Unfortunately, that's exactly who I was. A romantic loser freaking out over having fucked things up.

Just as I was filled with dread and feeling sorry for myself, she barged in.

'Buonasera!' she shouted.

I nearly fell out of my chair. 'You scared the crap out of me.'

'Why are you sitting here in the dark?'

'I...was—'

'No word from Vincent?'

'Not a single fucking one.'

Laura stared at me blankly for a little too long.

'We are going out!' she said, breaking the silence.

I looked her over and saw no sign of head injury. '*Huh?*'

'Out. Like out, out. Club. Lights. Alcohol. Dancing.'

'You spent the day dancing and now you want to go for a dance?'

'You'll find ballet is a teeny bit different from standing in a club drinking a vodka cranberry. Come on! It's not like you have anything better to do!'

'I'm in my pyjamas. I was about to have some camomile tea!'

'You're eighteen, Teddy,' she said, with exasperation. 'Go get changed. Wear something slutty and let's go!'

'Slutty? Are we going to a gay club?'

'Are there any other kinds?' she asked, as if we were living in a post-apocalyptic world where only the gays survived.

'Yes. Straight clubs. Where men buy *you* drinks.'

'I don't want to be around straight men. Not sure if you noticed, but straight men suck.'

'Gay men suck too.'

'You don't suck.'

'Then why isn't he messaging me?' I asked, quietly, the bottom falling out of my words, unable to look Laura in the eye.

She looked at me for a bit, her lips pressed together and her eyes soft with pity. She walked over and rested her hand on my shoulder. 'You have to give him space. He may be very confused. Just...give it time.' She gave me a little smile. 'But you can't sit and wallow over this, you've changed your life for a boy before, Teddy, and I'm happy you're here, but you can't stop living your life while you wait for Vincent to sort out his. So, in the meantime, we go out, we drink and watch boy candy. Come on.'

I smiled at her, rubbing circles on her back with my hand. 'Fine. But I won't dance with anybody.'

'You'll dance with me, though, right?'

'Of course.'

I stood up, wearing the opposite of sexy clothing and made my way to my bedroom to get changed, ready to start a fun night and forget about my issues.

A few hours later, Laura and I were on our fourth cocktail and watching people dance to *I Kissed a Girl* by Katy Perry. Clubs in Italy were a bit hit and miss. They were amazing during the summer, especially when near the beach and the temperature was a solid thirty-four degrees at eleven at night. Middle of winter?

Eh.

The dancefloor reminded me slightly of the dingy gym where we had our senior spring formal. Except my skin was slightly clearer and I wasn't wearing a *Sailor Moon* t-shirt. Other than that, it was roughly filled with the same number of boys ignoring me, although this time it hurt more, because all of them were gay.

The floor was sticky, the air was cold, and my date was a girl. What a flashback. Laura was sitting in front of me, looking dolled up and gorgeous. Her golden hair was down—which didn't happen all that often—her feline light green eyes were sparkling and her face was glowing with awe.

'You haven't stopped smiling since we got here,' I said. 'What have you done with my Laura?'

'I smile all the time,' she said. Dead in the eyes.

'You usually don't have the strength to smile. I guess someone is happy to kickstart their brilliant future as *prima ballerina* of the Royal Academy of Performing Arts?'

'I only got an audition, Teddy. It's hardly a done deal.'

I rolled my eyes up. She was so talented, I had zero doubts she'd make it big. 'It's a huge deal. And I couldn't be prouder.'

'Thank you. I'm a little proud,' she said, clinking her glass with mine. 'So,' she looked around. 'Any boys here you'd like to play with?'

'I don't think I'm in the mood,' I said, in a defeated tone.

'Edward.'

'Ew.'

'I know you're thinking about him, but there's no harm in having a little fun. You could make out with anyone here.'

'Yeah, I could do that,' I said, trying to picture it and getting myself hyped for it.

'You could.'

'I could do that right now!'

'You could do that all evening!'

'Like yeah. Fuck him! Ignoring me after our last call! That's not cool.'

'Okay, I don't think we should insult him now,' she said, with a giggle.

'I could have anyone I want. I'm going to find myself a guy. My prince charming! Right now!'

'Do that!' she said, raising her glass.

I skulled the last of my drink and made my way to the bar to flirt with some guys. It being my fourth drink of the evening, my walk was less of a runway one and more of a clumsy-trip-on-everything kind of stride, but I made it safely to the counter. I leaned on it and ordered myself a rum and coke.

As I waited for my drink to be made, I scanned the dance floor to find anyone wearing a shining armour. And just as I was about to huff and puff, annoyed in defeat, I locked eyes with someone. A tall guy with shaved head, a tight shirt and a general expression which all Italian gays shared. The *I'll-seduce-you-and-stomp-on-your-heart* kind of expression.

Perfect, really.

He smiled wickedly at me, cocking his head towards the dance floor. Though it wasn't an approach I'd normally go for, as my first instinct was to ask for his name, age, occupation, organ donor status and a recent fit note; this time would be different.

I smiled back, linking my fingers with his and letting him pull me through the crowd. We were in the middle of the club, toe to toe, his hand on my hip. I let my eyes fall shut and started moving, letting myself lean into his firm body. The music vibrated through me, the bass overtaking my pulse and setting its own rhythm. I finally let myself go. Strobe lights danced behind my eyelids and acrid artificial smoke combined to build me a new reality, one where it was just me and the rhythm of this nameless song.

A strong arm snaked around my waist, my hips against his, I felt his body against mine, moving as one.

I let my head fall back slightly, opening my eyes for the barest of seconds. Reality slapped me once again. It was not Vincent's gentle slate-coloured eyes I saw. Everything was wrong. It felt wrong.

Sexy, fit, beautiful Italian boys as far as the eyes could see, and my mind could not stop thinking about chalky skin and dopey hair. So, I sucked in a deep breath and smiled at him awkwardly, trying to convey that I had no intention of dancing with him any longer. A part of me wanted to tell him that it wasn't him, it was me. I was doomed to succumb to my own dumb romantic self, falling for a near-impossible guy. It wasn't his fault.

It was my silly heart's.

I walked back to the bar, collected yet another pair of drinks, and walked back to my trusted table.

'You weren't feeling it?' she asked.

'Nope. So, we drink,' I said.

We both sipped our cocktails without saying much to each other for a few minutes, and then it was as if a lightbulb lit up over her head.

'Look, alternatively...we could do this in London.'

'What are you talking about?'

'My audition in London? You think I want to go by myself?!'

'Oh! I've never been to London!'

'Exactly! We go see the city, eat terrible beige food and have fun!'

My eyes lit up. 'That sounds amazing.'

'There's only one catch.'

I knew it. Too good to be true.

'The academy will be having a celebration party on that weekend. You'll need to help me pick a costume and a mask.'

'I *love* a ball!' I shouted.

'No, Teddy. Not a ball. Just a party to congratulate everyone auditioning.'

'Yay, oh my god. A proper *ball*!'

'It's theatre kids just wanting to dress up in elaborate costumes to make us feel like we're auditioning for Versailles,' she said, eyes sparkling with excitement. 'So, are you in? A little sibling-bonding time abroad?'

'I don't think we have any more bonding to do!'

'I think it would be a lot of fun!'

I smiled at her and tapped my hands on the table with excitement. The prospect of seeing London for the first time made my heart pound with anticipation. I couldn't wait to tell Vincent, ask him about the best places to go, but then remembered he wasn't speaking to me. My face was just about to turn into a frown, and then my phone rang.

Laura looked at my display and laughed.

'It's our evening,' I said. 'I shouldn't.'

'You're dying to. Please tell Vincent I say hi.'

'I'll be super quick,' I said, while getting up and running away from the table, trying to find a quiet spot.

I walked outside, near the entrance of the club, where everyone was smoking or trying to catch a break from the endless pop music. My phone was still ringing, and I finally picked up the call, while kicking a few stones with my foot.

'Hello?' I said, trying my best to sound cool and detached.

'...I owe you an apology,' he said. No preambles.

'Are you okay?'

'Yes. No. No. I'm not. I'm the fucking worst. I'm sorry.'

'Vincent, what are you talking about?'

'You're really going to make me say it?'

I didn't say anything.

'I'm...what we did the other day on the phone...Teddy...'

'You can talk to me. We can talk it out.'

'I love our chats. I love talking to you. But after the other night...I've never felt more confused. I thought not speaking to you for a while would clear my head, but...'

'But...?'

'...it made me miss you.'

I missed you too, Vincent.

'...I feel like there's another 'but' coming,' I said.

'Do you think we can...take a little step back?' he asked.

I felt as if my heart was given a tight squeeze but I understood. Sure, in my head it seemed as if I had known Vincent forever, but we only had been talking for a few weeks. I had my entire life to come to terms with my sexuality. I had no business pushing him into something he wasn't ready for. I knew this, and yet...the idea of taking a step back hurt me.

'I'll do whatever you want, Vincent.'

'I just…want to clear my head. But I still want you to be part of my life. Just like before.'

'I'd be happy to do that.'

'Really?' he asked, sounding surprised.

'Look. I'd be lying if I said I didn't enjoy our last phone call and—'

'I did too.'

Wait, what?

'You did?' I asked.

'Try to be patient, Teddy. I just need to think things through.'

I nodded.

'You still there?' he asked.

'I'll be waiting for you. And I'll hold your hand through it all. Just don't shut me out.'

'I won't.'

'Perfect. We have a deal then,' I said, trying to smile through it. 'Has Hazel told you to call, by the way?'

'I got reprimanded a bit, yeah,' he laughed. 'I deserved it, though. Not speaking to you accomplished nothing. All I wanted to do was to sit in front of my laptop and talk to you about my day.'

'Well, you're here with me now. How was your day, Vincent?'

'Honestly? I can't remember at all. I feel much better now.'

'Happy to hear that. Uhm…I'm out with Laura, so I should probably head back. Don't want her to think I ditched her and left her alone.'

'Talk tomorrow?'

'You can count on it. Goodnight.'

'Goodnight Teddy.'

I put my phone back in my pocket, crossed my arms, leaned against the wall and took a deep breath.

I knew I was allowing myself to fall for him.

And there was nothing I could do to avoid that.

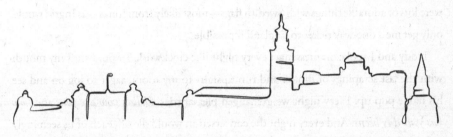

CHAPTER SEVEN

VINCENT
2009

The weeks leading up to Christmas flew by, filled with a blur of snow, visiting my host family's relatives, and eating grotesque amounts of Swedish food. The sun may have been reluctant to show up in December, but the bright twinkling lights, the delicate scent of saffron buns, and the warming taste of mulled wine were enough to make you feel like you were walking inside a snow globe.

My silly friends and I spent our time off from school walking down the decorated streets, watching the magical *NK* shop windows, always bursting with sounds and colours, and observing the bustle of the high street from the inside of a packed café, drinking hot chocolate and gossiping about the other exchange students around the country.

Christmas Day itself was an interesting one. It was Swedish tradition to watch Donald Duck cartoons on TV. Every year. Meanwhile, my darling Hazel was at a ski resort, trying not to kill herself on a snowboard. Daniel also went on a trip with his family, somewhere near Gothenburg. Both having the absolute best time, I often wondered why I had to have the tyrant host mother who, even during Christmas dinner, didn't miss a beat with sending side eyes and providing passive-aggressive remarks.

'How come you don't speak to your father, Vincent?'
'Have you done anything else apart from being behind your silly camera?'

'Could you say that in Swedish, please? You've been in the country long enough to know that phrase!'

And on, and on, and on. However, I did receive some nice presents from them. There were lots of adorable things with Swedish flags—most likely from Jonas—as Ingrid would only get me a one-way ticket to England if possible.

Teddy and I spoke on messenger every night like clockwork. I would stuff my mouth with the last scrapings of dinner and run upstairs to my room, eager to log on and see his name pop up. Every night we exchanged pleasantries. *Hellos, how are yous* and *how has your day beens.* And every night the conversation would die off, each of us seemingly unsure what to say. For as much as I desperately needed the separation and needed to give myself time to work out what the ever-loving hell was happening with me, I just wanted to talk to Teddy.

Instead, we just fished around for threads of normal conversation, sometimes settling into a debate about different movies or books. Sometimes the space between us was so much more than just the physical distance between his house and mine.

I wasn't quite sure how I'd gotten myself into this situation, where what I knew about myself was up in the air and in doubt. I looked at other boys when I went out, forcing myself to look at different parts of them. Comparing them to pretty girls. But nothing stood out, nothing gave me pause, and nothing made my stomach twist like seeing Teddy's name pop up as "online".

We hadn't spoken on the phone since the day I told him I needed to step back. At first, I just needed the time, I wanted my mind to be clear. Then it had been too long, and I wasn't sure how to get it back, how to tell him I wanted to call and hear his sweet voice and that lilting accent. Friends spoke on the phone; it was *normal* to speak on the phone. I knew that. But neither of us made a move to change that, so I settled for our often-stilted conversations, drawing them out for as long as I could. A little time with Teddy was better than no time with Teddy and I would take it, gladly with both hands.

Then after we had said our goodbyes and I had climbed into bed, alone with the dark and my thoughts, the confusion would creep in. I'd examine how I felt. What I'd said. What he'd said. Every heart flip and quiet stretch. Hoping they would line up to tell me what was happening. I'd lay there until sleep took me and the day started again.

I was in my bed, staring at the ceiling, watching the shadows of tree branches outside, moving with the wind. It was a sunny—probably fucking freezing—morning in January, and I was enjoying the last few minutes of a long, overdue lie in.

It was, after all, my birthday.

I yawned, loudly. Stretched my arms.

Eighteen. I was eighteen.

Officially an adult. And yet, I still felt like a kid. It was my birthday and it was a big one. I wasn't sure what kind of person I'd be at eighteen, but living in a house filled with people who didn't care for me much, or constantly questioning myself and my feelings, wasn't what I had pictured.

I grabbed my phone and looked at the little *Razr* screen. Texts and multiple missed calls, which made me smile. Family, friends from home, people from across Sweden all made sure I was feeling loved on my special day.

"Happy Birthday, mooch! We can both go out clubbing, finally!" popped up on my phone screen. Hazel was the first to turn eighteen, so she had been waiting patiently for me to join the adult club. I was very excited at the idea of being able to drink legally.

One had to be eighteen to buy alcohol at restaurants and clubs in Sweden, but had to be twenty to purchase bottles at the liquor store. Weird law, but I could live with it.

I was basking in the comfortable warmth that was being thought of by loved ones, when I heard a knock on my door.

Ugh. Go away.

'Come in,' I said, knowing full well I'd regret it. Like inviting Dracula in.

'*Grattis*, Vincent!' said Jonas, with a cake in his hands: strawberries, candles, the whole nine yards. Ingrid followed with a bottle of champagne. I had no fucking clue what was going on.

'Happy Birthday!' said Amanda with a big smile.

'Oh my goodness, thank you,' I said, awkwardly.

'It's Swedish tradition to have strawberries and champagne in bed for your eighteenth birthday!' said Jonas.

I blew out the candles and wished for a day of peace without Ingrid's constant scrutiny.

'What did you wish for?' she asked.

'I can't say, or it won't come true,' I said with a wink. 'Thank you so much for this. I wasn't expecting it at all!'

'Take your time and come downstairs. We have pastries and coffee,' said Jonas.

'Excellent. I'm just going to quickly call my mother and I'll be there.'

'Also, this came in,' said Ingrid, placing a box on the floor. 'All the way from Italy.'

I smiled, thrilled to check its contents as soon as the Lindbergs would fuck off away from my room.

They closed the door and left me alone with the champagne. I took a big swig and frog-jumped towards the box, which looked like it had been on a journey around the globe. I slashed it open with a pair of scissors, as if I was the killer in an 80s horror film going to town on an unsuspecting teenager.

And then it came out. Staring at me with kind eyes, was a fluffy teddy bear with a big bow around its neck. Imbued with what was obviously Teddy Clarke's aftershave, I hugged it as tight as I could. Perhaps I was already a little tipsy, but I couldn't get over how sweet it was. I put my robe on and had another sip of champagne, while I sat on my trusty chair, with the laptop on my lap and a bowl of fresh strawberries on the desk for me to snack on. Mid-morning wasn't exactly the usual time I'd talk to him, but I was hoping Teddy would be online. Being my birthday and all.

He didn't disappoint.

Did he ever?

'G'day mister,' he said. 'Quite the special day, isn't it?'

'Guess who came to me after a tumultuous couple of weeks lost in the postal system. He didn't make it for Christmas, but Mister Teddy bear has arrived to me in one piece. Precisely on my birthday.'

'It's a miracle!'

'Did you spray him with your aftershave?'

'Would the answer make you think I'm crazy?'

'We are past that.'

'Then enjoy Teddy's signature scent.'

'Thank you. It's lovely. I love it,' I said, with a smirk.

'I'm so happy. How's your birthday so far? Host family gave you any presents?'

'The best present they could give me is them going away on holiday in a few days!'

'Oh my god, you must be so happy about that.'

'Oh, you have no idea.'

'It sucks we won't get to speak as much,' I typed a sad face.

'What? Why?

I'm going to London with Laura!'

'Oh, yeah. Laura's audition. I didn't realise you'd be going too.'

'Sorry, yes, I must have forgotten to tell you,' he said.

Why didn't he tell me though...

Teddy was going to be 1500 km closer to me and we'd get to interact less. What was I going to do without our chats? Sleep? Study? *Actually* work on my documentary and not be the usual lazy fuck who hated editing more than anything?

This wasn't good.

'I'm so excited to see London. I wish you were there to show me around,' he added.

Funnily enough, I was too.

'I don't know London all that well,' I said.

'Well, we could get lost together and it would be just as fun.'

I sighed. It would be fun, yeah.

'Hey,' he added. 'Do you think we could do a quick phone call today? I know we haven't done it for a while, but it's your birthday, and I'd love to hear your voice. If that's alright with you.'

I wasn't sure what to say. I wasn't sure what to do. Why did everything have to be so damn complicated?

'Maybe later?'

He paused for a few seconds, then typed *'okay...'*

Ellipses.

I'm the worst.

'Thank you so much for the bear and the birthday wishes, Teddy. I just have to go now,' I wrote.

'Yep. I hope you have an amazing birthday, Vincent.'

I closed my laptop and I wanted to scream. I wanted to slap myself for being so weird with him. I drank another glass of champagne and felt its bubbles warm my body up. I sniffed the bear for just another second and then put it by my pillow.

Birthday pastries and coffee were waiting for me.

I walked down the stairs, famished, craving that awesome strawberry cake that was waved under my face. Everyone was sitting at the table, laughing out loud. I raised my brows in confusion and then realised Daniel was sitting with them.

'Hello sleepyhead! Give me a kiss,' he shouted.

Weirdo.

'What are you doing here?' I asked, baffled at his presence.

'That's no way to welcome a guest!' said Ingrid.

I sat down next to Daniel, who seemed incredibly excited for my birthday, far more than I was.

'Finally, our little baby turned eighteen! I'm going to take you out for the day.'

'...and night!' said Jonas. 'You're now allowed an extended curfew.'

'Oh really?' I asked. 'Thanks for that.'

'So...what's the situation regarding clubs? Where's "hot", Amanda?' I asked, doing air quotes.

'Well...there aren't that many I've been to, but there is a really fun gay club on a boat. I was there last week and had the best time.'

It was like I couldn't *ever* escape the G word.

'That sounds like lots of fun!' said Daniel.

My face scrunched up. 'Maybe we can ask Hazel where she'd like to go?'

'I want to go on the boat!' he chanted.

'Fine, Jesus! We'll go full gay. Hope you have glitter handy.'

'Glitter may be your birthday present, Vincent.'

'Please don't get me presents,' I said, while munching on cake.

Daniel smiled at me and then turned to the host parents. Everyone loved him, so keeping them busy and away from me was just a testament to how much he valued me as a friend.

'I hear you're going on holiday in Oman in a few days?' he asked.

'Yes, we are really excited to have some time under the sun,' said Jonas.

'Will you and Vincent be doing anything fun in the meantime?' asked Ingrid.

'Unfortunately, not. I'll be going to Helsingborg with my host parents.'

'Oh, that sounds like fun. Why don't you join them, Vincent?' she asked while staring at me.

I wasn't listening much, so I kind of looked at her as if I had just woken up. With a cinnamon roll in my mouth. 'What, now?'

'If it's okay with Daniel's family, you could join them for a little trip! So, you don't have to be alone in front of your laptop.'

'I'm more than okay with being alone.'

'I'd like it if you came,' said Daniel.

'I'll think about it, okay?' I said, trying to enjoy the rest of my birthday breakfast.

'I would hate to see you sitting in the dark, just spending the entire day indoors,' she pretend-worried.

'Ingrid, all you're going to see is a shining sun and crystal-clear water. Do not worry about me! I'll be sweet as.'

'...as what?'

Christ, was I adopting Aussie into my vocabulary?

'Don't mind me,' I said, ready to wash my plate, when Jonas took it off me.

'No chores on your birthday, Vincent. Just go have fun,' he said with kind eyes.

'Thank you,' I smiled. 'Daniel, want to get ready with me?' I asked, pulling his hair. Hard.

'Okay, okay!' he exclaimed. '*Vi ses snart!*' he said to the family, pretending to tip his hat off to them.

I rolled my eyes and dragged him upstairs with me to get sorted for the day.

It was a day of celebration. My friends made me feel special by taking me out for both lunch and dinner respectively. The two of them were the best thing to come out of my exchange year.

'So, what's your expectation from this evening, mister Stewart?' Hazel asked. We were having dinner at a Chinese buffet restaurant, my favourite.

'Frankly,' I said while biting on a spring roll. 'I kind of just want to get pissed and dance like an idiot.'

'Calm down. I can't even tell you how expensive it is to get drunk at a club here,' said Daniel.

'Damn. We should have thought about it earlier,' I said, worried.

'That is why we got a birthday bottle of vodka for us!' said Hazel showing a bottle inside her handbag.

'That's half a bottle,' I said.

'That's all my host sister had. Make do, Vincent,' she said with a smile.

'Alright, fill my glass, woman!' I said, passing her a glass under the table.

Daniel put an arm around me and gave me a kiss on the cheek. 'Happy birthday, you English bastard.'

Perhaps that was the reason why Amanda made the gay suggestion. She probably thought my bromance with Daniel was an actual full-blown gay relationship. I couldn't blame her. Daniel would randomly hug me and kiss me on the cheek all the time.

If only she knew *she* was the actual object of his sexual attraction. Along with any other woman on the planet.

We drank the bottle in no time, so quickly we all got tipsy at record speed. Soon after, a cab took us near *Slussen*, the area where *Patricia*, the boat, was moored.

The ship was massive: like a freighter and *The Black Pearl* had a baby. Fairy lights of every colour were woven through railings, wrapped around poles, and somehow attached to the black sides, twinkling a rainbow in the dark. We passed through a small room that acted as the entrance, music vibrating through the walls. We held our hands out for a little stamp showing we had paid the entry fee and were, in fact, of legal age. A tiny, inked ship saying I could now drink and be in this club.

The inside of the boat was just as colourful. Disco lights and a jam-packed dance floor made for a very sweaty experience. There were many older men, dressed in leather, in full drag make-up, or covered in sequins. I noticed groups of friends having the time of their lives, screaming and shouting around a birthday-hat-wearing blonde girl in high heels. Probably the same kind of crew my host sister would go out partying with.

The three of us were sitting in a red-leather booth, just looking at the packed dance-floor. Decent chance there were far fewer people, and I was just seeing quadruple from the alcohol.

'What about birthday girl over there?' Hazel asked. 'She seems hot, easy, and she's wearing a mini skirt that if it was any shorter you could see her lunch!'

'Hazel don't shame the beautiful screaming girls!' said Daniel.

'They shame themselves, Daniel.'

'What do you say, Vincent?' he asked, putting his hand on my shoulder. 'Shall we mingle and get ourselves some puss?'

'Fucking hell, Daniel. That's disgusting,' she replied. Then looked at me. 'But yes, Vincent. Why don't you dirty dance with a hot bimbo? It's your birthday and that's the closest you'll get to a stripper!'

'I...don't want to?' I said, slightly disgusted by the whole conversation.

'Why is that?' she asked, clearly alluding at something.

'Because—'

'Come on, bud,' he said, pushing me out of the booth.

'Alright, fine!' I shouted.

I drank a shot of tequila and followed him to the dancefloor, while Hazel stayed behind to finish her gin and tonic.

Daniel was his usual self. Except he was wearing a sleeveless tee and his muscles were the ideal chick magnet. He started dancing with the group of girls, making a tit out of himself, lip syncing to *Disturbia* by Rihanna. I was just a little behind when one of the girls started dancing near me.

My whole body went stiff, incapable of socialising in a natural way.

'Hi!' I screamed, hoping to talk my way out of how uncomfortable I was feeling.

'Hey,' she said. She looked a bit tipsy, but not any more drunk than I was. 'Where are you from?'

'England! I'm Vincent!'

'Nice to meet you!' she shouted over the music. I didn't catch her name at all. Didn't really matter.

I gazed across the wooden dance floor and with a sudden burst of confidence—exclusively due to alcohol levels in my body—I put my arm around her waist and began to dance.

The music was loud, the rhythm pounding through my head, hazy with alcohol and atmosphere. We moved through the crowd of sweat sticky bodies, hips together and our hands in the air. I looked like an idiot, but I couldn't bring myself to care. Today was a special day, today I stood proudly at the gates of adulthood.

My eyes fell shut, the strobe iridescent and otherworldly, my head swimming into a dream. And I thought of you. Your soft brown hair, golden where the sun hit. Cat-like eyes, warm and green. Your perfect cheekbones and sharp jaw. I could almost see you before me, your flushed skin shiny, teasing into your shirt with the buttons half done. Your fingers laced with mine, pulling me to you. Chest to chest, your heartbeat learning the tune of mine. I'd tilt my head back, your hand pulling through the loose strands of my hair.

But this wasn't real. You weren't here.

I opened my tired, glossy eyes, and you weren't there with me. The wrong person was in front of me. Heck, everyone was the wrong person.

I looked at my poor unsuspecting dance partner, still dancing seductively in front of me, getting close enough for us to kiss, and taste each other, when a shiver that felt like a lightning bolt went down my spine. I knew I had to get some fresh air.

'I'm sorry, I'll be right back!' I shouted.

She nodded, and I made my way outdoors, breaking into the cloud of smoke from people chilling outside with their cigarettes.

The heat I felt on the dancefloor was quickly replaced by the stinging cold of a Swedish night by the sea. I opened my phone and immediately looked for a number.

His number.

The two rings that preceded his voice felt endless. My heart was racing, fearing he wouldn't pick up my call, but Teddy's warm tone finally greeted me.

'Hello?'

'Teddy!' I uttered. 'My Teddy.'

'Hey, what's going on?' he asked, in a slightly amused tone.

'It's my birthday!' I screamed.

'It is! Are you having a good one, Vincent?'

'I'm just great! It's great! Everything is great!'

'I'm happy to hear that. What are you up to?'

'I'm at a club. Very drunk. A gay club.'

'A gay club?' he giggled. 'Never thought I'd see the day!'

'You and I both!'

I was walking in circles, nervous to speak to him, for some reason.

I sighed loudly, trying to gather the right words to say. A trying task, after ingesting my own weight in mysterious, colourful shots.

'Are you okay?' he asked, perhaps apprehensive about my state of mind.

'I don't know what's happening. Everything is so confusing, it may be the alcohol talking...honestly, I don't know. All I know is that one second I was on the dance floor, arms around a pretty girl, but I couldn't be there. I left her there and came out here. Outside. I ran out so I could talk to you.'

'Why is that, Vincent?'

'Because as stupid and crazy and a million other words that would describe the insane feelings, I have no business feeling...'

I took a deep breath, looked at the starry sky, looked down at the water. My heart was pounding, my mouth felt dry. I had no idea if words would come out, but I pushed them out.

'I need to see you, Teddy.'

'What?'

'I want to see you.'

'Vincent, I—'

'Is it crazy? Is it stupid?' I asked, trembling from anxiety.

'It's...neither. I...you know how I feel.'

'I don't know how you feel! We've been tiptoeing around each other and it's silly, because...I'm scared. I'm terrified of what I feel. Of what I could become.'

'Then meet me. Meet me in London. Don't tell me over the phone. *Take me somewhere we can be alone.*'

I smiled through my tears.

'*Baby, just say yes,*' he whispered, hopeful.

I took a deep breath, looked at the horizon, the moon shining onto the sea, the city lights gleaming around me.

'Yes.'

CHAPTER EIGHT

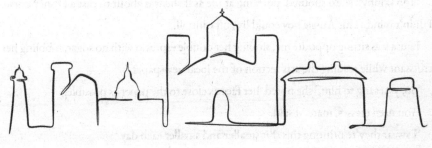

TEDDY

2009

B reakfast in Italy was a slow ritual. Back home, I'd be throwing a piece of brown bread like a frisbee, while trying to pass my giant feet through the unbelievably tight uniform trousers my mum had tailored for me. The gay little thing I was, I couldn't be caught dead in a lumpy get up like the other douche kids. But there wasn't a single day I managed to be up early for school. I'd often stay up late at night, watching *Desperate Housewives* or just adding glittery images and picking a new *Taylor Swift* song to Myspace.

Good old days.

It was toast and vegemite every day. Pancakes on weekends. It was just what I knew. I never thought one day I'd be slowly sipping a cappuccino while being fuelled by several pastries at once.

Laura and I used to go to this lovely little café near the house all the time, ran by our neighbour. We'd often skip school together or just skip the first hour of lectures. She could get away with murder because she was the darling ballerina and I...well, I could do whatever I wanted. Exchange student power.

The café was run by the oldest lady in the world. One hundred and seventy-five-years old easily. Giuseppina was tiny and round, she had kind eyes and a cloud of perfume followed her wherever she went. She made the best coffee in town; her sweet pastries were all homemade and the café itself was filled with knick-knacks she'd collected throughout her undoubtedly eternal life. She also really enjoyed my face and would often give me extra everything.

'Too skinny!' she'd shouted, pointing at me as if she was about to cast a Disney curse. I didn't mind. This Aussie boy could live off cannoli.

Laura was sitting opposite me, sipping her double espresso with no sugar, nibbling her croissant while reading the arts section of the local newspaper.

'So, you sang to him,' she noted, her face as close to the paper as possible.

'You need glasses, mate,' I said.

'I swear they're printing this shit smaller and smaller each day.'

'Honestly, eye doctor. See one. We could go after my haircut.'

'I don't need glasses. Have you ever seen a dancer with glasses?'

'Well, that seems like a trick question. I only watch *you* dance.'

'You don't wear glasses. They look dumb. I can't look dumb.'

'Contacts?'

'I'm fine!' she said, while closing the newspaper and putting it away. 'Here. Full undivided attention.'

'Thank you. I can't see why you'd be reading that when you have your brilliant brother in front of you telling you about his—cautiously—developing love life.'

'So, he called you while he was wasted—'

'Tipsy,' I interrupted.

'...hammered.'

'Potentially.'

'...and he said he'd like to see you.'

'Those exact words. Plus, the Taylor references.'

'Why are you like this?' she asked, smirking.

'What? What do you mean? I thought we loved this. I thought we liked me being romantic and having this moment with him.'

'We do, we do. I'm just—'

I widened my eyes, waiting for the rest of the sentence.

'...what if it was the alcohol talking? In vino...'

'Why would you put that in my head?' I asked, my voice changing pitch with mild hysteria. 'Like I don't have enough to worry about. I have Giuseppina making me fat, my hair is a mess, and I can feel a spot growing on my face. Now I have to worry Vincent didn't mean any of what he said?'

'Well. You know how you get when *you* drink.'

'Like what?'

'You kind of love everybody, that's what you do.'

'That's because I'm deprived of attention! That's my subconscious wanting to be loved!'

'It was weird when you did that with my cousin.'

'There was a lot of wine involved. Don't come for me. Your family was on a mission to get me *blotto*. Then they all made fun of my Italian.'

'That's because it sounded like Klingon.'

'You know, sometimes I feel like if you had spoken Italian to me like, oh I don't know, ONCE, I would have learned more.'

'Yeah, but that's no fun.'

'I taught you everything. And what did I get in return? Swear words.'

'There are some good ones. You can practice on Francesco one day. If he doesn't beat you up next time he sees you.'

'I could take on Francesco,' I said, raising my fists up.

'He lives near the stadium. You don't want to fuck with those people,' she said, dismissively.

'Woooow, someone just put classist in classic ballet!'

'That...doesn't even fit.'

'You know what I mean!' I said, pointing at her. 'Mean girl. What were we saying?'

'How strong you are.'

'No, that's not it.'

'Last night! You were telling me about the phone call!'

I inhaled half of my chocolate croissant and stared at her with giant hamster cheeks, forcing myself to swallow what felt like a heaven flavoured rock. I punched my chest trying not to choke on puff pastry. 'I think he's going to come to London!'

'Really?'

'Yeah, why are you surprised?'

'Remember the amount of shit we got from IESP for flying you to Tuscany? It was a Bible worth of paperwork.'

'Ha! Here's the kicker! I don't think he should tell IESP at all!'

'That's a great idea! Then he can just stay in the UK, because he'd be expelled from the program so quickly, he won't even need to fly back to Stockholm!'

'You are so negative sometimes,' I said, while standing up and brushing the crumbs off my purple turtleneck. 'I'll go pay.'

'Like she will let you.'

No joke, I went to Giuseppina a million times and maybe paid twice. Maybe my soulmate was in front of me all along. Complimentary, cooked incessantly, great stories. Screw men!

I walked over to the lovely old lady I could rest my own chin on comfortably, got called *bellissimo* and a bunch more words I couldn't possibly know, and managed to talk to her for over twenty minutes. I couldn't escape.

Afterwards, we headed to a salon. The only one in Cagliari where the hairdressers spoke some English. It was my go-to place to get my highlights done and to listen to hairstylists talking shit about each other.

It was imperative I'd look my best when going to London, so Laura and I decided to treat ourselves. Laura was sitting next to me, getting her golden locks trimmed by her usual guy. Meanwhile I was waiting patiently for Serena to come do mine. I was facing Laura directly, while she was looking at me via the mirror, as she couldn't move her head.

'So, what do you think we should do?' I asked.

'What are you on about?'

'You gave me anxiety over the IESP thing!'

'Oh that? Is that the only thing giving you anxiety? Nothing about the encounter itself? Or potential lack of encounter?'

'What about the encounter? It's Vincent.'

'What if it's a sixty-five-year-old dude pretending to be him? And you meet up in London and he's humming Taylor Swift songs while spitting his dentures at you?'

I just stared at her. Immobile. Traumatised.

'I'm just saying,' she added. 'You dive into things face first. I have to try and do damage control before you smack your teeth onto a guy you know very little about.'

'I know it sounds crazy,' I said, while leaning closer to her. 'You just have to trust me on this. Vincent is...amazing. And even though we are distant, I feel like I really know him.'

'I get it,' she said, turning to me and looking at me in the eyes. 'I just want you to manage your expectations. Don't forget this is the same guy who isn't even sure about liking guys to begin with.'

'He...likes *me*, though.'

'Just be careful, okay?' she said with a comforting smile, while touching my hand softly.

I smiled back, then heard a man's voice behind me, speaking in broken English.

'Serena's sick today. What can I do for you?'

I sat up straight again and locked eyes with him through the mirror. My fucking luck. Francesco's big muscle Mary boyfriend was standing behind me.

Of course, he's a hairdresser.

Laura started giggling, while I had pretty much made peace with the fact, he was going to shave my head bald.

Fuck.

I spent the rest of that evening and a great deal of the night thinking about Laura's words. My self-esteem had taken a few hits. Not only was my hair butchered by a vengeful homo with scissors, but I didn't get to speak to Vincent, as he had to have a "last dinner" with his host family before their trip away.

After a night of tossing and turning, adrenaline pumping through my veins, and pure anxious dread preventing my eyes from slipping shut for even a moment, I gave up on sleep altogether. I got up, took a scalding shower, tried to fix my hair, put on a slightly tinted moisturiser, and dressed in the cosiest knitted jumper, and jeans so tight you could see my chicken legs from space.

I left the house before anyone in the family woke up. I wanted to play some loud music, dance like a coked-up version of Kevin Bacon, and shout from the rooftops about how ecstatic I was at the thought of Vincent wanting to see me. I also wanted to smack Laura for planting a thousand doubts in my head. I was conflicted.

I needed to find peace.

I drove to the beach, hoping the early hour would afford me some quiet and let my mind settle. The whisper of a breeze rolled off the ocean, carrying the bite of winter and lacing the air with salt. I pulled off my shoes, dug my toes into the sand and sipped my to-go cup of coffee I'd brought from home. I leaned back on my elbows, crystalline waves breaking at my feet and the sky above me sifting through its morning wardrobe, trying every shade on before settling into its favourite worn blue. We could have this, Vincent and I. Sandy feet and sunrises, shoulder to shoulder. We could have this quiet alone, together, waiting for the world to awaken. I let my eyes fall shut, my mind at rest, just you and me and the world.

One day.

A seagull and a foghorn had few things in common, their ability to make me shit myself was one they shared, however. I woke with a start, seagull screeching and time missing. I dragged my satchel onto my lap and started to dig through it for my phone. The chances of losing my hand were fair, somehow a lifetime of receipts created the ideal nest for gum and energy bars to breed and multiply.

It was the perfect time to call my dear mother. One of the perks of being up so early was being able to communicate with the motherland without having to face a brutal time difference.

The phone rang for over a minute, before she finally picked up.

'Hello?' she said, in a soft-spoken, slightly husky voice.

'Mum! Were you asleep?'

'Uhm, yes. I guess I was.'

'It's...7pm over there. Is everything alright?' I asked.

'I'm not sure. I just don't seem to have a lot of energy at the moment. I'm up now, though. How are you, my darling?'

'Well, I'm a little worried about you now. You don't sound like you're doing too good. What's the doctor saying?'

'Oh, fuck all.'

'Mum!'

'Sorry, it's just been really frustrating. He thinks I'm depressed and not getting enough vitamin D, or some crap like that.'

'Do you feel depressed?'

'No, I feel annoyed! It's hard to focus at school. It's like a brain fog.'

'Maybe you do need vitamins, or iron, or whatever.'

'Yeah, maybe.'

'Why don't you go get a second opinion?'

'Yeah, I suppose.'

'Do you want me to call for you?' I asked.

'I can handle a phone call myself, Teddy,' she said, laughing. 'I promise I'll do that.'

'Good. Because I enjoy my upbeat mummy,' I said.

'Don't worry. But tell me about you! What are you doing up so early?'

I smiled just at the thought of it. 'Remember when I talked about Vincent?'

'The boy who lives in Switzerland?'

'Sweden.'

'Yes, yes.'

'I think I have a big crush, mum.'

'Of course you do. He sounds like a very nice boy. Unlike that other one. I never cared for him much.'

'You have to say that!'

'No, I'm serious! You deserve better! Are you guys planning to meet up?'

My whole body was trembling with excitement. I was about to scream YES as loudly as I could but decided to maintain my composure.

'...maybe.'

'Maybe? Do tell!' she said, almost squealing with joy.

'Oh, mum. I knew you'd share the same level of excitement. He called to tell me he'd like to see me.'

'Where will you meet? Will you be flying over?'

'Noo. That would be way too stalkerish. I don't want to frighten him. He wouldn't be able to cope with that amount of Teddy.'

'Any amount of Teddy is the perfect amount of Teddy. I, for one, could do with more Teddy. I miss you so much.'

'I miss you too mum. But I'll see you in just over two weeks.'

'I'm counting down the days! So, is this Vincent meeting you in Sardinia? Or London?'

'We haven't fully discussed it yet. And, full disclosure, he was a little tipsy when he told me.'

'Oh boy,' she murmured.

'No! No *oh boy*, mum. It'll be fine. And it'll be splendid.'

'Splendid.'

'Yup. Wonderfully splendid. In fact, I may call him soon just to check he still remembers me.'

'Trust me, no one could ever forget you.'

'Again, that's what you're supposed to say!'

'Give him a call. He'll love hearing your voice. I know I have,' she said.

'Okay. Please, please, please get your health in check! I'm going to need you in top form when I fly back to Australia. Have a nice evening, mum.'

'Goodnight Mitchell,' she said, before hanging up.

Huh?

Gosh, she was sleepy. She hadn't gotten Mitchell and I confused since I was in kindergarten.

My credit card was tired. I had been in all my favourite shopping spots in Cagliari to get myself a whole new wardrobe of pretty clothes to wear in London. Vincent or not, I still wanted to live my best Audrey Hepburn fantasy and wear amazing outfits while strolling around the amazing city. And sure, if Vincent did decide to come, I wanted to look my best for him. I walked inside the house with my twenty bags in one hand and a stack of pizza on the other. I closed the door with my foot and shouted to make my presence known.

'*Mamma*, Laura! I brought pizza!'

It didn't look like there was anyone home, but the bathroom light was on, and I was hearing strange moaning noises. I placed the pizzas on a table and put my bags down. I walked towards the bathroom and I found Laura in tears, sitting on the floor.

'Hey, what is going on?' I asked, worried.

'Hey. It's nothing...' she said while holding her ankle.

'Did you get hurt?' I asked, kneeling next to her.

'It's the usual. My ankle is playing up.'

'Shit, are you going to be okay for the audition?'

'I have to. I can't believe this is happening. I have been working on this for so long and now my body decides to betray me.'

'Hey, you'll be okay. Let me grab some ice for you,' I said while standing up. I ran to the kitchen to get some frozen peas. I felt so bad for her. Laura had been dancing since she was four years old. She was incredibly talented, and I hated seeing her suffer.

I grabbed the bag of peas and ran to the bathroom.

'Here,' I said while placing it onto her foot.

'Thank you.'

'What are you going to do if it doesn't get better?'

'It has to get better. I'll take a pain killer. Or a whole pill bottle of them.'

'Okay. Hey, I got us pizza. Would you like for us to have dinner here? In the bathroom?'

'I can't really move now. So...yes?'

'Well, that's just gross...alright!' I stood up and walked to the kitchen once again to grab the pizzas. I took a second to look at the photos of the family. I had seen them all before, but it was nice to see little Laura in her tutu when she was four, or photos of the family in various world locations. I was there too, in a few frames. Our best moments captured on camera proudly displayed as if I was a full-fledged member of the family.

A part of me was truly worried about the future and how long it would be for me to see them again, after going back to Australia permanently.

I didn't want to think about that. I had another two weeks. I still had some time to fill them with as many happy memories as I could.

I took the pizza boxes and carried them to the bathroom. Laura had luckily calmed down. Her eyes were no longer teary.

'There you go, my queen,' I said, getting myself seated on the floor.

'Thank you for doing this. I am so glad you're here.'

'Are you alright? This can't be just about the ankle.'

She sighed. 'I am freaking the hell out. I don't know Teddy. I have worked on this my entire life. This ankle has been hurting constantly. Is this it? Has my dancing career ended before it's even started?'

'Why are you talking like that?'

'Because I have done so much to fix this damn ankle and it's still hurting.'

'It will be better before the weekend. You are going to rock that damn audition and that's all there is. We will have an incredible time in London! You should be ecstatic!'

'I should be fasting, really.'

'I have just over two weeks left to enjoy the best pizza in the world. You're going to fucking eat it with me.'

She grabbed a slice and started eating it.

'Did you hear from Vincent?' she asked.

'I'll speak to him after dinner. This is our pizza time.'

'It's our ankle funeral time.'

'I can't stop thinking about him risking it all. He has another half a year left in his exchange. Those are precious memories I would not want him to lose. I would have been devastated if my year was cut in half. That's the half where you actually learn the language and make friends...'

'You said it yourself though. He's pretty smart. I doubt he'd get into it without having a solid plan.'

'That's true,' I said biting into a slice of pizza.

'But if he does go...you sure you should be stuffing yourself with carbs?' she said laughing.

'You fuck off and stop making me feel self-conscious about my body.'

'I'm joking,' she giggled. 'I'm actually quite curious to meet him. Unless you're just planning on locking yourself in a room with him, so you can have monkey sex.'

'Oh please.'

'Just remember I still want my ball with you. Even if you bring him.'

'Ha! So, you admit it's a ball!'

'I feel like you'd hurt me if I didn't address it as such.'

'Bloody would.'

We looked at each other and smiled.

'I should call him,' I said.

'Yeah, you should. You'll be fine. Just be mindful I may eat all of the pizza in the meantime.'

'They'll love you being all podgy and squidgy,' I said with a smirk.

She threw a toilet paper roll at me, but I managed to close the door in time.

Ha-ha!

I entered my room and immediately jumped on my bed. Vincent's phone was ringing, and my body was as restless as my pulse. I wriggled around until my butt was against my headboard and my feet were leaning on the wall above, toes to the ceiling.

'Hey!' he said, enthusiastically.

'Bad time?' I asked.

'No, no, no. Not a bad time at all. How are you?'

'I'm okay! Had a disastrous haircut, but I'll be okay. Tell me about you! Party animal!'

'Hardly. Although I had my first official hangover and I was not a fan.'

'That bad?'

'My head was still in the toilet twenty-four hours later. Then Ingrid left, and I felt rejuvenated.'

'Amazing. So, a good birthday, then?'

'It was perfect. I'm sorry if I sounded dramatic on the phone...I didn't—I didn't mean to.'

'Are you trying to say you didn't mean what you said?' I asked, heart dropping for a second.

'No...no, I did. I really did.'

'Are you okay, Vincent?'

'Just...talking about...this. Sorry, I'm just not used to it. It's all new. But I absolutely did mean it.'

'So, we're going to see each other?'

'Baby, I said yes,' he chuckled.

'So...it's official?!' I couldn't contain myself.

'We're working on the logistics here...but yes.'

'YES!!' I shouted.

'Teddy, I'm super nervous.'

'Why? Talk to me...'

'I can't wait to see you, I really can't. It's just my nerves. What if you don't like me? What if you regret everything?'

'I can promise you...I won't. Seeing you will be a wish come true.'

'It'll only be twenty-four hours, Teddy.'

'And we'll make them count. Just meet me. Meet me in London.'

'I will. I'll be there.'

We'll be there together.

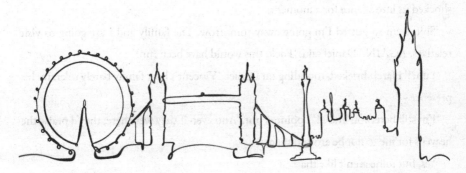

CHAPTER NINE

VINCENT
2009

'Are you out of your fucking mind?' Hazel blurted.

We were having lunch at my place, a much more pleasant location now that my host parents had fucked off to the Middle East to get their winter tan. There was no one to tell me off, no need for me to wash my cereal bowl the second I was done eating. I could hear the birds, the wood fairies, the naked little cherubs playing tiny harps. A guy could get used to all that.

I was munching on a bag of burger-flavoured crisps when I dropped the London bombshell.

'I thought we had already established I am. Why are you suddenly surprised?' I asked.

'Okay, Vincent. It's one thing to chat with a stranger living on the other side of Europe every single day until the early hours of the morning,' she said.

'Not every day. We had those two days where—'

'Whatever,' she interrupted. 'It's also one thing to be sniffing your bear every night.'

'Bro, I don't do that.'

'Yes, you do,' said Daniel.

Such rudeness.

'It's a completely different thing to fly to the United Kingdom without telling anyone!'

'I just told you guys.'

'That's because you want me to come with you!' she shouted. The intensity of her voice shocked us into silence for a moment.

'Shit, I am so gutted I'm going away tomorrow. The family and I are going to visit relatives, AGAIN,' Daniel said. 'Fuck, this would have been fun!'

'Fun?!' Hazel shrieked, rounding on Daniel. 'Vincent's host family barely tolerates his presence—'

'I'm still here, you know!' I pointed out. 'And even if they were here, they'd praise the heavens for me to not be around them.'

'Yes, but mine aren't like that!'

'Which is why you'd be telling them you're with me. To keep me company. The lonely, sweet and adorable Vincent all by himself because his meanie parents wanted to be miserable in the sand, rather than in the snow!'

'Should I try and get out of my parents' trip? Danny wants to go to London!'

'NO!' Hazel and I said in unison.

'Thanks a lot, guys,' he said with a frown.

'Do you really want to risk everything with this absolutely mental idea of yours?' she asked.

'I don't know...'

I really didn't know. I was blinded. This was going to be the only time I'd be able to see Teddy. If I didn't make the effort to see him, then I would most likely regret it in the future. I needed to know if what my whole body was feeling was actually real. I needed to know if we were made for each other.

'I think we can pull this off, Hazel,' I said.

'You're not just risking your exchange year, remember,' she pointed out.

'Okay, realistically, how could your family find out about it?' I asked.

'Well, there could be an emergency and they might go all *we need you home now* and I'm all like *sorry, I'm eating bangers and mash in Piccadilly Circus! Please don't kill me!*'

'Alright, first of all, you wouldn't be eating in Piccadilly Circus. That's tacky and overpriced,' I said.

'Yes, Vincent. That was exactly the takeaway of my story.'

I huffed.

'Haze, I think you should tell your host family you're going with me to Helsingborg. That way they can't just ask you to come back because you're with me. I am sure your family won't be calling us. You can say we are going to visit some sick relative and you're coming with me so that we can do stuff while my host parents do all the sad stuff.'

We all stood there, in silence, staring at each other.

'What?' Daniel said.

'...nothing,' Hazel said. 'I'm dumbfounded that you even came up with such a plan.'

'What?!' he shouted. 'You need to stop thinking of me as a dumb child!'

'Well...you look like one,' I said, poking him on the cheek.

'You two can fuck right off.'

I turned to Hazel. 'I think this may work...'

'I think so too,' she said. 'Look, I am not going to pretend I don't want to see London. I live on the other side of the world. I'd have to fly for twenty-six hours to get there.'

'You have big cities in New Zealand, it can't be that different,' Daniel said.

'I'm just going to ignore that.'

'Just picture it, Haze. You walk around the beautiful sights—'

'By myself,' she interrupted.

'No, I'll be there!'

'You'll be sucking face with Teddy. You would not be walking with me and crying in front of buildings.'

'Why would you cry in front of buildings?'

'Because they're historic, and pretty and I only read about them in books? Keep up, Vincent.'

'Okay,' I said, trying not to agitate the crazy.

'And the photos I'll take. Ah! My perfect portfolio...'

'*Will* take? So, it's decided?'

'*Would*. I meant *would*. In this senseless fantasy land of yours.'

'I heard will,' said Daniel.

'I think you want to go just as much as I do! You just want to see me begging!' I said, pointing a finger at her.

'I wouldn't hate begging.'

I chuckled and moved in slow motion, naively waiting for her to stop me at any point. But she was intent in seeing me kneeling in front of her. 'Please!'

'Oh, my. You really like this guy, then,' she chuckled.

I took a deep breath and decided to speak from the heart. 'Haze, I know you'd do anything for your friends, but I don't want you to lose your spot for me, and if you genuinely aren't okay with this, I can let it go, and go by myself.

'Fine, gosh. Of course, I'll do it. I just wanted to see if I could get you to beg.'

I couldn't believe my ears. There was a part of me that wanted them to talk me out of such an insane plan. If anyone told me I'd be jumping onto a plane to go see a guy I had never met in real life, I would have never believed it. But there I was.

'Worst case scenario, we have a hell of an adventure,' said Hazel.

'I am honestly a little jealous,' said Daniel. 'I kind of want to go too.'

'Hey, if we get away with this one, who's to say we won't be doing it again, somewhere else?' I asked.

'Me. I'm to say that,' she said.

'Hazel and Vincent are going on an adventure!' I announced with a big smile.

It *was* happening.

A sleepless night later, and the time had finally come. I had spent a great deal of the morning nervously trying to tame my hair. To say I was jittery would be the understatement of the century.

Hazel seemed a lot more at ease with the trip, even though it had put a considerable dent in both of our savings. Worse for Hazel, as her New Zealand dollars were virtually useless. I always expected that it would be me who'd be the one calming her, but she was completely relaxed. We were walking towards our gate, the airport being a stir of unknown faces, all rushing to their destinations. A roar of voices and service announcements, with a background of soft classical music playing, while we were walking steadily on the gleaming white tiles to get in the queue boarding the plane. It was the point of no return, the moment where in videogames you get warned you won't be able to go back.

Save now, you fool.

The inside of my mind was a roaring mess. I wasn't sure of anything I was doing. I almost wanted to abort the mission.

'You need to stop worrying,' Hazel said. 'We'll have lots of fun and you'll have lots of sex.'

Sex.

Sex.

Sex? I hadn't even thought about sex. Did I want to have sex? I had never had sex with a guy before. I wouldn't even know how to go about it.

'I am not going to have sex!' I blurted, low-key frightened of the word itself.

'What? Are you crazy? Why the hell are we going then?'

'I don't know. Why *are* we going?'

'You need to snap out of this,' she said while pointing at my face like some military sergeant. 'I won't be having you trembling like a leaf all the way there. You know why we are going.'

'What if I don't feel what I think I feel when I see him?' I questioned, apprehensive.

'Well, lucky for you, I will be there. If you guys don't get on, or get *it* on, we will just go on the London Eye and forget about it.'

'I'm not sure of anything right this second,' I said, about to rip my hair out.

'Stop! You'll have a few glasses of alcohol on the plane and you'll be fine and dandy. Hey, maybe we can focus on finding *me* a boyfriend in London. I could really use the green card.'

'I don't think it's called that in Europe...'

'Shhhh Vincent.'

'Okay. We can absolutely do this,' I said, trying to be positive, for once.

But I didn't know if I could do it. I just knew I had to get there as soon as possible. The quicker we'd start our adventure, the quicker I'd stop feeling a heart attack coming. It was a two-hour flight. It'd be easy.

And then I saw her. That indistinguishable mousey face I had the misfortune of seeing every morning. Panic ensued. I took Hazel's arm and pulled her around, so we'd face the opposite way.

'What the fuck just happened?' she asked.

'My host sister is over there!' I said, terrified.

Hazel's head slightly turned. 'That's not her, that's a middle-aged man with a toupee and a limp!'

'Oh yes, my mistake. For a second I thought that the blond girl over there wearing the orange trench coat was Amanda Lindberg!' I said, angrily digging my nails into her arm.

'Ohhh that. Yes, that's definitely her!'

'Fuck, shit, fuck. Fuckery fuck.'

'Vincent?' I heard from behind.

'Tell me I just dreamed that,' I whispered to Hazel.

We turned around and she was standing a foot away from us.

'Amanda! Hi!' I said, awkwardly.

'What are you doing at the airport?' she asked, slightly suspicious.

'That's an excellent question!' I said.

'I thought you were going with Daniel to Helsingborg?'

'We are! Host family just went to get some snacks for the flight!' Hazel said.

'Where's Daniel?'

I looked at Hazel and patted her on the shoulder. 'This is Daniel!'

I could feel Hazel's big *what the fuck* energy incinerating my face.

'I thought Daniel was the boy—'

'No, no, no. That's my other friend...Hansel.'

'Hansel?'

'Hansel. Yes.'

'We love Hansel,' said Hazel.

'See, I thought you were Hazel, and you were all going to Helsingborg?' she said.

'Yeah, that would have made sense. But nope. Daniel. Right here.'

'Okay, then...' she hesitated, looking at us with her beady eyes in confusion. '...well, you have a nice trip then. We're going now,' said Amanda, giving me a wave.

Hazel and I stayed still. In shock for what had just happened.

'Does your host sister even listen to you when you speak?' she asked.

'I'm sweating. Everywhere,' I said, robotically.

'She's a moron, Vincent.'

'She thinks you're Daniel now. Good. This will be an inside joke we'll laugh at someday,' I said, optimistically.

'Not today,' she said, in the driest tone.

'Nope. Not today.'

We made our way to our gate arm in arm, showed our passports to the gate agents and walked onto the plane.

The weather in London was far more welcoming than I had anticipated. Perhaps the Swedish climate had made me a lot more resilient to the cold, but I could swear it felt like a spring day. Hazel and I made our way to the hotel—using the term *hotel* loosely—and we both jumped onto the bed with our faces down. The trip had barely started and we both felt exhausted.

The room was very simple, white sheets, old wooden furniture in a dirty shade of beige, tiny little TV with basically five channels, a carpet that hadn't been cleaned since 1776 and a used plaster near the bedside table. Ideal.

I was also pleased to see we had a bathtub. I loved taking baths, but I didn't want to risk getting into this one where mushrooms were growing on the side of it.

'Shall we take a nap?' Hazel asked. 'All this lying and doing things in secret has already taken a toll.'

'I think I need to see him first. I'm terrified,' I replied. 'But I need to do it now, or I'll have a heart attack.'

'I suppose I could sleep while you're smooching with your Australian boyfriend.'

'He's not my boyfriend!'

'Fine, fine. Whatever you say.'

I stood up in front of the mirror, checking my face out, making sure it looked as close as possible to my photos. I hadn't even contacted Teddy yet. I needed to calm down first. My hands were shaking, my legs felt weak. I was one more shallow breath away from passing out onto the nasty carpet.

'You look fine,' Hazel said while sitting up on the bed. 'I have to say...it's so cool I get to see you meet your little love.'

'Shut up.'

'I am serious. You know, you have been talking about him for months now and, in a few hours, you will get to see him for the first time! What if you get married, have children and do all the lovey-dovey couple crap? I'll be witnessing the origin story. It's cute as.'

'So, you don't think I'm crazy?' I asked, turning around to face her.

'Oh no, you need to be fucking institutionalised,' she giggled. 'Where are you going to meet?'

'I don't know.'

'You're the English one, Vincent. You should really take charge!'

'When do I ever take charge?'

'Uhm, when you dragged me into this deadly situation and wouldn't take no for an answer!'

'Hazel,' I said, trying to find my words.

'Yes?'

'I'm really happy you came with me. This whole thing is crazy.'

Hazel got up and walked over to me. She looked at me with her kind eyes and smiled. 'We're in this together,' she said. 'And I'll be fine. You go find him. I'll call you later.'

'Are you sure?' I asked, worried.

'Absolutely. Now go!' she commanded, pushing me out of the room.

I took a deep breath and, one slow step after the other, I left the hotel to go find Teddy and meet him for the first time.

I arrived at Holland Park, the double decker bus journey a blur of London cliché. I had time to spare but fell into a steady jog, weaving around mothers with prams in athletic wear and, finally, through the gates. Crossing the boundary of the park, a physical mark on the earth moving me from one version of myself to another. A new version that included Teddy.

I followed the signs to the Japanese gardens, the path dappled with sunlight that had snuck through the imposing canopy of trees. A peacock wandered the pathway, a stunning multicoloured tail dragging behind him. It was Wonderland and I was Alice, determined to find the end. The trees gave way, and I was stunned by the Kyoto Garden before me. Nestled in the heart of the park, it was beauty in high definition. Water flowed steadily over purposely stacked stones, feeding into a wide pond. Cherry trees dotted the edges, their branches barren. I walked towards the pond, flashes of orange and white koi dancing beneath the surface pulling me in for a closer look.

'Vincent!' my own name in that familiar voice, clear across the park.

My pulse thrummed in my ears, and I sucked in an unsteady breath.

'Hey! Vincent!'

Closer this time.

I turned around and my eyes met his. Grey against green. He stopped in front of me, no longer out of reach and a brilliant smile tore across his beautiful face.

I took him in, his tall, fit body wrapped in a tight navy denim jacket, an oversized white knitted scarf and his thick, thick, tawny hair, the sunlight dancing off it.

'Vincent,' he said.

My name a whisper and salvation from his lips.

'Teddy,' I breathed.

He reached out, pulling my body against his, his nose brushing my neck, breathing me in. My heart thumping against my ribs. I dove into his scent, so familiar and secure, his arms were wrapped firmly around me.

'I found you,' he whispered.

I smiled, though he couldn't see me, and as he loosened his embrace, I tightened mine.

'Just a few more seconds,' I said, holding him as if he was my most prized possession.

My Teddy.

My Teddy was with me and everything else became background noise.

I stepped back out of his arms, catching his hands in mine so we were linked together. My eyes traced his features, committing them to memory so I could live in this moment again when he wasn't with me.

'You're tall!' I said, my voice breaking from emotion.

'Yeah. And you're just...beautiful.'

We both smiled while looking at each other. We spent months talking, every single night, and now that we were finally together, I was speechless.

'Vincent, you need to say something. When there's silence I ramble and it's not pretty. It's a whole avalanche of words thrown against you. You don't want any part in that.'

'I think I do!' I said. 'Sorry, I've been picturing this moment for a long time and it's hard to make peace with the fact that it's happening. Right now.'

'Any regrets?' he asked.

'Not a single one.'

'Good. That's a relief,' he said. 'This place...it's incredible!'

'Yeah...yeah...it is...' I said, looking around.

'Are you nervous, Vincent?' he asked, with a slight hint of tease.

'I'm dying right now,' I laughed, anxiously. 'I'm sorry. This is actually my first—'

'...time here?'

'Date. It's my first date. Ever.'

'Ohh,' his bright smile showing up again. 'It's a date!'

'No, I didn't mean—'

'I'm just messing with you,' he chuckled. 'Okay, how about I take Your British Majesty for a drink, and we let tipsy Vincent out for the afternoon?'

'I think it's an excellent idea,' I said with relief.

I put my hand out to hold his. An intimate gesture I had never shared with anyone before. He looked at me, laced his fingers with mine, and pulled me closer to him. I blushed, and he gave me a soft kiss on the side of my head.

Being in his proximity felt magical, like a daydream.

One I never wanted to wake from.

It didn't take long to find a cosy pub for us to enjoy a well-earned series of glasses filled with liquid courage. Not that Teddy needed any. He was charismatic, full of life and eternally optimistic, looking at me as if I were the most important guy in the world. His hand delicately touching mine over the table, while I inhaled gin & tonic as if it was sparkling water.

'I don't drink this quickly, usually,' I pointed out.

'Vincent, I live in Australia. Not only do we drink a lot, but we also drink the absolute worst kind of wine. Usually comes in a box. We call it *goon*. We hang it from the clothesline and spin it while we drink it.'

'I feel like you've lived your life a little more than I have,' I said.

'Oh yeah. That's some quality life experience right there,' he said, rolling his pretty eyes. 'I don't think we've ever talked much about your life here, really.'

'There isn't much to say. I'm an only child, I play video games, I spend a lot of time behind my camera...'

'I wish I was an only child...'

'I thought you didn't speak much with your brother?'

'I know, but he still exists. Which is irritating. My mum is great, though. Smartest person I know, an absolute force of nature. She can quote any book she's ever read. It's disturbing. It's very hard to compete with that. Especially when playing *Trivial Pursuit*.'

'I think you have more in common than you realise,' I said, with a cheeky smile.

'Nah. I'm more...free-spirited, I guess? I want to see the world, not read about it.'

'We could do it together, you know...'

'What?'

'See the world.'

'Care to pinky promise?' he said, ready for it.

'I pinky promise.'

As our fingers touched, he cupped his other hand over ours, sealing them together.

'Well, you can't take it back now, Stewart.'

'I don't intend to, Clarke.'

His eyes slightly shut from smiling.

'So, what did you do with Hazel?' he asked, crossing his arms and leaning back on his chair.

'I...sort of left her? At the hotel. She pushed me though. I swear I'm not a monster.'

'Vincent! Tsk tsk. You should know better than to leave a friend in a big city.'

'Oh, trust me, she's in no danger. She can handle herself.'

'Okay. I have an idea,' he said, clapping his hands on the table like a drum. 'How about...'

'Mmh?' I asked, intrigued.

'But you can't make fun of me!'

'Go on...?'

'I think...you and I...should go to a ball!'

'A ball?' I asked, suspicious.

'A wonderful, over-the-top, Disney-style ball,' he said, with confidence.

'Teddy, you know this is 2009 and not the sixteenth century, right?'

'I know.'

'Like we may have a queen and everything, but—'

'Oh, shush, you! I know what I'm talking about! Also, I thought you trusted me?'

I couldn't fault him. I had flown across Europe to see him, knowing damn well it'd be a dangerous and careless decision. 'I'm listening, I'm listening!'

'Well, Laura's future school is having a ball tonight. And she can take whoever she wants. And that whoever wants to take you, my Romeo.'

I cackled.

He stared at me with dead serious eyes.

'You're not joking,' I said, with a slight tear in my eye from laughing so hard.

'Vincent, I never joke about balls. Balls are great. I *love* balls.'

Still laughing.

'And this is where I'm going to leave this, as one more glass of wine, will make me say much naughtier things than what I just came up with,' he said.

'I mean, nothing wrong with balls.'

'Nothing at all. They're amazing.'

'...so, what would I wear at this ball?' I asked, terrified.

'I know a place,' he said, raising his eyebrows, excited. 'Text Hazel and we'll meet her there.'

'Hazel?'

'Yeah, she has to come with. Unlike you, Vincent, I'm not a monster. Everyone should experience my ball.'

'I thought it was—'

'Let's go,' he blurted. He took my hand and kissed it before I followed him to yet another unknown territory.

***

A few changes on the underground later, and after getting inevitably lost, we were at a little costume shop. Bright and colourful, tucked between a bookstore and a charity shop. We were trying things on. I was in my fitting room, trying on burgundy tights and a pair of knee-high brown leather boots.

'Can I see what's going on?' asked Hazel.

'You stay out of here!' I shouted.

'I can't believe you're taking this long!' she exclaimed. 'Teddy and I had picked our costumes over an hour ago!'

'I'm honestly unconvinced you hadn't planned this before!' I said, trying to hide my junk from sight. The rest of the costume was lying on a chair, waiting for me.

'Vincent, I'm too curious!' Teddy said.

'Well, curb that! I'm still not ready!'

'Do you need help with anything?' he asked.

'Absolutely not!' I said, while staring at my scrawny, pale shirtless chest in the mirror.

'It's been forever!' Teddy said, before pulling the curtain back and getting a full view of my half naked body.

'Teddy!' I shouted, trying to cover up with my hands.

He immediately recoiled and closed the curtain.

'I'm so sorry! I didn't mean to expose you! I'm not a weirdo, I promise!' he said, embarrassed.

I couldn't say anything back. I was so body conscious; I didn't want him to see me.

'Vincent, please say something!' he begged.

'It's okay,' I said, taking a slow deep breath to calm myself.

'You can take your time!' he said.

I looked at myself in the mirror one more time, worried about how Teddy would see me. But I wanted him to see me. I closed my eyes and took another steadying breath. 'Actually...'

'Yes...?' he asked.

'Could you like...give me a hand with this? It's heavy and I can't put it on!'

'Sure, you don't want Hazel to help you?' he asked.

'Bro, no!' she said, from afar.

'You can come in,' I said, my heart thumping in my throat.

He pulled the curtain slightly and entered the room. He was already wearing his costume; a white baroque Louis XVI-style jacket with gold embroidery and a frilly shirt with lacy sleeves. His trousers were short, with high white stockings and a pair of patent black shoes.

'You look ridiculous,' I said, trying to contain my laughter.

'And you look...lovely,' he said, while staring at my chest.

I looked down at the floor, heat crawling up my cheeks. His soft fingers grazed my chin, tilting my face up to his. I met his eyes, unable to look away, unable to breathe as he gently traced my jaw. Electricity was between us; my body was a live wire as each uneven exhale brought us closer together. Teddy's eyes slid closed, his thumb on my cheek as he inhaled deeply. He took a step back, face flushed and eyes darting.

I realised, for the first time, that Teddy was nervous.

'I...I...let me help you with that,' he said.

'That what?'

'The...uhm,' he said, pointing at the costume on the chair, but still locking eyes with me. 'That. Thing. Put on. Situation.'

'Guys, I'll meet you at the school!' Hazel shouted.

'Are...you sure?' I asked.

'Yes! Do you need me to take your backpack directly to the venue?' she asked.

'Is that so you can take a pair of flats to change into?'

'And my camera, maybe.'

'Sounds good!'

'You guys take your time!' she said, opening the front door and leaving us alone in the fitting room.

Teddy helped me with the gigantic upper velvet piece with humongous puffy sleeves. I had never been hotter in my entire life.

'This is a heck of a costume,' I said. 'It's like a spacesuit,' I said, while fixing my long cape behind me.

'You look...amazing,' he said, watching over me with sparkly eyes.

My knees became weaker, looking at his perfectly chiselled face, staring at me like I had never been looked at before. For once, I didn't feel shy, or awkward. My whole body tingled, my lips gravitating towards his, adrenaline pumping, begging me to kiss him. And just as I was about to make the first, courageous step to lean my head forward, to finally taste him, the shopkeeper woke us up from the fantasy, by knocking on the curtain.

'You guys okay?' he asked.

I couldn't utter a word, but Teddy was a lot more straightforward.

'We're okay, thank you! I think we've got a winner!' he exclaimed.

I looked at him and smiled.

'I think we do,' I whispered.

'You look incredible, Vincent. And I know it's stupid but—'

'It's not,' I interrupted. 'It's our evening, and I couldn't ask for a better prince.'

We remained in silence, for a second, waiting for the other to make a decision and leave this little, tiny world that was just for us.

'I have an idea,' I said, suddenly.

'You do?' he asked.

'We have some time before the ball, right?'

'Yeah?' he said, giant curious eyes.

'There's somewhere I want to take you. Costumes and everything.'

'Okay, I'm in.'

'You trust me, right?' I asked.

'Yeah, I do.'

'Let's get out of here, then,' I said. I grabbed his hand and took charge. A complete one-eighty from what people normally expected from me.

Hand in hand with Teddy, I could do anything.

CHAPTER TEN

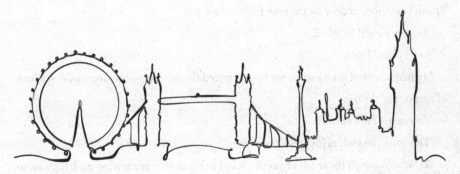

TEDDY
2009

Vincent was a revelation. I expected our encounter to be at least a tiny bit uncomfortable, but that was never the case. I had underestimated the power of the written—and sometimes spoken— word. I felt like I got to know this guy inside and out, in a way that was unconventionally pure. Yes, I was infatuated with his photos, and I did find him unbelievably attractive, but it's the person he'd shown me evening after evening through our conversations that I had grown so fond of.

None of it felt forced. He held my hand and he never let it go. In that moment, the world around us didn't matter. Nothing else mattered. We weren't in a foreign country; I was home, with him. If reality was different, this would have been our normal—walking around and exploring, sitting in a park kissing each other under a tree. That was what I wanted. Not just for that day, but for every day after that.

Perhaps not wearing big princes' costumes, but a guy could dream.

In fact, screw that. We would *definitely* be wearing princes' costumes.

I had no idea where Vincent was taking me, but I didn't care. I was happy enough just looking at him, his whole body smothered in a mountain of burgundy velvet, with his silky hair framing that stunning face of his.

'What?' he asked, probably feeling uneasy from my constant stare.

We were riding the underground to an unknown location; the train packed with passengers, warm air smelling of dust and metallic grease, and we stood face to face, a breath apart, forced close by the rush hour crowd.

'Are you okay?' he asked.

'I really am,' I said.

My hand stroked his hair and my fingers traced the outline of his face, pushing a lock of hair out of the way.

Next stop, Chalk Farm.

'This is us,' he said, as his eyes lit up.

We wove through the crush of people, hand in hand, Vincent towing my happy ass to the exit.

'Where are you taking me?' I asked, curious.

'I thought you said you trusted me!'

'What if I'm a terrible judge of character?' I teased, after a dramatic gasp.

'Bit late now, isn't it?'

'I do trust you, Vincent,' I said, with conviction.

'Good, because we're almost there.'

I looked around at the quaint little streets, lined with pastel houses and garden paths. Magnolia trees danced along the road ahead, their blossoming branches filling the chilly air with their scent. We ran in the middle of a quiet road, eyes of bystanders firmly looking at us, the crazy kids wearing over-the-top royal garments.

The setting sun spun the light around us into a glittery gold. An in person vintage filter applied to the world.

'It's...crazy pretty around here,' I gasped, my nose up in the air.

'It's about to get a lot prettier,' he said, his eyes on me, shining with excitement. 'Uhm, there's just one thing.'

'What is it?'

We slowed down, and I was presented with a beautiful park, green meadows, azure wildflowers all running up a steep hill, overlooking the grassy expanse.

'We're going up to the top, aren't we?' I asked, slightly daunted by the task.

'Yup. But don't worry, I'll be here to help you up if you're not fit enough to run!' he said, sticking his tongue at me.

'Not fit enough?!' I yelped, clutching my imaginary pearls.

'I'm just saying,' he said, walking backwards and looking at me. 'It's steeper than it looks!'

'Oh, it is on, Vincent. We're racing!'

'Teddy, I think I'd beat you even while wearing this enormous puffy costume! This is my homeland! I know hills!'

I gave him a faux-angry look and sprinted past him.

'Damn you!'

We started running alongside each other, our mutual laughter making it more difficult than it needed to be. My little French shoes were strangling my feet, while Vincent's cape was floating in the wind, like my own personal superhero. Two thirds of the way and that's when both of us dwindled. Laughter turned into panting, and neither of us seemed to have the strength to make it all the way.

'How about we call it a draw?' he asked, hands on his knees, face down.

'It was a good fight, Stewart. I'm very impressed,' I forced out between gasps of precious oxygen.

I wanted nothing more than to lie on the grass and catch my breath but was then reminded of my incredibly expensive rental costume I couldn't get dirty. The shopkeeper would have my head served on a platter if a single trace of mud was found on it. Which was fitting since I looked like Louis XVI.

'Come on you lazy! A few more steps!' he said, while slowly walking to the top.

'You couldn't have killed me any other way? Smothering me with a pillow, perhaps?' I asked, teasing him.

'You're so dramatic!' his voice echoing down the slope.

'Vincent, why oh why did you—'

'Just turn around,' he commanded, his eyes taking in the scenery behind me.

I obeyed; my eyes were greeted by a breath-taking view of the City of London. A series of shiny metallic buildings, all reflecting the orange hues of a winter sunset. The air was bitterly cold, but warmth rushed through my body, knowing I was here, standing near my special guy, surrounded by a picture-perfect view of what had already become my favourite place in the world.

'This is amazing!' I exhaled, my eyes not wide enough to take all of it in at once like I wanted to.

'You are,' he said, tending his hand to catch mine.

I turned to him, falling into those storm cloud eyes again. Close to him but not enough. I didn't think it would ever be enough. I took him in, this wonderful boy who made my heart dip, my knees weak. This boy who tripped into my life and filled it with magic.

'What?' he asked, whisper soft and his eyes on mine. Like he could see all of me, start to end, in a way no one had before.

'I'm...just so happy you came.'

'I brought you here, Teddy. Dragged you for a while too,' he teased.

'Not the hill,' I rolled my eyes, he was adorable. 'Here, London. I still can't wrap my head around it. What you're risking, it's crazy.'

'You caught me. I'm crazy.'

'And I'm crazy for you,' I said, cheesy and cliché and unequivocally true. I couldn't take my eyes off him, watching his beautiful face flush red at my words. My fingers danced along his jaw, down his neck, my thumb against pulse, beating faster than it had any right to. My other hand, still trapped in white regency silk, snaked around his slim waist, pulling him into my space. Hip to hip, crushed velvet and lace, his hands on my chest wrapped in the folds of my costume. He looked up at me, eyes wide and pupils blown.

'Teddy,' he whispered, breath soft against my lips.

My heart was thunder in my chest, nerves dancing, desire growing and all consuming. I wanted to know what he would taste like, how his mouth felt against mine. At once, we both moved, unable to resist and not wanting to. His lips were soft, unsure, and sweet. I nipped at his bottom lip; his breath hitched at the sensation. He pulled me closer, and I felt the tremble roll through his body as he parted his lips, his tongue finding mine, deepening the kiss. Our kiss, our first kiss. I savoured his taste, the tiny sounds he made, the way my skin felt alive and too small for my body. I wanted him with me, always. I wanted to reach for his hand on the sofa as we watched a movie, in the bittersweet evening, as we walked home from a date, in the quiet darkness of night when the world went to sleep, and it was just us. Him and me. I wanted him.

We smiled together, looking at one another, having just experienced a kiss so perfect, it was otherworldly. Vincent took both of my hands and encouraged me to sit beside him, facing a city clinging to its last few moments of daylight. He rested his head on my right shoulder, and I wrapped my arm around him, letting the world know that he was mine, and mine alone.

'You know...' he said, in a hushed tone. 'This was actually my first real kiss.'

'Yeah?'

'Yep.'

'So...?'

'What?' he giggled.

'You're just going to leave me hanging like that?' I whined, poking him with my finger.

'Well, not that I have a lot to compare it to...'

'Shall I just throw myself off the hill, Vincent?'

'It was a great kiss, with...a great guy,' he said, shy smile.

I held him just a little tighter and kissed him on the head.

'We should probably get going,' he said. 'We have a ball to go to!'

'Just a few more minutes.'

'You sure?' he asked.

'I'm just not ready to let go of this moment yet.'

'Alright.'

We didn't need to speak, content with each other's quiet. The sky— a soft purple blanket, wrapped us up and froze us in time—together.

A few cuddles, sweet words, and a lot more kissing later, Vincent and I made our way to the Royal Academy of Performing Arts. It was an imposing Victorian structure, like a Dickensian orphanage or a gaudy cathedral. I had never seen anything of the sort before.

We walked past an elaborate iron gate with twirling spikes on top, decorated in gold leaf, sprinted past dozens of people in costumes, desperately trying to find our —probably furious—friends. However, not the case. We spotted them leaning on the façade of the building, laughing as if they were the oldest of friends.

Hazel was wearing a black ball gown, with a plunging corset and a huge tulle skirt, and Laura opted for a pale pink silk mermaid-tail dress. Her hair was up in a bun, and her smile shone brightly from across the room. Her whole face finally looked relaxed and she, undoubtedly, rocked her audition.

'What's so funny?' I asked, jumping in front of them.

'Finally!' Laura blurted, punching me in the shoulder.

'Ow!' I lamented, rubbing the now sore spot.

'You must be Vincent!' she said, putting her hand out to shake his.

'Hi Laura,' he said enthusiastically. 'I can't even tell you how much I have heard about you. It's so good to finally meet you.'

They shook hands and I stared at Hazel, looking glorious. 'And you, Madame. You should wear that gown every day for the rest of your life!'

'Oh, I plan to, Teddy.'

'Can I just say you guys look ridiculous,' Laura said, bursting out laughing.

'Seriously, Vincent. Those tights leave nothing to the imagination and imagining your genitals is not what I ever want to do,' said Hazel.

'Are you sure you've not forgotten part of your costume cause I'm not sure we're meant to know your exact measurements,' Laura added.

'Who knew you'd have so much junk in the trunk!' Hazel said, still going strong on the penis jokes.

'I think trunk only refers to arse, Haze,' said Vincent, trying to cover up with his hands.

'Sometimes, cars have their trunks in the front, Vincent.'

'How do you even know that?' Laura asked, turning to Hazel.

'I'm from New Zealand. It's very boring there.'

'I'm so sorry,' Laura said.

'Not as sorry as Mister Stewart over here, now that everyone knows he's uncut,' she replied.

'Wow,' I said. I made this combo happen. I did this. These two should never be together again.

'Hey Laura.'

'Yeah Hazel?'

'Knock knock!'

'Who's there?'

'Vincent and.'

'Vincent and whom?'

'Vincent and his enormous wang.'

'Have you girls been drinking?!' Vincent asked.

'YES,' they said at once, falling over themselves laughing.

'I forbid you from being together again,' I commanded.

'Too late. We're each other's date now,' said Hazel, putting her arm under Laura's. 'And I have another eight or ten penis jokes if you want to hear them.'

'I think I'm good,' said Vincent, still cupping his—disproportionately sized—bits.

'No more alcohol, then,' I said, pointing at Laura.

'They're serving champagne, Teddy. I'm planning to swim in it. Shall we?' she asked, cocking her head towards the entrance.

The girls walked into the building, and I was left outside with tripod boy.

'To be fair, Vincent—'

'Don't say anything,' he interrupted.

'Can we hold hands, or do you still need to hide your salami from people?' I chortled.

'And I thought my balloon sleeves would be the issue,' he sighed.

I gave him a smile, holding out my arm so he could link his with mine, walking side by side into the school.

The foyer had marble columns supporting the vaulted ceilings, covered in murals, depicting ancient Greek theatre and philosophers throughout history. The main hall was decorated with a colossal chandelier, which would easily kill fifty people if it fell. All I was missing was an indoor balcony for me to profess my feelings for Vincent.

'Hey, hey, hey, hey,' Vincent said frantically, his arm shooting out in front of me before we could enter the dance floor.

'What is it?' I asked.

'Okay, with all the emotional finding each other and everything...I kind of just realised this is an actual ball.'

'Yes? I've been talking about a ball since we first met.'

'I know! Yes. And, well. Like any normally adjusted person, I imagined we'd never get to do this.'

'Vincent, a ball was always on the cards. And many more in the future!'

'How many people do you know who are having balls, Teddy?'

'I'm manifesting the reality I want to live in.'

'Buckingham Palace? With me tripping on your feet?'

'But I'll be leading!' I said, feeling proud.

'I don't think you understand the extent of how much I suck at dancing.'

'I am here for you. One waltz. And then we can leave.'

'Okay...' puppy dog eyes out in force.

'It's very easy,' I said, putting myself in front of him, his eyes staring at our feet. 'Hey no, no! Look at me!'

He slowly moved his head up. 'I'll step on your little Marie Antoinette shoes and then we'll trip, and everyone is going to point at us and tell Laura she can't be in this school because of me.'

'So, nothing dramatic then, huh?' I said, placing my hand on his side. 'Yours goes on my shoulder.'

'Like this?' he asked.

'Yes.'

'We are the only couple of guys,' he said, looking around.

'Are you uncomfortable?'

'No, not at all. I wouldn't want to be with anybody else.'

I couldn't stop my smile, feeling so damn lucky to be standing so close to him. 'It's a simple box-step. Waltz is really boring. We have this in the bag.'

'It's not a competition, Teddy,' he laughed.

'Ehm...have you not seen what our girls are doing?' I asked, pointing out Laura and Hazel working the dancefloor, twirling their gowns like pros.

'I should just stand in a corner,' he said, walking away.

'Wait, Vincent!' I said, catching his hand. 'Just give it a try. For me? Please?'

'Okay, but only because of that face of yours.'

'Hopefully not one you want to punch?'

'Fine. Teach me.'

'Left foot back,' I said pushing it with mine. 'Right foot back.'

'I feel like Bambi,' he said, wobbling.

'You guys need to hurry up!' said Laura, dancing with Hazel like an annoying tornado.

'You're a professional, Laura!' Vincent shouted.

'Not yet, I'm not!' she cackled.

'That's it, we're doing this,' he said, full resolve in his eyes.

With his newfound determination, after a few toe damaging moments, a near-fall and an endless stream of grunts later, we had finally found a rhythm. And I was in heaven. Nothing could compare to this moment. Vincent without inhibitions, moving in perfect harmony with me, as music swelled and ebbed through the ballroom. His beautiful face happy and relaxed, giving into this moment, to us.

Champagne showers and endless laughter. We danced until our feet wanted to give out. A perfect reverie, the four of us chasing the small hours of a quiet morning through the London streets.

Arms linked, high heels swinging from their free hands, the girls' voices carried back to us, incoherent and giggly. Hyde Park was waking up, colour returning after the cast of night faded. Vincent nuzzled into the sensitive spot below my ear, his nose cold and his arms around my neck, half empty champagne bottle hanging precariously from his hand.

'Bro, Hazel needs to sit!' she said, speaking in third person.

'I want to see the sunrise!' Laura shouted, doing *grand jetés* ahead of us.

'Where is it, Vincent?' I asked. 'Where's the best place for us to watch the sunset?'

He pointed straight ahead, near the water, where swans were resting and the moonlight reflection was still twinkling on the surface. We sat by the edge, Hazel surrounded by her tulle skirt and Laura lying on the grass, watching the stars above. I demanded Vincent rest his head on my shoulder, so that I could kiss it and breathe its vanilla scent.

'So, what's everyone's plans for next year?' Laura asked, raising her head enough to take a swig of champagne.

'That's the million-dollar question,' Hazel said.

'If that's New Zealand dollars, then it's quite a cheap question!' I said, teasing her.

'Ha-ha!'

'Vincent, will you be moving to London?' Laura asked.

'I...don't know. Maybe? I'm not sure.'

'I could do with a flatmate!' she added.

'Hey!' I said. 'You can't like him better than me!'

'Sure can. Next best thing!' she said, stretching her arms.

'Well, I've already asked Hazel to come to Australia with me. How do you like that?' I asked.

'You did?' Vincent turned to me. 'When did that happen?'

'Oh, Teddy and I go a long way back,' she laughed. 'Who do you think gave him your address for the bear?'

'That was so cute, by the way. Bravo, Teddy!' Laura said, clapping for me.

'I just wanted to surprise you!' I said, scratching the back of my head.

'I haven't made any decisions yet,' Hazel said. 'It would be nice to change scenery and photograph something different...'

'Yeah, there are snakes, humongous spiders, drop bears...' teased Vincent.

'Drop bears aren't a real thing,' she replied.

'Only one way to find out!' I said. 'But also, can we stop talking about the future? As far as I'm concerned, I'm staying in this forever. With these exact people in this exact location.'

'Then allow me to immortalise this very moment for you,' Hazel announced, whipping her camera out from her bag.

'I didn't realise you were carrying that with you, Haze!' said Vincent.

'I carry it wherever I go. I'm not a slacker like you and your video camera!'

'Rude!' he replied.

'Hazel, it's so dark. We're going to look crazy,' I pointed out.

'I'm a good photographer! I have night-time settings, you fool.'

'Eesh. That ego is showing,' I said.

'Everyone ready?' she asked.

We shuffled together, trying to make us all fit in the frame, and smiled at the camera, smiles of innocent joy, forever captured.

I wondered if they'd be able to see the pain behind mine, already picturing my parting with Vincent, only mere hours away.

I wanted to live in that photograph, forever in his arms.

'I'm going to need a copy of that,' I said.

'You'll have to wait until I work my magic, Teddy. I have the awful feeling that my makeup gave up on me hours ago.'

'I'd like to raise a glass—well, the one bottle—to you guys,' said Laura, as she raised her bottle in the air. 'Thank you so much for coming to London with me. And you're all invited to mine and Vincent's flat next year!'

'So, you've decided that, huh?' he asked, amused.

'Yep. Welcome to the Laura family!'

'I'll drink to that,' I said.

The bubbles helped with keeping our spirits high, and when the sun rose, filling the sky with strokes of magenta, orange and yellows, it was the inevitable sign that our time was coming to an end.

We managed to jam-pack the remainder of the day with adventures and the many stories Hazel shared about Vincent, until it was time for them to get back to Sweden. My heart ached, knowing each beat brought us closer to goodbye. Laura and I accompanied them to the airport to watch them leave.

The flight was from the much quieter Luton airport. The flurry of people running and speaking one would expect was replaced by a deafening silence, turning this moment into an excruciatingly noiseless background to my loud, miserable sadness.

'You have everything, right?' I asked him.

'Yeah, I think we do.'

Tears rolled silently down my cheeks, sorrow taking over my body and consuming everything in its path. I swiped at my eyes, frustrated that when I wanted one more chance to map his perfect face, my vision was swimming.

'Guys, it was amazing to meet you,' said Laura, while giving them both a hug.

'I hope you get accepted, Laura,' said Hazel. 'And you've been the best date I could ever ask for!'

'You guys liked each other too much. I'm still bitter about the level of mocking I received for my dancing!' he said.

'I am going to go ahead, leave you guys for a moment,' Hazel announced. 'Teddy, I will see you down under.'

Laura rubbed my shoulder for a second and walked away, setting up my goodbye with Vincent. The dreaded moment.

'We have been abandoned,' he said, smiling through his own tears.

'Vincent—'

'Let me go first,' he interrupted. 'I'm about to get a little corny here but allow me to say something.'

'I like corny.'

He held my hands, his sad, gentle greys, staring at me.

'I have had an amazing time with you these past days. You have given me something I didn't know I could have or even want. Thank you, Teddy, for waiting for me. For holding my hand and for the way you look at me like I'm something special. Someone worthwhile and important. I don't want to say goodbye. We haven't had enough time, or enough kissing. Enough anything. I don't want to go,' his words caught in his throat, his beautiful eyes red rimmed and tears dripping in a steady stream off his jaw.

I grabbed his face and kissed him. I kissed him like it was the last time I'd ever kiss him. I kissed him to let him know how much I wanted him to stay with me. I kissed him for as long as I could.

'I have felt so alone,' I sobbed. 'And then you came. This feels like I am reciting vows, but it's hard to say something witty, or funny, when the idea of seeing you go breaks me so much.'

'We will still talk, as we did before. We will always have each other in our lives. And we will do this again. We will meet in another country and bless them with our presence.'

I smiled a little.

'I'll come and see you, Vincent.'

'What?' he asked, furrowing his eyebrows.

'Before I fly back to Australia, I'll come and see you, in Stockholm.'

'Do you mean that?'

'Yeah. This can't be our last goodbye. I refuse,' I said, with conviction.

'So, I'm seeing you in two weeks?'

'Yes. I've decided. *Just* decided,' I said, wiping my tears. 'This is a see-you-later.'

'You promise?' he asked.

'Pinkie promise,' I chuckled. 'You'll show me around, we'll kiss the whole time and we'll be us. One more time. Vincent and Teddy.'

'It'll be the longest two weeks.'

'I'll be there before you know it, Vincent.'

I held tightly to his hand, softly kissing him just one last time. One last brush of my nose along his jaw.

'*Arrivederci*, my love,' I whispered into his skin, hoping he could carry how I felt back with him. 'You must go. You'll miss your plane.'

Hollow sobs forced their way out.

I let go of his hand and watched him go. I watched him walk away from me, until he faded into the distance.

'Are you okay?' Laura asked, wrapping her arms around me.

'I'll be okay.'

'How about I go buy us a terrible-tasting English pizza?'

'Ha! Yeah, that sounds perfect.'

I felt a vibration in my pocket, I took it out, hoping to see Vincent's name, even though he had just left, but it wasn't the case.

'Who is it?' she asked,

'It's my mum. I'm just going to pick this up really quick. Mum?' I said, answering the call.

'Hi, this is Doctor Rivera from Royal Hospital Hobart. Is this Edward Clarke?'

'Yes? Where's my mum?'

'I'm calling to let you know that there has been a head-on collision involving your mum. Currently, we have her in intensive care due to the nature of her injuries and we are doing a few tests to see what caused her to lose control of her vehicle.'

My blood froze and my heart stopped and, suddenly, I went from sad to desperate.

CHAPTER ELEVEN

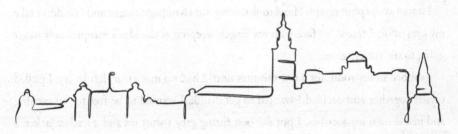

VINCENT

2009

I ngrid had just left my room after dropping her usual insults masked as concern. I was so tired of dealing with Ingrid, I was close to considering changing families. I had reached a point where the proximity to her was making my life harder than it needed to be, and I wasn't sure being so close to the city centre was a good enough reason for me to endure this torture day after day.

I hadn't been myself for two weeks. Grumpy and snappy, I felt like I was starting to alienate my friends. Hazel and Daniel understood what was going on. I was hurting. I was trying to forget. Seeing Teddy was amazing and one of the best—albeit most reckless—choices I had made in my life, but I never, even for one second, considered the consequences. I never stopped to think what life would look like once Teddy moved back to Australia. I never imagined how little we'd get to talk to each other, seeing as we'd have this massive time difference between us. But worst of all, I was unreasonably furious at the fact he never kept his promise to come and see me.

We'd only exchanged one bit of conversation since we said goodbye in London. There was something wrong with his mother. No details, no explanation. Just a *sorry, I have to fly back home immediately.*

I was, of course, worried about her, but I felt cast aside. We had shared everything until then, and now I was left in silence, riddled with doubts on whether we were actually connected, or if it was now just a lost memory.

I stared at the photograph Hazel took during our champagne night and I couldn't take my eyes off it. I traced his face with my finger, weeping at the idea I was probably never going to see Teddy again.

I sobbed in my room for a few minutes until I had no more tears left to cry. I pulled myself together and decided I wanted to get drunk. I wanted to be free for an evening and just drown my sorrows. I put my best fitting grey t-shirt on and a leather jacket. I pulled my hair back with gel and put on a pair of chunky brown boots. It was half past five in the afternoon, which meant I only had half an hour to find a *Systembolaget*—liquor store—and implore someone to buy a bottle of alcohol for me. Lucky for me, I didn't live too far from one. I ran out of the house and made my way to the shop wearing the camera strap around my neck, thinking I might go take some footage of my special little spot by the beach. While drinking something strong, hopefully.

It was a lovely evening, framed by a clear dark sky and a blanket of early stars. My eyes were puffy from crying but the fresh air on my face had a soothing effect on me. I was hoping I would have enough time to get to the shop and scout for someone to break the law for me.

The shop was ahead of me and there was a man sitting on the bench outside, smoking a cigarette; his hair and stubble were a mix of black and silver. I took a deep breath and tried to channel my inner charm, to convince him to do what I wanted. I walked up to the entrance and started checking my pockets nervously.

'Shit,' I said, trying to look for a reaction.

'*Är allt ok?*' he asked.

'It's nothing. I walked all the way here and realised I left my passport at home,' I said.

'They won't let you in without it, unfortunately.'

'I know. Fuck.'

I paused for a little bit and looked around me.

'Hey,' he said. 'Maybe I could go in and buy whatever you need? I need to get some stuff for myself anyways.'

Bingo.

'Really? Would you do that for me?'

'No problem,' he said, getting up and crushing his cigarette butt under his boot. 'I'd love to be of assistance to such a cute guy.'

Oh.

What are the odds? I scored a gay man. Hopefully he wasn't just pretending so he could arrest me. I had done enough damage in the previous month to kick my arse all the way back to England.

'What would you like me to get you?' he asked.

'I don't know...like vodka? Something I can drink straight from the bottle.'

'Oh, someone is planning a fun evening. Okay. Leave it to me. I will be right back.'

He went inside the shop and I sat outside. I couldn't believe how easy it had been. I wondered if he helped me because he found me attractive. Apart from Teddy, I had never entertained the idea of flirting or being particularly attracted to other guys. I was reading old texts on my phone, saying stuff like *I will see you soon* to Teddy, a cruel reminder of the pure happiness I was able to feel just a few weeks prior. The memory of us holding hands was still freshly embedded in my head, but the trip down memory lane was cut short by my phone's low battery. Annoying. All I now had to stare at were the pretty trees around me, as I waited for the guy to come back with the goods.

Around ten minutes later, he reappeared with two bags full of bottles.

'I went a little bit overboard,' he said with a big bright smile.

He seemed like a genuinely nice person, and now that I was looking at him closely, he wasn't that awful to look at. Both his hair and his beard were shades of grey and black resembling salt and pepper. He was a lot taller than me—probably six foot five—and had broad shoulders.

'Thank you so much,' I said, happy like a little schoolboy. 'How much do I owe you?'

'How about we drink some of these together and you don't owe me anything?'

'Seriously?' I asked, confused.

'Yeah. It's a beautiful evening. We can walk down by the beach and have a chat!'

'I don't really do that with strangers,' I said, cautiously. He was friendly enough, but I just wanted to make sure he wasn't a psychopath.

'You're right, I am Simon,' he said while tending a hand to me. 'Pleased to meet you.'

I looked at his big blue eyes and giggled a little. Swedish pronunciation of Simon sounds a lot like *semen*.

'I'm Vincent,' I said while shaking his hand. 'Thank you for helping me out, Simon.'

'No worries. Do you know of a nice quiet place where we can chat?'

'I do, as a matter of fact,' I said. My skin prickled and my mum's voice echoed in my head, reminding me not to talk to strangers. I shoved that aside, I was eighteen now. Not a child. I could do what I wanted and, right now, I wanted to get drunk. I was lucky Simon helped.

'So, you're British?' he asked, while leading the way.

'Yes. I am an exchange student.'

'That's cool. Do you like it here?'

'I love it,' I said, looking around.

'We are not too far, I just thought it will be very quiet there.'

We hopped past the little port with the boats. The night sky wrapped everything with a dark curtain, bestrewn with glowing stars. The moonlight, with its silvery shine, lit up the sea, velvety and silent.

The small beach was still as breath-taking as I remembered. Funny how last time I was here, I was mere few hours away from receiving Teddy's first message.

'How nice is this?' he asked with a big smile.

'Very nice!' I said with my nose up in the air.

'Let's sit over there by that tree, so you can tell me all about the reasons why you needed to get drunk this evening.'

'Sounds good,' I said.

Much of the evening was spent talking and getting to know each other. Alcohol fumes making it an unusually easy task, warming us up during an exceptionally cold night. Perhaps there were some advantages to not being a silly introvert all the time.

Simon had bought fruit flavoured vodka, which was extremely easy to drink. I didn't remember how, but we were two bottles in when I started rambling about Teddy.

'So, you haven't spoken since he went back to Australia?'

'We did, a little. He told me he was spending a lot of time looking after his mother, but he hasn't really told me much else.'

'Ah, so you're jealous of his sick mother?'

'No, of course not! I just wished he talked to me. Even for a minute. I don't know what to do. I had this tunnel vision idea that I needed to meet him face to face, and once I did, I had run out of objectives. Does that make sense?'

'No? I get you're young and everything seems so dramatic, but—'

'You think what I'm feeling isn't necessarily real?' I asked while chugging from the bottle.

'I think there will be so many Teddies in your life that you're going to look back at this little asshole and laugh about it.'

'He's not an asshole. That's the problem. He is the single nicest guy I have ever met.'

'Trust me when I say you won't even remember him in a few years,' he said, having a few more sips of raspberry vodka.

'Maybe...but tell me about you. What's your story? Are you gay or...?'

'Not quite. I work as a policeman, so I'm surrounded by straight men all day, every day.'

'Are you telling me I have asked a policeman to break the law for me?'

Fuck.

His smile was wolfish, as he leaned forward, running his thick fingers through my hair.

'You're okay. I think I needed company too.'

My eyes bounced around, nerves competing with the alcohol in my veins. I had to get home. Now.

'It's pretty dark now,' I said. 'I should probably start making my way back home.'

'Hey...' he leaned towards me. 'Do you think I could have a kiss?'

I wasn't too keen on the idea. 'I don't really think we should. We are both very drunk, it's probably best if—'

'Oh, come on. Just a little one. You can consider it my payment for the alcohol.'

I took a deep breath and figured it wasn't such a big deal.

'Absolutely. I am incredibly grateful for it,' I said with a forced smile.

I kissed him hesitantly on the lips for a few seconds and then moved my face away.

'You call that a kiss?' he said, with his big bright white teeth. 'Come here.'

He grabbed my head and kissed me in a much more sexual fashion. His tongue was inside my mouth, rolling against my tongue.

'Wow,' I said. 'Thanks for that, I should really—'

'Just a few more minutes, Vincent.'

He climbed onto me, sitting on my thighs and pinning my hands down. I couldn't move. He was too heavy for me to move my arms or legs.

'Hey, I think we should stop here,' I said, nervously.

'Come on,' he said, unbuttoning his jeans. He reached in, groaning as he touched himself.

'I don't want to, Simon.'

The crack of his hand across my face stunned me.

'Let's relieve you of some of these clothes Vincent.'

My whole body clenched in fear. Why did I put myself into this situation? Did I make this happen? Was my flirting the thing that got him to think I'd be up for this?

I clamped my jaw shut, eyes closed, hoping he would get off or something and leave. His meaty fingers trailed down my throat, slipping under the neckline of my shirt. The bite of cold metal on my skin sent a jolt through me. The tip of a knife cutting the threads of my shirt; a tiny nick meaning he could tear my top like it was nothing. My exposed skin pebbled from the unwanted caress of the Swedish night and his rough hands. He leaned down, his mouth at my ear. I strained to move my head from his, pinned under his weight.

'So, pretty Vincent. I can't wait to see what else you're hiding.' His warm breath blew across my face, foul and soaked in alcohol. 'Turn around,' he sneered.

I had to leave. I tried to scream, but no sound came out. I was petrified, the salty air burned my lungs with every frantic breath. My hands dug into the ground, failing to grab onto anything solid. I was fully at his mercy. I closed my eyes again, there was no way I could escape him, no way to avoid what came next. Tears rolled down my face, the ocean was the only soundtrack I wanted. I willed my mind to take me anywhere else while my body couldn't.

He stood across from me, zipping his jeans, straightening his clothes. Boots. Belt. Sparing me not the barest glance. So normal. Unhurried. Like he hadn't just stolen something from me, hadn't just cut away the fabric of who I was, so it would never fit quite right again. In this moment, Vincent from before and Vincent after this, met and separated. Before and after. That's how it would be now.

I felt like I was being torn in two, my conscious mind locked on the points of pain, indelible on my skin. Left by this repulsive man, I was used and undoubtedly thrown away. Terrified that this would be my last few moments alive, or that they wouldn't be, that

I'd have to exist each day with the memory of his hands and mouth on me. Knowing that I had walked myself into this hell and my body had given itself over to him, no matter how badly I wanted to escape. He ambled over to me, crouching down by my head. Fingers sliding into my hair. Knife in his other hand, an unnatural shine in the dark night.

I didn't want to die like this, I didn't want my mum to know this was how my life ended. I didn't want her to be disappointed by the choices I had made.

Then he leaned close to my face and whispered into my ear.

'You will never talk about this. To anyone.'

My eyes flitted around, desperate for something to look at that wasn't his face. I never wanted to see his face again. My camera lay a few feet away, a shining black lump I could focus on.

'Tell me you won't say anything,' he said, wrenching my head back, forcing my eyes to his.

'I promise. I promise!' I screamed.

'Good,' he pushed my head down, a silent sob begged for sound in my chest. Sand in my mouth, on my teeth, in my nose. I never wanted to feel sand again.

He walked a few steps, stopping and turning. I dared not look up at him, my eyes glued to my camera.

He raised his booted foot and brought it down on it, my lifeline.

Destroyed, splintered pieces were all I had left.

I lay there until I was sure he had gone, his footfalls were no longer within hearing range.

Slowly and shaking I dressed myself. My body felt raw, one giant open wound, the material abrasive. I fell back to my knees and gasped for air. Hoping it wouldn't come.

I was alive, he hadn't killed me. He hadn't taken my life. Just everything else.

No one would believe this. This didn't happen to men.

Men aren't victims.

I'd been drinking. I'd brought him here to this spot. No one would believe me. He was in the police force. I was nothing.

Maybe he said he was with the police so I wouldn't call them. But maybe it was the truth, and he would be there when I went in. Waiting for me. I'd have to see him. They wouldn't believe me; they wouldn't understand what had happened. I'd led him here, spent time with him.

My body shook and my mind was a snarled mess of panic and shame.

This was on me.

I took a shuddering breath. And then another.

Pulling the pieces of the new Vincent into place.

Each day that slipped by after that night was hollow. I waited for it to stop hurting. To stop waking in the middle of the night in panic, imagining the ground beneath me instead of my bed. I didn't want to see Daniel or Hazel; I didn't want to go to school and I sure as hell didn't want to be anywhere near Ingrid. It was like she could sense something had happened, her hounding of me for every offensive step I made seemed to take on a life of its own. I hadn't heard from Teddy, he hadn't answered my calls or even read my messages. I didn't know what it meant, and I didn't think I cared right now. I missed the UK. The familiar town, the people. My mum. Home.

Each day I left for school, knowing I wouldn't be going. I was putting my place in the program in jeopardy. Ingrid would find out sooner or later, the school would notify her of my absence and that would be that. I had swallowed my feelings day in and day out to stay here and now I felt nothing.

I walked into a department store; one I had been in every day this week. Out on the street, I looked for him. Checking over my shoulder every few minutes in case he was there.

It felt like he was always there.

But inside felt better. I walked down the aisles, touching things as I went past, like I was browsing. So they wouldn't ask me to leave.

I stopped to try on hats, pretending I was interested. Did I want blue? Would green look better? I looked around, feeling like an idiot in a pantomime and no one was watching.

Nobody cared. I could walk out right now, and it wouldn't matter, hat on my head and all.

For the first time in days, my heart raced for a reason that wasn't fear. I wasn't numb.

I looked around again, still nobody anywhere near me. I pulled out my phone and put it to my ear, like I was on a call, and strode to the entrance. Every step my heart leapt, waiting to be caught. I crossed the threshold of the store and darted around the corner, tearing the hat off as I did.

Nobody came. There were no cries of "thief", nor security guards in sight.

I leaned against the wall, hat in hand, my emotions a mess. I knew this was wrong.

But it was exhilarating.

Tears rolled down my cheeks. I was filled with shame and guilt.

What the fuck was I doing?

PART TWO

2014

PART TWO

2011

CHAPTER TWELVE

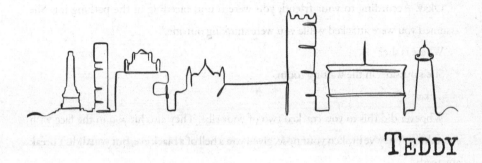

TEDDY

2014

My head pounded. I was disorientated and nauseous.

I opened my eyes slowly, barely able to see through the left one. My face felt numb, my body was aching. The neon lights in my room were artificially bright and it took me a few seconds to realise where I was. The smell of sterilisation and rubbing alcohol was pungent but it was the dead giveaway I was lying on a hospital bed.

The night before was a blur. I couldn't remember much.

I pressed the button to call a nurse, or a doctor, hopefully to let me know what was going on. I didn't have to wait long before someone entered my room, with a big smile and a clipboard. My eyesight was blurry, but I could sort of see her dark teal scrubs and her bleached blonde hair in a ponytail.

'Hello, Teddy. How are you feeling?' she asked.

'I'm...tired, in pain.'

'Do you know what happened to you?' she set about taking my blood pressure and temperature.

'I only remember being out, clubbing. Then I woke up here.'

'You don't remember being attacked?'

Attacked?

I didn't remember anything, aside from the fact that I'd been drinking a lot. I was upset about my mum's condition and just skulled a few.

'Not really,' I murmured.

'Okay. According to your friend, you were found bleeding in the parking lot. She assumed you were attacked while you were smoking outside.'

'Where is she?'

'She's outside, in the waiting room.'

'...okay.'

'Whoever did this to you cracked two of your ribs. They also hit you in the face with something. They've broken your nose, given you a hell of a black eye, but you didn't break any teeth.'

'Are you serious?'

'You're currently on morphine, but if the pain becomes unbearable, we can sort you out with some more.'

'I'm so confused...could you let my friend in?'

'You need to rest, Teddy,' she said in an almost motherly tone.

'I just need a few minutes, please.'

'Okay, I'll tell her to come in,' she said on her way out.

My head was pounding. Perhaps I need more morphine. As much as possible, so I could be unconscious again.

The door opened and there was Hazel, with her messy hair and a weekender bag in hand. She had probably stayed up all night worried sick.

'Hey. How are you feeling?' she asked, putting her bag down and dragging a chair next to my bed.

'How do I look?' I joked.

'Do you want the truth?' she grimaced.

'What happened? I thought we were having a good time?'

'I wouldn't say that. You were drinking to forget, and from what I can see, you achieved that.'

'Who did this to me?'

'Frankly, I have no idea. You went outside to smoke, and when I didn't see you come back in, I went outside to check on you and the ambulance was already there.'

'Fuck...'

'Jesus, Teddy you scared the living shit out of me. You're lucky they didn't do anything worse.'

Her voice wobbled at the end and I felt like shit for scaring her, even if I didn't know what had happened.

'I'm sorry,' I managed to choke out, tears rolling silently down my face.

'Hey, hey. You'll be okay. I am going to take good care of you.'

'My life is so messed up, Haze.'

'I know,' she stroked my hair softly, comforting me.

'Would you mind going to my mum's? I don't know when I'm going to get out of here.'

'Yeah, of course I can. I'll drop by as soon as I leave the hospital.'

'Thank you,' I said with a little smile. 'Do you know where my phone is?'

'I have it, but I don't think it's such—'

'Please.'

'Okay,' she said, placing it on my bedside table. 'Just don't think about it.'

She leaned towards me and gave me a kiss on the forehead.

'I will be back later, okay?'

She left my room, and I was alone once again. I reached for my phone, pain shooting up my side and scratches were all over the back of my hand. A memory flashed through my mind. I knew why I was so mad the night before. It was plastered all over social media. Vincent had gotten engaged to that guy. It had come out of nowhere and hit me like a ton of bricks.

There were photos of engagement rings, and of the two posing in matching shirts. It was just happiness all around, while I'd been living in a hell I couldn't get out of.

I took a "poor-me" selfie to post but wasn't sure if that would be a good idea. I felt so abundantly sad and alone, but under it all, I was just so angry; angry at my circumstances, angry about what had happened to me, angry at what my life had become over the past few years. I was stuck. My life was frozen in time. All my hopes and dreams had to be put on hold to make sure my mum was okay. I loved my mum; I would have done anything for her. I just wanted there to be a piece of life for me, where I could just be Teddy. I really wanted someone by my side to make it all feel better, but it felt like I had missed my chance before I'd even had one.

I missed Vincent so much.

I wasn't sure if it was because of the morphine, but my fingers tapped on their own. I opened his profile and typed *"Congratulations on your engagement."*

I put my phone down and closed my eyes.

Maybe I'd wake up to something good.

I woke up to a truckload of notifications. Turns out Morphine Teddy did eventually post the selfie and more than one person had taken an interest in what had caused my injuries. I had quite the array of missed calls from Laura, a few acquaintances sending me thoughts and prayers but nothing from Vincent. He was probably out celebrating with the fiancé. My soul ached in a way I didn't think was possible. Our conversations weren't like they used to be when we were teenagers, but there was always a part of me that thought we'd be reunited one day. That fate would somehow step in. Now I had to hope for a divorce on top of that. How awful a person did that make me?

My phone started ringing; the noise not helping the dull pain in my head. I really couldn't face speaking to Laura yet, so I was ready to reject the call. I looked at the screen and realised it wasn't Laura. It was Vincent.

Shit. I didn't know what to do. I wasn't sure if I'd be able to bear hearing his happy voice, while I felt like my life was falling apart.

But I *did* pick up.

Masochist.

'Hi there,' I said.

'Teddy!' his voice layered with stress. 'What happened?'

'Nothing much, just Australian homophobia at its finest.'

'That's it?'

'I don't know what happened.'

'What do you mean you don't know? How can you not know?' he asked, his voice an octave higher than normal.

'I was out drinking. I went outside for a smoke. I woke up in the hospital.'

'And someone...what, attacked you? How? You went outside alone?'

'Vincent, what do you want me to say? We haven't spoken in forever.' I didn't appreciate the Spanish inquisition joining the throbbing in my head.

'And whose fault is that?' he asked, getting his hackles up.

I hesitated. As much as I was annoyed at him, part of me was relieved to hear his voice after all this time. To know that he cared enough to call.

'Look, I don't want to argue,' he sighed. 'I know it's been tough for you...'

'You have no idea what it's been like for me.' I snapped.

'Then tell me. Tell me, Teddy.'

'It's...a long story and you wouldn't understand,' I explained, trying hard not to cry at his gentle voice. 'What happened last night...is nothing. I may have deserved it, even.'

'Is your mother okay?'

'I really don't want to talk about it, Vincent. I'm...very grateful you called, but it's probably best if you go back to your wonderful life. Forget me.'

'My wonderful life. Teddy you know nothing—'

'I have to go, doctors are knocking. I mean it. It's time to forget about me. Goodbye Vincent.'

I hung up, dropped my phone onto the bed and cried.

He tried to call me again.

I ignored it.

I knew I was acting like a child. I was just so tired. Being in that hospital bed was the most rest I'd had in the last few years. I'd felt so fortunate when I lived in Italy. I thought I had all the opportunities in the world ahead of me. That there was no limit to what I could do or the time I had to do it in.

Fucking hell. I couldn't stop the pain that coursed through my body, physically and mentally. The fragile whisper of hope I had, that Vincent and I would one day fall in love, pick up the threads we had left all those years ago and come back together was gone. It wasn't going to happen and the sooner I accepted that, the better. It was for the best. That didn't stop how badly it hurt to close the door on one more of my dreams for good.

At some stage, someone did actually come knock on my door.

'Come in,' I called out.

I saw his stupid long blond hair entering the room and I rolled my eyes. Well, the one eye.

'Hey, bro,' he said.

Funny how I would get the "bro" treatment only once every few years.

'What are you even doing here? Ran out of money? Located a conscience?' I was snarky and unapologetic.

'When you receive a phone call hearing your baby brother has been beaten to a pulp, you tend to go visit them,' he said, indignant.

'So, let me get this straight. You fly out to see me for this, after years of not speaking to each other, but you don't bother with mum whatsoever? Mum, who has actually sponsored your bullshit trips around the world all these years?'

'Your friend Hazel called. I came as soon as I could,' he said, walking towards me.

'Great. That's fantastic. So where have you been, Mitchell? Did you miss the phone calls and messages where I told you about mum?'

'The situation with mum is...complicated.'

'Ha!' I couldn't believe him.

'Look...one thing at a time. Who did this to you?' he said, now sitting on the red leather chair next to my bed.

'Please don't sit down. Just...leave.'

'I won't. I am here to stay.'

'You're back in Tassie? Whatever happened to your raging acting career?'

'I need to spend some time with you. When Hazel called me, it scared the shit out of me.'

'So, you were already in Australia? For how long?'

'I have only been back for a few weeks. I'm crashing with a friend in Sydney.'

'Mum would be so proud of you,' I said, sarcastically.

'Enough with this shit, Teddy. I'm sorry I couldn't deal with her,' he said with his eyes on the floor.

I wanted nothing to do with Mitchell. He was an idiotic, arrogant piece of garbage I had the misfortune of sharing DNA with. As far as I was concerned, I was an only child.

'Teddy, we only have each other. I am here to stay, and I will look after you.'

'...you want to move back home, don't you?'

He paused, then sighed.

'Just for a little while. I'll help you out with your recovery.'

'*I* don't need your help, mum does. Do you have any idea what it's been like for the past five years? I had to put everything on hold! My whole life is on fucking hold.'

'I know.'

I was already tired of seeing his dumb face. Mitchell had used his looks to his advantage his entire life. His light honey brown curls, his bronze skin, his muscular body were all great assets for someone with such a small brain.

'I need to rest. Please leave.'

'Okay...I will be back later,' he said getting up.

I didn't have the energy to speak to him anymore, I turned my head the other way and waited for the sound of the door closing. My whole body was shaking with rage. I was in so much pain. I just wanted to cry and disappear.

Then the door opened again. He wasn't quite done yet.

'You're so fucking unfair, Teddy.'

'Oh, here we go.'

'You left mum too if you remember.'

'She hadn't fallen ill when I left for Italy.'

'Oh, so you thought that car accident—'

'I didn't know then, and you didn't either.'

'Don't be naïve. I'm sure mum had been displaying symptoms for months. You just didn't see them. When the disease started taking over, it was already too late. You could have put her in a home or hired someone.'

A small part of me couldn't blame him for staying away. Even I wanted to get as far as I could. I didn't want to see my wildly funny, intelligent, resilient mother wilt away in front of my eyes. But I knew I had a duty to stay. I had to be there with her when she was terrified about losing control of her body. When the loss of her co-ordination resulted in injuries. When she saw the pain and frustration I couldn't hide in my eyes when she had forgotten something important. I wish I could erase those moments. But she was my mum, she had raised me and loved me without limit. She needed to be cared for by someone who loved her.

'You're so fucking selfish...' I said, with disgust.

'You've lost half of your twenties already. You've put your life on hold. Whatever happened to becoming a flight attendant? Seeing the world? Neither of us should have to deal with mum's burden.'

'Do you think I haven't thought about it? Do you think playing nurse with mum was what I planned to do? I can't just leave her. She's terrified.'

'You have to live your life before it's too—'

'I understand, Mitchell,' I paused to take a breath. 'You can sleep in the pool house, so I don't have to see your stupid fucking face.'

'I think I will sleep in my old room,' he bit back.

'Hazel has your old room. But you're welcome to use mum's old room. She sleeps downstairs now.'

'Okay. Maybe the pool house is best.'

'Suit yourself. You usually do,' I said, dismissively.

'Hey, I'm here now. It's going to be alright, Teddy.'

Mitchell smiled for a second. I didn't smile back, but for a mere moment, I felt a faint sense of relief about having my big brother back in my life. I had felt so alone. I was seeing everyone moving forward with their existence, while I had been here, trapped inside a life that didn't feel like mine. Maybe this would be okay.

CHAPTER THIRTEEN

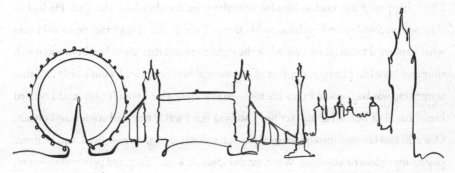

VINCENT

2014

Today was the big day. The second *big* day of my week. I was sitting on the hard, wooden floor wearing pure black and purple polyester in the middle of July. Graduation. The end of an era. University life had been harder than I had expected, but it was all coming together for one last big celebration. My mum and Kyle were already sitting in the audience, waiting for hundreds of names to be announced on stage, listening for mine.

The room was buzzing, the air uncomfortably warm, thick with excitement and nervous energy. Parents trying to take their best photographs with their children, graduates looking for their hats and friends, and people changing everywhere. Yet there I was, sitting on the floor in the corner of the room, staring at the screen of my phone. He hung up on me. I was hung up on by a person I cared about so much.

I had no idea what had happened to Teddy. Our relationship, friendship, had gone stagnant over the years and had become a case of a quick messenger catch up occasionally. Our lives had taken different paths and, as neither of us had changed the country we lived in, we had to deal with a god-awful time difference. I still found myself looking at his photos from time to time. He hadn't posted much of late. I knew he was helping to look after his mother who had fallen ill right after he went back to Australia. He never told me what her ailment was, no matter when or how I asked. Hazel didn't tell me either, always stating it was up to him. Time tripped on and he grew colder and colder, and I let it happen. I was mad at him for something he couldn't have changed. He had to skip out on Sweden and go back to his mum. I knew that. I had also never told him what happened to me, it never felt like the right time and then there had been too much time and I couldn't bring it up. Part of me wanted him to notice I wasn't okay and that something was happening in my life too—to *just notice* that I wasn't okay, and I needed him. I couldn't be mad at him for not knowing but I was. I was mad at him, and myself. Our calls had become infrequent over the years. Because of where we lived, and he never posted any videos or anything. When we did speak, it wasn't deep and personal anymore, so my last memories of his voice—*my* Teddy's voice—were at the airport saying goodbye. And then, today. For the first time in years, I finally heard Teddy's voice once again and *oh*, it was so painful. So beautiful and smooth and broken. Full of the emotions I'd missed without realising I had. I wanted to be there. I wanted to know what had happened and who had hurt him. I wanted to demand some sort of justice. But I wasn't a part of his life anymore. He had made that clear.

I was still thinking about our chat when an incredibly stressed-out Laura ran towards me.

'I can't get through to him. He won't take my calls,' she said.

'I did.'

'You did? When?' her eyes were wide, worried for our friend.

'A few minutes ago, it wasn't a long call.'

'What did he say?' she said, while sitting down in front of me.

'Not much. He told me to mind my business, essentially.'

'Yeah. That's Teddy, alright. He's been so angry lately. I wonder if he got into a fight or something.'

'Would he do that?'

'I can't tell you. He is so different from what I remember my "brother" being like.'

'I'm just really worried.' I sighed, letting my head hit the wall behind me.

'It's our graduation, Vincent. It's a happy day. Remember all the work we did to finally get here.'

'I mean, speak for yourself. I have another year or so to get my Master's degree.'

'I am thinking I might go for a Masters too.'

I scrunched my face up in confusion.

'Since when?' I asked.

'I don't know. It's just something I've been thinking about.'

'Alright. I guess we are all being a little mysterious today.'

'I'm sorry. I'm going to try to call him again. See if he finally picks up. I'll see you later,' she said as she got up.

She left me there, sitting by myself with thoughts of Teddy swirling through my head. The Teddy I loved so much and missed so deeply but didn't know how to reach. I didn't know how to fix what was between us and now he didn't even want that. I was over the moon about being engaged to Kyle but seeing the photo of Teddy in the hospital brought back way too many feelings I didn't realise I still had. It didn't feel right to be so happy, while a person I cared so deeply about was hurt and miserable on the other side of the world.

I got up with a sigh and fixed my gown and hat. I was sweating buckets. The building had no air conditioning, so I was stuck with hundreds of other people dying under their garments. And I'd have to stay there for another two hours. I put my phone inside my pocket and walked ahead.

It took every fibre in my body not to pass out from the heat inside the venue. Hearing name after name after name was exhausting. I felt sorry for the families and friends that had come to see us. I was one of the first people to get the hell out of there and I waited outside, sucking in air that didn't taste of old people, for my invitees to meet me.

Kyle was wearing a charcoal suit with a pink floral shirt. He would hardly ever look that dashing. An All-American boy would often be found in beige cargo shorts and green Hollister t-shirts, perfect to accentuate his scorching red hair and slightly darker stubble. My mother looked incredibly elegant, with a black dress we picked together at a super expensive department store. I could tell from her blotchy face that she had been crying during the ceremony.

They walked over to me, massive smiles on their lovely faces.

'Oh, mother. What have you been crying about?'

'It's so good to see you graduate!' she gave me a big kiss on the cheek.

'Weren't you guys bored to death?' I asked.

'Oh no, we definitely were,' said Kyle. 'Although your mother spent most of the time making fun of my Southern accent.'

'You have to admit, it's pretty fun to listen to, and we don't get that many Americans from the deep south in Bath so it's kind of like watching an American TV show,' she said. 'But we laughed a lot as well. So many students dress so bizarrely!'

'They act bizarrely too. The joys of an art school.'

'Did you manage to get in contact with your friend?' she asked.

I hesitated for a second.

'What friend?' Kyle asked.

'Uhm,' I looked at him a bit sheepishly. 'A friend of mine who lives in Australia has gotten into some sort of accident, but I couldn't find out more.'

'Do I know them?' he asked.

'...Teddy. He...shares a house with my old friend Hazel.'

'Well, you can always call again later,' my mum said. 'If he's at the hospital, he may still feel groggy or he may be busy with people visiting him.'

'You're right, I'll try again later.'

'Maybe you could send some flowers? Can that be done online?'

'Yeah, we'll see.'

'Should I be jealous of this secretive boy of yours?' Kyle wrapped his arm around me. 'You're officially off the market as of yesterday.'

I didn't want to lie, but it was probably a smart idea not to share the *tales of Vincent and Teddy*.

'It's not like that.'

'Okay, just checking,' he said, shrugging.

'Are you ready to go, Vincent?' asked mum.

'Could you guys go without me, and I will see you at the restaurant? I have a few people to see. You know, it may be my last chance to see them.'

'Sounds good,' said Kyle. He gave me a quick kiss on the cheek. 'But don't keep us waiting.'

'Of course not,' I said with a smile.

I went back inside the venue, looking for Laura. I needed to know if she'd managed to get through to Teddy. Seeing him wounded and in pain brought back memories I would have rather not remember. I was walking over to Laura and her family when my phone vibrated with a text from him saying "I'm sorry".

I came to an abrupt stop, not caring if anyone was behind me, and immediately gave him a call. Hearing the soft anger in his voice directed at me wasn't how I wanted to leave things with each other.

'Hey Vincent,' he said so softly.

I sighed as relief flooded my cells.

'Hey. Are you okay?'

'I'm sorry about earlier. I'm just so frustrated. Everything hurts.'

'Can you tell me what happened?'

'I...don't know,' he said. He sounded so defeated. Nothing like the sunny Teddy I fell for years before. 'I...was out. I was upset.'

'Teddy...' guilt twisted my stomach.

'No, no. I know. I'm pathetic.'

'Don't talk like that, please.'

'You're not responsible. I just went a bit crazy with the drinking and I acted like a dickhead.'

The story sounded more familiar than I expected. Was I the reason he was so drunk he lost control?

'Who did this to you?'

'Australia isn't always the friendliest when you're as publicly out as I am. It happens more than you think.'

'I'm so sorry, Teddy. I...'

I wanted to tell him that I knew. I knew what it felt like to be helpless, on the receiving end of meaningless violence. But I couldn't tell him. I couldn't tell him that I'd lived under paralysing fear since that night. And more so, I wanted to tell him how angry I had been at him for so long. Angry at the fact he wasn't there for me when I needed him the most.

'Tell me about you, Vincent. Everything is happening for you right now. What's this lucky guy like?'

'Kyle is...' I hesitated for a second. 'He's a really nice guy. We met during my gap year in the States.'

'Love at first sight?'

'Something like that.'

It wasn't anything like that. Kyle had become someone I used to stay mentally afloat. The only person I felt could protect me, like a big American security blanket. I owed him everything.

'How was the proposal?'

If roles were reversed, I never would have wanted to know the details of the way some other guy put his hands on the guy I, well, cared a whole lot about.

'He came over to London from Orlando for my graduation, he asked my mother and, next thing I know, he's down on his knee in a restaurant.'

'I don't know if I would have done a restaurant, but...he sounds like a nice guy.'

'He is. We struggle with the distance, but it'll be over soon once he moves in with me.'

'You do like your men living far away from you.'

'Teddy...'

'I know, I know. Inappropriate. Can I blame the morphine I'm on?'

'Hey,' I said. 'Do you remember when we met in London?'

'Of course I do. One might say it's a pretty damn vivid memory.'

'Did you ever think that would be the last time we'd see each other?' I asked softly, a tear escaping.

'You know I planned to see you. I...well. I'm sure Hazel must have told you what happened—'

'It wasn't just not seeing each other, Teddy. Not hearing from you...made me feel incredibly alone.'

'I'm sorry, I was just so overwhelmed.'

'You know...Hazel never really wants to talk about your mother's condition...'

'It's...awful. You don't want to hear about it. '

'But I do.'

'Gosh. Sometimes I just think of a world where life wasn't so damn difficult. A world where I would have started my flight attendant training and would be flying over there every chance I had.'

'Is that still your dream?'

'I don't really think I have dreams anymore,' he said quite abruptly.

'Don't say that—'

'Don't let me keep you. You have a lovely celebration. Both the graduation and the engagement. I'm glad you're happy. You found a Romeo to save you after all.'

'Teddy...'

Was I happy? There were so many things I didn't tell Teddy. So many things that were hiding behind the happy photos and the stories I'd write on social media. How did we let this happen? We used to talk about everything, and now I was just hopeless, numb and listening to him suffer in a hospital bed.

'What do you say we have another chat later, or tomorrow and we fill each other in on what's been going on?' I asked.

'Vincent, I think you'd be better off just being with your family, I'll be fine.'

'We'll talk later.'

'Okay,' he said with what sounded like a smile.

'Bye, Teddy.'

I hung up the phone and felt a sense of relief from hearing his voice once again. Calmer. Not the angsty person I spoke to a few hours earlier.

I removed my gown and returned it. Looking around at all the hopeful students surrounding me I couldn't help but feel a sense of joy and finality, for at last being done with my studies. At least until I'd start my master's degree in a few months' time.

I made my way towards the exit, weaving through the groups of people, when something like a switch flipped, my world stopped cold. I saw his face through the crowd. That giant leering smile, the grey hair, the bristly beard. Right in front of me, staring at me, mocking me. The sweet scent of fruity vodka flooded my mouth. It was suffocating. A scream caught in my throat, choking the air out of me. I couldn't move. Cold and clammy, a sheen of sweat coated me like second skin. I dropped to my knees, palms on the ground opening and closing, the grains of sand sticking under my nails.

I gasped for air; each sucking breath harder than the last.

It couldn't be.

It can't be.

I closed my eyes, forced my terrified mind to focus.

Five things I could see. I needed five things I could see. I looked around quickly.

Tears streamed down my face, eyes burning like fire.

One more breath.

A cap on the ground. Water bottle. A tree. A bird. The gutter.

Breathe. In. Out. Four things I can feel.

A soft breeze. The hard ground under me. A stone pressing into my knee. The sun on my neck.

He wasn't there. I was imagining things. *In. Out.*

Three things I could hear.

Traffic. People talking. A car horn.

My chest felt freer, the tightness receding. *In.*

Two things I could smell.

Exhaust fumes. My own disgusting sweat. *Out.*

Simon's ghost would always be my prosecution. He was always there hiding in the darkness, whenever I let my guard down.

There was one thing I could taste.

Well, I couldn't taste anything right now. I closed my eyes once more. Strong arms around me, lovingly. The taste of Teddy on my tongue.

Could I ever forget?

The panic attacks were less and less frequent the more time passed, and I was thankful that I could get myself through them. It didn't make them any more bearable, it didn't fix the hollow feeling in my chest or the shaking of my hands. I stood back up, brushed off my knees and slowly walked away. How many more of these moments would I have to endure?

I arrived at the restaurant right on time for our reservation, my body aching from the panic attack, flustered and angry that Simon still featured in my mind. It wasn't the first time, and it would most definitely not be the last. Seeing Simon amongst crowds was something that happened more than I cared to admit, though not every time ended on the pavement working through my grounding exercise. I felt watched and followed almost every time I'd be on my own walking outside.

I waved at my mother and Kyle, who were already seated. It was one of those restaurants where the chef cooked things in front of you throwing utensils and shit around for the entirety of the dinner. Kyle loved it, while I wasn't too keen since you had to sit with other random people. Not ideal. I sat in between the two, as I was the guest of honour.

'Finally!' My mum exclaimed. 'We've been waiting for our little graduate.'

'Sorry, there was a queue to return those stupid gowns,' I said, aiming for a normal tone.

'Well, I'm very happy we came back here. With the whole proposal thing, I couldn't enjoy the food yesterday,' said Kyle.

'I wish someone had recorded it, I would have loved to see Vincent cry,' said my mum.

'He actually didn't,' Kyle pointed out. 'He was just surprised.'

'I just wasn't expecting it at all.'

My mum gave me a suspicious look.

'Right, I'm gonna head to the washrooms before the cooking show starts,' said Kyle. 'Join me,' he whispered in my ear.

He got up and made his way through the tables.

'I'll go too,' I announced.

'Are you okay, little one?' mum asked, catching my hand in hers.

'Yeah. Yeah, of course. Why?'

'I just—'

'I'm fine, mum. Really,' I said, faking a smile.

I quickly bolted to the bathroom, where Kyle was washing his hands.

I looked at him in the mirror and he cocked his head to join him in the stall. My heart started beating faster, but I complied. He locked the door behind us, and I immediately pulled my trousers down, and unbuttoned his.

'Lube or—' he whispered.

'You should know the answer by now,' I said, facing the wall. 'Just hurry up.'

He quickly entered me dry. A pain so familiar, which I was now able to isolate. His hand pressed my head onto the wall, while I told him to fuck me harder. And harder. Until he wrapped his arm around my neck and tightened his grip until I could no longer breathe. With a muffled moan, he came inside me. I guided his hand to my cock and prompted him to give me a quick hand-job.

'I love you,' he said soon after.

I nodded, still facing the wall, and quickly pulled my trousers up.

'I'll see you at the table,' he said, leaving me inside the cubicle.

I closed the door again and sat on the toilet. Head between my legs, fingers digging into my scalp. I wanted to rip my hair off, what was left of it. He liked it short, cropped. No more "scruffy" Vincent.

I was tidy, polished. Perfectly obedient Vincent.

I left the toilets and ran into my mother. She looked radiant with her shiny long dark hair and long-sleeved black dress.

'There you are,' she said.

'Hi, mum. What's up?'

'I just wanted to make sure you're okay? You've had that face all day.'

'What face?'

'You just...don't seem to be particularly excited. You got engaged! Graduated!'

'I am. I'm very excited.'

'You know you can tell me anything, right?'

I didn't know how to express myself. It all had happened so quickly; I didn't have enough time to fully digest the rapid changes in my life. I didn't know how to tell her I just wanted to scream. All the fucking time.

'I'm very happy, mum...'

'And you're sure he's the one.'

'What's the one, mum?' I asked, doubtful such a person existed. Remembering it was Teddy my mind presented me with, in the midst of my panic attack, and not Kyle.

'I don't want you to rush into anything you're not ready for. You're my baby,' she said, caressing my face.

'I'm not a baby,' I said, flinching. 'I'm a grown man. Don't worry about me.'

'Are you sure you've given it enough thought? I wouldn't want you to have said yes if you didn't feel like it one hundred percent.'

I sighed.

'You still have time to think about it. Kyle's flying back to the States tomorrow. You can take all the time you need.'

'Think about what? It's done now.'

'Vincent. You're not obliged to do anything—'

'Mum. It's decided,' I said, snapping at her. 'I'll see you at the table.'

I walked away from her, every step a different doubt.

Was I doing the right thing?

Chapter Fourteen

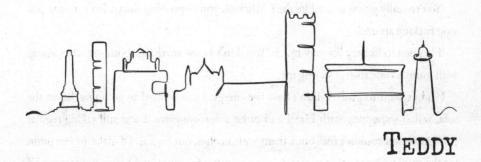

Teddy

2014

I was staring out the car window not seeing anything, thinking about my life. Getting my face pounded like dough had allowed me to reassess my existence, during the weeks of recovery. My ribs were finally healing, my eyes were able to fully open, and my nose had started deflating. I still thought I needed to go to a plastic surgeon to fix it and bring it back to what it used to be, but Hazel didn't seem to think I needed it.

Mitchell was driving mum's car like a maniac. I had survived my attack, but I certainly wasn't ready to die at his hands.

'Would you slow the fuck down?' I snapped.

'Don't be boring. We are hardly going above the limit!'

'I'm not—it's not about being boring. I still have broken bones.'

'As if! We all heal quick as in our family.'

'All except mum' I pointed out.

'I currently do not have any desire to depress myself, thank you very much.'

'You're such a dick.'

Mum's disease had ruined everything. My life in Italy was such a distant memory. Gone were the days where I had the freedom to lay about at the beach, attempting to read books in Italian, drinking *Aperol Spritz* and flirting with cute boys. Dealing with the first stages of her ailment had been soul crushing. The woman I knew so well, who baked banana bread and sung loudly, who loved teaching English and literature, had become nothing more than a shell. Someone who could barely emit sounds that made sense. She didn't even recognise me anymore and hadn't for a while now.

'You're really going to act like this? Mitchell, you're pushing thirty. Isn't it time you stop fucking around?'

'I happen to like my life very much. You don't know anything about my relationship with mum. Please stop pestering me.'

I didn't want to push. I didn't have the energy. I just wanted to go home, lie on the sofa, watch something with Hazel and order a massive pizza. I was still taking regular painkillers, so I couldn't really mix them with alcohol, but fuck it, I'd make an exception for the evening. I was going to interview a new nurse for mum, so I had to prepare myself to rehash the entire journey she had taken these last five years. I needed to get drunk.

'We're almost home,' he said.

I sighed, staring back out the window once again. I was starting to wonder what drove my brother away. I couldn't imagine how mum could be responsible for it.

It didn't take long for the three of us to overdo what was meant to be a chilled evening with a few drinks. I wasn't sure if it was my painkiller cocktail, but I was legless. Hazel and Mitchell had actually managed to get along in the house—which I thought was pretty bizarre—as Mitch turned what used to be a pretty neat two-floor house into a fucking pit, and his dirty socks were just about everywhere in the house, possibly growing their own lifeforms.

'Hope you'll appreciate I got some cleaning done today!' he said.

I looked around disgusted.

'Did you?'

'Oh, he did. It was hilarious,' said Hazel. 'There's video evidence of it as I was asked to record him as he vacuumed half naked.'

'You're joking,' I said, looking at him. 'Come on.'

'What? My Insta needs some action. How else am I going to get myself a missus?'

'No woman will be impressed by your vacuuming skills, mate,' she said.

'I was talking about my pecks, babe.'

Hazel rolled her eyes. 'How long will I have the pleasure of spending all my waking time with you for?'

'Hey, it's not my fault we're both in between jobs,' he said with a cackle.

'I am a photographer. I've been working this whole time.'

'Oh, they pay you for that?'

'Yes, Mitchell. They do. You should try it some time.'

'I'm just not very inspired at the moment. Also, going to auditions fucking suck since Tasmania is hardly a TV hub.'

'Really?' I asked. 'No inspiration?'

'None.'

'You could find a director and shoot a documentary, or something. You could pull a Joaquin Phoenix.'

'Doc on what?'

'I don't know, perhaps a fucking disease that nearly no one has?' snarky Teddy was out.

'God, you're so depressing, Teddy. No one wants to watch that.'

I huffed. Took a few more sips of beer.

'You know, that is actually not a bad idea,' said Hazel. 'You could really raise awareness and do something important for once.'

'I want to do something fun. I don't want to make the viewers sad. That's not my brand!'

'Forget about it,' I said.

I picked my phone up and flicked through social media. A photo of Laura and Vincent together filled my screen. I missed her dearly. I was glad she'd found Vincent when she moved to London, so she had someone. It was almost as if we'd swapped friends. Hazel had been an absolute star, helping me out with mum's stuff.

'What you lookin' at?' he asked.

'Nothing. Go away.' I couldn't take my eyes off their happy faces.

'Are you arranging a booty call?'

'No, piss off. Also, in case it escaped your notice, Mitchell, my body is a fucking shipwreck. I couldn't even if I wanted to.'

'Also, it's not like Tassie is gay-central,' Hazel piped up.

'Oh!' Mitchell turned to her. 'You're saying you too...?'

'My god. Teddy, how long do we have to put up with this urchin?'

'Just saying,' he said. 'I haven't once caught you staring at my abs!'

'Right, and on that note...' she said while standing up.

'Oh come on! Don't leave on my account! I'm just teasing.'

'I have some work to do and—' she turned to me. 'Please don't kill each other.'

I nodded, though no promises.

'Aww, don't be a *piker*, you!' Mitchell said.

Hazel ignored him.

'Oh, and Teddy?' she asked.

'Yes?'

'Tomorrow is Berta's last day and you have to interview the new nurse!'

'Right,' I said, giving her a thumbs up.

'Alright, goodnight, love,' Mitchell said while puckering his lips for a kiss.

Hazel looked at him, her face a mask of disgust. She must have been the first woman to fully, out-right reject Mitchell to his face. Bless her. She headed upstairs into her room, leaving me alone with him.

'You alright, mate?' he asked, while sipping his beer.

'Why are you asking?'

'I saw the way your face turned when you looked at your phone. Is it because of that *pommie* you're hot for?'

'What are you even talking about?'

'Hazel told me you and her friend used to be in love and now he's getting hitched to some other guy. Is that the one?'

'No! No. Don't speak to Hazel about me. You don't get to do that. Mind your fucking business.'

I was bone tired. I knew the sensible thing would be going to bed as soon as possible, but I didn't want the night to end. The morning after was going to be a huge ball-ache and I wasn't quite ready.

'Why are you being so defensive?'

'Because it's dumb alright? He's just someone I used to chat online with. It's not like we had a relationship or anything.'

Mitchell stretched his arms and his neck. Leaning back in his chair with his legs crossed in front of him. 'It's a new age, mate. Being able to communicate with people online around the world is a cool thing. I met so many awesome people during my trips. I think it's normal at least.'

'Talking about relationships? You ever had one where you didn't make a girl move out of the fucking country?'

Mitchell slammed his beer bottle down onto the wooden table, smashing it in his hands. His face hardened, his breathing savage and nostrils flaring. My heart stuttered, alarmed by the sudden change in his behaviour.

'What—'

'Sorry. Didn't mean to,' he said quietly, dabbing a napkin onto his bleeding hand. 'I'll wash this off and go to bed.'

He stood up, looking at me. 'I'll get everything cleaned up before the morning.'

I was on the edge of my seat, stunned, wondering what the fuck had just happened, but he was probably too drunk to function. So was I, to be fair. I staggered all the way to bed, falling somewhat painfully into the covers. Everyone had been acting so weird. I closed my eyes, pushing away thoughts of my insane brother and letting sleep take me.

I was tapping my foot on the floor incessantly. Agitated. My head felt like it was filled with rocks and lava. I hadn't slept well at all. Two hours after going to bed I'd stumbled into the bathroom and emptied the entirety of my guts into it. Hazel, however, woke up fresh as a daisy, like she hadn't skulled a bottle and a half of wine. Bitch.

I sat at the table in the little main street café, waiting for my interview prospect to arrive. The walls were a pale blue; the same shade that used to be on the downstairs room at home that mum now slept in. Mum's new space had been painted a painfully bright shade of yellow, her favourite. Frames of relaxing landscapes with water, mountains, and pine trees were hanging on every wall. She loved to take us out to explore the countryside when we were small, pointing out different trees and wildlife. Little did she know she wouldn't get to see another real landscape ever again.

I was lost in memories of far simpler times when a waitress stopped at my table, trailed by a tall, handsome guy wearing a shirt and tie.

'Mr Clarke?' he asked.

'Take a seat,' I said pointing to the white IKEA chair opposite me. 'And call me Teddy, please.'

'I'll just be back to get your order shortly,' the waitress smiled, leaving us alone.

'I'm Aidan, I just transferred from Sydney.' said the very young-looking guy opposite me, hand outstretched for me to shake.

His big ocean blue eyes were locked on me, undoubtedly waiting for me to proceed but I was a teensy bit distracted by the defined pecks hiding under his shirt.

'I'm sorry...how old are you?' I asked, dragging my eyes up.

'I'm twenty-nine?' he phrased it liked a question, his smooth voice picking up at the end.

'Oh.' *Not so baby then.* 'Okay. Do you have experience with Huntington's?'

'I do actually.'

'Well...my mother's condition has gotten a lot worse throughout these last few months and I could really use the help. I need someone strong and able to step in when needed,' I took a calming breath. 'She can get quite violent at times as she doesn't quite understand where she is. It's important to try and keep her calm, but there are times where she may need to be restrained, for her own safety mostly. But you seem like you know a thing or two about lifting,' I noted, staring at his buzzcut and shirt straining biceps.

Stop staring Teddy.

'I have to lift people fairly often. It's routine, really,' he replied, as his cheeks gained color. We looked at each other for a couple of beats, assessing one another. A cup clattered into a saucer a couple of tables over, bringing me back to present and the very real situation I was in. I cleared my throat.

'Well, you won't be bored with her. She's quite...the handful,' my eyes a little teary.

'Is everything alright?' he made to get up, but I waved him away.

'Yeah. Yes. Sorry. I just hate this disease so much.'

He smiled softly. 'Could you tell me about her, Teddy?'

'Did I not send you our previous nurse's notes?'

He slipped the stack of notes out of his bag and sat them on his strong legs.

'This won't tell me a whole lot. This disease hardly ever operates in the same way, so I need to know when it started and how it developed from a person who knows what the patient used to behave like, before.'

'I'm not sure when it started. I was out of the country for about a year and a half. I now know that there were symptoms during that time, but she wouldn't tell me much.' I was digging my nails into my thighs, I couldn't shake the undercurrent of anxiety when talking about this point of the past. 'At some stage of the symptoms developing, she had a car accident. She lost control of the steering wheel and ended up in the other lane. I thought it was just stress or fatigue, but it was later associated to some sort of incontrollable spasm.'

'Was she diagnosed straight away?' he asked, jotting down some notes.

'No. They thought she suffered from schizophrenia. With her attacks of psychosis and all...'

He lifted his eyes from the notebook and looked at me. 'Are you okay?'

'Yes. Sorry. It took a few months before they discovered it was Huntington's disease,' I said with glossy eyes. 'She said it was "liberating" to know. She was almost relieved when she found out. She was being treated for something that didn't make sense to her, but the real diagnosis was so much worse. I hadn't even heard of it before then.'

'It's definitely a rare one. Although it happens to more people than you think.'

'My brother never came back home...I looked after her. I've seen her wither right in front of me, day after day.'

'I'm truly sorry, would you like a tissue? I'm sure I have some in my—'

'I'm alright. I am used to this,' I interrupted, sniffing.

'What was she like before?'

'She was a teacher. She had such a great mind, a voracious reader. She wrote a few books too. She also kept these incredibly detailed diaries, so she would always remember students and their personalities. She loved being an inspiration to her pupils. They adored her. They'd come to visit us at first, and she loved it. Then the months slipped by and we saw fewer and fewer visitors. It was... painful for people.'

'Yes. Yes, it is.'

'She started to forget things. At first it was little things, stuff that didn't matter. It was noticeable, but nothing major. She is the kind of person who remembers actors' names, the year different movies and music had come out, names of random monuments around the world. Heck, Trivial Pursuit was her favourite board game.'

'...but then it wasn't just the small stuff. Was it?'

'She called me Mitchell one day and apologised to me for something she believed she had done. And I told her I wasn't him, that it was Teddy instead and she was like *"Teddy is still a child"* and it broke my heart. I couldn't deny what the disease was doing to her anymore. You know, you think she's the exception. The doctors tell you that she's...doing great. She's beating the odds. But you know, deep down, that the woman you're taking care of every single day is drifting away one piece of brilliance at a time,' my voice broke a little, emotion and reality choking me.

'Was she ever violent?' Aidan asked softly.

'She was frustrated when her body started doing things. When her hands could no longer grab things, when she couldn't turn the pages of a book, or when she couldn't walk upstairs anymore. She was trapped in her own body. Her brilliant mind was in a prison,' Tears were streaming down my face. I was sobbing. I didn't like to talk about her. I hated this horrid disease. It ruined both of our lives. My hands clenched into fists with no conscious thought, I was devasted this was life, and furious. 'Her body actually gave up before her mind did.'

'What do you mean?' he asked.

'When she was no longer able to wash herself, her mind was still switched on. She was humiliated at having to be bathed by her son. She would be crying under the water, screaming in anger because something that she couldn't control was taking over both of our lives,' I paused, drawing in a deep breath. 'Then one day she hit me, in the face. Full strength. She was mortified. Her arms were just moving of their own accord. I saw the horror in her eyes.'

'That's when you asked for help, I assume.'

'Yeah. It was her idea,' I said. 'She didn't want me to have that life anymore, that burden. She didn't want to risk hurting me. But I said no. I told her I needed to take care of her. Because only I knew how to deal with her.'

'It's good to hear she retained judgment. Many patients who suffer from HD...they don't really know what's happening to them. They are completely oblivious to their symptoms.'

'Yeah. Unfortunately, it didn't take long for her to fall and really hurt herself. She hit her head and suffered a fairly big laceration. I felt useless,' I said, dabbing at my eyes with my sleeve. Embarrassed I was losing control so openly in public.

'Teddy, you made the best choice about bringing a professional nurse into your home. You may even consider sending her to a facility.'

'She would die, if she were put in a hospice, with old people...'

'That's, unfortunately, another downside of the disease. It targets much younger people than, let's say, Parkinson's for example. Patients with Huntington's often feel lonely and misunderstood.'

'I know.'

'So, it would appear that Ms. Clarke has lost many cognitive functions,' he said while going through the notes. 'Dysarthria was one of the first speech impairments she's encountered. Her speech is slow and weak, often interrupted by spasms of her face muscles. She can still eat some solid foods, which is great at this stage.'

'How did this happen...' I said, dropping my head into my hands, staring at the wood grain pattern of the generic grey table.

'Well, it's genet—'

'I know what it is. I just don't understand,' I said rubbing my eyes again. 'I'm sorry, you're not here to hear *me* complain.'

'Teddy, this is exactly why I'm here,' he said, reaching out like he meant to touch me. 'The issue with this disease is that we have to take care of the rest of the family as well. Seeing a loved one going through all these changes in behaviour is extremely harrowing. I'm here to support you, and your family—'

'Sure,' I said. 'Thanks. So...when can you start?'

'I'm happy to start right away.'

'Oh, that's perfect, I said. 'I still have a few more candidates to go through, but I'm definitely keen to see you for a second interview; you seem to know your way around the disease and that's—'

'This *is* my second interview,' he noted.

'But this is the first time I'm meeting you,' I said, confused.

'Yes, but I met your brother first. A couple of weeks ago.'

'Mitchell?'

'Yes? Oh. I know you said on the phone when we set this up that you had been in the hospital, well, you never cancelled my first interview. So I showed up to the address you gave me, and the previous nurse answered. She said you were unavailable, but your brother Mitchell was at home and able to see me.'

'Mitchell at—what?' I asked.

'I'm so sorry, I thought you knew.' Aidan's face was twisted in guilt, undeserved entirely. It wasn't his fault Mitchell had pretended he hadn't seen mum, when apparently, he had.

'You guys want to order?' the waitress materialised tableside, sunny smile in place.

'No, thank you, I need to leave,' I sucked in a breath. Forced some composure when anger and pain burnt beneath my skin. 'Aidan, I think it's safe to say you'll be hired. I'll be in touch later to arrange things. I'm sorry but I need to get home.' My heart was erratic, and I craved fresh air to clear my head.

'Of course, Mr. Clarke. Teddy. Absolutely.' Aidan got to his feet and shook my hand. 'I hope you're alright.'

No Aidan, not quite.

But I didn't say that.

'Yeah, absolutely. I'll be in touch.' I gathered my things and rushed out the door, dragging lungfuls of sharp oxygen in as soon as I was clear of the café.

Fucking Mitchell.

CHAPTER FIFTEEN

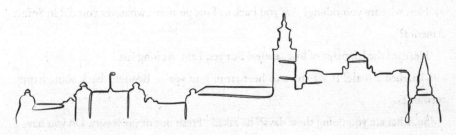

VINCENT

2014

Throughout my time in university, I got to use all kinds of equipment for free. Free access to all sorts of filming facilities. Since that night, I hadn't owned my own camera. I was staring at a display of the newest models in a shop, trying to feel that magic I used to feel once again. Mum had given me enough money as a graduation present to get a very nice set up. But each one I picked up, held in my hands, and thought of as maybe being mine, dragged those memories to the surface. The moment he snatched it out of my reach, throwing it away, before—

I shook my head, trying to push that particular image away, when my phone started ringing.

Daniel.

Talk about a blast from the past.

'Hello?' I said.

'Hey wanker!' his voice sounded like he hadn't been through puberty yet.

'Are you alright?' I asked.

'Of course I am! Why do you ask?'

'I don't know. It's been a minute!'

'Yeah, I know, I know. I've been a bad friend,' he chuckled. 'What are you up to?'

'Like...right now?' I asked, still walking aimlessly down the store aisles. 'Or...in life...?'

'I know you just got engaged. Congrats, man!'

'Thanks. I'm...super happy,' I responded, my tone monotonous.

'Yeah? You sound like you're about to be crucified!'

'Hey, why are you calling? Are you back in Europe after...whatever you did in South America?'

'I learned the language of love, *amigo*! But yes, I am. At long last.'

I laughed a little. It was nice to hear from him again. Brought back some happy memories.

'So, what are you doing these days?' he asked. 'Fresh out of university. Do you have a job lined up?'

'Well, Kyle—my boyfriend—works for the BBC. He's working on getting me through the door.'

'Fiancé.'

'What?'

'He's your fiancé now.'

'Oh. Yes. Sorry. Yes. It's still new. I have to get used to it,' I said, awkwardly.

'Good job on snatching someone who can get you the job of your dreams!'

'Yeah. I'm very lucky...'

'So, hey, listen. I'd love to chat some more. I'm actually about to get on a plane to Stockholm.'

'You're going back?' I asked, surprised.

'I haven't seen the host parents in months! I need to show my face!'

'Wow. That's really cool. I haven't been since I—'

'Went home?'

'...got sent home.'

'Right. This may be a little last minute, but you know it's how I roll...'

'I'm listening...?' I asked, weirdly nervous.

'Why don't you come with me? Like a pre-stag do. My host parents would love to see you again.'

'The only people in Sweden who would!'

'And we can go crazy, and I get to see your dumbass face.'

'You don't pronounce the B in dumbass, you dumbass.'

'I just came back from Argentina, baby!' the G said as an H. 'I pronounce everything!'

I chuckled. 'Alright, alright. And...I don't know. I don't really—'

'Hey Vincent, I'm boarding the plane. Have a think! I'd love to see you again.'

'Okay. I will. Have a safe flight,' I said closing the call.

I sighed. I couldn't go back. I never wanted to go back. All my happy memories were tarnished, wrapped in foul flashbacks that broke into my daily life. I had become a different person. I was ruined. My soul still felt like an open wound. The happiness and excitement this stage of my life should bring were unable to settle into place, while ugly, vulgar pain seeped out. Some days the wound was held together with butterfly stitches, no flashbacks came to cripple me: a movie night in with Laura, or a carefully time-zone-dictated late night call with Hazel. Others, it was days old, brand new. A slideshow of my failures, all leading to Simon, the suffocating panic, and flashes of him in a crowd.

The feeling I would never be free.

At the start of uni, I had a few sessions with a psych consultant on campus. Every time I tried to go through that night, to articulate in actual words what had happened so I could get some help, I was back on that sandy patch of earth with my vision tunnelling. She taught me how to ground myself, how to get myself back to the present. Once I figured out what I needed to do, I stopped going. I was never able to force the words past my teeth and get the help I needed, so I took the counting tool and I never went back. Being with Kyle helped me cope on a physical level with what had happened to me. I was finally in control. Even if what we had was violent, I was in *full* control, and it was on my terms. I wasn't the harmless kid anymore. *I* was in control of my life.

I left the store empty-handed, thoughts rabbiting through my head. Perhaps I did need a change of scenery.

I booked the first flight available while on the bus back home. I flew into my flat and into my room. I pulled out my navy weekender bag and tossed it on my bed. Turning around, I opened the top drawer and started grabbing underwear, throwing it into my bag.

'Hey, what's going on?' Laura said coming in, her delicate brows bunched up.

'I need to get away,' I said, frantically.

'Away where?'

'Daniel called me. He said he was heading to Stockholm to visit his host family, and he said I could stay with them too if I wanted.'

'Are you sure it's a good idea?'

'It's a great idea. I need to think about a few things, and I can't do it here. Plus, I haven't seen Daniel in forever.' I sounded a tiny bit frenetic to my own ear.

'You were a wreck after Stockholm. Why would you want to go back?' she asked, her hand landing on my shoulder.

'Don't!' I pulled sharply away from her touch. Her eyes were wide in her face, following my movements, as I took a deep breath. 'Sorry. Sorry, I didn't mean to do that.'

She had no idea what had happened to me in Stockholm. No one did. I just knew that I needed to go, to get closure, perhaps. I wasn't sure, I just needed to go.

'Will you be okay, Vincent?'

'Yes, of course I will. I just need to see an old friend, before my life turns into a cake tasting and venue picking montage.'

I kept throwing random pieces of clothing inside my bag as quickly as I could.

'So, when do you leave?'

'My flight is in less than three hours.'

'Holy shit!' she exclaimed. 'That is soon. What's the rush?'

'I just want to get out of here. I'll be okay. I just need some time with my old friend to get drunk together, and just not think about my stupid wedding or my future.'

I zipped my bag and put it over my shoulder. I looked at Laura and smiled.

'I'll be back in a week. I'll call you when I land, okay?' I said, giving her a little kiss on the cheek. 'I have to go now.'

I left the flat, walked down the stairs and hailed a taxi. It wouldn't be long before I'd get to see my friend.

Arlanda airport was as eerie as I remembered it. Swedes weren't the loudest of people, so walking through a nearly silent airport was always a slightly unusual experience. Daniel's flight had landed in the morning, so he'd already been settling in his host parents' guesthouse. Once I passed through the arrivals area, Daniel was there, waiting for me with a paper sign saying *Välkommen Vincent*.

'Hello, you,' the first genuine smile I'd had in a long while crossed my face.

'Hey sexy thing!' he was hugging me, nearly crushing my spine.

'Put me down, you shitbag.'

Standing in front of him for the first time in so long, I realised that so much time had passed. He was taller than me, sporting a blond man bun with colourful tattoos all over his arms and hands, and dip dyed rainbow trousers. He had also been working out a lot, making him look much manlier than I remembered him to be.

'Look at you!' I gestured in his direction, mostly at the trousers. 'What did you do to my friend?'

'I ate him. For protein,' he smiled. 'Thanks for coming. Being back by myself felt...'

'...wrong?'

'Yeah.'

'It feels weird for me too. I have a lot of emotions going on right now.'

'Well,' he said, putting his arm around me. 'My host parents are making dinner. We can eat, have a few drinks, and then we can go out and have fun. What do you say?'

I smiled and nodded. It was as if no time had passed. I was eighteen again.

Seeing Daniel's host parents was an absolute treat. They were some of the nicest people I had met during my year abroad. This was my first experience of summer in Stockholm, my exchange year had come to a screaming halt in winter. We had a beautiful plant-based dinner on the balcony and spoke about our lives after our exchange year. Daniel had somehow become a political activist. You could often see him shouting through a megaphone or helping refugees around Europe. His host family looked at him as one of their own children. They were proud and genuinely happy for him to be there. And they made me feel more than welcome; something I couldn't say about my own host family.

I had never spoken to Ingrid or the rest of the family again. They despised me and part of me couldn't blame them either.

After cleaning up the table and helping with the dishes, Daniel and I walked up to the rooftop with alcohol and snacks. We sat on deck chairs, looking out at the city, still bathed in sunlight despite it being the middle of the night.

'I can never quite get used to this,' he said, sipping from a beer bottle. 'This light...it's unnatural.'

'I know. This is the first time I've experienced this.'

'That's true. I forgot you didn't finish your year.'

'I got kicked out, Daniel.'

Silence ensued. I could only hear my own heartbeat.

'Could you blame them though? You were never the same after you came back from London...' he pointed out.

'I was hurting. I wasn't really myself.'

'And are you now?'

'Myself?'

'Hurting.'

Well, fuck. Was I hurting? Probably not. Pain wasn't an issue anymore. My relationship with Kyle was a clear example. I was in complete control of how he hurt me. And I liked it. I wasn't the child who gets taken advantage of anymore. What Kyle and I had, that was real. None of that fairy-tale bullshit I had made myself believe in.

Princes don't get raped.

'I don't know...'

'I just wish you'd reached out more back then. Hazel and I were right there. Why shoplift?'

'Daniel, I can't express how much pain I was in. I...I just needed to feel something. Anything. I...it's hard to explain, okay?'

'So you don't want to talk about it. Understood...' he said, trying to break the tension seeing as I had gone silent, lost in memories of a different sort. 'What's the deal with this engagement of yours?'

'Well, I took some time off before starting uni. I went to the States for a while. That's where I met Kyle.'

'Part of me thought you'd move to Australia instead.'

'I don't think there was much for me there, to be honest.'

'I believe there was a certain person you were very much infatuated with.'

'Damn, where did you learn that word?' I smiled, mockingly. I rolled my eyes, drank a sip of whisky, and took a breath. 'When Teddy went back to Australia, we spoke less and less. He was busy and I just moved on. I needed someone to be there, to help me through stuff. We wished each other *happy birthday*, or *merry Christmas*, but there wasn't much to talk about. He became more distant. Hazel told me that he was dealing with family problems, but she said it wasn't her place to tell me.'

'Do you still love him?'

I hesitated for a second. 'Can you really call that love?'

'I would.'

'I think two people should really know each other, go on dates, and all that stuff before calling it love. Teddy and I...I don't know. I think it's stupid.'

'You're someone who likes stories. I don't think it's that far-fetched for you to be able to convey feelings through *a meaningless Facebook chat*, like you called it.'

'We spoke on the phone a few weeks ago. He was in the hospital. Hearing his voice really brought me back. It felt like regression in a way.'

'You were just talking. It doesn't mean you don't love Kyle.'

'Maybe,' I finished my whisky in one big gulp. 'Hey...there is something I need to do.'

'What, tonight?' he asked.

'Yeah. I'll be gone for a few hours if you don't mind.'

'Sure. Do you want to tell me what's happ—'

'I just need to go." I said cutting him off, 'I can't tell you. I'm sorry.'

'Okay, fair. See you in the morning?' he said while putting out a fist to bump him.

'Absolutely.'

I returned the fist-bump and quickly left the rooftop. There was somewhere I needed to be.

The journey didn't take long, or I possibly closed my eyes for a second and found myself at the destination. The sky was a light shade of cyan, no sun, but neither was there a moon. It was late, or early, I couldn't tell which. It took every ounce of determination in my body to take myself to the place I had nightmares about almost every night. My legs were lead, heavier with each step I took. Alcohol was definitely in charge of my decision making. I went past the *Systembolaget*. Past the cute little port, walking with purpose, until I finally found myself at the tiny little beach of horrors. Nothing had changed. That place still existed unperturbed by what had happened on its watch. My pulse was a thoroughbred in my veins, each breath a knife to my chest. I kneeled, my hands hesitating above the sand, and I was shaking. Sobbing. I could still feel the sand in my mouth, the cold of the blade against my neck, and the finger shaped bruises on my arms.

Over five years had passed since that life altering night and I couldn't move on. I still saw Simon everywhere I went, I still felt his touch when I was naked and under a guy, even if they were gentle. He had become a part of me, fused with me and I couldn't forget. Silly little eighteen-year-old Vincent; forever fucked by the stupid, idiotic choice he'd made from heartbreak.

I got to my feet, brushing off my hands and walked. Step by step, I walked towards the water. It was still, silent. A glass blanket stretching out from the sand. There wasn't enough wind for waves to split the smooth surface. I stepped into the water with my shoes on. The glacial sea lapped at my ankles, my calves, up my legs. I kept walking, tears swimming in my eyes and a fire within me. Each step became lighter and lighter, until the water reached my neck. My whole body was engulfed in the frigid water. Water that watched me that night, giving me no help, giving me no avenue of escape.

I took one deep breath, my eyes unfocused and I screamed, as loud as I could. A scream I should have let loose that evening. A scream that acknowledged the five years it had taken me to realise that I was trapped. It was inhumane, ear-piercing and blood-curdling. I screamed for what seemed like an eternity, until my voice cracked, and my throat burned. I screamed until my head felt like it would explode, the pressure in my skull was beyond belief. Water sluiced into my ears and mouth as I kept myself upright, legs moving in the cold.

My body shook violently, my teeth grinding together, I could barely feel my fingers. For just a moment, a fleeting heartbeat, I let go. Eyes closed, my arms spread wide, the water all consuming. I sank down, somehow warmer and without fear. Almost unnatural how calm it was. I propelled my body up to the surface and dragged myself back to the land. I sat on the little beach of personal hell, looked at the horizon, and waited for the sun to rise. I was waiting for a new day, so I could finally put the memory behind me. I probably wouldn't be able to, but I was going to try.

There was something else I needed to do before going back to Daniel though.

Something I should have done years before.

I power walked all the way to that driveway; the same one I walked years before, day in and day out. The sun was now up, but my clothes were still drenched; dripping a trail where I went, breadcrumbs for sober Vincent. The fumes of alcohol were fading, but I still had more than enough in me to give me the courage to confront her. I stood still in front of the main door. Nothing had changed, so I was positive they still lived here.

I took a deep shuddering breath and knocked. At first, I used my knuckles, gently, and then I started tapping faster and faster, until I used my whole fist. I hammered at the door continuously, until frustrated, I gave it a hard kick.

That's when she finally opened the door. I knew it would be her. She was the brave one in the family. The one who made all the decisions. The queen of pure disappointment. She was wearing a silk robe and her short bleached hair was messy. Her eyes were angry, burning clear through my skin.

We didn't say anything at first. We just stared at each other, sizing these newer versions of each other up. The experience was unnerving. I had imagined speaking to her candidly without fear of consequences for years. All the times I held myself back from calling her a cunt straight to her face could now be realised.

'Hello, Ingrid,' I said, with a shallow breath.

'Vincent? What are you doing here? And what in the hell has gotten into your head?'

'I have pictured this moment for years. I have imagined a thousand scenarios in which I'd be in front of you telling you exactly what I think of you. But now that I'm here—'

'Leave, or I'll call the police.'

'Did you know I was raped?' I spat at her. The first time I had said the words out loud to anyone.

'What?'

'Five minutes from here,' I said while pointing in the general direction. 'There's a little beach down there. That's where it happened.'

'What are you even talking about?' she said rolling her eyes, like I was being dramatic.

'I was going through something horrendous when I lived under this roof. I couldn't confide in you about anything at all. A man forced himself on me, threatened my life and is walking free because I was, and still am, too fucking broken to be able to report it. Because men don't get raped.'

'Is this another one of your lies? What lengths will you go to, to paint yourself as a victim and be absolved of all blame?'

'I felt like dying. You didn't give a fuck about what was happening to me.'

'All I know is that you were found guilty of shoplifting. You went to school drunk and trashed your room. Care to explain what happened there? Was that a misunderstanding too?'

My eyes filled with furious tears. My hands started to shake, and my whole body burnt with anger.

'I thought...I couldn't live with the fact that someone had done something so horrible and had gotten away with it. I couldn't stand it. I figured I too, could do it without fear of retaliation. Why would I, someone who was stripped of their personhood by a man no better than a feral beast, be punished for something that didn't actually hurt anyone?'

She didn't say anything. Her eyes were as cold as the water I emerged from.

'You should have come to me. You should have asked me what was wrong, but you didn't care. You just wanted me gone.'

'I did. I never liked your attitude, I never liked you as a person, and from what I can see, you haven't grown at all. You're just the same useless kid who makes up stories in order to—'

'You don't believe me.' I interrupted. 'You are so self-righteous and self-centred. You can't even fathom that you may have been wrong. I had been seeking your approval all those months. I am so stupid.' My volume had steadily risen as I spoke, my frozen fingers grasped at my hair which was too fucking short. I started laughing, hysterically and uncontrollably. 'It was you, all along. *You* are the one with issues. I am...so happy I got to tell you exactly what I think of you. You have a nice fucking life, Ingrid, you awful human being.'

I turned on my heel and quickly left with a hint of a maniacal smile on my face. She'd reinforced all those awful memories, the feeling of being powerless and broken, the times I'd shoplift just to feel alive, the times I stood in front of the police station trying to find the courage to report my abuser, the time I looked at the rail tracks, fantasising about being decimated by a speeding train. I survived.

I spent endless nights trying to go over what happened in my head; when I stole a random book from the shop, instead of the little things I could slip into my pocket unseen. I pondered why I jeopardised my year abroad for something so futile. I would probably never have all the answers I was seeking, but confronting Ingrid was the closure I so longed for. I'd finally be able to override my awful experience with happy memories made with Daniel.

It felt like I could finally breathe again.

I was going through my Stockholm photos and smiling, while sitting on the bus that was taking me home. It had been a nice few days away from everything. After subjecting myself to "exposure therapy" to get over my issues with Stockholm, I'd had an incredible time with Daniel. We'd partied hard and caught up on everything that had been happening in our lives, more his than mine since he had so many adventures under his belt. It was daunting to think that the next time I'd see him would be at my wedding.

Even thinking that word caused my skin to prickle slightly.

I got off the bus and walked the familiar streets toward my flat in Shepherd's Bush, past the smelly *KFC* a few metres from my front door. I was looking forward to seeing Laura and sharing all the Swedish sweets I had bought for her. She'd try to avoid them at first, but she would crumble eventually.

I opened the door and heard the hum of multiple voices.

'I'm home!' I shouted. I walked through the narrow off-white corridor and pushed through the door that would lead to the kitchen.

Laura was sitting on the sofa. I looked to her right and there was a guy standing up, with two mugs of tea. He turned around and I dropped everything to the floor.

'Teddy!' I gasped.

'Hi Vincent.'

CHAPTER SIXTEEN

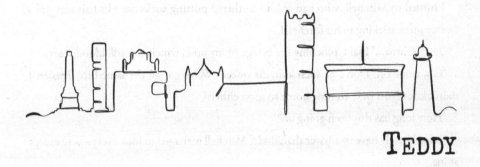

TEDDY

2014

The taxi driver was driving as fast as the law would allow him. I was so beyond pissed off, however, that it still wasn't enough. I had a brother to throttle after all. Why did he lie to me? What was he trying to prove?

I was the one who had taken care of our mother for years. Did he really think I wouldn't find out that he'd visited her while I wasn't home?

The taxi pulled up to the curve of our driveway, and I hopped out before it even came to a stop. I took the steps two at a time, opening the front door with a bang and storming into the living room ready for an argument with the dumbass. Instead, I stumbled into a sight I could hardly believe and would likely never be able to erase from my mind.

'Guys, what the fuck!' I yelped, slapping a hand over my eyes.

My very naked brother was fucking my best friend. Sweet Jesus.

'Oh my god, Teddy!' Hazel screamed, quickly trying to pull her clothes on.

Mitchell didn't bother moving and remained sitting on the plush floral couch I lay on to read, butt-naked, as if I had just caught him relaxing.

'Please, for all that is holy, put something on,' I shouted. 'How long has this been going on?'

'Like forty minutes, I reckon?' he said.

'Teddy, I am so sorry!' Hazel groaned, pulling Mitchell's hoodie on.

'Hazel, could you leave us alone for a minute?' I asked.

'Don't worry, I will sequester myself in my room. I'm never leaving it again,' she mumbled, quickly running upstairs.

I turned to Mitchell, who had at least bothered putting socks on. His hair was still a sweaty mess, sticking to his forehead.

'Jesus Christ...' I said, pinching the bridge of my nose, which was still bloody sore.

'Oh, come on. Don't be such a drama queen. We've got all the same bits, *Tedster*. I didn't know you were coming home so soon either.'

'How long has this been going on?'

'I don't really have to answer that, do I?' Mitchell managed to look everywhere except at me.

'Really? Because that was my best friend you decided to take to pound-town on my sofa, so I am interested in what the fuck is going on here.'

'You need to chill, mate,' he said, standing and stretching, dick just hanging out in the breeze. Zero fucks given. He made his way to the kitchen.

I followed him, naturally, and watched him open the fridge and chug milk from the bottle. Cretin.

'What's going to happen now?'

'Nothing! Why the hell are you acting like this? It's not like I stole your wife! It was just sex. Very much consensual. Back off.'

'What are you doing here, Mitchell. Seriously.'

'I am trying to look after you, you little shit.'

'I don't fucking need you!' I shouted.

Mitchell came right up to me; in my personal space, towering over me.

'Listen to me. I don't give a fuck if you appreciate my presence or not. Just know I won't let you get beaten to a pulp by some *randos* again. You're my only brother and you're the only fucking family I have left, so get over your controlling bullshit and sit the fuck down.'

'Why did you lie about seeing mum?' Fuck him.

His body went slack, face pale. '...what?'

'I was told you went to see her a few weeks ago. Any chance you want to tell the truth this time? Assuming you know what the truth looks like.'

'Now this is definitely *not* your fucking business,' he said while walking away.

Oh no sir, he was not walking out on this conversation. I followed him down the familiar hallway, past our smiling school photos hanging on the walls.

'Why would you lie about that? Did you think I'd find you "less cool" if I discovered you actually cared about our mum? Or maybe you thought I'd take advantage of you being here? That I would fuck off for half a decade like you did, travelling around the world, not giving a shit about anyone or anything? What the fuck is it, Mitchell?'

He whipped around, pushing me into the wall. His face a breath away from mine. He didn't scare me and I was sure my expression communicated that.

'Our mother isn't the fucking angel you have romanticised her to be in your stupid little prick head. Mum has done some pretty fucked up stuff, I'd tell you to ask her about it, but even her brain has decided to fucking leave her,' he sneered.

'Wow. What did she do, Mitchell? Did she not give you enough money? Were you forced to get a little part time job to pay for your recreational drugs? Poor little boy!' Part of me was desperate to know what it was, what had driven Mitchell out of this house. But a bigger part of me wanted to kick his fucking teeth into his head.

'You want to know what she did?'

'Oh yes please Mitchell. Tell me please,' I fake pleaded, voice high and breathy.

'You know what. Forget it.' His eyes roamed my face, looking for I don't know what.

'No Mitchell, for fuck's sakes, tell me. What can she possibly have done to you?'

'Fine! Do you remember my girlfriend Olivia?'

'You had a girlfriend? I remember you fucking my entire school, but I don't remember anyone you called a girlfriend.'

'That's because she paid her off to leave me, leave the country, never to be fucking seen again.'

'You think mum had your girlfriend whacked?' absurd, even by Mitchell's standards.

'No, you dense shithead. She paid her a shitload of money to leave me alone.'

'Why would she even care?'

'Because she was pregnant!' he shouted, eyes wild and face red with rage. 'She was pregnant with my fucking kid, Teddy. And mum just sent her away.'

'You're full of shit,' I said, dismissively.

'Mum knew she was getting ill! She knew what was happening to her. She said she didn't want me to waste my youth trapped in parenthood. She arranged all of this behind my fucking back. I told her I'd never forgive her, and I'd only come back when she was finally dead.'

'And yet you still used her money. Quite the independent spirit you are!'

'Fuck you, Teddy. I'm sick of your judgmental bullshit just because you played nurse for a few years. What the fuck have you accomplished in your life so far? Where's your motherfucking flight attendant training gone to? Do you think you have all the time in the world or—'

'Get out,' I cut him off, my voice pure steel.

'What?'

'Get the fuck out of this house. I don't want to see you anymore.'

He looked me straight in the eyes then, his expression deadly. I was almost frightened.

'Teddy, I'm not going anywhere. I told you the truth. If you don't believe me—'

'What? Should I ask what remains of our mother? Because I'm *sure* she'll tell me all about your fucking fantasy tale!'

'Find her goddamn diaries. Do you know where they are hidden? You know she used to write about everything.'

'I'm leaving,' I shoved past the naked fucker. I was done with this.

'You know I'm right!' he shouted at me.

I stuffed myself into my puffer jacket, opened the front door, and stormed out, slamming the door behind me hard enough the little stained-glass panels shook. I never wanted to go back in that house again, and I certainly never wanted to sit on that couch.

A million thoughts rushed through my mind. I couldn't believe Mitchell. Mum would never do anything like that—that would be some next-level-mafia shit. I knew she wanted Mitchell to get his shit together, but I just couldn't picture her taking his choice away like that. He had to be lying. Wanting to appear the victim had always been his modus operandi. But what if he was right? What if he was telling the truth and I'd been looking after a woman who had done something truly despicable. A woman who made decisions that resulted in her own solitude.

Mitchell could have a child out there in the world and he had no real chance of ever finding it.

I needed some time to think.

So, I did something wholly unthinkable and did something Mitchell himself would.

I bought a plane ticket through my phone and hopped on the first flight to the UK. I needed to get away from this place, this small town on this godforsaken island. My life here was suffocating, this never-ending loop of mediocrity where I was never first, second, or even third on my list of priorities. I couldn't think here, I couldn't see life beyond the borders of my home. I needed to re-evaluate so many things about my life, and I absolutely couldn't be under the same roof as my brother.

Twenty hours later, I landed in London.

Exhausted mentally and physically, I knocked on the door in front of me. My heart hadn't received the memo on being tired, and was—at present—trying to escape my chest. Laura opened the door straight away.

'Teddy!' she screamed, throwing herself at me. Hugging her felt like home, her scent a whisper of happier, simpler times, when it was just us living under Sardinia's hot summer sun.

'I am so happy to see you!' Fighting tears, I pulled back. Overwhelmed to be with my friend again.

'Please, come in,' she said, perfect white smile and damp eyes.

Her flat was one long corridor with navy carpet and doors on both sides. I followed her all the way to the end, where it opened onto the living room and kitchen.

'It's pretty small,' she said.

'No, it's adorable. I'd much rather live here with friends, than having to share my mum's house with my brother.'

'Hazel is there too though, that must be nice.'

'It is. Although she is currently having sex with Mitchell.'

'Oh wow,' she said, giggling.

'What?'

'Well, there are worse things to have sex with.'

'Laura, I swear to God...'

'Oh, relax. I'm joking. Sort of,' her grin wolfish, as she dropped to the sofa. 'Sit down, tell me everything.'

'Do you have tea?' I asked, staring at the dated kitchen.

'Yeah, of course, just in the cupboard in front of you.'

'You're having me make us tea? After a gazillion hours of travelling?' faux outrage, I could do.

'That's exactly what I'm saying.'

'Aww, how I missed my spoiled little princess,' I said, putting the kettle on. 'Are you sure it's okay I stay here with you for a while?'

'Of course it is, I wouldn't want you anywhere else.'

Seeing Laura again was like being transported to the old times. Nothing had changed between us. I could relax, talk shit with her, and joke around. She was still the sister I never had.

'Your hair's changed,' I said.

'Yeah, I haven't had time to go for my highlights. Sporting the natural,' she gave the ends a flick.

'It looks good!' I grabbed the fresh cups of tea and made my way over to join her.

The corridor door banged open, scalding tea spilt over the edge of both cups as I jumped slightly at the noise.

'Teddy,' eyes wide in that achingly familiar pale face.

'Hi Vincent,' I said. My entire body lit up, every nerve at attention. The years were pure blessing to his gorgeous face. He was sporting a short stubble, along with shorter and darker hair. His arms looked toned too, as if he'd been working out. His giant grey eyes were harder; flint rather than storm clouds, but as beautiful as they had always been. My heart, which had quieted somewhat since I had arrived, woke back up. My pulse was lightning, and my feet were lead, unable to move at all. Seeing him was a waking dream. A dream I knew could turn me inside out in one short second, and soothe every ache I'd ever had in another. He was my ailment and my cure, wrapped together in an unforgettable package.

Time was nothing, as we stood there. Our eyes were each taking the other in, studying each detail and comparing it. Now and then, them and us. I set the cups down on the little table, a quick breath in, hope and promise woven together on the exhale as I looked back up at him. There was no distance between us now, as we melted together, my rough edges against his. One of his arms was wrapped around my neck, and the other around my waist, holding tight. I curled my hand into the fabric at his back, pulling him into me so I could feel his chest against mine.

'Holy shit. What are you doing here?' his breath danced along my neck.

'I had a bit of a crisis and had to see my little sister.'

'So, this has nothing to do with me?'

'You, Vincent, are an added bonus,' I pulled back to look at his eyes. It had been too long.

'Why didn't you say anything?' he asked Laura.

She stretched her arms and giggled. 'Frankly I only found out yesterday. Mr Aussie didn't exactly give me a lot of notice.'

'What happened?' he asked me.

'It's a long story. We can talk about it later.'

'Actually,' said Laura, 'I have a couple of errands to run, so why don't you two have your much needed catch-up and then *maybe* I'll come back for dinner.'

'I thought we had time to have tea together?' I asked.

'I am sure Vincent will be more than happy to keep you company,' she said while getting up.

'Hot date?' I asked, winking.

'Yeah, with my pointes!'

'We need to talk,' he whispered to her, while she was exiting the room.

'By the way,' she said, then lowered her voice as if I couldn't hear her anyways. 'Your uhm appointment tomorrow? They called to say it's been moved to nine o'clock.'

'Okay, thank you,' his voice dropped a little.

Disappointed?

'You two behave,' she shouted from the corridor.

Vincent caught my eyes and together we burst into laughter.

'Shall we have this tea then?' he asked.

'I'd very much like that.'

We sat next to each other on the tiny sofa, our legs touching.

'So,' I said.

'So!' he sipped the tepid tea, nervous.

'You coming back from somewhere?' I asked.

'Yes, actually! I was in Stockholm, with Daniel.'

'Fun! Stockholm!'

'Yeah.'

Once again silence ensued.

Who knew we would have so little to talk about? Had our relationship rusted so severely we couldn't even start a decent conversation? Or was he as nervous as I was? I could barely control myself. I wanted to jump on him, but I was very aware of his whole not-being-single situation. I had to respect that even though my whole body was *begging* me to jump him.

'How was Stock—'

'Teddy, what are you doing here?' he interrupted.

'I told you, I—'

'What are you *really* doing here.'

'Older Vincent really likes to interrupt, aye?'

'...sorry. Seeing you is just—'

'I know,' I said, taking his hand.

He took a deep breath and locked his eyes on mine. He held my hand tighter, as if he didn't want to let it go.

Oh, how I wanted to kiss him, bite his bottom lip and feel his little gasp into my mouth when I did. I wanted to slide my fingers into his hair and have my tongue meet his, but I knew I couldn't. I wondered if he was thinking the same thing. I wondered if there was still a part of him that burned for me as much as I did for him.

The silence between us thickened, hand in hand, eyes drinking each other in. His tongue darted out, running along that bottom lip I craved so badly. It was like someone had dropped a match between us, the fire growing and devouring. Neither of us moving to break the spell it wove.

Until he did.

'Hey, listen...would you like to take a walk?'

I tilted my head, chuckled a little. 'Yes, I would *love* to go on a walk with you.'

'Okay just let me change. The bathroom's right there if you need it. I'll be right back,' he said, darting away and heading to his room.

A walk was a good idea. It would work to distract me from the sexual tension I was having to deal with while sitting on the same sofa as my long-lost love. Yeah, I needed to walk.

I made my way down the corridor, detoured into the loo and went to wait at the front door. Movement caught my eye and through the partly opened door I was presented with a visual treat—a shirtless Vincent picking a t-shirt to wear. My eyes ate him up, his toned back, the elegant column of his neck and whatever the fuck those weird dimples just above his ass were called. I needed to look away, so I wouldn't seem like a creep.

And then he turned around and giggled.

'Sorry, I'm taking forever,' he said.

'No worries,' I cleared my throat, suddenly very interested in the ceiling but my eyes flicking back to him of their own volition. 'Take your time.'

He pulled on a tight black t-shirt on and threw me a cheeky grin on his way out of the room.

'Let's go, perv,' he said, throwing his arm around my shoulders.

Damn, Vincent.

It was a warm evening, this quiet piece of earth soaked in soft orange sunlight. I had turned my phone off, no desire to deal with Mitch's phone calls, deciding instead to fully enjoy my little impromptu British holiday. Hazel would call Laura or Vincent if something dire happened, so I wasn't concerned. Vincent and I made our way down a long, straight road. Heading somewhere, although Vincent wasn't sharing much on the destination front. Hearing his sweet English accent was a delicious treat I so gladly craved.

'Where are we going?' I asked. 'You're power walking. Remember my body is afflicted with jet-lag!'

'Sorry, just trying to leave Shepherd's Bush, so we can get to a prettier area.'

'Shepherd's Bush is quite a name.'

'You know us Brits love naming things in the most curious way.'

'What's beyond *Sheppy B*, then?' I asked, slightly out of breath. This power walk was bordering on a jog, I swear.

'You'll see.'

I wasn't one to appreciate surprises. Most surprises I had been subjected to in the previous five years had all been crap. My mum's Huntington's diagnosis, the bastards who decided to use my face as a punching bag, and the sight my brother's bare ass while he fucked my best friend were just some highlights. But I trusted Vincent. And I trusted him enough to take me somewhere where people surrounded us, so I could clamp down my primal desire to make sweet steamy love to him.

His phone's jingly tone sounded from his jeans. I caught a glimpse of the screen as he pulled it out, not surprised to see Kyle's name. Vincent rejected the call and shoved the phone back in his pocket.

'You don't want to take that?' I asked, not really wanting him to take it.

'No, it's fine.'

I smiled.

'So, I need to ask,' he said. 'How are you recovering from...?'

'My attack?'

'Yeah.'

'It's fine. They never caught the assholes. We are not as big as you guys in the UK when it comes to CCTV. I also didn't particularly remember their faces. I was pretty damn drunk.'

'I completely understand, trust me,' he said, in a slightly more serious tone. 'How are you feeling about it?'

'Oh, it's fine. I honestly don't remember much. The only reminder is my new disfigured nose.'

'What? Don't be ridiculous!' he turned on the spot, forcing me to stop dead.

Again, I was so tempted to kiss him. He rubbed his finger along my nose and I shut my eyes.

'Does it still hurt?' he whispered.

'Not right now.'

'There is nothing disfigured on this face, Teddy,' his voice low and silky.

I gave a small smile, just for him. 'Thanks.'

We took off walking again taking a right, heading up a slight hilly road.

'You trying to kill me, Stewart?' I asked. 'Not again with another hill!'

'We're nearly there! Don't you Aussies walk?'

'No, we get fat in our cars, eating *Maccas* on our way to the *servo*,' I replied sarcastically.

He laughed, hopefully remembering all the Aussie slang I'd taught him. I trailed behind him, a little bubble of happy forming. I glanced up and was promptly smacked in the face with 2009. A time that felt simpler, and the last year I'd had truly happy memories in. The weight of the last five years came crashing down on me, tears burning my eyes.

'Hey, what's happening?' Vincent's hands were on my biceps, rubbing up and down, trying to comfort me. 'What is it?'

'I'm sorry,' I said, quickly wiping my eyes. 'I'm here. I'm very happy to be here. Pardon the jet-lag hormones.'

'Are you sure?'

'I'm sure.'

He gave me an odd little look, then walked through the main gate of the park, heading once again to the Kyoto Garden. The very same place where he and I had spent the most wonderful first date together.' The air was crisp, the flowers were in bloom and the trees were cheerfully greening. The park felt familiar; London with Vincent felt like home.

We found the Koi pond where our eyes had met for the first time, half a decade prior, and sat on the small wooden bench. We were both older, although I didn't know how much wiser. Real adult issues were a part of our everyday lives and, while I got lost in his beautifully haunting grey eyes, I came to the realisation that another man had made my love his. Vincent was not for me to touch, or to have feelings for. He wasn't mine and he never would be.

'I haven't been here since, you know,' he said. 'There was something so special about the memory of this place; I couldn't replace it with anything else. It's our place, I guess.'

'You never came here with Kyle?' I asked, wishing I could call the words back as soon as they were out.

His face darkened. 'No, I haven't,' he said, eyes on the ground, hands curling on his knees.

'Right, since I've mentioned him, would you like to tell me how you guys met and everything? Make me live through your quaint romantic fantasy, Vincent,' I said with a fake smile.

'We met in America, during my gap year before uni. He was really confident and so headstrong. We had a great time while we were there, but then I had to move back to the UK and we've only seen each other maybe two or three times a year for a few weeks each time ever since.'

'...and it's been okay? The distance?'

'Sure...although...'

Oh. Tell me more, please.

'I don't know. I got used to being without him for the majority of the time. When he said he had something to tell me, I actually thought he wanted to break up. He proposed instead.'

'That's nice to hear,' I said, trying my very hardest not to be jealous.

'I'm sorry, this is really boring. I don't want to have a whiny conversation where I discuss my doubts for—'

'Doubts?'

'Is that what I said?'

'It sounded a lot like you said *doubts*,' I teased. 'I'm curious to hear all about those.'

'I can't. It's not fair. I said yes.'

'You're still free to change your mind.'

'...and then what? What am I supposed to do? No one is going to want someone who is so damaged by what happened in Stockholm...'

'What happened in Stockholm?' I was curious now.

Vincent's entire body was shaking violently. I wrapped my arm around him, my turn to rub his arm in comfort apparently.

'Hey, hey Vincent, it's okay. You're alright.' I soothed. What the hell had happened in Stockholm?

'Yes. I'm alright. Please. I want to know about you,' he turned towards me, pale and jittery. 'How has it been? You glossed over what dealing with your mum's condition is like; or rather you glossed over the condition itself. What is wrong with her?'

I took my arm away from him and jointed my hands together. Now I was the one staring at the ground. I sighed.

'Is that too personal?' he asked, hesitantly.

'It's...it's just hard to talk about it. For me.'

'Don't worry,' he said while putting his hand on my knee. 'We don't have to talk about it if you don't want to.'

'She...' Words were stuck to the roof of my mouth. I was stuck, almost petrified. I was so used to not talking about it to anyone that wasn't Hazel. It was eating me from the inside. 'She has a horrendous disease called Huntington's.'

'I'm sorry, I'm not very familiar—'

'Imagine your body having spasms. You can't control any muscle in your body or your speech, or the way you walk, none of your movements. All gone. You're like a broken machine. You have trouble eating, saying things, even staying still in bed.'

'Oh my god.'

'And that's not all. Your brain fails too. You start forgetting things. You start forgetting people, notions, rules. Heck, you even forget who you are. And it goes on until there is nothing left of who you used to be. You're just a damaged body, a shell of the person you were. Just waiting to die.'

Vincent's eyes saddened. He didn't know what to say, and I knew that feeling, because when I'd found out, I hadn't known what to say either.

'I am so sorry, Teddy.'

I took a deep breath; I was trying my very best not to cry in front of him.

'She taught me everything I know. She was a firecracker, shouting correct answers at every game show on TV. She would quote writers, philosophers and even rap lyrics. She made my childhood magical...and now she is making my twenties a nightmare.'

'Does she...recognise you?' he asked.

'At first, she was stronger than the disease. She would hand write things every day, she would read all the time, she would test herself. Then her hands started acting up, the *chorea* started. Such a stupid word. It means "dance" in Greek. Like her spasms could be considered a dance. She wasn't dancing. She was losing control of her body, day by day.' I said, as I took a deep breath. 'It was only every now and then at first, and then it became a daily occurrence. She was frustrated and would get angry, throw things and break stuff.

And it just got worse, and worse, and worse, until I could no longer take care of her. She was not safe in my care. So, I got her a nurse, as per her request. She didn't want to be a burden to me anymore. But it got worse each day. Her disease completely took over much faster than we thought it would. Than *I* thought it would. So...' I paused. 'To answer your question. No, she doesn't really recognise me anymore.'

'That's horrible. I'm so sorry,' he shuffled closer to give me a hug, eyes shiny with unshed tears.

The moment my face was resting on his shoulder, safe, I couldn't hold my tears back. I was vulnerable, and I was exhausted. I was so tired of my life being the way it was. And I felt so guilty for wishing it were different, for fantasising about leaving Australia and never going back. I was so fucking selfish.

'Teddy, I'm so sorry,' he said, once again. 'I wish I could do something.'

'Can you hold me for just a bit longer?' I whispered, tears soaking into his shoulder, hugging him tighter and feeling safe in his unique Vincent scent.

'I could hold you forever,' he said, so quiet I wasn't sure I was supposed to hear.

CHAPTER SEVENTEEN

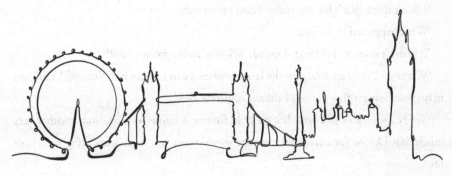

VINCENT

2014

I ran my fingers along his back, feeling for the little bumps of his spine. His head was tucked into my shoulder, and he was crying like he hadn't let a single tear fall in the entire 1,825 days we'd been apart. Give or take a few. When I saw him at my flat, it was as if I'd forgotten I wasn't the eighteen-year-old kid who'd jumped on a random plane and went abroad without telling anyone. But I was a grown man now. I went through adult things and, hell, I was engaged to another man. But this was Teddy. My sweet, radiant Teddy. So broken, so lost, and desperate for what could put him back together. I knew somewhat how he was feeling, I knew what it was like to be broken for so long. We weren't the same people as we had been five years before, but being near each other felt right; it felt like peace; from the surface of my skin, into the depths of my soul—the tiny scrap I had left—stretching out to touch his, knitting together to form one imperfect soul.

'Alright,' Teddy sniffed, pulling away and swiping at his teary cheeks. 'Sorry, I'm okay,' he gave me a hesitant little smile, resting his hands on my knees, staring at me with his verdant green, albeit bloodshot eyes. 'What's going to happen with you this year? Apart from the engagement?'

'I've been accepted for a masters in screenwriting. It will be tough, but Kyle is a film director, and he will help. Then hopefully I'll get to work with him at some point.'

'What happened to *you* becoming a director?'

'I don't think that's for me, really. I don't even own a camera.'

'What happened to the one—'

'It doesn't matter,' my heart skipped. 'What is *Teddy* going to do?'

'Whatever I've been doing for the last few years. I can't...leave her, Vincent.' The pain in his voice was gutting me. My brilliant sunshine Teddy.

'Teddy...you can't put your life on hold forever. I know you love your mother very much, but I know for a fact that even she would want you to do something with your life.'

'I know...'

'If you want to be a flight attendant and finally see the world, I really think you should start applying. You know Hazel will support you too.'

'I think...part of me is using my mother as an excuse. I don't want to face rejection and I guess I'm just a coward.'

'No! You're absolutely not,' I said, tilting his head back so I could look him in the eyes. Ignoring the way his jaw and his skin felt under my fingers. 'It's time for you to take that next step, you need to do something for you.'

'I don't know...we'll see. I just wish...other things would be different,' his low voice so sad, fingertip tracing my engagement ring.

We sat there quietly, turned towards each other, our hands between us. Both watching his strong hands over mine, over my golden ring.

'Hey, it's starting to get cold, and I am a teensy bit tired from the journey,' he broke into our trance. 'Do you think we could maybe grab a bottle of wine and chill at your flat?'

I knew deep down it was a bad idea, but my brain lit up like Christmas, declaring it a brilliant one.

'I would love that, Teddy,' I said with a smile. 'Let's go.'

I stood up, looking around once more at this magical spot where we were an *us*.

Maybe we could coexist as friends, it didn't need to feel hard. We were a bottle and a half into our evening, just sitting on the sofa with our feet on the coffee table, laughing hysterically at a stand-up comedy show on TV. Two mates just hanging out. I mean, sure, his arm was around me, and I could hear the tattoo of heartbeat in his chest, but other than that we were just friends. Buds. Hanging out.

'There's a tiny possibility that alcohol may have a *little* smidge of an adverse effect when mixed with my extreme tiredness, just so you know,' he said, dopey sleepy smile on his now much relaxed face.

'You're being stubborn. I told you to take a nap.'

'What am I, eighty?'

'It's eleven at night. And you've been awake for a thousand hours. You're practically falling asleep on me.'

'Uhm...maybe. Okay. Fine. I guess this sofa has Teddy written all over it,' he said with a yawn.

'It gets really cold at night here. You could sleep in my bed,' I offered, regretting it straight away.

'Oh, is that so?'

'I mean, I'll be sleeping on the floor,' I pointed out.

'Not the couch?' his brow furrowed.

'I...uhm. I would rather stay close by, if that's okay...' I could feel the heat in my cheeks.

'Oh. Thanks,' he said, eyes on the floor. 'Um, me too. I would like you close. So yeah. That sounds great.'

'You won't even offer to sleep on the floor?' I teased, trying to lighten the mood.

'I'm not an idiot, Vincent!' he smiled. 'Where was your room again?'

'I'm sure you remember since you were there while I was getting changed and all. Pervert.'

'My memory is not what it used to be, you know.'

I didn't know what to say, my eyes flew wide open.

'Sorry, this would have been a funnier joke if—'

'Yeah, no. I got it,' I wrinkled my nose and chuckled. 'Alright then, Gramps, follow me.'
I could feel his body behind mine, big and warm and solid.

'This is it!' I said with much more flourish than was normal.

He climbed onto the bed and buried his face in the pillow. 'Oh, this is the good stuff,'
he inhaled deeply, and I tried to not catch fire on the spot.

I hurried to my wardrobe and pulled out a bunch of pillows and a spare duvet, throwing
it onto the floor, where I'd be sleeping for the night.

'That doesn't look very comfortable,' he noted.

'I'll be fine. It'll do wonders for my back!' He looked at me, sceptical.

'Yeah, you'll be so rested in the morning,' he said, rolling his eyes.

He got back off the bed and left the room.

'Hey! Where are you going? It's fine Teddy, it's just the floor!' I yelled. I didn't want
him to sleep out there. He muscled back through the door with the two butt cushions
from the sofa and put them on the floor, making a little mattress.

'There. I'm not going to refuse your bed Vincent—I am dead tired—but I can't sleep
if you're on the actual floor,' he explained, voice quiet. My stomach twisted, emotions I
couldn't name tangling together.

'Thank you.'

We smiled at each other, and he started taking his t-shirt off, giving me a full view of
his lower abdomen.

'Ehm, what are you doing?' I practically shrieked, flustered by the expanse of tanned
skin.

'I'm getting ready to sleep?'

'Of course,' I said, clumsily trying to find the light switch behind me, yet unable to
move my eyes from the little trail of hair that snaked its way down.

He stalked towards me, his face hovering near mine for the barest second, stretching his
arm over my shoulder.

'Here,' he breathed, flicking the light off.

We were in complete darkness, but the space between us was alive. His soft breath
against my forehead and the warmth of his skin, just a few inches away from me. I closed
my eyes. Waiting.

He yawned loudly and moved back, slipping under the covers. I stood there for a second, trying to take deep breaths and trying to corral my braincells.

'Are you planning to lay down to sleep or...?' he asked.

'Yes. Yes,' I said, crawling under my duvet, then lying still, staring at the ceiling in silence, as I attempted to breathe evenly.

'Vincent?' a whisper into the dark.

'Yeah?'

'Do you ever think about what our lives would be...could be... if we didn't only exist in the shadows of our own nightmares?' he asked.

'What makes you think I've been through a nightmare?'

'I can see it in your eyes. In the way you hold yourself.'

I hesitated, unable to let the words pass through my lips.

'It's okay. You don't have to tell me about it,' he whispered in the dark room. The blankets shifted and his hand popped over the side of the bed, the outline of half his face barely visible.

I took a deep breath and wove my fingers in with his. 'I do.'

'Do what?'

'I do think about it. Like what our time in Stockholm would have been like if you came as you promised.'

'I'm so sorry, Vincent. If things were different...' anguish was clear in his voice.

'It is what it is, Teddy.'

'Are you angry at me because I went to care for my mother?'

'Of course not. I'm angry because...I'm an idiot.'

'What do you mean?'

'I just missed you so much. And...I resented you for making me believe that we could have been something.'

'We *could* be something.'

'Oh yeah?' I asked. 'And what would that be like?'

'We walk hand in hand in the beautiful streets of London. We wear big coats and matching fluffy scarves. We tease each other and we say sweet things. And I'd be the luckiest man alive because my Romeo picked me.'

I closed my eyes. Memories spinning through my mind, of us watching the sunset together, our dance, our magical kiss, giving way to the brutal and the harsh. The ones I would erase, me crying, face buried into my pillow, my assault, my year in America.

'Life isn't a fairy-tale, Teddy.'

He sighed. 'Hoping for a fairy-tale is all I have left.'

Lord.

I stayed quiet, unable to say anything of substance to him.

'Are you asleep?' he asked.

'Nah. I'm just trying to imagine living in that fairy-tale you were talking about. And I just can't. That sort of life isn't for me. It's too good and, Teddy...I don't think I deserve it...'

'What?' his voice pitched high. 'Vincent don't be ridiculous. Of course you do. I still remember a sweet romantic under that veil of sharp sarcasm.'

'Oh fuck off,' I said with a chuckle, eyes rolling.

'Do I need to come down there?' he asked, sounding like his old playful self.

'Goodnight, Teddy,' I said, turning my back at him and pulling the covers over my head.

'Uh, no? Take it back. You take it back and say you deserve that happy!'

'I won't take it back. I am twenty-three years old, and this is reality.'

'Well, don't say I didn't warn you!' he said, rolling off the bed and onto me. His legs over my waist.

'Did you lose your damn mind?!' I asked, pulling my duvet off my face and looking up at him sat on me. My eyes—now used to the darkness—could see his chiselled torso perfectly.

'Come on...just say it!' he said, his smile shining.

'I can't, now get off me,' I said, placing my hands on his sides, his skin warm and so, so tempting. I wanted to shove him away from me, but my hands missed that memo, moving down to rest on his toned thighs.

'Why can't you?' he asked, his face leaning close to mine, our eyes challenging each other.

'Teddy... come on.'

'No, Vincent. Why can't you say it? Come on.' he needled.

'Because there is no fucking fairy-tale without you!' I snapped at him, my heart erratic and blood burning inside my veins.

Teddy stared at me for a second, stunned then moved off me to lie on the floor beside my makeshift bed, both of us looking up at the dark nothing, avoiding each other's gaze.

'I'm so tired of life getting in the way of my happiness,' he whispered. 'Why can't I just be free...'

'Because you're a good person,' I said, facing him. 'And you're doing what's right.'

'I'm just so unhappy,' he said, his eyes glimmering. 'And seeing you...just reminded me of how much I—'

'Don't,' I interrupted. My hand on his warm chest, I felt his breathing pick up. I intended to push him away, ask him to move back onto the bed, but I couldn't sever the connection between us.

His fingers traced the shape of my face, so gentle, like I was the finest glass, and a puff of air would shatter me. His thumb moved along my jaw, the same way he used to before he'd move wayward strands of my hair behind my ear. I felt his soft breath across my skin and his forehead resting against mine. His lips were so close, I could nearly taste him.

I drew closer, our noses touching, and my eyes closed.

It was wrong, there was no redemption available and yet, I fell right into it. I pressed my lips against his, so tender and sweet. His hand, gently pressed into the dip of my back, pulled me closer, his smooth sun kissed skin pressed against mine and I lost myself in his familiar embrace. Our tongues fought for control of the kiss, our hard-undeniable bulges rubbing and our legs tangling together.

It was us, Vincent and Teddy, once more. We were whole and undamaged, a wild assortment of impossibilities fused into one possible. I could no longer think straight. This is what I wanted. It's what I needed.

I was addicted to him, to us, and his beautiful lips, made me feel like I was the only guy in the world. Except I wasn't. He wasn't.

I splayed my hand against his chest and gave it a little push, going against what my senses were telling me to do.

'I...can't,' I said, unconvincingly. 'I can't, Teddy.'

I looked at him, so handsome and pure, raw emotion painted on his face. He wiped the single tear falling down my cheek. I turned my back to him and stared at my wall.

I wanted all of it. I wanted us. But we couldn't. And it wasn't fair.

'I'll just go back to bed, then,' he said, his voice trembling.

'Teddy?' I whispered.

'Yeah?'

'I know it isn't fair. I know. But. Could you just stay here for a while? Next to me?'

'Of course,' he said. His breath warming the back of my neck.

I closed my eyes, forcing sleep. We were us, separate. Never one. Teddy and Vincent, lying in the silent darkness.

I got up early, managing to sneak out without waking him, surprised I didn't trip and drown in all the guilt pouring out of me. I closed the door behind me and left the flat. The fresh air felt amazing on my skin, though it was in harsh contrast to a warm night spent next to Teddy.

I grabbed my phone to return Kyle's call. *Calls*. Perhaps to find a way to lessen my guilt. His name flashed across the screen as he called again.

'Hello?' I said, picking it up.

'Finally!' Kyle said. 'Where have you been?'

'I was just having a few drinks with Laura!' I said, heading towards the tube station.

'You two...always trouble.'

'Yeah,' I said, with a little nervous giggle.

'Hey, so...I've been thinking...what do you say we have our ceremony with only a few people, and then a bigger celebration later on?'

'What do you mean?'

'Well, we could do the small ceremony, so I can apply for a visa as soon as possible. I'm having talks with the BBC for an executive producer position. It could be good for the both of us.'

'I don't know if I'm comfortable with you trying to get me a job, I'd like to earn it myself.'

'Don't be stupid. This is the industry. It happens all the time.'

I remained quiet.

'But hey, later we can do something more...majestic, once I move to the UK.'

'Yeah...yeah, that makes sense.'

'So how does twelve weeks time sound?' he asked.

'What?!' I shrieked.

'Is that a problem?'

'It's just...quite soon.'

'I thought you wanted me there as soon as possible. The quicker we get married, the quicker we can start our lives together.'

'I guess you're right,' I muttered, waiting on the sparsely populated platform for a train. Everything was happening too quickly. It was overwhelming.

'I can do most of the work from my end. You just need to get a suit and show up to say *I do*. Does that sound reasonable?'

I paused for a second, having a full colour flashback of Teddy and I kissing the night before.

'Yep. Completely reasonable. I'm heading to the store right now.'

'You'll look dashing in whatever you pick.'

'Sure.'

I jumped on the first train to central London and made my way to Knightsbridge.

I entered a swanky department store. The ground floor was inebriating with its beauty products and fragrances being sprayed everywhere, the vile taste coating my throat.

It was so familiar, yet disturbing.

It wasn't the same department store. Far from it. But I could easily see myself walking aimlessly along the aisles, looking for my next fix. The little worthless thing I'd take away from the store to feel alive. I'd never realised that stealing was an addiction until I'd had to stop it.

I could still feel the hands of the store guards pressing against my skin the day I got caught. The humid air I breathed as I sat in a dark basement room, where they kept all the shoplifters on hold until the police would take over. I could hear my sobs, my pleas. I could still see them dialling my host family's telephone number and telling them what I had done. And then the storm. The end of my program. A slap into real life.

That was then, a different me. I had grown. I was stronger now. I wasn't the same kid.

I took a deep breath and looked ahead. Everything was fine. I was fine.

I jumped on the escalator that took me down to the lower level and I was greeted by a tall, curvy girl with a black fringe.

'Can I help you?' she asked in a thick Essex accent, smacking gum with her mouth open.

'Hey, I have an appointment with...Dominic?' I screwed up my face, like maybe that would enhance my memory.

She rolled her eyes and stalked away. I stood still, not quite understanding what was going on. I considered following her but couldn't see where she was heading to. An attractive guy with dark brown hair and neat stubble came towards me, his face split in a big, wide, white smile. I wondered vaguely if looking like one had slept wrapped in the pages of Vogue was some sort of employment requirement.

'Hi! I am so sorry about my colleague. She's trash!'

'Oh, that's fine,' I laughed, instantly relaxing. 'She probably didn't think I belonged in this store...'

'What?!' he squealed. 'Nonsense. You must be Vincent.'

'Did we speak on the phone? Are you Dominic?'

'Dominic called in sick this morning. But not to worry. He gave me a vague brief about you needing a suit?'

'Yep.'

'Okay, follow me.'

He walked swiftly, tight black trousers and patent shoes clicking with each step as he led the way to the tailoring section.

'So,' he said, pulling his hair back. 'What sort of occasion are you—'

'Uhm...my wedding.'

'Oh! Amazing. Congratulations.'

'Thank you.'

He power-walked around the section, grabbing suit after suit.

'I assume you're after a skinny fit?' he asked, looking me up and down.

'Thanks,' I said, with a giggle.

'I'm grabbing a bunch of different ones. You have a specific budget in mind or...?'

'I haven't thought about it at all,' I said. 'I am hoping putting one on will just...feel right or something.'

'Let's do that then!' he said, while putting a mountain of clothes inside a changing room.

'I just want to be clear and say I may not buy one today. I don't want to waste your time.'

'Hey, look around. There's no one else here. We can play dress up for a while, so I can pass the time, and who knows, you may fall in love with one.'

I smiled at him and entered the fitting room. I decided to try a charcoal one first. It was the only one under a grand. This store was freaking fancy.

'So...' he said while leaning on the door. 'Who did the proposal?'

'Uhm...my boyfriend,' I said, trying to fit my thighs into a pair of tight-ass trousers.

'Romantic proposal?' he asked.

'I mean, sort of. It was at a restaurant.'

'Classic, then.'

'I suppose, yeah,' I said, buttoning up my shirt.

'I actually recently got engaged myself.'

'Oh? That's great. And here I thought I was the youngest person ever getting married,' I said with a giggle.

'No, you aren't the only one,' he said.

'What's her/his/their name?' I asked, cautiously.

'His name is Jake.'

'Sorry, didn't want to make assumptions or anything,' I opened the door and stepped out.

'Very dapper,' he said. 'It's quite the fabric. It reflects light slightly. It's so elegant.'

'I'm just trying to figure out how I could possibly afford it without selling a kidney.'

'I can relate,' he said. 'Even with discount, some of these are impossible to purchase.'

I was glad I could speak to someone who didn't really know me or my past. This guy probably didn't kiss another guy who wasn't his fiancé like I did.'

'Can I ask you a question?'

'Yeah, of course,' he said.

'Did you know it was right? The engagement thing.'

'It's a big decision, but...yeah, I think I knew it was right. He's a special guy. He's the kind of person I imagine having children with, or like, a puppy.'

'That's nice.'

'You shouldn't force yourself to do anything you don't want, even if you've already said yes. It's your life, after all. Imagine being with this man for years to come. Who do you see when you picture the future?'

I looked at his gentle eyes and started thinking about the future like he said. I saw Kyle, but my mind kept dragging Teddy's face into the frame too.

It was never going to work with Teddy. I needed to stop chasing such a fairy tale. I needed to get my master's, Teddy needed to tend to his family, and finally go after his dream of becoming a flight attendant.

'You should get paid more,' I said.

'Don't I know it!'

I stepped back into the fitting room and started getting changed. I wasn't going to try the other suits. I needed to go home and speak to Teddy.

'So, who was the girl who spoke to me when I arrived?' I asked. 'She seems an absolute treat.'

'Oh, don't mind Katherine. She's here only "temporarily". She's a singer or so she says.'

'You're a good co-worker, for taking over and all.'

'I try.'

I grabbed all the suits, opened the door and handed them to him.

'Sorry I didn't buy any,' I said.

'Don't worry. Time flew for a while there.'

'I'll be back. I'll try to guilt-trip my mother into paying for the charcoal one.'

'I will most likely still be here,' he said.

I smiled at him. 'Thank you for the chat as well.'

He ran his hand through his wavy hair and nodded.

'Hey,' he said.

'Yeah?'

'You never told me the name of your fiancé.'

'It's uhm...' I looked over the sales assistant's shoulder and caught *his* emerald eyes. 'Teddy!' I gasped.

Teddy smiled, making his way towards us.

'Did I miss the fashion show?' he asked.

I took a sobering breath, trying to mentally prepare for this inevitable goodbye.

CHAPTER EIGHTEEN

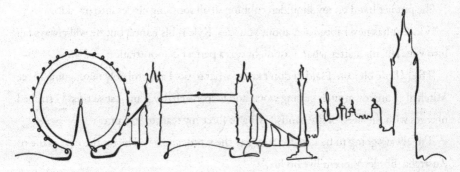

TEDDY

2014

Vincent practically fled the flat this morning, leaving me alone in the room. I dragged myself to the kitchen for a glass of water, my back wishing I had slept in the bed, but I wouldn't trade a night wrapped around Vincent for anything.

Laura was sitting on the sofa, reading a magazine and, as I gulped half a glass, I couldn't help but note that her expression didn't seem too friendly.

'Teddy, what are you doing?' she asked.

I looked around, setting my glass on the counter. 'What do you mean?'

'You know I love you. You're my brother, that's never going to change. But what are you actually doing *here?*'

'Laura...'

'Vincent is with Kyle. He's probably downplayed it for you because you guys have this...past together. But Vincent is happy.'

'Oh, come on.'

'Don't do that. You know exactly what I'm talking about. You can't come here, mess his life up, and then leave again. It's not right. You can't stay here, and he can't move there. At least not anytime soon.'

'I know,' I said, heading over to sit next to her. 'I didn't know it was going to be like this. I didn't know how much I cared for him still, until I flew here. It's like I'm alive again, Laura.'

She put her hand on my shoulder, rubbing small soothing circles into my skin.

'Vincent has never forgotten about you. Yes, Kyle is his fiancé, but he will always fall into your lap, no matter what. Last night was a perfect demonstration of that.'

'I feel a little bit lost,' I said. 'I don't know what to do. I am probably never going to see Mitchell again; my mum is getting worse and worse each day. I am just so tired.' I rubbed my eyes with the heels of my hands, trying to force my tears to stay put.

'I'm always going to be here for you. Say the word, and I will be on the next plane to Australia. But let Vincent live his life.'

I couldn't hold it in any longer. My already damaged heart was splintering into another hundred pieces. I loved the fantasy of us. Vincent and me, one whole beautiful life. I had let myself live in it last night, just for a while. Living with Vincent, waking next to his sleepy smile, days falling willingly into his big grey eyes, him in front of me instead, suit, flowers and polished shoes, an 'I do' for me instead...but that wasn't real life. It wasn't *my* real life. That was not how things were planned for us and I felt so stupid for pretending they could be. Laura was right. I had no business being here.

'I've been so damn lonely,' I said. 'Could you really blame me for falling for Prince Charming? For wanting Vincent, just for myself. Nothing in my world is just for me.'

'I think...it's always the case of not being at the right place at the right time for you two. It won't always be like this, but for now—'

'Yeah,' I sniffed, wiping a few tears with the back of my hand.

'I don't mean to kick you out, but you need to go back home. You have so many things to sort out. Find out the truth about your brother's story; apply for flight academy or whatever. Start your life, Teddy. It's well overdue.'

'You're right...'

Laura gave me a kiss on the cheek. 'You know I love you, right?'

'I do, yeah.'

Laura left me sat there, still, trying to reassess my choices. I loved Vincent so much, but I had to let him go.

It took me a while to find him at the department store, but I finally saw him exiting a fitting room, talking to a cute sales assistant.

'Teddy!'

'Hello,' I said with a wave.

'I'm just going to put these back,' the guy said, carrying a tonne of clothes.

'Thanks for your help, uhm...?' Vincent said with a smile.

'...Leo.'

'Thanks, Leo.'

We were left alone, staring at each other, an odd tension filling the air between us.

'I had this booked already—'

'You don't have to explain,' I interrupted. 'Care for a walk?'

'Another one, this can't be good,' he said, following me outside.

We walked side by side, under a grey-skyed morning, in what seemed to be the richest area in London.

'Does everyone drive a Ferrari here or...?' I asked.

'Yeah, lots of celebrities live around here. The party kind.'

'I love that...'

'I wasn't expecting you here. Did Laura—?'

'I'm going home,' I interrupted. Blurting the phrase like peeling a plaster.

'Your carbon footprint will be through the roof,' he said. 'What happened to drinks and dinner?'

'I can't stay, Vincent.'

'Yeah...' he said eyes locked on the ground. 'We have never been lucky, Teddy.'

'You're telling me.'

'I'm going to get married.'

'I know.'

'If things were different—'

'No, you don't need to explain,' I said, brushing away a stray tear. Or two. We came to a stop, I let myself touch his face, just one last time. 'You are so special, Vincent Stewart.

You've been rocking my fucking world since 2008. You always will. Being on the other side of the world for less than a day was worth it. Seeing *you* was worth it. You will always be worth it. I am so sorry I created confusion. You have a good life, Vincent. You made good choices. Don't let me get in the way of your happiness.'

His body shook, tears flowing freely down his cheeks. 'I really, really wish we could just, be...together,' he hiccupped.

'We will always have each other. I will be ready to speak on the phone, like we used to. We can still keep each other that way. Pinkie promise.' I held my little finger out, ready to link with his.

He stared at my hand, like I had offered him a grenade.

'I...I can't do that. I can't hang my heart on that promise again Teddy, I'm sorry.'

My mind tripped back half a decade to an airport promise I couldn't ever keep but didn't know then. 'Right, of course. I'm going to go, Vincent.' I swallowed my sob, the pain, my own and what I had caused him.

I leaned forward, his lips mine one more time, as I gave him a soft, tiny kiss. Tears were streaming down our faces, combined heartache and loss. I could feel our hearts beating together, this time in pain. I didn't want to let him go, holding his slim waist with my arm, his soft skin against mine, just one last time until he'd be out of reach forever.

I wished I could freeze time, go *back* in time, give us *more* time. I pulled away from him, leaving a piece of my soul with him always.

'I'm just...going to go and pack. Please...don't come with me,' I said.

'You want this to be our last—'

'I can't...I won't leave. I won't be able to, if I see your face. And I have to do this.' I tried to smile, knowing it was weak. I reached out to touch his jaw, stopping myself, hand raised between us. 'Goodbye, Vincent.'

I walked away, as quickly as I could, hands shoved deep in my pockets. My tears streamed down my face and the entirety of my being screamed at me to go back. I wanted nothing more than to be with him. And now we were apart once more. This time for good.

My last conversations with Laura and Vincent were constantly replaying in my head. My house was empty. Hazel wasn't in and there was no trace of Mitchell. I was sitting in my mother's office. A room surrounded by books upon books. Classics, first editions, and guilty pleasures. I was running my hand across the mahogany desk, reminding myself how polished it was, when she was around. How angry she would be about the dust and neglect. I'd kept the office locked for years. I didn't want to go in. It didn't feel right. The oil painting of Mitchell and I was still hanging on the floral wallpapered wall right in front of me. She loved it so much. She loved looking at us, while she worked hard on her lesson plans.

Her cave, she called it. She'd come out and take us for ice cream so we could see the sun without the barrier of the window. She would take one each of both our small hands in hers and run with us to the water's edge, toes digging into the sand of a mile-long beach. Let us feel long grass tickling our ankles as we tore around an empty field, playing tag, while she lay on the blanket, living in those moments of joy with us.

I missed her. So damn much.

I took a deep breath and unlocked her chest of drawers, where all of her diaries were kept. There were so many. I turned the desk lamp on and grabbed one. I opened it and smelled its pages, paper and perfume, undeniably mum. I read a few lines and for a second, I felt like she was there, leaning over my shoulder.

Her words were always carefully chosen, conveying her voice, style, and emotions. I read and read and read, until my eyes closed from tiredness.

I was up early. As I stood in the shower, boiling water falling down my body, it hit me just how utterly alone I was. Laura was right. I needed to start living my life, any life. Something where I existed beyond the walls of this house.

I walked into mum's room, wearing my crispest white shirt. Mum loved when Mitchell and I would put an effort in how we wore our clothes. I saw her looking my way and I smiled at her.

'Hi mum,' I said, closing the door behind me. 'How have you been?'

I knelt so I could look her in the eye, but her gaze was absent, unseeing. She had no idea who I was, or even where I was. Trapped in this bed, the world moving while she stayed still.

I caressed her hair and sat on the chair next to the bed.

'I am sorry I went away. I was trying to deal with a few things.'

She tried to talk, but nothing coherent came out.

'Don't worry, mum. Don't stress,' I said, smiling at her. 'These last few years have been so difficult. I watched your light fading away, I saw this disease taking over, little by little. I have been here every step of the way. I don't regret a thing. It's been hard, but I am glad we had a chance to talk to each other before it became too late.'

I paused for a second and looked around the room. 'You know, a few years ago I fell in love with a boy. It didn't make any sense, but it happened. Life has kept us apart, and life will continue to do so. I can't really blame anything but our circumstances, but I can make peace with it.'

I stopped smiling, my expression slipping into a frown. 'But what you did to Mitchell? Mum...how could you? You wanted what was best for him, I get that, but you took that choice away from him. From them. You took away his chance to be a dad, mine to be an uncle. I wish you could really explain yourself, but all I have is your words, written by a person that almost doesn't exist anymore. You can't defend yourself, and it sucks.'

My eyes were damp, and I held her hand, gently. She was looking up at me.

'I know it's your biggest regret. I hope it is. You thought you were doing what was best for your son, but it backfired. I don't know how I would have reacted if you'd interfered with my life like that. Mitchell was right, all these years.'

Someone knocked at the door, and I turned my head.

'Hey,' Mitchell said, slipping into the room. He had his hair tied in a bun, wearing a big, shearling brown jacket and beige cargo pants.

'Hi,' I said.

'How are you?' he asked.

'I'm okay. Where have you been?'

'I've been crashing at a friend's house for a while. It's not bad,' he said walking towards me. 'This is awful, isn't it?'

'I never thought I'd ever see the both of us in here.'

'Me neither,' he turned to her and stared at her. 'I can't believe this. I still can't.'

'You should move back home, Mitch. I'm sorry. I'm sorry about everything.'

'What made you change your mind?' he asked.

I stood up, moved to him.

'You were right. You were right about everything and I didn't believe you. I didn't want to believe you.'

'How do you—'

'The diaries,' I interrupted. 'I'm so sorry.'

'What did she say?'

'They're all in her office, you can read them yourself.'

Mitchell started tearing up. 'Did she regret ever doing what she did?'

'Yeah,' I said, resting my hand on his arm. 'She regretted it. She hated herself for it. She hated losing you.'

'Good,' he said while sobbing. 'God. Now that I'm here I'm like...I waited too long.'

'There is something,' I said, reaching my hand into my pocket. I grabbed a folded piece of paper and handed it to him.

'What is this?' he asked.

'It's an address and a phone number. She actually managed to find Olivia and your daughter, Mitch.'

'I have a daughter...'

Mitchell dropped to his knees, crying, grabbing my legs. I held his head, while he sobbed without interruption.

'You can go find them, now,' I said.

'Thank you for finding this,' he said. He stood back up, furiously wiping his face and unfolded the piece of paper. 'They're in Sydney,' he noted.

'Yeah,' I said with a smile.

'You know I need to go find them, right?' he said, looking at me.

'Of course,' I said, my face falling, tears flowing. Alone again, I looked back to mum.

'We could both go,' he said.

I faced him, unsure of what he had just said.

'We could get mum transferred to a facility. I'm sure there are places in Sydney where she could go to. We could take turns taking care of her and you'd have endless opportunities to do what you want to do.'

'Are you serious?'

'Why not? She needs more care than we can realistically give her and is there really anything keeping you on this god-forsaken rock?'

'I'm just...I would have never thought you'd want to help her.'

'I will never forgive her for what she did,' he said, then put his hand on my head. 'But it's not fair. I haven't been fair. She shouldn't be just your responsibility.'

I looked at him and smiled a little.

Sydney could be a good idea for the both of us.

Weeks went by, flowing into months. I kept myself busy by selling furniture and junk we had hoarded over the years and packing the stuff we wanted to keep. The house itself was sold quickly. Mitchell, Hazel, and I worked hard, many long days in a row but eventually we managed to empty it out. Mum had already been transferred to a really lovely facility in Sydney. It wasn't as scary and clinical as I had thought it would be. She had a room pretty similar to the one she had back home and had settled in as best as we could expect, given her condition. All that was left for us Clarkes was to say goodbye to our childhood home.

Part of me was happy I got to focus so much on packing and getting the house ready for sale. I didn't have even the slightest opportunity to think about Vincent and his upcoming wedding or the oddly *Vincent-shaped* gaping hole in my chest. Hazel flew out on our last day at the house. She wouldn't miss Vincent's special day for anything.

Mitchell and I sat on the grass outside the house, drinking a couple of beers and toasting to our lives.

'I wonder who's going to live here, what they'll be like,' I said.

'They won't be as cool as us. Remember when we both demanded a tree house?'

'Yeah. Mum didn't know where to start, so she called fucking professionals.'

'It was awesome! I may have actually lost my virginity there.'

'That's fucking disgusting, Mitchell.'

'I thought you did too…who was that neighbour kid who used to come to ours all the time because we had the big TV?'

'Oh my God, no!' I cackled. 'Not bloody Timmy!'

'Oh yeah, Timmy and Teddy. Cute.'

'I'll never forgive our parents for giving me such a stupid name.'

'It was me, by the way,' he said while smiling at me. 'I gave you that nickname. I thought it was cool to name you after a stuffed bear.' My mouth fell open.

'I could have avoided years and years of bullying!'

'No one ever bullied you, I'd beat them up mostly.'

'True…'

A beautiful day in Tasmania was beyond comparison, our house - our former house – was surrounded by nature, every green on the colour wheel present and accounted for. Closing my eyes, I let my head fall back, the sun warmed my skin almost too much and the softest breeze blowed through my hair. I took a deep breath and looked back at the house. I saw Mitchell and I chasing each other in the garden. Our old dog, Lulu, drinking water from the sprinklers. Our mum reading books on the front steps, drinking ice water and checking that Mitchell wasn't actually going to kill me.

'You know…during my years away…I really missed you, our family,' he said. 'When you're travelling by yourself…sometimes you get lonely. You see people celebrating Christmas and whatever. It makes you miss home.'

'I don't think you would have wanted to celebrate Christmas here.'

'I wish I came earlier.'

'I'm glad you came. I missed my big brother.'

'Right back at you, Tedster,' he said, slapping my shoulder.

Sweet Jesus.

'So, what's going to happen with Hazel now?'

'Oh, I don't know. I mean, she is bloody hot. And you know, funny, smart, crazy talented…'

'Calm down, you.'

'I know. I doubt she'd be cool with me trying to find my lost ex-girlfriend and our child…Bit much, ain't it? I don't know if she'd want something with me anyway.'

'You'd be surprised,' I said. 'She's pretty great.'

'Well, she's moving with us, so...we shall see.'

'Please don't fuck on the sofa, there isn't enough fabric cleaner in the world, and I actually like that one,' I said, while gulping the last of my beer.

'What will you do with your fella?'

'I don't have a "fella", Mitch.'

'You know what I mean.'

I grabbed my phone. Laura's Facebook was filled with photos of the venue, her outfit, Vincent and Kyle getting ready. It was really happening.

'Think I let him get away,' I could barely get the words out. 'I need to get my shit together man, become a flight attendant. Everyone has had their chance to do what they want to do. It's my time. I'm going to date, maybe go to the gym finally.'

'We could both go. I'd help you get rid of those chicken legs.'

'I can't think of anything worse.'

I looked at the time on my watch. It was almost time for Vincent to get married.

'Do you think I should call him?' I asked.

'I don't know if that's such a good idea... Maybe text him?'

'Yeah, maybe,' I said, disappointed.

I sent him a text, just to say *good luck*. I couldn't believe someone else would get to call Vincent their husband.

'Are we set to go? Shall we get a cab to the airport?' he asked, getting to his feet.

I held my hand out, letting him pull me to my feet.

'Let's go.'

CHAPTER NINETEEN

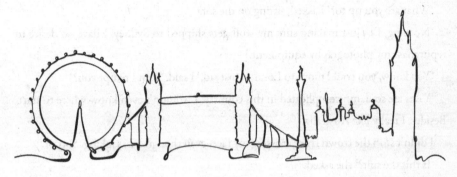

VINCENT

2014

Sunlight streamed through the break in the curtains, throwing a pale-yellow stripe across the bed I was currently dying in. I may have been ever so slightly hungover from the night before. My head was a throbbing wound and my mouth felt like it had grown fur overnight. Today was going to be the day. Kyle had spent the night at a cheap hotel. He thought we'd have this piece of tradition, at least. He didn't want to see me before the wedding.

My charcoal suit was hanging from a door hook, all ready for me to wear. I rolled out of the bed and peaked out my window, the light was agony for my hungover eyes. It would seem London was shooting for perfect today. I stretched my arms above my head, twisting side to side, trying to force life back into my muscles. I shuffled to the kitchen, desperately seeking water.

'Good morning, groom!' exclaimed Hazel, pushing past me to reach for a mug.

'You're chirpy,' I said.

'It's the jet-lag, I'll be crashing in a few hours. Bang in the middle of your wedding, I imagine.'

'I'll probably do the same, to be honest,' I said with a smile. 'Is Laura still asleep?'

'I think she went to grab some breakfast.'

I nodded, which was a bad idea, given the state of my head, and pulled my fluffy black robe on. Hazel kept checking her phone.

'What are you up to?' I asked, sitting on the sofa.

'Nothing, I'm just making sure my stuff gets shipped to Sydney. I have no desire to repurchase my photography equipment.'

'You know, you could move to London instead,' I said. 'Can I tempt you?'

'Visas are so damn complicated in this country, I wouldn't even know where to start. Besides, I really like Australia.'

I didn't stop the frown from crossing my face, even though I was joking. Sort of.

'Is this the suit?' she asked.

'Yeah, mum bought it for me from a fancy *schmanzy* department store.'

'Nice!'

'Hey, Haze...'

'Yes?'

'How's—'

Laura barged into the flat, with two bottles of champagne and bags of groceries.

'I'm home!' she shouted.

Hazel looked at me to finish the question, but I let it go. It was stupid anyway. I went to rummage through the bags Laura had.

'Oh, this takes me back,' Hazel laughed.

'You know it.'

'Not this again,' I rolled my eyes.

'Your mum will be here in an hour,' said Laura. 'We have time to get a few drinks in and celebrate.'

'I don't know if I can drink. I'm a little nervous about today, and I feel less than ideal after last night.'

'We will have a drink, you'll get changed, and it's all going to be fine,' she said.

'It sounds like a good plan, Vincent,' said Hazel.

'Do you mind if I go for a walk first?' I asked. 'I have to clear my head.'

'Sure, just don't be too late, today is the day,' Laura said.

Today was *definitely* the day. There was just somewhere I wanted to be first.

I got to Holland Park faster than I thought I would. It was still quiet, the early morning light filtering through the half-dressed trees, the wind kicking up their discarded leaves. I sat on our bench, painfully aware that he was missing.

I pulled out my phone and looked at his photo. My mind kept handing me vivid memories, like the last time we held each other's hands and how much it hurt to say goodbye so soon after. I pressed the call button without putting much thought into it. It rang for a bit and then I finally heard his voice.

'Hello?'

'Hi,' I said.

'What's going on? Isn't today your big day?'

'Yeah, it is. I just...'

'You got my text, right?'

'Yes, yes I did. Thank you.'

We both paused for a few seconds.

'I'm in Holland Park,' I said, looking around. 'I must say, it feels different.'

'Oh, yeah? I bet it does.'

I hesitated, unsure what I should say or what I even thought would happen here. I scratched the back of my head nervously and took a deep breath. 'Okay, sorry I bothered—'

'Hey, Vincent,' he interrupted.

'Yes?'

'Why did you call?'

'I think...I want to know that I'm doing the right thing.'

'You're asking me?'

'I know, I know,' I said with slightly teary eyes.

'I think it's the right thing if you feel it's the right thing. You seem to love Kyle very much and...I think he can make you happy, but it isn't for me to decide, it isn't fair.'

'Will we still speak to each other?' my voice was small, nervous.

'Yeah, I think so. I am, first and foremost, your friend, Vincent. I will always be there for you. I just, I can't be there for you when you're marrying another man. Not right now. But hey, if you get married again, I'll be there for that one.'

I smiled again, my eyes watery. 'Thank you, Teddy.'

'For what?'

'For...loving me. For waiting for me when we were young, for being there for me now. For making me feel special and for just...making me feel safe in your arms.'

He didn't respond straight away, we sat in silence, half a world apart.

'Vincent, I have to go now. I meant what I said, though. Best of luck today.'

I nodded and looked at the sky.

'Take care, Teddy.'

I hung up and put my head between my knees. I wanted to scream, but I thought it wouldn't be fair to scare the peacocks. I got up, took a deep breath and made my way back home. I had a wedding to attend.

I was in a taxi with my mother heading to Baker Street, where the Old Marylebone Town Hall was located. Kyle and I had booked one of the venues and Laura had helped to decorate it. I had yet to see the room. I was wearing a white bow tie and an orchid boutonniere. Mum was sitting next to me, holding my hand.

'Aren't you happy it's not raining?' she asked.

I was staring out the window, watching people walk, jog, and talk to each other. Watching the other cars rolling past. I had a sense of unease curling through my stomach, an anxiety that would not go away.

'I'm really nervous about this, mum.'

'Of course you are,' she said. 'It happens to everyone, it's a big deal. Just enjoy the day.' She smiled at me and fixed her hair behind her ear.

'And it's not just the wedding you need to be excited about. In a few weeks you'll start your masters course. You've worked so hard to make your dream come true.'

'What if we hate each other when we start living together?' I asked.

'You do whatever is necessary to keep the peace. That's what everyone does.'

I guess her words made sense. Maybe I was exactly where I was supposed to be. Deep down, a piece of me felt awful because I had never told Kyle about my kiss with Teddy. The sense of guilt had been eating me up and part of me really didn't want to start a new life together with a secret between us.

The taxi pulled to a stop in front of the town hall, so I gathered myself and got out.

I needed to talk to Kyle.

'I'll be right back!' I shouted to my mum.

I walked up the stairs and looked around. The hall was beautiful. The stairs were a cool marble, a red carpet perfectly fitted on each step. Historical statues were planted around the main hall and white flowers were bursting with perfume on each oversized planter.

On the first floor there were a myriad of rooms, so I walked along the corridor to find some sort of changing room. It took a bit of wandering, but I eventually managed to find the room where Kyle and his best man Josh were changing. I took a deep breath and knocked.

Someone shouted, *'one second!'* from beyond the door. It didn't sound like Kyle. Josh opened the door. He was a tall guy, with a blotchy face that looked like a horse. He was only half dressed. An unbuttoned shirt and grey sweatpants.

'Hey, man!' I said. 'Is Kyle in there?'

'Yeah, but I thought y'all didn't want to see each other,' he said in a Southern drawl.

'I really need to speak to him,' I insisted.

He looked back, inside the room and then looked back at me.

'Could you come back in like, five minutes?' he asked.

'What is going on?' I asked, suspiciously.

'It's just our ritual, we are not quite finished.'

'Josh, let me in,' I commanded.

'Fine,' he threw his hands up and let me through.

'...and could you leave us alone, please?' I asked. He threw me a look, left the room and closed the door behind him.

Kyle was lying on the sofa, eyes fixed on the ceiling. The room felt like a greenroom. Like the ones you'd get backstage at a theatre. The big mirror was lit up and numerous beauty products were disseminated. There were clothes tossed all about the room.

'God, what happened here?' I asked. 'Kyle, are you okay?'

'Yeah, I'm all good. Just have a bit of a headache. Hey, you look beautiful!' he said, sounding somewhat drunk.

'You need to get ready, and fairly soon too.'

'I am going to, I am going to.'

I walked towards the mirror and noticed there was a plate with a few speckles of powder on it, along with two colourful thin straws cut short.

I turned to him, my face flushed, my jaw clenched. 'Are you guys doing drugs?'

'No...I would never.'

I grabbed the plate and showed it to him. 'What the fuck is this then?'

'Okay, Okay,' he said while standing up. 'It's not what it looks like.'

'So, this isn't coke and you're not tripping balls right now?'

'I was just very nervous about today. Josh helped me loosen up a little.'

'I can't believe you'd pull this shit on the day of our wedding!'

'I'll be okay, don't worry! Hey,' he said while pulling me closer to him. 'It's going to be great! Are you nervous too? Is that what this is about?'

'I am nervous that I'm about to get married to a man who does drugs when under pressure. It really doesn't feel like the best way to start our lives together.'

'Look,' he said, moving into my personal space. 'I'm sorry. I have been very stupid about this. It will never happen again. I *promise*. All I want is to have an amazing day with you.'

I pressed my lips together and let out an exasperated sigh. 'Get your shit together, okay?'

'Of course,' he said, giving me a soft kiss on the lips. 'Was there something you needed to tell me?'

'What?' I asked.

'The reason why you came here? I thought you wanted to tell me something. I thought it may have been something important, since we are breaking the whole not-seeing-each-other thing.'

I hesitated with an answer, I was so mad at him. I couldn't tell him about Teddy. Perhaps it'd just be something I'd forget eventually.

'Nothing, I just missed you. I needed to see your face.'

'That's so sweet. I missed you too,' he said.

We kissed once again, this time with tongue. I swear I could actually taste the cocaine a little. It was vile. I looked at him and told myself I was doing the right thing.

'Okay, well. I'll see you out there, Kyle.'

'I'll see you later, future Mr. Meadows.'

I turned around and shook my head.

The time had finally come. Kyle and I entered the room from different doors. Kyle had cleaned up nicely. His ash blond hair was pulled back and he was wearing a little bit of make-up. His satin pink shirt matched his socks.

My mother, Hazel, Laura, and Josh were sitting in the room, all smiling at us. It was an emotional setting, and for a second, I had no doubts at all. I looked at Kyle and imagined myself spending my life with him.

The Registrar was a tall man, with grey hair and a goatee, wearing a beautiful navy suit.

'Good afternoon, ladies and gentlemen, and welcome to the Marylebone Town Hall. We are gathered here today for the marriage of Kyle Meadows and Vincent Stewart,' he said, reading the text in his leather-bound folder. 'I must, first of all, tell you that this room in which we are now met has been duly sanctioned, according to the law for the celebration of marriage. You are here to witness the joining in matrimony of Kyle and Vincent.'

I turned to my mother, and she was already dabbing her tears. Laura and Hazel were smiling at me.

'Marriage joins two people in the circle of its love. It is a commitment to life, the best that two people can find and bring out in each other. It offers opportunities for learning and growth that no other opportunity can equal. It is both a physical and an emotional joining that is promised for a lifetime. Happiness is fuller, memories are fresher, and commitment is deeper. Marriage understands and forgives the mistakes that life is unable to avoid.'

My legs were shaking. It was really happening, and my mind kept going back to Teddy and I holding hands in Holland Park. My heart was so violent in my chest, I was sure that if you opened me up there would be bruises.

'I ask you now; Kyle, do you take Vincent to be your lawful wedded husband, to be loving, faithful and loyal to him for the rest of your life together?'

'I do,' he said with a big smile.

'And you, Vincent, do you take Kyle to be your lawful wedded husband, to be loving, faithful and loyal to him for the rest of your life together?'

Blood rushed in my ears. My tongue dry and awkward and I was panicked I wasn't going to emit a single sound. The seconds I stayed silent felt like minutes, hours. My answer would be the one that would bind me to Kyle.

I took a deep breath and the words finally came out.

'I do.'

'The exchanging of rings is the traditional way of sealing the contract that you have just made. It is an unbroken circle, symbolising unending and everlasting love, and is the outward sign of the lifelong promise that you have just made to each other.'

My mum was full-on sobbing, I could hear her trying to contain herself. Kyle's eyes were also tearing up, but I didn't feel like crying. I was...happy, perhaps.

This was a year of self-discovery. I was able to face my fears for the first time in half a decade. I had been in the worst place on earth and managed to leave unscathed, albeit drenched. I'd told Ingrid exactly what I thought of her, and I had a very significant moment of happiness with Teddy. It was our last goodbye, and something I'd always carry in my heart. All of that had led me here.

Kyle was a decent guy. He was spontaneous, happy-go-lucky, and one I'd be able to rely on. It was like I had finally woken up from a nightmare, and I was finally going to get my happy ending.

'Today is a new beginning. May you have many happy years together, and in those years, may all your hopes and dreams be fulfilled. Above all, may you always believe in each other, and may the warmth of your love enrich not only your lives, but also the lives of all those around you,' the Registrar said. 'It now gives me great pleasure to tell you both that you are now legally Husband and Husband. Congratulations.'

I held Kyle's face with my hands and kissed him passionately while everyone clapped loudly.

Then, holding my husband's hand; we were covered with colourful rose petals thrown by our friends and family as we walked out the door.

It was a picture-perfect start to our future.

CHAPTER TWENTY

TEDDY

2014

Mum's room in Sydney looked a lot better than the one in Tasmania. Her walls were painted a soft shade of pink, the TV was a larger flat screen, and the mattress was a lot more comfortable. Mitchell and I had tried our best to make it as homely as we could. We filled her desk with framed photographs of us, a stack of books, both her favourites and the ones she had published earlier in her life. I often enjoyed reading to her. It would calm her so much she'd often smile at me. I couldn't be sure if my voice was reaching her, but it was still a nice image.

I was there early, filling the vases in her room with sunflowers. The hospice wasn't too far from a lovely flower market. On sunny days, I enjoyed taking her there in her wheelchair, so she could touch and smell a little corner of nature.

She was lying there, staring at the wall. The last few months had been hard on her. She had been having trouble swallowing food and, as such, she had lost quite a bit of weight.

'It's a great day outside, isn't it?' I said, 'The flower market was really lovely this morning. I'm sorry you didn't feel well enough to come with me,' I continued while cutting the ends of the flower stems. 'Sunflowers are just so pretty. I bought an extra bunch to put around the new flat. Hazel likes them quite a bit as well. And Mitchell, surprisingly! Although he would probably never admit that.'

I filled the vase with some water and placed it next to the window.

'You're probably wondering what the hell I've done to my hair. I saw a guy online with silver hair and just thought how cool it would be to have it myself. So far, I just feel like I have *fried* my hair. Don't be alarmed if you see me with a completely shaved head in a few weeks.'

I smiled at her and pulled a stool next to her bed, taking a seat.

'You'll be happy to know Mitchell has managed to track Olivia and the little girl down.' I said while caressing her hair and she slowly closed her eyes. "Her name is Emily. I saw photos and she's the double of Mitchell. She has gigantic light blue eyes and dark blond curls. I even watched cartoons with her one afternoon and she's an absolute delight. You would have really liked her.'

Someone then knocked at the door and I turned around.

'Sorry, am I too early?' he said.

Aidan had transferred back to Sydney. He wasn't mum's caretaker anymore, so there were no issues with us seeing each other.

'No, I'm ready to go.'

'How is she?' he asked.

'She's alright. She seems very relaxed today.'

I turned to her and gave her a kiss on the forehead. 'I'll be back to visit very soon. I love you. Have a lovely day.'

I stood up and walked towards Aidan and gave him a kiss on the lips. He held my hips and tickled me.

'Not in front of your mum, Clarke!'

'Oh, I forgot you're my dirty little secret.'

He grabbed my hand and we walked next to each other, making our way out of the nursing home.

'You know,' he said while looking at me. 'I am really starting to dig the grey hair.'

'Oh yeah? Is that so? You don't think I look infinitely younger than you?'

'Oh, is that what this is?' he laughed. 'You would never be able to compete with my baby face.'

'Your baby face is indeed endearing,' I commented. 'Hey, if you're not working later, what do you say we spend our afternoon painting my room?'

'You want me to spend my precious free afternoon doing manual labour? What do I get in return?' he said, squinting his eyes and smiling at me.

'My infinite gratitude, of course.'

'And does infinite gratitude include a lap dance?'

'Aidan Jones. Never thought you'd fall under the slutty nurse cliché,' I said with a giggle.

'I have to memorise what you look like under those clothes as I'm hardly going to see you for the next eight weeks!'

'Don't remind me, I am nervous as fuck.'

'Whatever they teach you in training school, don't tell me anything I don't want to hear. I'm scared of flying as it is. I don't want to hear anything that is going to traumatise me for life. Like planes flying with no fuel or engines or whatever.'

'I'll only share the good news.'

I looked at Aidan and smiled. It was nice to have someone so easy-going, kind, and attractive by my side. He wasn't a complicated person; he didn't have a crazy family history, or psycho exes. He was just a nice guy who enjoyed his job and going to the gym. It was a nice change for me.

We made our way home, where Mitchell and Hazel had been working around the clock to turn our flat into somewhere liveable. There were still boxes everywhere, but the living room had been officially repainted.

Hazel was wearing a red bandana on her head. Her entire outfit looked like the *"we can do it!"* poster, albeit dirty with paint. Also including a handprint on her ass.

'What happened to you?' I asked, trying to contain my laughter.

'Your brother happened,' she said while pressing her lips and frowning.

'You two...'

I could hear Mitchell's heavy steps, running downstairs. He was shirtless, with his hair tied up. His chest was also stained with colourful paint.

'Hi brother,' he said, while opening up a beer. 'What do you think?'

'I think I'm tired of seeing your tits hanging about! But yeah, the living room is coming along nicely.'

'Hey nurse!' he said, trying to get Aidan's attention. 'Do you think you could help me out with some heavy lifting upstairs?'

'Sure,' he said. 'Make way!'

'Sweet!'

They both walked upstairs, leaving Hazel and I alone in the living room.

'I could also do with a beer, to be fair,' she said while grabbing two bottles. 'I'm exhausted.'

She offered me one and we both sat on the sofa, observing the rest of the room.

'Sorry for leaving you to do this,' I said.

'It's all right. You need to focus on getting your dream job.'

'Yeah...I'm nervous, you know.'

'It makes sense, but you'll do great,' she said. 'You've been waiting for this moment for such a long time.'

'How's the situation with Mitchell? Have you guys actually talked? I don't want to live in a house where you two are avoiding each other.'

'It's alright. We will always be friends, no matter what. He just needs to spend time with his daughter and try to figure out what life will be like in the future.'

'For what it's worth, I really don't believe he has any feelings for Olivia.'

'I know. It's just a little complicated,' she said, staring at her bottle.

'Can I ask you a question?'

'Of course.'

'Did you move to Sydney with us for Mitchell?'

'I moved for many reasons. I am mainly here for you, to support you with your mother's stuff. I love her very much. I want to be there for her until the very end,' she said. 'But yeah, maybe I do have feelings for your brother. Is that gross?'

'Yes,' I said while taking another sip. 'But he's also changed. He's no longer the selfish guy I thought he was. He's demonstrated that he's grown, and he's become a fairly decent person. And if I had to have a sister-in-law, I'd be incredibly pleased with you being her.'

We gave each other a hug and I gave her a kiss on the cheek.

'What do you want to do for your last weekend of freedom?' she asked.

'I think I'd like to go dancing. I haven't been in such a long time.'

'You sure?'

'Yeah, it's time I stopped living in fear. I just want to have a good time. I can't let a few idiot homophobes dictate my life.'

'Mitchell will be absolutely thrilled about going!'

'Oh, I'm looking forward to seeing that,' I winked.

I grabbed my phone from my pocket and checked my Facebook. Vincent and Kyle had also found a new place to live. They were starting their life. I'd be lying if I said it didn't hurt to see Vincent with another guy, but I was confident it'd hurt less and less with time. I hoped so at least.

Gay clubs in Sydney were truly something else. Bigger, louder, and a lot more crowded. As someone who grew up on a tiny island, it was quite the adjustment. The guys were also very different. There were a lot more gays going shirtless and showing off their six-packs. I also didn't feel very special with my silver hair anymore, as it seemed everyone else had gotten the same memo.

Hazel and I were on our third round of shots, while Mitchell was in the middle of the dance floor being a dickhead. He was so damn vain and—with a series of guys complimenting his body or buying him drinks—his ego only grew larger.

'How are you feeling? Ready for another round?' I asked Hazel.

'I think I'll throw up if I get one more drop of tequila inside my body!'

'Oh, come on! We're celebrating!'

'I need to go to the loo! How about we discuss the possibility of other shots after I come back?'

I rolled my eyes. 'Don't leave me alone! You know I do stupid stuff when I'm alone!'

'How about you call Aidan and say goodnight to him?'

'Oh yes, poor thing needs to be up early for work!'

'Does drunk Teddy care?' she asked.

'He does not. All right, go. Do whatever you need. I'll be outside smoking.'

'Be fucking careful. Okay?'

I made my way to the outside smoking area and lit a cigarette. I grabbed my phone and looked for Aidan's number. My drunken brain had, however, different plans.

Calling Vincent while drunk at a club? Full freaking circle.

'Hello?' he said.

'Hi stranger.'

'One second.'

He put me on hold for almost a minute and then spoke again. 'Hey, Teddy.'

'Did you go into another room?' I said, while puffing out a little cloud of smoke.

'I did. It was a bit noisy.'

'So you're not hiding from your husband?'

'Teddy...'

'I'm sorry, that was inappropriate. Hey, I'm calling to let you know I'm at a gay club and have not freaked out!'

'That's really good to hear. How are you feeling?'

'Amazing. Sydney is pretty cool. You should come visit someday.'

'Yeah, I'd like that...' he said. 'Hey, I noticed you got into training school to become a flight attendant! Congratulations!'

'Thanks, I'm super excited to start. What about you? How's married life treating you?'

'It's alright.'

'I miss you, you know. And I'm sorry. I know I shouldn't be saying this, but I just have our last meeting replaying in my head over and over again. Sometimes I wish I'd never left.'

'I sometimes wish you didn't leave either, but...'

'That night I got attacked...it *was* about you. I got incredibly drunk and probably said something stupid to set someone off. I denied it to look cooler, but I thought you deserved to know the truth.'

'I'm really sorry.'

'What I'm getting at is...seeing you moving on with your life without me...it'll never stop hurting.'

He didn't say anything. I could hear him breathing, but no words were coming out of his mouth.

'This is the last time I'll call you, Vincent. You're like a drug I can't quit, and it needs to stop. I will never be able to go on and live my life, if every time I get sad, drunk or upset I call you to hear your voice. There's a guy here that I really like. He's not you. He will probably never be you, but I have to give it a chance.'

'Teddy...' he uttered, his voice dwindling.

I turned around and I saw Hazel walking towards me. My eyes were watery, but it was something I had to do.

'Best of luck with everything. You'll...do great. I can't wait to see what you do next.'

My voice was cracking. 'Vincent, you're so incredibly special. Saying goodbye to you is the hardest thing. Never give up on that fairytale ending.'

'Goodbye Teddy.'

I hung up and it was truly bittersweet.

Hazel and I walked back inside and danced our sorrows away.

On Monday I'd start a new chapter of my life and, as heart-breaking as it was, it would not involve Vincent.

PART THREE

2020

Chapter Twenty-One

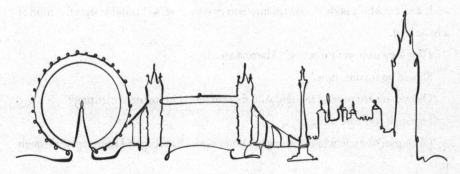

Vincent

2020

I yawned for the hundredth time that day. Work hadn't been particularly eventful, so I had mostly been checking the news online. I was sipping my fourth cup of coffee, but it seemed like no amount of caffeine could save me from the exhaustion straining my body. My co-worker—and my only friend there—Martina, was instead looking at recipes. She was very close to getting her culinary degree, so she had to create something phenomenal to show for it.

'Are you planning on making chocolates? Isn't it a bit understated?' I asked while peeking at her screen.

She turned around and smiled at me. She was still sporting a tan from visiting her family in Italy. I was so jealous. I couldn't remember the last time I had been on holiday.

'No, I'm making chocolates as a side hustle!' she said. 'I have to start building a clientele, don't you think?'

'They are pretty good chocolates, to be fair.'

'Thanks. I've been trying to nail a good variety, so I'll be fully ready for advent calendar season!'

'Is that a thing in your world?'

'It should be a thing in everyone's world!'

I was nervously checking my watch; my legs were restlessly tapping onto the floor. I couldn't stay still. Perhaps I'd finally hit that sweet spot where my tiredness would step aside and my whole body would fall into energy overdrive, so I could at least function at a basic level.

'How long until your meeting?' Martina asked.

'Should be anytime now.'

'Okay, you need to relax though! And fix your hair. Do you need hairspray?'

'I mean, if you have some…'

'Of course!' she said while opening her humongous handbag and rummaging through it.

'Got a shovel in there I can borrow?'

'You think it's funny, but you try leaving the house and forgetting your son's favourite toy. You'll never make that mistake again.'

'Is that what's in there?'

'Yeah, it's mostly stuffed with Pokémon crap.'

'Oh, now I'm jealous of your bag,' I said with a smile.

'Here,' she said while handing me the hairspray. 'You can also use concealer for your eye bags.'

'You think the concealer you use on your beautiful olive skin will somehow work on my ghost-like appearance?'

'Yeah, better not.'

I sprayed my hair and filled the office with its "tropical" scent. 'Thanks,' I said, handing it back to her.

'Anytime, my dear.'

The door to our office opened suddenly and my boss, Bradley, entered with a big smile which gave too much attention to his ridiculous black moustache.

'Vincent? Can you come to my office for a few minutes?'

'Sure,' I said while pulling my hair back.

'Good luck,' Martina whispered. I smiled back at her and followed Bradley into the corridor.

'It won't take long,' he said.

He walked so fast I could barely keep up with him. He showed me the way to his office and opened the door.

'After you,' he said.

I entered and took a seat on the black leather chair facing his desk. I gave him a smile, hoping it would help me out. He sat down in front of me and pulled a little folder out of his drawer.

'How are you, Vincent?' he asked.

'I am very well, thanks for asking.'

'Things at home okay?' he probed.

'Uhm...yeah, sure.'

'You know you can take time off if you—'

'No, no. I need to be here. Honestly.'

'Okay, let's get down to business. How long have you been with us at the BBC, Vincent?'

'Over four years,' I said, grinning.

'Over four years...'

'Bradley, just let me know if I got it. We don't have to—'

'You didn't get it,' he quickly interrupted.

'I didn't—'

'Vincent, I'm so sorry. This business is extremely competitive and there were so many people after the position.'

'I have a master's degree in screenwriting! I have worked in this company for nearly half a decade.'

'...in human resources,' he pointed out.

My face flushed red. 'I thought it'd be easier to move internally. Jesus, Bradley. I barely took any holidays! I basically live here.'

'Vincent, you know I value you very much, but—'

'What?'

'You know,' he said while rubbing the back of his neck. 'These last two years, and especially these last few months...your situation at home...'

'I'm doing my fucking best, Bradley.'

'I know,' he said, nodding. 'It just wasn't enough to get into the writers' training program.'

The news hit me like lightning. Everything I had worked for was a complete waste of time. I couldn't do anything right. I was just so sick of it all.

'Are you sure I can't help you with anything at home?' he asked, tending his hand to mine. 'If you need some time away from it, you can stay at mine. I have a spare room.'

'No. I'm fine,' I said, putting my hand away. 'Same as it always is? I have to wait another year to apply again?'

'Yeah, you know the drill by now.'

'Did they even read my script, Bradley?' I asked, while standing up.

'Yeah, of course they did. Perhaps you need to find something new. They weren't thrilled enough from what I heard. I'm sorry.'

'Okay, thanks,' I said. 'It's been an absolute blast.'

'Go home for the afternoon. Get some rest.'

'I don't want to go home!' I lashed out. Bradley's eyes widened as if I scared him. 'I'm sorry. I'm sorry. Sure, maybe you're right.'

'Vincent, I can't help you if you don't tell me what is happening.'

'What are you going to do? It's my mess. Only *I* can clean it up.'

I hesitated for a second and took a deep breath.

'Thank you, Bradley. Actually...I *will* take the afternoon off, if you don't mind.'

Bradley nodded, I left the room and closed the office door. I walked slowly down the corridor, passing all the people randomly gossiping with each other, until I finally reached my office.

I opened the door and Martina's face looked like she was ready to celebrate, but my expression quickly dulled hers.

'No! You're joking!' she said.

'Nope. Nothing. Again.'

'What will you do?'

'Well, for one, I'll be buying myself a gigantic bottle of wine and I'll drink it in front of the TV, by myself, in my room. My therapist will love that.'

'Why don't you come for dinner at mine? Come play with the baby! That'll keep your mind off things.'

'Martina, I'm used to this kind of rejection. I've been with this company for so long. I know how things work,' I said while grabbing my backpack and putting my laptop under my arm. 'Bradley told me I could leave early, so…I'll see you tomorrow?'

'All right. Don't go crazy with the wine!'

'I won't…' I smiled at her and left as quickly as I could. It was pouring down and I didn't have an umbrella. I put my laptop inside my bag and made my way home. Nothing could stop me from napping in the middle of the afternoon now.

For once, the train journey was a breeze. By skipping rush hour completely, I was home in no time. Unfortunately, the walk from Wandsworth Town station to my flat was the moment where the heavens decided to take their shit out on me and pissed cats and dogs like it was the end of the world.

I finally reached the front door to my building and escaped the torrential rain. I grabbed the post and walked up a flight of stairs. I was about to open the door to my flat when I heard footsteps coming down from above.

Fuck.

'Vincent is that you?' she shouted on her way down.

'Yes, Georgina.'

She took a look at my drenched self. 'Is it raining outside?'

I paused. 'What can I do for you, Georgina?'

'A few things. First of all, the music, it's so late at night…it can't go on. It's too loud!'

'Got ya.'

'And one more thing, Vincent.'

I raised my eyebrows to prompt her to tell me.

'The rent. It's now over fifteen days late. I've given you the benefit of the doubt, but this is seriously late now. I have a mortgage to pay—'

'What do you mean you haven't received the rent?' I asked, quite abruptly.

'Well, it usually gets deposited into my account at the beginning of each month. Has something happened?'

I closed my eyes and took a deep, steadying breath.

Why, today of all days? Couldn't the universe just give me a break? I was on the edge of mental collapse. I shoved my hands into my jacket pockets to hide how bad they shook.

'I will make sure you get the rent money, Georgina. I promise. I'm sorry.'

'Thank you, darling. And take a nice warm shower, or you'll catch your death.'

One could hope...

'I will,' I said, giving her a tight smile. 'Have a nice evening.'

I entered our flat, hanging my jacket on the hook by the door. Kyle's room was locked, techno music pulsing from behind the door, instantly setting my teeth on edge and kicking my mood even further into the gutter. My heart was beating at a sonic rate. One deep, soothing breath in, and I knocked on the door.

The music cut off and Kyle's head appeared in a gap between the door and the frame. His hair was a mess, unkempt and shining with grease. Bleary, bloodshot eyes he could barely keep open.

'Hey,' I said, fighting for calm. 'Listen...I'm going to need you to tell me the truth, so don't lie. I had a disgusting day. I gave you the money for rent weeks ago. Have you given it to Georgina?'

'Oops,' he said with a giggle.

'Is that a no?'

'Sorry, it slipped my mind,' he slurred.

I looked at the ceiling, trying to calm myself down so I wouldn't choke him.

'Do you still have the money?' I was vibrating with anger.

'I...could get the money. I just need some time.'

'You spent it?!'

'Maybe?'

I turned on my heel and stalked into the kitchen. I needed to calm myself down. I couldn't believe it. I looked around, taking in my surroundings finally. Maybe I could believe it. The house was a tip. There were pizza boxes scattered on every available surface, dishes that needed washing and dirty clothes everywhere. Kyle staggered in behind me, the smell rolling off him made my eyes almost water.

'I can't do this anymore, Kyle.'

'What do you mean?'

'You!' I shouted. 'This shitty behaviour! You're a fucking junkie and I can't take it anymore. I am done!'

'Oh, you don't mean it,' he scoffed.

'I mean it. I have meant it for the last two years! I am done with you and your shit!'

'You don't understand how I feel!' he screamed.

'Kyle, your sister died...two years ago. I have helped in every way I can. I gave you space, I offered to take you to counselling, I have tried to get close to you and listen to you. I have turned a blind eye to all the fucking random drug addicts you bring around every evening—'

'They're my friends!' he shouted. He grabbed a dusty vase off the counter and threw it clear across the room with a guttural roar, smashing it against the wall.

I took a few steps back, looking at him. He was not the man I married. A part of me was actually frightened of him and what he could do to me.

'I'm done, Kyle,' I said, my voice shaking, disbelief at the reality of my life. 'Either you go, or I go. But I refuse to be under the same roof as you for one second longer,' I said, taking the stairs two at a time.

'Vincent, please. Don't be like this! I'm in pain!' his voice twisted with anguish.

I turned around, halfway up the stairs, looking down at him. 'I have also been in pain. For years, Kyle. Soul destroying pain. I have poured myself into this relationship, I have tried to get you to get help, and you want none of it. You're content to sit in your own filth, fill your body with fuck knows what, and stick your dick in any willing hole. I am so beyond fucking done. It's over. Leave, or I'll call the police.' My voice was sharp but as soon as the words were out, I knew they were true.

'You fucking leave!' his voice was laced with pure rage.

I looked at his face, his skin flushed and veins protruding. His once bright eyes, full of life, now hollow pits in his gaunt face. The ghosts of all the doubts I had before marrying him were suffocating me. I truly wished I could go back and slap myself, force myself to follow my instincts.

'I should have known you'd never change,' I said, turning my back on him. Like a vice, his hand wrapped around my arm. I ripped it out of his grip, adrenaline flooding my body. He lost his balance, out of shock or from whatever he'd flooded his system with, and fell down the four steps below him, landing on his ungrateful ass.

'Don't. Ever. Touch me,' I didn't bother to hide my utter disgust. The unexpected touch an instant flashback to a dark night on a Swedish beach. 'Look at you! You can't even stand on your feet! You're a fucking joke. Just tell me if you're going to leave or if I am. I promise you, Kyle, if I lay eyes on you in hell it will be too fucking soon.'

'Fine, I'm going out,' he staggered to his feet, slamming the door on the way out.

I sat on the stairs, wrapped my arms around my head and screamed. Screaming gave way to crying, ugly open mouth crying. I was so tired. I was tired of not being valued at work, I was tired of weekly therapy, I was tired of all my friends moving away from me and I was so fucking tired of being trapped in a marriage with a monster. I pulled my phone out and scrolled down my contacts to find his other sister, Amber. It rang for a bit, until she finally picked up.

'Hello?' she said in a Southern accent.

'Hey, it's Vincent.' I tried to not sniff in her ear.

'How are you?' she asked.

'I'm going to need you to fly to London and pick your brother up.'

'What?'

'You need to come here and take him away from me. Before I call the police and get him arrested for drug possession or selling, or who knows what.'

I didn't give her a choice. Whatever shred of affection I had left for Kyle had officially left my body. I wanted no part in such a shit life anymore.

It was time to sort my life out.

Hanging up from Amber's assurances that she would get the next possible flight, I broke into Kyle's room. The windows were covered with blankets. Apparently, he'd had the coordination to nail the bastard things to the wall. The only light source in the absolute pit of a room was a string of fairy lights, haphazardly woven through the slats of his headboard. For the first time in a year, I was in the room my husband slept in. Initially, when his younger sister passed, he had slept in the spare room downstairs so he wouldn't bother me with his night terrors, but I knew he wanted to be alone more than anything.

The death of his sister was due to an incredibly tragic car accident, no doubt at all, but he had already been dabbling with a few recreational drugs before that. It had started small; nothing really, just a joint here and there when he felt "stressed" mostly. Then that wasn't enough. Nothing was enough; and he spiraled out of control with crystal meth.

I'd gotten him into rehab the first-time round, but it didn't take. No matter how much he promised me he wanted to stop, when he was high off his face all that he wanted was the next high.

I pushed stuff around with my foot, not entirely willing to plunge uncovered hands into the ankle-deep sea of who the fuck knows what that covered the ground. Takeaway containers, empty glass bottles from various types of alcohol – some had graduated from the floor to be packed full of cigarette butts. Condom wrappers, shoes, plates. I could see syringes scattered from a box of "repurposed" NHS needles. I was horrified. This was what had been happening under my roof for over a year now. This had been happening while I spent my days and evenings at work, trying to get noticed for a freaking job that wouldn't drive me insane. Work didn't notice me, and Kyle was too deep in his own rubble to remember I existed, unless he needed money. That was the sum of my life.

I grabbed a bunch of bin liners and rummaged around until I found a pair of thick gardening gloves. Back in his room, I ripped the blankets off the windows and shoved them open, light and breathable air flooding into the room. Any drugs I found, I tossed in a shoe box I rescued from the floor. I knew what his priorities were.

I was unstoppable. His clothes, shoes, CDs, and everything I could put my hands on, were dumped inside the bags.

I didn't stop until late evening, when the room was basically emptied, and the bed stripped back. Kyle wasn't going to come home that night. He went to his "friend's" place, where they'd spend the night smoking from a pipe or sticking needles in their arms and fucking each other blind.

I grabbed a piece of paper from the printer and wrote in thick black letters '*I want a divorce.*' I placed the note above his bags of stuff, packed a bag and left. No desire to share a space with even the lingering scent of my failed marriage.

I found myself around Notting Hill, where Bradley lived. I knocked on his door and he opened it.

'Vincent...' he said, with raised eyebrows.

'Hey. Can I take you up on that offer of staying the night here?' I asked with tears in my eyes.

'Yeah, of course. Come in.'

He let me inside and gave me a hug. As soon as I felt his touch I started sobbing uncontrollably.

'Hey, hey. It's okay,' he said while patting me on the back.

I needed that.

After taking the longest shower, I sat on his sofa, with my hair still wet. He sat next to me, pouring red wine into two glasses. Bradley's home was cosy, with a grey fluffy carpet and a wallpaper covered with sunflowers. He lived by himself, with a chubby ginger cat. There were a few Jesus statues disseminated around the room, along with a few crucifixes hanging on the wall. I didn't realise he was such a devoted Christian.

'Thanks, Brad. And thanks for letting me borrow a pair of pyjamas,' I said with a smile.

'You're absolutely welcome,' he said while taking his glass and offering me mine. 'What happened this time?'

'I don't want to bore you with my marital problems.'

'You can tell me anything!'

'Well,' I said after taking a sip of wine. 'Kyle has taken my rent money and spent it on drugs.'

'God.'

'It's done. I'm done. It was long overdue...'

'You did the right thing. You've stayed there long enough.'

'I just felt so bad. He was grieving, at first, but now...he needs help, and I can't provide that for him.'

'You need help too,' he said, putting a hand on my thigh. 'You gave it your all. You tried everything you could.'

'I like to think I did.'

'You did, Vincent. It's time for you to move on.'

'Thank you.'

I gulped the entire glass and sighed. 'Thank you for letting me crash, this is perfect.'

'I'm glad,' he smiled. His hand was still on my lap. He looked at it and then looked at me. He moved a little bit closer, so I panicked and got up quickly.

'I'm going to brush my teeth and go to bed, I think. It's been an exhausting day.'

He nodded. He seemed to understand nothing was going to happen between us.

I walked to the bathroom and looked at myself in the mirror. I was looking forward to a night of absolute rest. I couldn't remember the last time I'd managed to have an uninterrupted night's sleep. I'd spent so many nights locked in my room worried Kyle's friends would come upstairs and bash me in the head during a drug trip.

I brushed my teeth and smiled at the mirror, wondering what I'd do next with my life.

I left Bradley's flat before he woke up. I was in the backseat of a taxi, looking through the window at a London that hadn't quite woken up yet. We passed a still sleepy Westminster, with the sun shining onto the Thames and reflecting into my eyes.

I grabbed my phone and scrolled for Martina's contact.

'Vincent?' she said, sounding sleepy.

'Sorry, did I wake you up?' I asked.

'I have a two-year-old. What do you think?'

I smiled. 'Hey, listen—'

'Are you okay?' she interrupted.

'Yeah, yeah I'm fine. Uhm...I need to ask you a favour.'

'Sure, anything.'

'I'm not coming back to work, Martina.'

'What do you mean?'

I scratched my head and looked at the road ahead. 'I'll be going away for a while, but I have no plans of coming back to work. Would you be so kind as to put my office stuff inside a box and keep it safe for me?'

'Of course, but...are you sure you won't be coming back?'

'I can't stay. There's nothing there for me. I promised myself I wouldn't wait another year to have a shot at my dream.'

'You better still see me outside of work!' she said.

'That goes without saying.'

We remained in silence for a few seconds.

'...so, where are you going to go?' she asked.

'It's a secret for now,' I chuckled. 'I'll send you a postcard.'

'Well, good luck, my love.'

'Thank you,' I said. I hung up the phone and quickly looked for another contact.

'Hey you!' I said, enthusiastically. 'I know we haven't spoken in some time, but I just wanted to let you know that I finally left my husband, my shit job, and I am on my way to you. I'm really looking forward to seeing your pretty face again. Call me when you get this message.'

I closed the call and put my headphones in. I played some music and focused on the beautiful view from the window.

I couldn't wait for what was to come.

Chapter Twenty-Two

Teddy

2020

Wearing a suit outside work always felt wrong to me. I had the privilege of wearing a navy suit for fifteen hours at a time when on an aircraft, so I'd usually stay away from them on my days off.

But this was a special occasion.

I was standing there, by the altar, wearing a skinny dark burgundy suit I'd bought on a layover in Singapore. My hair was slicked back, my face was freshly shaven, and I could not stop smiling.

Everyone looked impeccable, and part of me laughed a little, as I couldn't quite believe how many gay guys were sitting inside this church. Paddington Uniting Church in Sydney had already celebrated quite the array of same-sex ceremonies in the few years since gay marriage had become legal in Australia. Had those ceremonies been as gay as this one? Probably not.

The string quartet started playing Canon in D and the notes echoed around the inside of the church. It was whimsical.

Aidan started walking down the aisle accompanied by his mother. His face was glowing, with a bright smile and shiny shoes tapping slowly heading towards the altar. His mother was filled with emotion and looked as if she was trying not to cry.

Aidan and I locked eyes and smiled at each other. I fixed my bow tie and waited patiently for the groom.

It was a day celebrating pure love and I couldn't be happier for Aidan and his soon-to-be husband. Aidan had become a really good friend of mine after we'd decided dating wasn't for us. So, I stood still, with the other best men. My feet suffered inside a pair of new faux leather shoes, but I was excited to see yet another friend being married off.

The reception was outdoors; the grooms capitalised on a beautiful spring day. I was standing in a corner stuffing my face with crab cakes and drinking the only glass of champagne I was allowed, as a few hours later I would have to get my ass into my uniform and jump onto the inaugural flight to London. The airline I worked for had just opened the new route and I was going to be the flight manager on its maiden trip.

I couldn't wait.

Aidan walked towards me, probably worried I wasn't having enough fun.

'Hello handsome,' he said, slightly tipsy.

'You can't call me that anymore. You're a taken man.'

'I am!' he smiled. 'Tell me you're having fun.'

'I am having the most fun, Aidan. Everything is beautiful and you're positively dashing. You know, this could have been us,' I said, pointing at the reception.

'Oh, for sure! You missed out on all of this,' he said, pointing at his body. 'Am I the only one who's had like six glasses of champagne or...?'

'I can only have one. I'm going to visit my mum and then I'll head to the airport. There's a direct flight to London I have to be on.'

'That's so exciting!' he shouted while putting his hand on my shoulder. 'You've finally made it, Clarke.'

'Thanks. And...I'm really happy for you, Aidan. You're the nicest guy I know. You really deserve to be happy.'

He smiled at me.

'I have to go now. Please be responsible with how many more drinks you have. Wouldn't want for your parents to pick you up in a catatonic state.'

'I will try,' he said, doing a peace sign.

'Enjoy your special day,' I said, sending an air kiss.

I walked away and headed to my parked car, my trusted old Jeep Wrangler, which desperately needed a wash. I jumped in and quickly made my way to see my mother.

I walked up the corridor in the hospice leading to my mum's new room. They were still doing works to expand the structure, and my mum was currently in a different wing, so she wouldn't hear the noise. It'd really upset her. I got to the room and had to squint to see because of the dark.

'You doing a ritual to Satan, Haze?' I asked.

'Do. Not. Speak,' she said while working on her laptop and holding her forehead.

'What happened?'

'Nothing here. Your mum has been asleep for a few hours. I think the new medication makes her even sleepier.'

'I see,' I said while getting close to mum and caressing her hair. 'Hi, mum.'

I turned to Hazel and raised my eyebrows.

'So why are you still here? You didn't have to stay.'

'Well, first of all, this silence is amazing. I've gotten so much work done, you wouldn't believe it! But mainly,' she stood up, holding her pregnant belly. '...I have stayed because I'm so close to the toilet, for whenever I have to throw my guts up.'

'Morning sickness has moved into the afternoon?'

'You know it!'

'Oh, that's all right, though! Another five months of this and you'll be done! Isn't that a nice thought?'

'I would hit you in the head if I could walk over there without vomiting.'

I smiled at her and changed the water for the flowers.

'How was the wedding? Did you guys lock eyes and realise you were actually made for each other all along?'

'God no. Do you think Aidan is the one who got away?'

'Oh no. He is nice to look at, though.'

'That's what Instagram stalking's for. I don't have to marry him to see his shirtless photos at the gym!'

'I'm avoiding Instagram at all costs. If I see a photo of avo on toast, I'll heave on the spot.'

'Christ, woman. This won't be a fun pregnancy.'

'You're telling me. Anyways...you look good! You excited about your flight? You're a senior now! You get to be flight chief bitch and all!'

'Yeah! My first time in London in forever and I will get to spend it sitting in my hotel room pulling reports out of my ass and answering stupid e-mails.'

'But who else gets to call themselves *chief bitch*?'

'This bitch,' I said pointing at myself. 'Where's the baby daddy by the way?'

'He's gone to the gym. He needed some time away because every time I go to the bathroom to vomit, he feels like vomiting too.'

'There have been so many mentions of vomit in this conversation today, Hazel.'

'It's because there has been so. Much. Vomit. Teddy!' she shouted.

'Oh my god, even I am about to gag,' I said, putting a hand in front of my mouth. 'Will you and Mitchell be all right checking in on Mum? I know you're all baby-crazy, but I will be in Bali for a few days for my layover on my way back to Sydney. I figured two direct long-ass flights in a row would destroy me.'

'I want to go to Bali now.'

'Maybe we can all go one day when the little monster pops out of your uterus.'

'No, Mitchell and I can go, and you look after it.'

'It?'

'Yep.'

'Shit, okay. I'm really hoping my good old happy friend Hazel makes a comeback by the time I return, because this one is terrifying.'

'Just...being pregnant is horrible.'

I leaned towards her and gave her a kiss on the cheek. 'You be a good girl, okay?'

'Good luck with your bossing around. You'll do great. Enjoy the power trip!'

'Can't wait!' I said while opening the door. I looked at my mum peacefully sleeping and thought about how much I missed speaking to her. Like *really* speaking. There was nothing left of her, just an empty body that she could no longer control. I really missed my mum.

* * *

The flight was a success. I was really lucky with the team I had been assigned, so it mostly went smoothly. Apart from the hen party celebrating the last of a Sydney yummy mummies group to get married. They terrorised the entire flight. Never had we ever been so close to completely finishing our whole alcohol supply mid-flight. I still managed to laugh at the whole situation. No old man had a heart attack and only a few babies cried.

The rest of the crew all went out for drinks and I was left alone in my hotel room staring at my laptop trying to get all of the paperwork done. Throughout my career I'd meet hundreds upon hundreds of new people, but there would always be a little part of me that felt lonely. So many nights spent in a bland hotel room, scrolling through a list of headless torsos on Grindr, chatting to one or two for a bit and maybe, just maybe, inviting one around for meaningless hotel sex. That's if the jetlag didn't bash me in the head, forcing me to fall asleep in the middle of the afternoon.

I didn't have enough energy to make any sort of English hook-ups happen. I was wearing a fleecy white robe, along with the little soft slippers that I'd found in the bathroom, for which my feet were way too big to fit into. My hair was still wet from the hour-long bath I'd taken, and I was lying on the bed, staring at the ceiling. The TV in the room was turned up loud, playing Disney Channel of all things.

I had dedicated the latter half of my twenties to juggling between the job and visiting my mother; but seeing Mitchell and Hazel starting a family together really started to make me wonder at what point I would be able to start one of my own.

I got out of bed and walked towards the window. There wasn't much to see. The hotel was very close to Heathrow, so my view consisted of highways and other gigantic hotels. I really needed to do something. I'd spent a day and a half without leaving the hotel, and I had pretty much only been to the pool, the sauna for a few seconds, and the gym for even less time. I was bored, but at the same time I didn't want to do much else.

I was in London, staring at its grey sky, thinking of the few other times I'd been here. Thinking about how long ago it felt. I was a different person then. I was spontaneous, and probably in love. I wondered if I would ever fall in love again.

I closed the curtains and jumped back onto the bed. I grabbed my phone and opened Grindr.

The night eventually passed. I was arranging for a guy to come over, but that was the exact moment when I fell asleep. Phone in hand and all.

I was excited about spending a few days in Bali, so I was hoping the plane would get me there as soon as possible. I was standing up, looking at all the passengers from the end of the aisle, ready to recite my script, which no one would listen to. One time I'd even cursed in the middle of it, and no one noticed.

'Hello and thank you for flying with Osprey Airlines— This is flight OA1091 from London Heathrow to Bali,' I jazzily said. 'A few announcements as we begin our flight. Everyone should have a look at the safety card that is in the seat pocket in front of you. Not only does it have pretty pictures, but it also has important information about the location and how to operate all exits and explains the safety features of this aircraft. Please keep your seatbelts fastened whenever the seatbelt light is on. To be safe, we recommend your seatbelt stays fastened whenever you're in your seat, just in case there is unexpected turbulence.'

Everyone was still looking at their phones. I had just walked past dozens of people telling them to remove their earphones, but as soon as I went past, they'd put them back in. I'd slap them in the face if we *actually* had to land on water.

'Also unlikely, is the possibility of a water landing,' I announced. This would usually be the part they'd actually listen to. 'But just in case, a pouch containing a life vest is located under your seat. In first class, they're between the seats at floor level. Take it out of the plastic bag and place the vest over your head. The strap goes around your waist and attaches with a buckle. Pull on the end of the strap to tighten. As you leave the aircraft, pull sharply on the red plastic handles to inflate. The vest can also be inflated by blowing into the red tubes at both shoulders. A water-activated locator light is attached at shoulder level. Keep in mind that your seat cushion is not a flotation device, so please, don't take it home with you! It won't match your furniture anyway,' I laughed.

'As the crew comes through to make a final cabin check, please let them know if you need any help. My name is Edward and I'm your flight manager; if you have any questions about our flight today, please don't hesitate to ask one of our flight attendants. Thank you.'

After putting all the demonstration crap away, I sat in my seat and fastened my belt.

I closed my eyes ready for take-off and waited for the plane to fly. I'd still get a rush every time I'd finish my speech.

We were in the middle of the flight when my colleague Kate came to see me while I was just getting dressed after a quick nap. It was time for hers, so she seemed quite eager to get me out of bed.

'Everything alright?' I asked.

She rolled her eyes. 'It would have been perfect. Almost everyone is asleep, except for the guy in 14A who keeps pressing the call button.'

'What's wrong with him?'

'He keeps ordering glasses of wine,' she said. 'Relentlessly.'

'Maybe he's trying to knock himself out. Not everyone can sleep on a plane. I had to teach myself at first.'

'I think I've served him like ten.'

I giggled. 'That's nothing. It's probably some *bogan* going crazy with the free wine button. I'll take over, anyways.'

'I am so tired!' she said with a yawn.

I buttoned up my shirt and tightened my tie knot. I checked my hair and surprisingly it didn't look too bad.

Kate climbed into bed still wearing her uniform.

'Girl, get into your pyjamas or you're going to look as if you just came out of a tumble drier when you get up!'

'Fine, fine!' she said.

Then the call button was pressed again. 14A was at it again, apparently.

'See? I told you! He's getting faster at drinking them too. Maybe you should cut him off!'

'I'll see if he's cute or nice enough, and make a decision based on that.'

I looked at the screen to see what he had ordered, and this time it was two glasses of wine, and a bag of chips. 'I need to go tell him he can't order two at a time.'

'Just put it into a drip and give it to him, so we can all rest for once.'

I poured the wine into a glass and placed it on a tray, along with a bag of ready salted chips. I walked down the aisle to find the guy's seat. He had two free seats next to him, and he was gazing out the window.

'Sir? I have your order. We couldn't bring two—'

And then he turned around.

I thought I was dreaming or hallucinating from being recently awake. His hair was a little bit longer, his face a little paler, but it was him.

'Vincent...?'

He looked at me for a second, widening his eyes and raising his eyebrows. Then quickly grabbed a sick bag and loudly hurled into it.

I stood there incredulous.

...and a little grossed out by the vomit.

CHAPTER TWENTY-THREE

VINCENT

2020

It didn't make any sense. I didn't plan for it to happen. Flying to Bali was an incredibly spontaneous thing I had decided on a whim that morning. I had taken many planes in the last six years since Teddy had become a flight attendant and I had never seen him on board. Literally the day after I decide to get a divorce and leave Kyle forever, there he was. Bearing alcoholic gifts and witnessing me regurgitate my dinner into a paper bag.

Was it fate? Was it the kind of crap people bang on about when they wanted to be romantic? Was the last decade just some sort of trial to get me on a motherfucking last-minute flight to Bali of all places?

'Wait for me outside,' he said to me. I'd left the aircraft in a hurry, so I could hit the bathroom to fix my face and hair as quickly as possible before he'd come out looking like a perfect Hollywood actor dressed as a flight attendant.

So I sat just outside the arrival area, close enough so that I could see him as soon as he came out. My whole body was shaking in trepidation. I kept twisting one of my rings, biting my lip, and my legs felt fidgety.

Then there he was. Walking and talking to his co-workers, looking impeccable, as if we hadn't been on the same god damned sixteen-hour flight. I stood up and cleared my throat. I walked towards him, and he stood still, looking me in the eyes and smiling.

I wasn't sure what I was going to say; I wasn't sure what I was going to do. I got close to him and after a pause for a split-second, we hugged each other.

We hugged for long.

'Judging from your face earlier, I'd say you weren't aware I was working that flight?' he asked.

'I was so drunk I didn't even know *I* was on that flight.'

We looked at each other and I realised how much we'd both changed. Him? For the better. His face just looked a lot more grown-up, with a square jaw and sharp cheekbones. His body also looked a little bit more buff than I remembered. His hair was slicked back, and his eyes were as piercing as they had always been. There he was, looking like that, while I was barely able to stand up on my stupidly trembling legs, freaking the fuck out that Teddy was once again in front of me.

We hadn't kept in touch these past few years. Neither of us posted much on social media anymore. The days of over-sharing were truly gone. I had so many questions to ask him. I wondered what his life was like now. I wondered if he was with somebody. I wondered if he still cared about me.

'Do you want to share a car? So, we can talk?' he asked, as we reached the taxi rank outside. 'I assume we are going to the same place!' he smiled.

I nodded and followed him. Why the hell was he so chilled about our ridiculous encounter? No one would believe me if I told them Teddy fucking Clarke was on my flight. I was truly speechless, and that didn't happen very often.

'You know the way, then?' I asked.

'Yeah, I get to come here quite often, actually.'

'You do? Damn, I'm jealous.'

'I do love it, although sometimes I'm a little too exhausted to enjoy it. I just lie by the pool and try to get a tan.'

'How's this new life of yours treating you?' I asked.

He looked at me, squinting his eyes from the sunlight. 'It's good. I think I have finally managed to do something right, if that makes sense?'

'Yeah. It does.'

'So, what about you? What's been happening? How's marriage?'

'It's—'

'We almost there!' the driver interrupted.

'Yeah, it's not very far from the airport,' Teddy said. He looked at me once again. 'I can't believe you were on my flight. I'm...I don't even know what to say, really.'

'Me neither. I'm still partially convinced I'm having a weird drunken dream.'

We remained in silence for a few minutes, until the car parked in front of a little resort.

'Is this it?' I asked, looking outside the window.

'That's the one!' he said while handing the driver some cash.

'Oh, I can—'

'Don't worry. I get spending money through the company,' he said.

We both opened the doors and exited the car. It looked like we had just reached the jungle. The resort was small and made of big round wooden huts, surrounded by greenery. We both entered the reception area, walking side by side.

The place was called *Ahimsa* and it was so damn quiet, my own thoughts were echoing inside my head.

'Mister Clarke,' said a peaceful receptionist talking like she was on one too many Valiums.

Teddy smiled at her and approached her. I was incredibly confused as to where I was. My whole stressed being was physically rejecting such a quiet, chilled place.

'My men!' we heard coming from behind us.

We both turned around and there she was, barefoot, wearing some sort of beige kimono and with her hair tied up with what looked like a bamboo stick. Laura was the owner of the entire resort.

'Hey, gorgeous,' Teddy said, going towards her and giving her a hug.

'Vincent, I haven't seen your stupid face in almost two years!' she said.

'Mate, what the fuck is this place?' I said, while also giving her a hug.

'This is where I, and city douchebags like you, come to find inner peace!' she said. 'I can't believe I get to have you both here with me.'

'I cannot wait to get pampered,' said Teddy.

'Amazing! I hope you guys don't mind, but I only have one room available,' she said while smiling at us and raising her eyebrows. 'You didn't give me a hell of a lot of notice, Vincent.'

'Sorry, it was a bit of an impromptu voyage for me.'

'I'd say! You didn't bring anything?'

'Oh yeah,' said Teddy, looking at me. 'No luggage?'

I blushed and looked away. 'I was in some kind of rush. I'll get some clothes from this shop, or something.' I said while pointing at the little shop next to reception.

'You'll look great in a sarong, Vincent.'

'Okay, I'm sorry, I have to ask. What is this about?' I asked, pointing at the resort around us.

Teddy was giggling silently.

'We can talk about it over dinner. Why don't you guys get settled first?'

'Alright,' I said. 'Do we get keys?'

'There are no keys here,' she said while holding her palms up to the sky.

'You have got to be shitting me, woman.'

'Come on,' Teddy said. 'Let's get London boy to relax.'

He put his hand on my shoulder and led me away from the reception desk.

'See you guys later!' she shouted.

◦ ❦ ◦

The rooms of the—let's just call it a hotel—were also little standalone bamboo huts surrounded by trees and mosquitoes. A little bit like glamping— just without the Wi-Fi.

'Isn't this amazing?' Teddy said, trying not to laugh.

'Who was that woman and what has she done to my Laura?'

'She had a difficult time before managing to get this whole project started. I'm sure she will explain it to you at dinner.'

'Alright. Is there a shower, at least? Please tell me there's a shower.'

'Yeah. It's very cool actually. Let me show you,' he said. 'Close your eyes.'

'You serious?'

'Yes, come on.'

I closed my eyes and let him guide me. He held my hand and pulled me to a different part of the room.

'Open them,' he commanded.

I opened my eyes and my jaw dropped open. My eyes were graced by a gigantic view of mountains covered in greenery, exotic birds and, best of all, free-roaming elephants eating leaves. I turned to Teddy and saw the look of satisfaction on his face.

'This is the only room where you can take a shower while looking at the elephants. Sometimes they come really close and you can pet them,' he said.

'This is incredible,' I said, my eyes still drinking in the beauty in front of me.

'They-re all rescued from circuses or abuse for the sake of tourism. They get to live here in peace. That's why I love coming here so much. Apart from seeing Laura, of course.'

'And she did all this herself?'

'Pretty much.'

I was speechless.

'Hey, Teddy...'

'Yes?'

'It's really good to see you,' I said with a timid smile.

He smiled back. 'Right. I'm going to leave you to your shower.'

'Is this it?' I said, pointing at the completely open shower. 'I shower in what is essentially a terrace, facing a herd of elephants?'

'Yeah,' he giggled. 'It's oddly liberating. Being naked in front of such spectacular nature? You're never going to do anything cooler than that.'

'Alright, fine. Then you must take me somewhere where I can buy some clothes, please. I can't go another minute in this outfit.'

'Sounds good. I'll leave you to it.'

He left me alone and I just stood there, staring at the elephants. I took all my clothes off and felt like I had lost my mind. I was completely naked in the middle of the jungle.

'Well, that was one of the best experiences I've ever had!' I said, as I came back inside the bedroom, trying to tie a sarong around my waist.

Teddy was getting undressed. He was only wearing a shirt and a pair of boxers.

'Oh, sorry,' I said, as if I had never seen Teddy's thighs before.

'Are we doing that?'

'What?'

'The whole walking-on-hot-coals thing with each other,' he said while walking past me. 'By the way, sarong looks great. Bit transparent, perhaps!' he giggled.

I looked down and realised my knob was basically on full display.

'Shit!' I said, covering it with my hands. 'So, I guess I won't be wearing this down by reception.'

'Try not to frighten the other guests with that. It's a temple of peace,' he said while joining his hands together. 'I'm off to take a shower too. I'll be quick.'

He went to take his shower and I lay on the bed, turning my phone on for the first time since I had left the UK. There were dozens of missed calls from Kyle and a few worried messages from Bradley. I didn't want to deal with anyone. I turned it back off and enjoyed the fresh breeze blowing through the hut.

I closed my eyes for what I thought were a few minutes and when I re-opened them Teddy was lying next to me with a towel around his waist, reading a book.

'Was I asleep for long?' I asked.

'Like half an hour? I mean, you must be tired. You were up drinking while the whole plane was sleeping!'

'I can't sleep on planes,' I said, sitting up on the bed next to him. 'It is mad hot in here.'

'Yep. You'll get used to it!' he said. 'You still up for some shopping or...?'

'Sure. I'd love to cover up.'

'Can I ask you something?'

'Of course.'

'Why are you here by yourself? Last time I checked you were getting married and everything. Are things—'

'I'm done with that.'

Teddy looked as if he was trying to contain a smile.

'That's terrible!' he said.

'Is that a smirk, Clarke?'

'No, no. I would never. This is my upset face!' he said. 'Really, what happened?'

'Boy meets boy, boy meets drugs...you know...'

'Shit, really? Like serious addiction or like every gay on a Friday night?' he asked.

'Using my rent money for drugs kind of addiction.'

'Wow.'

'His baby sister died a few years ago and he never got over it. But there was a huge shift between grieving and actually turning into a shadow of his former self. He needs help; far more than I can give him. And using my money for drugs was unforgivable.'

'Do you still love him?'

'I think the horrible memories of the last few years have cancelled out whatever positive feelings I had for him. I just want him out of my life.'

'Fuck,' he said while looking at the empty space. 'Life hasn't been the kindest to either of us, has it?'

'It hasn't. Hey,' I said, turning to him. 'How's your mother?'

'We are at the end of the road. It's horrible what that disease has done to her, what it's done to our family. Part of me hopes she is actually gone and not trapped inside this nightmare. Does that make sense?'

'Does she ever...remember you?'

'No. Those days are long gone. We are just playing the waiting game. I just hope she goes...without pain.'

He turned to me, his eyes starting to tear up. 'I'm sorry, this is really depressing.'

'Hey, you can tell me anything,' I said putting my hand on his lap. 'I missed you. I missed talking to you. It used to come so naturally.'

'I know. It's my fault, really. I thought I'd get over you if I no longer spoke to you. I thought...I thought I'd forget you and forget what had happened between us, so I'd stop comparing you to every guy I met.'

'And did you?'

'Did I what?'

'Stop...'

'I thought I did...then I saw your pretty face on my flight.'

I looked at him and put my hand behind his ear.

'...and I'm an eighteen-year-old boy again,' he said.

'Teddy,' I whispered, half a breath between his face and mine. He leaned into me, his lips brushing against mine, gentle and sweet. I froze, more aware than ever at what was within reach. 'Teddy,' I said again, my voice firmer as I sat back. I watched his brow furrow, confusion on his lovely face.

'I'm sorry. I thought we were on the same page here.'

He traced my cheekbone, cupping my cheek like he had something fragile in hand. I suppose I was in a lot of ways.

'We are. We are, I'm sorry. But I just need to tell you this,' I said, swallowing hard. The number of times I'd alluded to what had happened to me all those years ago out loud were few, the number of times I said it out right, plainly were non-existent. I knew I couldn't drag all that... trauma into this, whatever this was. Teddy deserved better than what I had to offer, which was nothing, But I was selfish, and I wanted him, my wonderfully patient Teddy.

'Whatever you need, take your time.'

'Okay,' I took a deep breath. 'You know I was kicked out of the exchange program, right?' My pulse was racing for all the wrong reasons now.

'Yeah,' he nodded, taking my hand in both of his. Lending me his strength. I could tell him this.

'Something... happened to me in Sweden. With a man.' My mind took me back there. The sand under my nails. The water rippling in the dark. Teddy squeezed my fingers, bringing me back to him. 'I can't tell you everything just yet. I'm working on it, or I will be. But I've never had this before. You're so gentle with me Teddy. You look at me like I hung the moon and I'm afraid. I'm afraid of how much I want this when all I've had is pain.'

I felt the tears making their lonely trek down my face, heating as embarrassment coloured my cheeks.

'Oh Vincent. I'm so sorry.'

'Please don't pity me, Teddy.'

'Never. I admire how strong you are. You've pulled yourself from hell the best you could. How could I pity that?'

I sniffed, not at all graceful or sexy. I was sitting here with this gorgeous man, and I dragged up hell. Gosh I'd blown this, hadn't I?

'I've blown this haven't I?'

A laugh popped out of Teddy, surprised and pure.

'No, Vincent. Not at all. I'll always want you. You deserve gentle.'

His fingers gently touched the back of my head and I was done.

I pressed my lips against his, licked at the seam of his mouth asking silent permission to enter. A little gasp huffed out and my tongue slipped in. And oh, the taste of Teddy was heaven, pure sin and consuming desire. His hand skimmed down my side, electrifying my skin. I groaned into his mouth, rocking my hips forward, searching for friction, desperate for more.

It was powerful and consuming, and so incredibly right. He rolled on top of me, settling his firm body into the V of my open legs. Kissing my neck, licking, nipping, breathing on it. I skimmed my hands down his naked back, moaning as he playfully bit my ear lobe.

'You appear to be overdressed, Mr Stewart,' he smiled into my shoulder, pulling the thin fabric off my hips, leaving me bare and exposed for him. My cock was rock hard, laying against my stomach, twitching with need. Teddy's eyes devoured my body, pupils wide as he looked his fill. I was so impossibly turned on; I could barely contain myself. I had been denying myself his naked body for years, and now it was on top of me, waiting for me to touch and enjoy. I trailed my fingers down his muscular back, grabbing his firm ass with both of my hands. I pulled his towel off, desperate for his skin to be entirely against mine. His hard dick was against mine, delicious friction sending sparks of pleasure up my spine. We kissed again, I was frantic with desire, but Teddy seemed content to slow down, forcing me to as well. He pulled my bottom lip between his teeth, a bite of pain soothed with a gentle flick of his tongue.

He kissed down my neck, his tongue running along my clavicle. He kissed my chest, traced my nipple with his tongue, sucking it between his perfect lips. His hands were everywhere, dancing across my skin lighting my every nerve ending on fire. He nipped and kissed down my body, his hands on my thighs, pushing my legs wider. I looked down my own body, his brilliant green eyes bright and wild. Eyes locked together, he took my aching cock into his mouth, sucking, swirling his tongue around the head. He swallowed more of me while his hands traced imperceptible shapes on my skin. My hands clawed at the bed, hips desperate to thrust up, prevented only by my desire to not hurt him. No one had ever taken their time with me, looked at me the way Teddy did, some emotion I dared not even consider brimming in those magical eyes. He wrapped a hand around the base of my shaft, squeezing just enough to drive me crazy, his mouth sucking and biting the head to slowly send me over the edge. Torturously slow. His fingers grazed the overly sensitive skin behind my balls, my back bowing off the bed. He felt incredible, he *was* incredible, and I wanted nothing more than to get inside that tight body of his. I tugged on his hair, forcing his eyes back to mine and pushed him onto his back. I wasted no time swallowing his hard dick, the taste of pre cum making my own cock leak like crazy. Sliding my hands down his legs, I pushed on the backs of his thighs, moving them out of the way so I could get to my goal. I licked my way down, stopping only to suck each ball into my mouth, my body lighting up when he moaned and bucked his hips.

I held his legs up and put my mouth against his tight hole, licking, sucking, teasing. I pushed my tongue inside his body, rewarded by the uncontrollable, sexy sounds coming from his mouth, my name mixed in and desperate. I sucked my finger into my mouth, then pushed it into him, working him open. Two fingers and he groaned loudly, almost a sob. My name falling from his lips a plea. I pulled my fingers out, rubbed my spit into his now relaxed hole and crawled up to catch his mouth in a kiss. Our bodies were slick with sweat, needy, desperate to be joined.

I pressed the tip of my cock inside him, slipping past the first ring of muscle. I paused, giving his body time to adjust even though all I wanted to do was to slam my hips forward and take him. I kissed him again, pushing inside his body until I bottomed out. His hole was absolutely strangling my cock, and I sucked in air, desperately trying to not cum. I looked down at Teddy, his beautiful face a picture of ecstasy, eyes glazed. I rocked my hips, testing the movement, and started to fuck this perfect man until he was absolutely beyond speech. I pushed a leg back, changing the angle and he almost came off the bed, eyes rolled back in his head. His foot was right in my face and I couldn't even stop myself licking his sole, sucking and licking his toes. His other leg was over my shoulder and my cock was slamming into his ass. I wrapped my hand around him, squeezing his poor neglected dick and jerking him off. When I felt his body begin to tighten around me, I slowed down, licked the sweat off his smooth glistening chest and kissed him once more until he was breathless and needy. I pulled almost all the way out and fucked back into him, the angle shallow and he cried out my name. He pushed my hand off and started pumping his own cock, as I fucked him faster, harder. I ran my nose up his foot and my hands down his legs. His body arched, tight as a bow, choking my cock. My vision was blurry, stars and colours were all I saw as I unloaded every drop of cum in his impossibly tight ass. I was gasping for air, my chest tight and dripping with sweat. Teddy was completely slack under me, his stomach and chest striped, white with cum. I pulled out slowly, not wanting to hurt him, sitting back on my heels, I watched my semen drip from his used hole.

I wanted to do it all over again.

I put my arm under his head and moved it closer to me. I kissed him on the cheek.

'Fuck...' I muttered.

'Yeah,' he whispered, snuggling into my body.

We both lay there, staring at the hut ceiling, trying to gain our strength again. We were both exhausted, so I closed my eyes and fell asleep next to the only man I wanted to be with. His eyes fell shut, perfect lashes stark against even his tan skin. I traced my fingertip along the feathered edge, smiling as his eyes twitched at the contact. Thumb tracing over his cheekbone, palm against his cheek. I slipped my fingers through his hair, pulling his face closer to mine, and he came willingly, eagerly.

We had dinner on a platform that overlooked the sea. It was the kind of place you'd find on Instagram, photographed by insufferable travel bloggers. I was now being that type of arsehole, wearing a white linen shirt that wouldn't quite button all the way up and a sarong that was a little bit less see-through than the previous one. Teddy indulged me and bought a similar outfit himself, so I wouldn't feel too self-conscious about wearing an oversized skirt with my dick hanging out. The sound of the waves lapping the shore was incredibly special, and the table was decorated with a fruit basket and large red flowers.

Laura was wearing a long flowery dress with a matching headband and her incredibly long blond hair wrapped in a bun.

'I still can't get over this new you, Laura,' I said.

'You all should be thankful. These are the only bottles of wine available in the resort. It's a relatively strict no alcohol destination.'

'You're kidding me?' I asked.

'Nope, she is not,' Teddy said.

'So...how did this whole thing come about?' I asked while gesturing at the surroundings.

'It wasn't too long after you moved in with Kyle that my ankle really, really started to give me hell again. Dancing was no longer my escape. It became my torture. My whole body was struggling under the pressure of being a better, skinnier, or even taller person. Auditions were just a formality. Companies already knew who they were going to hire,' she gulped a whole glass of Chenin Blanc. 'I was done. I was done with it all. With the pain, with the industry. I was so tired and just overwhelmed by the city. Yeah, I could have moved back to Sardinia, but I was looking for a different culture altogether.'

'I'd say you found it,' Teddy said.

'This place! This place spoke to me. I loved the food, the people, and the culture. I loved doing yoga, meditation, hiking...it was just such an escape for me. I felt like I'd found my true self.'

'A hippy?' I asked.

'No! I created a place where more people could find that...element. We have a lot of classes where we just teach you how to simply breathe. I felt like I belonged here. Then, when everything started coming to fruition and this place was being built, a freaking elephant was roaming around the area! I couldn't believe my eyes.'

'Where did it come from?' I asked. 'Do elephants just roam around the island or...?'

'She'd escaped. I think she was used to carry tourists around or something. She was covered in scars. We looked at each other and there was this weird connection. I really responded to her expression. I promised her I was going to take care of her and...the rest is history. This place became a sanctuary, not just for people, but also to the beautiful giants who just want to live their lives in peace. I got a huge investment from the government and bought a shitload of land so we can save as many elephants as possible.'

'This is the coolest thing I have ever heard, Laura. I am so fucking proud of you,' I said.

'I'm proud too,' Teddy said while raising his glass.

'You guys...I'm so happy to see you both,' she said, slightly teary, holding our hands. 'I'm sorry about the whole Kyle situation, Vincent. I never would have thought...'

'It's okay. It wasn't always bad...we had some happy memories, at the beginning, at least.'

A waiter came around to our table in a hurry. The first time I had seen anyone do anything in a rush at the resort.

'Laura, we have a bit of a situation with a few guests. They were put on an earlier flight, so they'd like to spend an extra night here.'

'I'll sort it out,' she said while getting up. 'I will just give them another room.'

'I thought you didn't have other rooms!' I said. 'Isn't that the whole reason why you put Teddy and I in the same room?'

She winked at me. 'I'll be right back,' and she walked away.

I was left alone with Teddy, drinking my wine and staring at him being illuminated by the glow of the candles and the moonlight. My heart was racing with emotion, but at the same time I was completely relaxed by our beautiful surroundings.

'I don't know why it took me so long to come here. This is great,' I said.

'It's a very special place. This time a little bit more special,' he said, touching my leg with his foot.

'What we did this afternoon—'

'Yeah!' he said with a smile.

'We should do it again,' I said while raising my brows and smiling flirtatiously.

Time seemed almost to stand still. Now that the sun had set, the air had finally cooled, and I was now tipsy enough to cast aside all of the negative emotions I'd endured over the past few years. I was living in the present, enjoying that little bit of serendipity that had brought me back to Teddy.

I took a deep breath and stretched my arms.

'So, Teddy—'

And then his phone started vibrating on the table. He grabbed it and looked at the screen.

'I'm sorry, it's my brother. I have to take this.'

'Sure, go ahead,' I said.

'Hello?' he said, picking up the call. 'What happened?'

His expression changed, and he rubbed the back of his neck and started trembling.

And just like that, we went from the perfect evening to a full-blown nightmare.

CHAPTER TWENTY-FOUR

TEDDY

2020

The last few days had been filled with emotion, both good and bad. I was walking alone, in an empty school. I was walking in the middle of the corridor, surrounded by posters, sports memorabilia and lockers. I could smell the varnish of the mahogany staircase, being preserved year after year, and constantly needing work. Her office was upstairs, first room to the right. Her door would always be open, for students to just drop by and have a chat. She'd double as some kind of consultant or therapist sometimes. She loved the school. She loved seeing her students grow up, become adults, become someone she'd be proud of.

I walked into her office; her desk still a mess with papers everywhere and folders scattered around the room. The one window was huge, facing a park. She'd sit there on the windowsill, drinking her black coffee, no sugar. She'd have a blanket over her shoulder as the old frame let a draft in, but she never wanted to change offices and lose the view.

She was right there, with her short blonde hair and oversized black glasses, watching the sun go up in the sky.

'Are you okay, my dear?' she asked, turning her head to me.

'You're here,' I said, my heart filling with joy. 'I've missed you so much, mum.'

'Yeah, yeah. I know I've been working heaps, but this is the only place where I can concentrate and get some writing done!'

'I know.'

'Although when I'm here, in silence, before anyone comes in, it's a little bit too quiet. I miss you and your brother screaming at each other,' she said with a smile.

I sat down on her brown leather chair, gliding my hands alomg the seat and closing my eyes.

'Where have you been, mum?' I asked.

'I've been with you, all along. I've seen you grow into the beautiful boy in front of me.'

'I have so many questions...'

'Of course you do. You're my curious Teddy. You always were the little investigator trying to figure out how things work.'

'Why did you leave me alone? I needed you. I still do. I want to tell you things. I want your advice. I want a god damn hug.'

'You don't need me, Teddy,' she said while walking towards me. She put her blanket over my shoulders and gave me a kiss on the head. 'You are a grown-up. You always have been. I am so sorry I can't be there. I would have loved seeing you fall in love, giving you advice, walking you down the aisle.'

'You had a dress in mind you wanted to wear, didn't you?'

'Of course I did. Such a beautiful gown! A tight silk number. Maybe I would have grown my hair too.'

'You would have tortured my husband-to-be with a million questions too.'

'Oh, I don't think so. Vincent is such a nice guy.'

'Mum!' I said, putting my hand on my face and shaking my head.

'Oh, come on. Don't think I don't see you smiling thinking of him.'

'Can we not talk about my love life, please?' I said, giggling.

'I will always be by your side, Teddy. Please remember that.'

'I just don't know if I'm strong enough, mum,' I said with tears streaming down my face. 'I don't know if I can live in a world where you're not in it.'

'Listen to me,' she said while kneeling in front of me, her hands on my knees, her gaze stern, yet gentle. 'I am so proud of you. Not just for what you have accomplished, but also for the incredible human being you have become. I know how much you sacrificed to look after me and I will always be grateful.'

'Please don't go, mum.'

'I love you very much, Teddy,' she said with glossy eyes. 'Always be kind. Don't ever forget who you are.'

'Mum, I—'

I opened my eyes slowly, found myself sitting in the back seat of a car.

'We're here,' Vincent said, tapping my shoulder with his hand.

I looked outside the window and we were parked outside the hospice. I rubbed my eyes.

'You okay?' he asked.

'Yeah, I think so.'

I opened the door and got out of the car. I stood still, staring at the building. Vincent walked up to me, gently touching my hand with his. I turned to him and gave him a little smile.

'Thank you for being here,' I said.

He nodded. 'You ready?'

We walked inside, together. We walked down the corridor, all the way to her room door. Hazel and Mitchell were waiting just outside. Mitchell's eyes were red. Big brother had surely been crying.

Hazel stood up and gave me a hug, without saying anything.

'Has she gone?' I asked Mitchell.

'Not yet,' he said. 'But it could be a matter of minutes, an hour, perhaps.'

'Okay,' I said. 'Mitchell, this is—'

'Vincent,' Mitchell said tending his hand to him. '...heard a lot about you, mate.'

'Nice to meet you,' he said.

'Hey...' I said, turning to Hazel and Vincent. 'Could you guys just wait here while Mitchell and I say goodbye?'

'Of course,' Hazel said. 'We'll be here when you need us.'

'Thanks,' I turned to Mitchell. 'You ready?'

He nodded and entered the room with me. She was on the bed with her eyes closed. A machine breathing for her. A female nurse was standing next to her, writing things in her file.

'She looks like she's sleeping,' I said.

'I'm afraid that as of last night, there isn't any brain activity,' the nurse said.

'Can we have a moment with her?' Mitchell asked her.

'Sure, I'll be right outside.'

She left us alone with her. Both of us were standing in front of the bed, next to each other.

'Here we are,' he said.

I sat on the stool next to her bed, while Mitchell decided to stand on the other side. I didn't know what to say, my dream with her felt so real, I almost felt like I had said my goodbyes already.

'Wouldn't it be crazy if she just woke up now and was absolutely fine?' he asked.

'I think the funny thing is...I can imagine exactly how it would go down.'

'She'd remove all these tubes and pipes and cuss like crazy.'

'Yeah, then she'd ask us to go have a cocktail with her.'

We both laughed briefly, then Mitchell's face darkened.

'She's never going to meet this baby...this will be my first time actually being there day and night for my baby. I want to do it right, but...I won't know anything. I'm going to need her guidance, but she won't be here.'

'You'll do a great job, Mitch. And if you won't, you're lucky Hazel will probably do a half decent job herself.'

'You're such a little shit,' he said while smiling at me.

'Do you remember that time she took us to the zoo, and you were so terrified of snakes, so she thought the best course of action would be to get a handler to put a python around your neck?'

'Remember? It's the number one reason I need therapy!'

'She wanted you to be fearless, so you could look after me.'

'That didn't really work, did it?' he said.

'You came back to me when you discovered I was in the hospital. You've been looking after me since, really.'

He took a deep breath and then put his hand on mum's head.

'I've been angry at her for so long...'

'It's understandable.'

'I could have spent some extra time with her, before the disease completely took over.'

I looked back at mum, suddenly her vitals dropped and her heart stopped beating.

We panicked, we called the nurse, but it was too late. She couldn't be resuscitated, and in a matter of seconds, she'd died peacefully in her bed.

I hugged Mitchell; we both cried on each other's shoulders. We watched the nurses and the doctors work as quickly as possible, but it was an expected outcome.

We both walked out of the room in a state of semi-shock. Vincent hugged me and, as soon as I was wrapped in his arms, I cried incessantly. My heart ached, I was shaking with sobs and he held me tighter. I couldn't even breathe.

'Hey, why don't we go home, guys?' Hazel said. 'This day has been heavy for the both of you. You should take a moment of quiet.'

'We...have to think about funeral arrangements, what sort of coffin she should be buried in, or if we should cremate her, and call our relatives...' I said, trying to have a string of coherent thoughts.

'I think Hazel is right,' Vincent added. 'You guys should take at least the evening to just grieve and rest.'

'Let's go to the *bottle-o* and get a shitload of alcohol, Teddy,' said Mitchell.

Of course, his course of action would be getting drunk. Perhaps he wasn't wrong. I needed to shut my thoughts up. I just needed to sit somewhere and breathe again.

I looked at Vincent and kissed him, with tears still streaming down my face.

'Thank you for being here,' I said.

It had been a few days since mum died and I'd become some sort of android; I went on with all the things I needed to do and tried to keep my emotions to a bare minimum. Nothing had prepared me for how exhausting and difficult it was to arrange a funeral. Mum was a private person and she'd never mentioned that she wanted a funeral; but once the news spread around Tasmania, it was imperative that we'd arrange some sort

of celebration so that her students could pay their respects. We cremated mum the day
before. Mitchell and I hadn't quite decided what to do with the ashes, but we decided
not to talk about it until we'd spoken to the lawyers. We were going to read her will and
check for whatever she'd saved for us in her security box.

I was in yet another suit. A black one, this time. Black shirt, black tie and even a black
hat. I didn't want to wear one, but I remembered my mum liked me in it. She said I had
a "hat head". Mitchell wasn't taking the situation so well. He was quiet and angry at the
same time. He hadn't had the few extra years of memories like I had. He blamed himself
for being so stubborn and was already tired of being pitied. I understood. I felt that in a
similar way.

In an alternative universe, I'd be spending such precious days with Vincent, who
without hesitation had followed me across the country just to stay close by. I was riddled
with anxiety even thinking what would become of me if he left me alone, once again.
Something which was bound to happen at some point.

'*Ciao ciao bella,*' I said before hanging up the phone. I walked towards Hazel and
Vincent, who were sitting on the sofa.

'Brushing up the Italian?' asked Hazel.

'You wouldn't believe it, but the old lady who owned the café I went to every day
during my time in Italy. She just gave me a call to express her condolences. That lady was
a thousand years old then. I'm shocked she's still alive and remembered me.'

'You have a remarkable face,' said Vincent.

'Thanks, but I have checked myself in the mirror today. It isn't good.'

'Is that why you're wearing a porkpie hat?' asked Hazel.

'Yeah, I'm hoping it shrouds my face in darkness,' I smiled and checked my watch.
'Where the fuck is Mitchell? The lawyer will be here any minute.'

'He needed a moment. He went for a run an hour ago,' said Hazel.

'Oh, great.'

Mitchell came back, completely sweaty, in full jogging kit.

'Hello peeps. How are we?!' he shouted, still with music playing in his earphones.

We all looked at him.

'You don't think you're a little bit late? Go get changed!' I commanded.

'Alright, alright.'

He started making his way to the bathroom, when Hazel stopped him.

'Wait, the lawyer's outside!' she said.

'Oh, crap,' Mitchell said. 'Well, surely he can wait until I take a shower. He's paid enough.'

'Mitchell, let's just get this over with,' I said to him.

He rolled his eyes and looked at Hazel and Vincent. 'Hey, could you guys—'

'Say no more,' said Hazel. 'We'll leave you to it.'

They both left and opened the main door, where Russell, our family lawyer, was waiting.

'Please, come in,' said Hazel.

'Hi, boys,' said Russell. 'How are you, guys?'

'Well, we're orphans now, Russell!' said Mitchell.

I turned to him tilting my head. 'Are you on something, Mitch?'

'No,' he said while sitting on the sofa. 'Please Russell, let's just get on with it.'

'Okay, let me just get the paperwork out.'

I sat down on the chair opposite Mitchell, and Russell sat on another, in between the two. He placed his briefcase on the coffee table and grabbed a bunch of documents in it.

'Some of this will be already familiar to you. You got the house in Hobart as soon as you got your mother's power of attorney, Teddy.'

'Yeah, we've already sold that, mate,' said Mitchell, while biting his nails.

'Right. Upon your mother's death, as the only heirs to the Clarke name, you will also get your grandparents' Claremont house in Perth, valued at five million dollars, all of your mum's bonds and investments, along with all of her savings, which altogether amount to just over three million dollars.'

'Is that it?' I asked.

'What do you mean? We're rich!' said Mitchell.

'We have always been rich. That's how you get to live your life without a job.'

'Oh, yeah. Thanks Teddy.'

'What the fuck is your problem?' I asked, looking at him in the eyes.

'...nothing. Go on, Russell.'

'There is also a letter. It's for you both,' he said, showing us an envelope with a wax seal.

'Jesus. I forgot how swanky our family could get,' said Mitchell. 'But then again, everyone fucking dies in this family, so that's probably why I forgot.'

'Okay, Russell, would you excuse us for a second? I just have a few words to share with my brother.'

'No problem.'

'Mitchell, would you be a dear and follow me to the other room?'

He got up huffing and puffing and we both walked into the adjacent room. I closed the door behind us and pushed him against it with my hand.

'What the fuck is up with you?' I hissed.

'Nothing! Can I not grieve in my own way? Do I need to follow the fucking Teddy Clarke handbook on how to be a god damn robot?'

'What are you even talking about?'

'It's like this whole thing has completely gone over your head! Mum has died. Everyone in our family is fucking dead.'

'Yeah. We already knew that.'

'No. You don't get it. We only have each other. And how long until we both die because of this motherfucking family curse?'

'Mitchell...'

'I have gotten to a point where I have so much to lose, Teddy. I managed to reconnect with my child, I have fallen in love with an amazing woman who is currently expecting a baby, and I have my baby brother back in my life again. I am scared shitless of losing it all.'

'So, you...*don't* know. You have never—'

'No,' he interrupted. 'And I didn't want to know. But now that it's just us, and two new lives that could inherit our genes, I'm like...maybe it's time. To know, to plan.'

I turned away from him and put my hands on my head, running them through my hair.

'You're on your own with this. I'm not ready. You weren't here watching mum turn into...' I hesitated for a second. 'It was awful. It did things to me. I don't want to live my life having to think about it.'

'We have to do this, Teddy,' he said while putting his hand on my shoulder.

'Mitch...not now. Please let's get back out there and read what mum had to say to us.'

'Okay...'

We looked at each other in the eyes and left the room. We took our seats again and I grabbed the envelope.

'*I* need to break the seal,' Russell said.

I nodded. He opened the letter and handed it to Mitchell.

'I can't read that,' he said.

'I'll do it,' I said, grabbing the letter and opening it up. It was mum's writing, although a worse version of it. It was probably written when the chorea was taking her hand coordination away.

I took a deep breath and looked at Mitchell. I put my eyes down on the letter and started reading out loud.

My dearest boys,

Writing this letter is something I have been postponing for quite some time. I did not want to write it; I did not want you to read it. But unfortunately, life doesn't always go the way you want. Sometimes life forces you to make hard choices or forces you to give up on things that you hold so dear.

Something happened to me that I couldn't control. A disease that's so ugly and so vicious that its name barely gets spoken out loud. It's a disease so awful, it takes away every single aspect that makes you...you. You're no longer a human being, you're...a liability, a shadow of your former self. You still look like you, for the most part, but everything else isn't there. It sucks.

I have watched this disease take over my life and, unfortunately, yours as well, Teddy. I can't help but feel an incredible guilt over what I have done to Mitchell. If I had never driven him away with my stupid, inappropriate actions, he'd be here by your side supporting you and letting you live the life you deserve.

Instead, you're here. Day after day, looking after me, trying to make me feel better, trying to downplay the horrible ways I act and move. I have noticed that I have started forgetting things. I used to have so many things memorised. Names, dates, locations...now it's all slipping away from me and there is nothing I, or anybody else, can do to stop it.

So, why am I saying all of this?

Well, if you are both reading this letter (and I truly hope it's the both of you, together again), it means that the disease finally won and I am no longer with you. You may feel an array of contrasting emotions today. I get it. You're going to wonder whether I suffered, or whether I died years before, when I lost my speech, or when I lost the ability to walk, or when I lost the ability to swallow. These are all things that are going to happen to me, but for you, my amazing children, this would have been the reality you lived in for the past few years.

You both deserved so much more from me. I thought I was doing my best, I thought I had all the time in the world, but regrettably, no one has enough time in this world. Even without this disease. I watched myself postponing things, prioritising the wrong things, thinking there would always be more time.

I can only hope that, despite these circumstances, you have managed to become two great men; I hope you have become kind men, respectful, and courageous. I hope you have both found love and I hope you'll be there for each other, for better or for worse.

This was supposed to be the letter where I'd tell you what to do with my body and my funeral, but I know for a fact you're already aware I'm not into that sort of stuff. Instead, I'd like for you to take a trip together. Get a car and drive around the southern coast of Australia. It's so beautiful and I so regret not ever taking you to see the beautiful spots of Perth, where I was born and where I spent some of the happiest years of my childhood.

Take it slow, enjoy the ride. Make special memories together, because when you sit in a hospital bed and your body starts to fail you, memories are all that remain. When money can't buy the thing you most desire, you will at least have those great moments to rely on.

I truly hope neither of you will have to succumb to this. I wish I could have the assurance that neither of you will have to deal with Huntington's ever again, but I'm afraid I do not have the power to promise that.

I am immensely proud of you both. Teddy, I'm so proud of the gentle soul you're growing up to be. Your empathy and resilience are an inspiration and I know you have become an outstanding man worth looking up to.

Mitchell, you're my little rebel. You never played by the rules and your spontaneity is something I have always admired. You love in a way that is raw and passionate and you were born to be a protector.

I could fill a book with the number of things I would like to say to you, but I think I have exhausted my allowance of coordinated movements for the day.

I am not a religious person, I haven't raised either of you to be, but I find myself praying that I'll be able to look after you after my death. Whichever deity allows me to do that, that's the one I'm praying to.

I love you both so very much. More than you could ever imagine.

Be strong,

Mum.

Mitchell and I remained in silence. We looked at each other and we didn't know what to say. It felt like someone had just stabbed me in the heart and I could barely move, let alone speak.

Reading the letter was soul-crushing, but I finally knew what we needed to do to celebrate Mum.

Chapter Twenty-Five

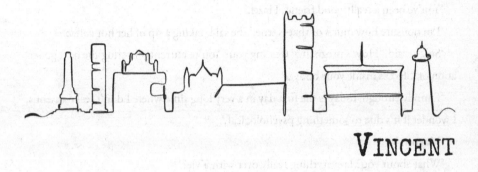

Vincent

2020

Grief is a hailstorm. It's unpredictable and can be devastating. I didn't have much experience with it. I couldn't remember feeling the pain of a grandparent dying or being particularly affected by the death of a pet. After all, I'd only ever had goldfish. When Teddy found out about his mother's condition getting worse, his face changed, his mannerisms dulled, and words of joy weren't spoken for days.

I felt useless. I was, once again, in the wrong place at the wrong time; so much for the incredible coincidence of meeting Teddy.

Hazel and I went to a café. We didn't want to be in the way of the two brothers having to deal with their feelings of desperation and sorrow. I, especially, was an outsider to it all. I wanted to be there for him, but I had to respect his wishes of being alone for the time being.

The café was an American diner-style joint, with red booths and old rock songs being played on a vintage jukebox. Hazel and I were sitting facing each other. She was sipping on a decaf flat white, while I went for a double whisky on ice.

'This is a nightmare,' she said.

'I feel incredibly useless,' I said, while moving the ice around the glass. 'We're out of the way, but is that what they really need?'

'I'm not sure. I also don't know how to feel myself. I have met Veronica. We would have so many conversations about books, stuff on TV, politics...just about anything. I saw the disease develop, I saw her forget things more and more each day.'

'You've been a really good friend, Hazel.'

'I'm not sure how much of that is true,' she said, taking a sip of her hot coffee.

'So...' I said. 'How's pregnancy treating you? You're currently hosting the next generation of Clarkes inside your body...'

'Funnily enough, today is the first day in a very long time where I don't feel nauseous. I wonder if it's due to something psychological.'

'Maybe...'

'What about you? Is everything really over with Kyle?'

'Yeah...yeah it really is.'

'What happened to you guys?' she asked.

'It wasn't right. Kyle needs far more support than I could ever give him. He himself was also affected by grief, and he allowed for it to take over his—our—lives. He disappeared behind drugs. The nice guy I had met years ago has vanished, replaced by a person I can't love or respect.'

'What if this happens to Mitchell as well? He isn't exactly the master of handling bad news.'

'Hazel, this is only temporary. They have each other, and they will get over this. I'm sure of it.'

'Yeah, I hope so.'

Hazel's phone started to vibrate on the table. 'It's Mitch,' she said. 'They must be finished with the lawyer.'

'Why don't you wait for me in the car and I'll pay the bill?' I asked.

She nodded and left the café while answering the phone.

I picked up my phone and scrolled down my missed calls and texts. Kyle had finally stopped texting. I decided to call his sister to get a quick update on the situation at home.

'Hello?' she said.

'Amber...you alright?'

'Yes. Sorry for the lack of contact...it's been fairly intense over here.'

'Are you still in London?' I asked.

'Well, we're at the airport. I finally managed to make him understand that going back to our parents' is probably the best course of action.'

'Oh, so this is it.'

'Yeah...our dad found him a spot at a local rehab center, so hopefully that should help. I have to say, Vincent, I can't thank you enough for calling me. We've already lost a sister, I didn't want to lose my brother as well.'

'I probably should have called sooner...'

'Hey, you did what you had to do. He should have known better.'

'I'm sorry you'll have to deal with this from now on.'

'Don't worry. He'll be better soon.'

'I am probably never going to be able to forgive him. It sounds awful, I know.'

'I get it.'

'Hey, I actually called to get his new address. My lawyer is going to need it to send the divorce papers.'

'I can text it to you before we board.'

The waitress came over to the table to take the payment. I handed my card to her and smiled.

'Let me know if he improves, Amber.'

'I will.'

'And if it ever gets too much, just call me. You can talk to me anytime. Good luck to you both.'

'Thanks, I will,' she said. 'Oh, one more thing. I found a teddy bear in the room, but Kyle said it wasn't his. I left it in the living room for you to get it back.'

I smiled for a second.

'Thank you for all this. Goodbye Amber.'

Goodbye Kyle.

It felt like the day that wouldn't end. So many people dressed in black, so many people crying in every corner of the house. The boys somehow managed to convince the new owners of their old house in Tasmania to allow them to have the wake there. It was, after all, the house where they both grew up and where they had made most of their memories.

The house was filled with sunflowers. We bought so many, there were probably none left on the island. Classical music was playing in the living room, loud enough to muffle a few cries. Former students of Veronica were exchanging stories and adding a few bits of laughter to what would have been an otherwise depressing event.

I floated from room to room, listening to people's stories and trying to make sure Teddy was eating something. Mitchell and Teddy were two different people, but grief made them look fairly similar. Both were trying to get drunk as quickly as possible, and both were being as cold and distant as they could.

It was difficult being there and not being able to help them in any way.

I found Teddy in the kitchen, filling up a tray of chalices with champagne.

'Do you need help with that?' I asked.

'No...no, thank you,' he said while pouring.

'Teddy, I think you should just sit down and relax for a while. Let me deal with all of that.'

'I can't,' he sighed. 'I can't.'

I walked towards him and touched the bottle, so I could take over with the pouring.

'Vincent...I need to do something. Or I'll go insane,' he said, looking straight into my eyes. 'I appreciate your help, but I feel like I should do this alone.'

'I'm just conscious you haven't stopped for even a second.'

'It's how I operate. I'm trying to go through this moment as quickly as I can, but,' he slammed the bottle on the table. '...but I can't. It's much harder than I thought, Vincent.'

Teddy started crying, with his head kept down. I moved closer to him and put my hands over his shoulders.

'Hey, hey. It's okay. It's okay to break down,' I said.

He hugged me and started sobbing on my chest. I held his head and caressed his hair. He couldn't stop weeping. I hoped it felt somewhat liberating, as holding him tight, was the only thing I could do for him.

We remained still, in the kitchen, until Teddy's sobbing finally came to an end. He was overtired, so the emotions he was feeling were raw and incontrollable. Then we heard a noise coming from the other room and it sounded like something bad was going on. Quickly we ran from the kitchen to see what we could do.

Mitchell was walking on the dining hall table, drunk out of his arse swinging some sort of Japanese sword.

'There's my baby brother!' he screamed, while making the sword rotate.

'What the fuck are you doing up there, you moron?' he shouted.

Hazel was pressing her lips together in anger. 'Mitchell, get the fuck off the table before you stab someone!'

I didn't know what to do; I stood there, waiting for him to at least drop the fucking sword.

'So many students here!' he said with a smirk. 'You all loved my mother; it makes me so happy! It's like everyone here has a happy little episode that involves my mother, the Mary Poppins teacher of Tasmania!'

'Mitchell, please stop,' Hazel said.

'I'm just sharing stories! Like everyone else! Now, does any one of you know the story of how my dad killed himself in a car crash when I was seven years old? No? No one? It's so funny how such a "great" woman drives literally everyone around her away or to their fucking death!'

I could see Teddy clenching his fists. I was terrified he too would do something stupid.

'Does anyone know the story of how my mum paid my ex-girlfriend to fuck off away with my child? Yes! She thought I'd become some sort of loser if I stepped up to raise my daughter so young! Ha. Joke's on her. I became a loser anyways!'

Teddy walked towards him and tapped his leg.

'Alright, Mitchell. You've made your point,' Teddy said. 'Please stop embarrassing yourself and allow these fucking people to mourn without a clown show.'

He looked right through him and completely ignored him. That's when Teddy grabbed Mitchell's ankle and pulled it towards him, making Mitchell fall on his face on the table.

'Jesus Teddy, he could have impaled himself!' Hazel shrieked.

Mitchell got up and off the table. He touched his nose and noticed it was bleeding. 'You're a fucking dead man,' he said as he punched Teddy in the face, making him fall backwards.

'Hey, you two, stop!' I bellowed, putting myself between them.

But they weren't finished. Teddy ran towards Mitchell and tackled him, making him fall on his back. That's when Teddy punched him in the face. They rolled around the room trying to get on top of each other and exchanged a few more punches.

I walked behind Mitchell and tried to hold him by immobilising his arms, but he then head-bashed me, hitting my nose and making my eyes water up. He then pushed me, and I stumbled into Hazel, who fell on her back as well.

'Fuck,' Mitchell said. He walked towards her, helping her get up, but she refused to take his hand.

'Get the hell away from me,' she said, helping herself up. 'You two are unbelievable. It's not just your mother's funeral. It's also someone that everyone here knew and—ah!' she said while holding her stomach.

'Are you okay?' Teddy said.

'Let's take her to the hospital,' I commanded.

'Alright, everyone! Get the fuck out!' shouted Mitchell. 'Mate, can you call an ambulance?' he asked me.

I took my phone and dialled 999, but quickly realised it wasn't the right number. I looked at Teddy in slight panic and he grabbed my phone, quickly dialling 000.

'Hey, my idiot brother has pushed my pregnant best friend on the floor, so we'll need to get her checked out. How quickly can you get here? See you soon,' he said, handing me the phone back.

I made sure everyone left the house in the meantime, so we could all jump into the ambulance as quickly as possible.

The doctors saw Hazel almost straight away. In the meantime, I was stuck with the Clarke brothers, who were both covered in bruises and blood. Mitchell was holding a bag of ice on his eye, while Teddy was dabbing his nose with a tissue. Both were quiet, and angry at each other.

'You know, you could have fucking skewered somebody,' Teddy said, all of a sudden.

'I know how to handle a fucking katana. I trained in Japan.'

'That's what you did while I was home dealing with mum's shit?'

'Yep.'

'Wonderful,' Teddy said.

I wasn't sure if it was my place to intervene, but I felt like if I didn't, the two would murder each other. I was about to speak, when Teddy interrupted once again.

'Like...you have a child. And another one on the way! What the *fuck* were you thinking?'

'Jesus Christ. I was wasted!'

'You two ought to get it together, or I swear I'm going to slap the living shit out of you both,' I said.

They both looked at me as if I were a mean teacher.

Shortly afterwards, Hazel was escorted back to us by a doctor. Teddy and Mitchell stood up in unison.

'How are you? How's the baby?' Mitchell said.

'It's alright,' the doctor said. 'They're both absolutely fine.'

'Thank you, doctor. We were both terrified there for a second,' Teddy said.

'I was told you had a sword fight?' the doctor said.

We all looked at Mitchell for a second.

'It won't happen again,' he said.

'Thank you,' Hazel said.

The doctor walked away and left us in the waiting room.

'Are you two going to get your faces checked?' she asked.

'I think we're fine,' Teddy said. 'Aren't we, mate?' he said, flicking Mitchell's eye with his fingers.

'Right, can we go home, before you two punch each other again?' Hazel asked.

We all started walking towards the exit, when Teddy stopped suddenly.

'What's wrong?' I asked, turning around.

'I have something to say,' he responded.

We all turned to listen to what Teddy had to say. He scratched the back of his head and sighed.

'I'm going to scatter mum's ashes in Perth.'

'What?' asked Mitchell.

'She said it herself. She wanted for us to go there and to drive down the coast. I am going to fulfil her wish,' he said. '...and I'd like for you guys to come with me.'

'Mitch, how hard did you bash his head?' asked Hazel.

'I'm not crazy. Look, Perth is...what? A twenty-hour drive from Sydney?'

'Try fucking forty-five, Teddy,' she replied.

'Well, we could take turns driving! Look, I am going to do this with or without you all, but I feel like doing it together would be more fun.'

'I'm keen,' Mitchell said.

I looked at Hazel and shrugged. 'Yeah, I'd love to go with you guys.'

'Haze?' asked Mitchell.

She rolled her eyes. 'Sure. But be aware that I will have to pee incredibly often and I'll most likely be nauseous for ninety percent of the trip.'

'Okay, then!' said Mitchell. 'I'm excited! Let's head home and grab mum's urn.'

'Could you guys call a car?' Teddy asked. 'I have to speak to Vincent for a second.'

'Alright,' said Hazel. She and Mitchell walked out of the hospital, leaving me behind with Teddy.

'Is everything alright?' I asked.

He walked towards me and held both of my hands, standing in front of me. His poor beautiful face was bruised, and his hair was a mess, but his eyes looking at me? Those were still gorgeous, filled with emotions.

'I just wanted to thank you,' he said. 'These last few days have been a bit of a roller-coaster, but I am so glad you're here with me.'

'Really? I kind of felt like I was in the way of things—'

'No! No, no...I...I'm sorry I acted like a moron with Mitchell, but that's us. That's how we do things.'

'I'm happy to be here, with you,' I said, while looking at his eyes.

He leaned forward to kiss me, but Mitchell shouted at us from outside.

'Yo! Car's here!'

I smiled at Teddy and held his hand. We both walked towards the exit and headed to our next adventure together.

CHAPTER TWENTY-SIX

TEDDY

2020

Saying goodbye to our childhood home was a cathartic moment for the both of us. We would most likely never go back to it again. We all flew back to Sydney and headed to the flat. We had to get supplies for the trip. Mitchell pushed for us to get tents as well, as he was particularly eager to do some camping at some point. I wasn't thrilled, but he said it would be a good experience for us all.

I mainly said yes, just so we could hurry up. The jeep had been packed with snacks and clothing. Vincent had been creating a long enough playlist, so we wouldn't want to murder our ears listening to the same song over and over.

I was the first one at the wheel. I was fairly used to the god-awful traffic in Sydney, so it made sense for me to be the one leading the way. Vincent was sitting next to me, while Hazel was sitting at the back with her feet in between the front seats. Mitchell had been munching on Pringles since we left. Mum's royal blue urn was in the glove compartment, waiting patiently for us to scatter its contents by the *Crawley Boatshed*, a few days later.

The sun was shining on Vincent, who was wearing sunglasses and a navy baseball hat. He called himself "the best road trip companion" as he would never be able to sleep in a moving vehicle. It was the same reason why he was the only person awake on that infamous flight to Bali. He had his elbow on the window, looking at the scenery outside while his other hand was holding mine.

We were on the road for almost seven hours when I realised I could barely wait to be in a hotel room alone with Vincent. Having my brother and best friend always around, kind of minimised the amount of making out I felt I was entitled to.

'Hey, hey, hey!' shouted Mitchell, all of a sudden.

'What?' I asked.

'We are not too far from *Fowles Winery*! Why don't we stop for a bit?'

'You're not serious...' said Hazel.

'Why?' he turned to her.

'Wine is literally my favourite thing. Are you really going to have my favourite thing while I suffer in a corner drinking a glass of water because I'm incubating your demon baby inside me?'

'Sure you could have one!' said Mitchell. 'Hey, Vince. Google that for me?'

Vincent tapped on his phone. 'I seriously don't think—oh!' he exclaimed.

'What did you find?' I asked.

'It looks like you could probably have one, Haze!'

'Get this fucking car to that god damn winery right now!' she shouted.

'Guys. We're an hour and a half away from Melbourne. I don't think stopping to get hammered now is a good idea,' I said. I could see Hazel's death stare through my rear-view mirror. 'Hey, but if you guys are outvoting me...by all means...'

'I'll drive next if we make the stop,' she said.

'For the next six hours?'

'I mean, I'll drive to Melbourne.'

'...And for the first few hours tomorrow?'

'Sure...fine. Yeah. Just get me some wine now.'

'Sweet!' said Mitchell.

I drove for another half hour on the Hume highway, waiting for the exit to the winery, so we could take a little rest after going through what felt like no more than one percent of our journey.

I parked in front of the winery restaurant, overseeing the central Victoria plains. The sun was scorching hot and the crickets were singing for dear life. We all got out of the car and entered the restaurant, ready to get some of that sweet, sweet wine into our bloodstream.

We walked through the restaurant and got seated in a lovely leafy courtyard. It was breezy and fresh, a lovely combination for wine and various types of cheese.

We were served our glasses and Hazel observed hers. She grabbed the glass, she smelled the wine, moved it around the glass and then put it back down.

'I can't,' she said, defeated.

'What?' I asked, incredulous.

'Look, this baby already has the odds stacked against it, with Mitchell's dumb genes...'

'Hey! What the hell?' said Mitchell.

'You guys enjoy your alcohol heaven. I'll have some bullshit apple thing.

'Alright then!' said Vincent, while pouring Hazel's glass into his.

Hazel rolled her eyes at him. 'As soon as this thing comes out, I'm buying a barrel filled with red wine.'

We sat there for two hours, trying every single fermented grape they presented to us. Hazel only got to have a few mocktails, but she made Mitchell give her an-hour-long foot massage, so she was just as merry as we were.

The boys and I were around four glasses in, which made us all incredibly tipsy and chatty.

'Have you guys started thinking about names yet?' Vincent asked.

'Yes! Names, names!' I shouted, tapping my hands on the table like a drum.

'No! We haven't thought about it at all,' said Mitchell. 'Although she loves to call it a "demon", so maybe Damien?'

'No. I knew some asshole from school named Damien who would always call me fat. Fuck him,' she said.

'There's still time, anyways...am I the godfather by the way?' I asked.

'I don't think we have to decide that now. This thing is as little as a mango right now,' she said.

'I am the godfather!' I mimed to her.

'Hey Vincent,' said Mitchell. 'What are your plans regarding this whole Australia thing? You staying?'

'Uhm...I don't know, really.'

'I'd really like for you to stay,' I said with a drunken smile, holding his hand.

'I'm not too sure,' he said. 'I didn't plan much. I was just going to see Laura in Bali. I didn't expect I'd be transported to Australia and get to be with you guys. I have loved every moment so far. I just haven't done a lot of thinking regarding what I want to do in the future,' he said sipping from his glass.

'What would you like to do, then?' Mitchell insisted.

'I don't know. I was hoping I'd get into a screenwriting program back in London, but I didn't get in, unfortunately.'

'You're a scriptwriter? That's amazing!' he said.

'I'm not, I'm not,' he said. 'I just...I wanted to be a director. I don't know, I haven't done much, to be honest.'

'We should do something together, then!' Mitchell shouted, slamming his hand on the table.

'What the fuck is going on, here?' asked Hazel.

'Yeah, I'm confused too,' I said, drinking the last of my wine. 'Did someone spike my drink, by any chance?'

'No, listen to me,' said Mitchell. 'I have a bunch of camera equipment waiting to be used. We could create something by uniting our skills. We could do a documentary.'

'On what?' I asked.

'Funny you should ask. I think we should do a documentary on Huntington's disease.'

'Huh?' I said with a frown. My lips contorted in confusion.

'I think we are done with the wine, Mitch,' said Hazel.

'I'm not kidding. Look, this disease is incredibly rare, and we both know what little information is out there. We could shed light on it and do something great! We could interview people who have it and even provide our own story!'

'I don't want to do that,' I said.

'Why not? It was your idea!' he asked.

'Because it's not something we should be going through again. We have just lost our mother to it!'

'I think that's exactly why we should do it. And what better way to start with this road trip we're on?'

'I don't know, Mitchell,' said Vincent. 'I don't think I should really get involved with something this big.'

'I have some equipment I don't even *know* how to use. I think it's a brilliant idea. We could really help people!' he said.

'How?' I asked.

'I think it would be good for people to know what's going to happen to them. I think your input is invaluable in this, Teddy.'

'I'm getting some fresh air, excuse me,' I said while getting up.

I walked outside and sat on top of the hill, overlooking nature and the clouds moving in the sky. The alcohol fumes were already abandoning me. Talking about the disease would always make me feel like shit. It had taken so much away from me; I couldn't dedicate any more of my life to it.

Mitchell followed me outside and sat next to me. He untied his bun and let his curls free, enjoying the wind flowing through his hair.

'This is a nice place,' he said. 'I'm glad we took a break.'

'Mitchell...I don't want Huntington's to come back into our lives. With mum no longer here with us, we don't have to deal with it anymore. We can live, move on...'

'Teddy, we will never be able to move away from its shadow. You know that.'

I hugged my knees and put my chin in between them, rocking myself back and forth.

'I know what you're going to say,' I said. 'I don't think I'm ready.'

'Do you not think it's time? It would be a lot easier if you were by my side.'

'One day.'

We remained in silence for a few minutes, listening to the whistling sound of the wind rushing past our ears. There were barely any other sounds, apart from birds singing and dragonflies touching water.

'Think about it, Teddy. People out there could feel a lot less lonely if they found some sort of representation. We are driving through half of Australia. We could touch so many people.'

'You involve people who have a disease, and they will be dead before the documentary comes out.'

'Okay. What do you say we visit a Huntington centre in Melbourne? We give it a trial run, and depending on how you feel about it, we go ahead or shelve the whole thing.'

'Why is this so important to you?'

'You know why,' he said while getting up. 'So, deal?' he asked tending his hand to me to pull me up.

'Deal,' I said, grabbing it. 'Now get your girlfriend to drive us, because I need a nap.'

He smiled at me, and we both made our way back to see the others.

I wasn't convinced yet, but I was glad to see Mitchell being passionate about something.

<hr>

We managed to arrive in Melbourne ridiculously quickly. Hazel was a maniac behind the wheel, but I was still surprised we managed to reach the city as fast as we did. Mitchell and I were asleep the whole time, while Vincent stayed in the front to keep our driver awake and happy.

'Where are we?' I asked, rubbing my eyes trying to understand what decade I was in.

'That's where we're staying for the night,' said Hazel.

'Yeah, you should have seen her. GPS said nearly two hours and I think we got here in forty-five minutes,' said Vincent.

'Shall we get a room, then?' asked Mitchell.

'Rooms,' I pointed out. 'I have no desire of hearing you snore all night or listen to Hazel go to the toilet every twenty minutes.'

'You make a fair point, little Clarke,' said Hazel. 'Fine. Let's all get some fucking sleep. I am exhausted.'

We all got out of the car and stared at the building we were supposed to go into.

'Mitchell?' Vincent asked.

'Yes?'

'Is this a gay hotel?'

'Yeah!'

'Why?' I asked, squinting my eyes and crinkling my nose.

'Because you guys are gay. Thought you'd appreciate being here.'

Vincent and I looked at each other. We both burst out laughing. Hazel quickly followed suit and put her arm around Mitchell.

'You're such a fucking dingus,' she said.

'What? It's colourful! It's fun!' he said.

He wasn't wrong.

The hotel itself looked as if Elton John had designed the whole thing. The staff uniforms were bright pink; there were paintings of divas such as Madonna, Celine, and Cher hanging all around the main hall. The walls were lit up with red and blue lights and there was music pumping out, as if we'd just entered a late-night club.

We checked in as quickly as possible and ran to our rooms. They put us next to each other, which usually would have annoyed me, but since music was playing in the hallway, then maybe all noises from inside the rooms would be muffled.

I closed the door to my room and dropped my bag onto the table. Vincent collapsed onto the bed face down.

'Oh look,' I said while grabbing a door hanger. 'We can put a "please disturb" sign outside our door!'

'Hey, I know it feels like we have been together for ten years, but I thought we weren't quite at the "inviting strangers into our room" phase.'

'I was just checking. I want you to be fully aware of all of our amenities,' I said while sitting next to him.

'I gather you haven't noticed the bathroom is surrounded by glass walls?' he said with a giggle.

'Oh, what the fuck? That's not ideal.'

'This is killing a lot of the mystery I thought we'd get to enjoy for some time.'

'Who's into this?!'

'Your main ally next door, clearly,' he said. 'Hey,' he sat next to me and held my hand. 'So you were asleep while we talked about this...'

'Huh?'

'There's a centre for Huntington's here in Melbourne.'

I let go of his hand and ran mine through my hair then dropped with my back onto the bed.

'Vincent...I don't know.'

'Can I say something you may not necessarily want to hear?' he asked while lying next to me with his elbow on the bed and his hand holding his head.

'Shoot.'

'I think what Mitchell wants to do is a really good idea.'

'Those are some of the worst words in the English language, Vincent.'

'No, hear me out. We are driving down the coast to honour your mother's wishes, which is great. But don't you think it would be an amazing act to collect the stories of different people with the disease? Not just people who suffer from it, but also their families. It's a devastating topic, but I think fewer people would feel isolated if we managed to get some stories into the doc.'

I sighed. 'Okay. Let's give it a try in the morning, then.'

He smiled at me and sat on top of me. I grabbed his thighs and smiled back at him.

'I still can't believe you're here,' I said. 'I can't even tell you how many times I've found myself in a hotel room completely alone and imagined what it would be like to have you here.'

'Hotels like this?' he said, while pointing at the room.

'Of course,' I giggled.

Vincent leaned forward and gave me a kiss. His hair dropped down to the sides, so I ran my hand through it and put it behind his ears.

'Thanks,' he said. 'What do you say we take this shower for a test drive?'

'Fuck yeah!' I shouted with enthusiasm.

We quickly ran into the shower, throwing our clothes all over the room.

The rain was pounding against the roof of the car, making the previous scorching hot days a distant memory. We were parked outside the centre. Hazel was mounting her favourite lens onto her camera and packing a few extra into her bag. My heart was racing.

'You ready to go in?' Vincent asked, slipping his hand into mine.

'Yeah.' I sucked in a deep breath.

We all left the car in a hurry, trying not to get soaked by the rain. One of the doctors said that we could pretty much walk around the entire structure, as long as we had staff acting as chaperones and each wore a little visitor badge. It was a larger hospice than the one in Sydney; a little older too. We passed a few people fighting to take a few steps using a rollator walker, but my blood froze in my veins when we walked past a kid who was maybe twelve at most.

'Hey Oliver,' said the doctor. 'Are you done with your check-up?'

'Yeah,' his voice lower than I expected for his age.

'Are you waiting for your mum?'

'I'm w-w-wai...ting,' he managed, his wide innocent eyes looking at our motley group.

I turned to the doctor in horror. 'Is he...?'

'Yes, unfortunately.'

'How?' Mitchell asked. 'I thought—'

'Oliver is actually the person I was hoping you'd get into your documentary,' the doctor said. 'I spoke to his parents, and they were more than happy to share their story.'

'I can't do this,' I turned on me heel, walking away.

Mitchell followed me.

'Teddy, stop.'

'Jesus, Mitchell. It's a fucking child,' my eyes burning with unshed tears. 'I didn't even know this could be a thing. Did you know about it?!'

'I called last night, and the doctor mentioned that Oliver was diagnosed two years ago with Juvenile Huntington's. It's rare for young people, but it can happen.'

'I can't believe it...'

'You should speak to him. Really.'

I looked at him from afar and watched Oliver talking to the doctor, his smile innocent even though he had experienced more than most would in a lifetime already. I was heartbroken.

I nodded and walked back with Mitchell.

We arranged for Oliver and his family to sit in a well-lit room. His mums were sitting on either side of him and he seemed fairly eager to start.

Vincent had written a few questions and was standing with Hazel behind the camera. Mitchell was checking lights and sound. I was going to be the one talking to Oliver and his parents.

'You can start whenever, Teddy.'

I was sitting in front of him, ready to start our chat. 'How are you feeling today, Oliver?'

'Not bad, today has been alright,' he shrugged.

'And why are you here today?'

'It's my monthly check-up. I have trouble doing things.'

I turned to one of his mothers. 'When did it all start?'

'Well,' she hummed the word, hesitant.

'We noticed these spasms,' the other continued. 'We weren't sure what it was at first. It took us months to get the right diagnosis. Huntington's isn't exactly something doctors search for in children.'

'And it came from...?' I asked.

'His biological dad. We didn't know he had it. It wasn't disclosed.'

'How do you feel about it all, Oliver?'

'It's frustrating, people at sc-school know an-and can be weird about it. My mums often cry about it. I think they think I can't hear them but they're not really that quiet.'

'Well, they're just super worried about you, aren't they? That's pretty normal when you're a mum I think.'

'I know, I'm 12, I know w-what happens at the end.' His brown eyes were on mine, wide like only a child's could be.

I looked at Vincent, whose eyes were glossy. I didn't know what to say.

'You know what happens...?' I asked.

'I die. I won't be around.' he swallowed, brave face on. 'That makes me s-s-sad, and maybe a little scared.'

I took a deep breath and put my hand out for a fist bump, trying my god damned hardest not to cry. 'You're a really brave young man, Oliver.'

'Hun...hun...tington is stupid,' he whispered, slowly bumping his fist into mine.

'It really is,' I nodded.

'Do you have it too?' he asked.

I hesitated, trying to find the words. 'My mum did.'

'Is she okay?' he asked and even though he said he knew how it ends, there was unbridled hope in his eyes.

'She...she passed a little while ago,' I said. 'She's why we're talking to you, and other people who have it. That doofus over there is my brother.'

Mitchell waved at him.

The rest of the interview was a blur. I couldn't understand. I didn't want to understand. Oliver had just started living. It wasn't fair.

As soon as we were done filming, I left in a hurry and locked myself in a toilet. I couldn't stop crying, I couldn't breathe. I was having a full-blown panic attack and couldn't help but throw up into the toilet.

Mitchell knocked on the stall door. 'You okay, mate?'

'Go away,' I shouted. 'I'm fine.'

'Hey, I understand it was difficult. But...'

'But what?' I said, opening the door.

Mitchell shrugged. 'Imagine other children like him. Not knowing what's happening to them. They see a smiling Oliver, telling them not to be afraid.'

'They *should* be afraid, Mitchell. Their bodies and their minds will be crushed like a ball of paper! Did you see him? Did you see his face?'

'Yes...'

'No, because if you did, you'd know I can't be doing this. And neither should you.'

'I want to do this. Have you ever thought that putting something like this into the world may urge more people to donate to research and maybe, just maybe, we may get a cure for it at some point in the future?'

He was making sense. For once, I was being the unreasonable one. I took a deep breath and closed my eyes.

'I know why you're being like this, Teddy,' he said.

I shook my head. I didn't want to hear it.

'You're terrified, because now that mum is dead, you know what you have to do, but you don't want to, because now you have something to lose.'

I closed the door of the stall on his face and put my back against it. I looked up on the ceiling, trying not to cry out loud.

'Teddy...there's a *fifty percent chance* we have the disease ourselves.'

And there it was. The sentence I never wanted to hear out loud. Just like that, my heart felt ripped from my chest. The potential of having the disease was now a real thing, thrown into the world, ready to manifest.

'Teddy, we have to. *I* have to. I need to know if I'm going to be around to see my kids grow up. We both need to know.'

I opened the door again. My tears were no longer coming out.

I nodded and took another deep breath.

'Not here, not now. We'll do it in Perth, together.'

'Okay,' he said, also trying not to get emotional.

'Please don't tell Haze and Vincent. Not yet.'

'Okay. We'll do it before we scatter mum's ashes. And whatever the result, we will deal with it.'

'Alright.'

We both hugged for a while.

I really couldn't shake off how right he was.

I had *so much* to lose.

CHAPTER TWENTY-SEVEN

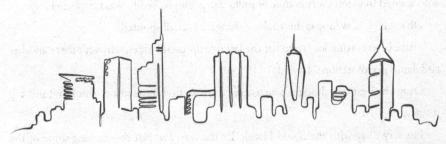

VINCENT

2020

Australia is a gigantic country. I'd never quite realised just how big it was when I'd studied geography. It was there, at the very bottom, looking like it could easily fit in the middle of Europe, but that was not the case at all. We drove for miles and miles and, so many times, we hadn't seen a single thing, other than camels or kangaroos on the side of the road. I wasn't quite used to seeing such an array of animals. I had yet to see a koala, but we still had a fair way to go before we reached Perth, so the opportunity could still arise.

Four days after we'd left Melbourne, we passed something which I didn't think was an attraction, but Mitchell swore it was, as he was blogging his entire road trip. The *Nullarbor*—which means "no trees"—is comprised of the largest limestone bed in the world, through which the *Eyre Highway* runs from *Ceduna* to *Norseman*. It is flat, arid, and remote.

It was the part of the road trip where one would be scared shitless, wondering senselessly whether they'd got enough petrol, water and food. It was a whole lot of nothingness, stretching for what seemed a million years. Hazel had finally got over herself and her fear of peeing on the side of the road, as petrol stations were quite scarce and far between. Definitely not close enough for a pregnant woman to hold her constant flow of urine.

I was once again in the front seat, trying to entertain the driver, which at that point, was Mitchell. Hazel was lying in the back with her legs over Teddy's, while he was reading a book. I wanted to do that too, but I didn't think we could have two people in the car who wanted to vomit every couple of miles. Surprisingly, Teddy, was unaffected.

'Oh my god, how long is this fucking thing?' Mitchell shouted.

'I have been craving ice cream for the last five thousand miles, why isn't there another god damn petrol station?' I asked.

'Okay, the next one shouldn't be too far. I say we find some sort of shit hotel and call it a day.'

'I'm very okay with that,' said Hazel. 'By the way, I'm just re-watching some of the footage we took in Adelaide and it's looking pretty damn good.'

'Don't remind me,' said Teddy. 'Another family whose mother is about to die and leave her children. I can't get used to it, still.'

'I don't think we are going to find a happy story with this disease, Teddy,' said Hazel.

'I know, I know.'

'Hey, random question,' said Mitchell. 'Do you guys hear the noise the car is making or is it just my brain being fucked?'

It was some sort of whistle, which kept sounding noisier and noisier as we went along.

'Guys, I don't feel too good about this piece of trash car,' said Mitchell.

'Mate, it was brand new when I got it. What did you do to it?'

'Nothing! It's just—'

The car stopped all of a sudden. Mitchell tried to turn the engine back on, but it wasn't having it.

'Oh no,' said Hazel. 'Please, not in the middle of the desert.'

'I'll go check,' Mitchell got out of the car and opened the bonnet, to reveal a fuck-ton of smoke coming from the engine. 'Oh, great. We're fucked.'

We all got out of the car and looked around us. We looked at the big fat nothing that was surrounding us for the next gazillion miles.

'We were so close,' I said.

Teddy sighed. 'My poor baby. She didn't deserve to die here, in the middle of nowhere. She's a city girl.'

'It probably just needs some oil change or some shit like that,' said Hazel.

'I have no clue,' said Mitchell.

'Yeah, same,' said Teddy.

'Wonderful. Can someone call the pick-up thing then?' I asked.

'Right, I'll try to get a *ute* to take pity on us. Start praying.'

Teddy dialled a number and walked away from us, trying to get a better signal.

'How far are we from Perth?' asked Hazel.

'Last I checked, something like fourteen hours,' said Mitchell. 'We really should have just taken a plane. Mum's description of the southern coast is absolute bullshit.'

'I can't stay here, under the god damn scorching sun,' said Hazel. 'How about we walk to the next servo and wait there? I doubt the pick-up "thingy" will get here anytime soon.'

'You want to walk for a kilometre?' asked Mitchell, surprised.

'I want an ice-cold tea and I want to sit in air conditioning.'

'It's not a bad idea,' said Teddy, coming back. 'They're on their way, but it'll probably be over an hour before they get here. You should definitely go and rest. I can stay with the car.'

'I'll stay too,' I said. 'Can't have you eaten by drop bears!'

He smiled at me. Mitchell looked at the straight long road ahead and looked at Hazel sheepishly.

'Are you sure?' he asked.

'Yes! When did you get so lazy?'

They both went on their way and left Teddy and I alone.

'Want a piss-warm beer?' Teddy asked, while opening the boot.

'Sure, why not,' I said, sitting on the bonnet. Teddy followed suit, handing me a bottle.

We both sat and looked at the nothingness ahead of us. If we weren't so screwed, it would have been almost romantic. Almost.

'Are we sitting up here because of snakes and tarantulas?' I asked, my eyes widening in fear.

'It's just a precaution,' he said with a giggle. 'Hey, thanks for being here. I know it hasn't been the love fantasy you'd envisioned probably...'

'I'm just happy to spend time with you. For once, neither of us is in a rush to go anywhere.'

I kissed him softly, holding the back of his neck with my hand.

'I'm a little scared of what is going to happen once we're done with this journey. You're going to have to go back to London, and I'll be alone again.'

'I haven't decided anything, Teddy. I'm here right now. That's all I want to focus on.'

'Living in the present? It isn't exactly my forte,' he said, looking down on the ground and sipping his beer. 'I really just wish you never had to go.'

I also didn't want to ever go. I never wanted to live in a reality without Teddy. Spending day after day together was an adventure I never wanted to see the end of. I wanted it all with him. Loving Teddy was easy, and it came naturally. My heart was safe with him. After everything I had been through, I never thought I'd get to trust someone again, blindly and fully. Now was the time.

'Hey, Teddy?' I asked, my voice a weak tremble. A sign of what was to come.

He turned to me, his feline eyes watching me with anticipation.

'What happened to me in Stockholm—'

'You don't have to tell me, Vincent. You know I'll wait forever for you,' he interrupted, as his hand gently touched mine.

'I want to. It's...such a huge part of me, of who I am. It sneaks into my thoughts daily, a smell or a sound or a hair colour takes me right back there, Teddy. It'll never go away.'

'You can tell me anything.'

'After you came back here...I was lost,' I said, touching each of my fingers to my thumb. My whole body revolted against my memories; even after all these years when I let myself think about it, it was as fresh as the night it happened. I was upset and just wanted to get out of the house. I was so foolish, Teddy. I got a stranger to buy me alcohol and we went to this beach. And it was nice, I thought he was nice. Until he pushed me down. I didn't have a choice, Teddy, I couldn't get away from him. He wouldn't let me go.'

'No...' he whispered, his kind eyes started glinting.

He knew already. His expression was full of pity and sorrow, but I knew I needed to say it out loud for it to be real, for both of us. I needed to get rid of this secret I'd carried under my skin and let weigh me down.

'I was sexually assaulted,' I said, the words flew out in a hurried breath, unwilling to linger between my lips. 'I blamed myself. I still blame myself. Every single step that brought me to that exact moment was freely mine. If only I had stayed home. If only I had been content with just walking and hadn't wanted a drink. If only I wasn't so weak. Just that one day... if only I had made better choices, then perhaps I'd be free.'

'Vincent...what the hell,' he said, full blown tears streaming down his perfectly shaped cheekbones. 'I could have prevented this. I should have been there for you. I should have—'

'Hey,' I cut him off, my hands holding his face, our eyes locked. 'This isn't your fault, and it isn't your trauma to wear. It took me... a little while to realise I couldn't get better on my own. To realise there was no "better" and it was just a different version of okay. It took me countless sleepless nights, endless hours spent talking in therapy and a handful of hard days where I wasn't sure my life was worth living. I wasn't sure I'd get to do it, or if I was just doomed to be a prisoner of my own trauma.' I took a deep breath, steadying my heart and focusing on what I needed him to know. 'But I got through it, Teddy. I may not ever be perfectly okay; I might have to leave a crowded space if I see someone who reminds me of him. I might still have nightmares. But I have dragged myself through to the other side of this and I am proud of that. I want a life with you and that means I have to share all of me, even those parts I wish I didn't have.'

My body was shaking with every single word as I felt my blood burn through my veins, the corners of my lips lifted, a hint at the smallest of smiles.

'The truth is, it wasn't my fault. I never asked for it. I never...even remotely wanted it. I was miserable, but all I wanted was to be heard, and understood. And before you say anything, Teddy...it wasn't your fault either.'

'But if only I was there.'

'We can't live in the "if only", Teddy, because any one of those may have taken me away from you. This way, no matter what, I know that I get to love you.'

'I love you,' he smiled, the soft smile that was just for me. 'And I'll always do my best to keep you safe.'

'I know.'

We lay on the car together, enjoying the quiet and stillness. It felt like nothing stood between us, all the things I never wanted him to see were out in the open and we were better for it. I pulled him into me, lightly kissed the part below his ear I knew he liked, and we waited for our quest to start again.

The pick-up lorry eventually arrived. We were dropped off at the petrol station that Mitchell and Hazel walked to. Surprisingly, there was a motel too, which is where we would stay for the night, as the repairs wouldn't be completed until early the next morning.

It was the dodgiest place we could ever find, and they only had one room available. Luckily for us, it had two queen beds. The feeling of luck faded quickly, replaced by the dreadful image of the four of us sharing one room.

Mitchell opened the door to the room, and we all looked at it slightly disgusted.

'Well...isn't this a delight?' Mitchell asked with sarcasm.

Hazel quickly ran inside into the bathroom. 'Move, move!'

She slammed the door and we heard her violently vomit.

'Well, that sums up how I feel about this motel,' said Teddy.

He wasn't wrong. The carpet was a bizarre dark red colour, with clouds of dust releasing into the air with each step we took. The TV was showing static, the rubbish bin hadn't been emptied and I was confident the sheets hadn't been washed.

Hazel exited the bathroom holding her stomach.

'It's very possible there was vomit in the toilet even before I vomited on top of it,' she said.

'Mate!' said Teddy.

'I wonder if we can easily get rid of the fleas once we sleep on these beds,' I said.

'I have something that could get us to forget about how shitty this room is and help us sleep,' said Mitchell waving a bag of weed.

'Oh, I miss weed...' said Hazel.

'I can't,' said Teddy. 'I'm the one driving tomorrow. But you guys can enjoy it,' he said pointing at me and Mitchell.

'Oh, I don't think—' I said.

'Come on, mate. Let's share a moment together,' he said, while putting his arm around me.

I wasn't too keen on smoking weed, but I thought I'd keep Mitchell company outside.

'Just don't make out, please,' said Hazel before diving into bed.

Mitchell sent an air kiss and walked with me outside. We sat together at the back of the motel, where there was nothing but the starry sky looking down on us. I finally found a positive to being in the middle of nowhere. The night sky was filled with stars; something I didn't get to see in London often. Mitchell lit up a joint and took a few puffs, blowing the smoke while looking up.

'I feel like a hypocrite for getting stoned, after leaving my ex for drug abuse,' I said.

'I don't know you that well, but you strike me as someone who doesn't really do this all that often,' he said with a smile. 'It's okay to let loose sometimes. As long as you don't let the search for pleasure take over your entire existence. I know I did at some point.'

I smiled and looked up at the stars again. 'Wow...'

'Maybe this is what my mum meant. Maybe this sky is what she was so fond of,' he said while passing me the joint.

'I think she just wanted you and your brother to share something together.'

'She probably broke the car herself, then.'

'You think she really wanted us to sleep with bed bugs?'

'I wouldn't put it past her. She may be punishing me for being so shitty.'

I turned my head and looked at him. 'Mitchell, I think it's fair to say you've already had your share of shit happen to you. No one expected you to act normal.'

'Teddy did. He stepped up.'

'Teddy is special.'

'Yeah, he is...' he said while leaning towards me to get another puff as I was still holding the joint. 'He is stubborn, though.'

I smiled at him.

'Can I ask you something?'

'Sure,' I said.

'Have you given it any thought? What being with Teddy might look like in the future?'

'We haven't discussed it fully, I guess. I know it might be difficult, with me being from the other side of—'

'It's not just that, Vincent,' he paused and looked around to see if there was anyone listening. 'There's something else you need to keep in mind.'

'What's that?' I asked, my heart racing in fear.

'Teddy and I could potentially carry the Huntington's gene. It's a 50/50 chance.'

I clasped my hand over my head. 'You guys—'

'...haven't been tested.'

'Why not?' I questioned.

'We're terrified. The both of us,' he said, trying to keep a brave face. 'We've both seen what the disease does. Teddy has seen way more than I have.'

I felt a sense of sadness, with my whole body aching at the idea they could both be doomed to their mother's fate.

'Why are you telling me this now?' I continued.

'Because once we reach Perth, we'll finally know the truth. I need to know whether or not you'll be by Teddy's side. Knowing what that could entail.'

'I—'

'You don't have to answer now. Just know I'll be there. Don't feel like you're forced to do anything,' he said, getting up. 'Think about what you're getting yourself into, Vincent.'

I looked at him speechless.

'Oh, and please don't tell him we had this conversation.'

He walked away, while I stayed there, sat still for another few minutes. I had a lot to think about that night. Much more than I'd bargained for when I said yes to smoking with Mitchell.

The night eventually passed, and we got to jump into our trusty jeep once again. The road ahead started showing signs of life, but we took a detour to absorb more of the Australian nature. We reached *Esperance*, where we saw kangaroos jump around the beach, passed *Cape Le Grand National Park* and watched some of the most incredible sunsets. We spent a night at *Lucky Bay*, slept in tents and ate marshmallows around a fire.

I noticed that the closer we got to Perth, the longer the streaks of silence would become. I wasn't sure if Mitchell had forgotten what he had told me, but it was sculpted into my brain and impossible to ignore. I held Teddy's hand tightly. I wished I could do more for him, I wished I could tell him I'd always be by his side. I waited and waited for him to share his fears with me but, like a stoic hero, he kept it all to himself.

That was until our very last dinner before reaching Perth.

We decided to have alcohol and dinner inside Hazel and Mitchell's room. We bought all the junk food we could possibly get and the cheapest boxed wine. We moved the two queen beds together and sat in circle, already reminiscing about the beginning of our trip and how far we had come. Every smile felt slightly bittersweet, as I was certain nothing would be the same the morning after.

'We did it,' said Hazel. 'I never thought we would drive for over fifty hours without killing each other. I'm so proud, you guys.'

She cheers'd with a glass of orange juice, while us guys got to enjoy the vinegar-tasting purple liquid.

'I thought we had established you could enjoy a glass every once in a while,' said Teddy.

'Yeah, wine. Whatever you guys are drinking looks like it's going to set my foetus on fire!'

'I have enjoyed every moment,' said Mitchell with a smile. 'Speaking and connecting with people with *HD*, getting stranded in the middle of the road, sleeping in the tiniest tent with my feet coming out of it...it's all been great fun.'

'Tomorrow will be a very long day,' said Teddy. 'We can finally scatter our poor mum's ashes. She's been cooking in our glove compartment for so many days, bless her.'

'At least we have some time to chill,' said Hazel. 'I think we should do *Crawley* at sunset. No clouds forecasted as well. It's going to be beautiful.'

'So,' said Mitchell. 'Teddy and I have a few interviews to go through in the morning; we'll be busy for a few hours.'

'You don't want us to come with you?' asked Hazel.

Mitchell looked at Teddy, waiting for him to say something.

'They've only allowed two of us. It's a few very bad cases. Mitchell can handle the camera, while I'm more versed in handling someone at the final stages of Huntington's. It's not something you two really want to see.'

'Well, I don't mind just having brunch with Vincent for a few hours, right?' she said. 'Vincent?'

I was lost in thought when Mitchell tapped my shoulder.

'Right, mate?'

'Yeah,' I said. 'I love brunch.'

'It's decided then,' said Mitchell. 'We should probably get some sleep now.'

'Okay,' said Teddy. 'We'll leave you to it. Come on, Vincent,' he tended his hand to me.

We walked together and entered our room. I couldn't say anything about what Mitchell and I discussed a few nights before, but I really wanted Teddy to know I was there for him. I stood by the door, while he took his jacket off. My palms were sweating, and my legs couldn't move. My mouth became arid.

'Teddy?'

'Yes?' he turned to me and walked towards me. 'What is it?'

I looked into his gorgeous green eyes. They were trying to hide sorrow and pain, and my heart ached with him.

'I love you,' I said.

He smiled and his eyes filled with glee.

He put his hands on my shoulder and leaned to kiss me, with his eyes closed.

'I love you too, my Vincent.'

CHAPTER TWENTY-EIGHT

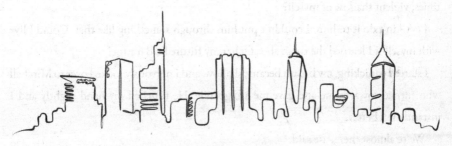

TEDDY

2020

I couldn't sleep much that night. I tossed, I turned, I got up, I drank some water, and tried again. My conscious eyes kept staring at the ceiling of our hotel room, while Vincent was sleeping peacefully, naked next to me. I caressed his back with my fingers and traced a heart. I smiled watching him unfazed by my touch.

I tried to fall asleep once more, but it was evident it wasn't going to happen for me. I got up, walked to the bathroom and washed my face with cold water. I looked at myself in the mirror, brushed my teeth and tried to get my hair to follow a set direction. I quickly got dressed, put my shoes on and left the room as quietly as I could.

As I was closing the door, I noticed Mitchell was sitting outside the door of his room.

'Big brother can't sleep either?'

'Hey, what are you doing up?' he asked.

'It's a loaded day. Hard to sleep through it.'

'Shall we—'

'Yeah. Let's get it over and done with,' I said, with my eyes staring into space.

I followed Mitchell into the car and let him drive us. I didn't have the strength or the focus to do it myself. I was watching the city through my window, still asleep, still wrapped in silence. We didn't speak during our drive; we didn't have any music on. We were both

317

thinking about our own lives, how they may be affected. I started thinking about Vincent, who'd told me he loved me. Would he still love me? Fully? Would he love me if I turned into a glorified puppet? Would he still love me if I turned into a forgetful, angry, and at times, violent shadow of myself?

I couldn't do it to him. I couldn't put him through something like that. Could I live with myself if I learned the truth about what my future held for me?

I started panicking, my breath became shallow, and I nervously looked over to Mitchell who turned towards me and gave me a big smile. He touched my hand slightly and I instantly felt better.

'We're almost there,' he said.

I nodded and looked ahead. The clinic was ominously staring back at me, ready to throw my hopes and dreams into the garbage.

Mitchell parked the jeep and turned the engine off.

'We've arrived,' he said.

'Yep.'

'Today is just the first step. We won't have a result for weeks.'

'I know.'

We both got out of the car and entered the hospital. It looked pretty fancy, considering we were in Perth. It didn't smell so much like a hospital, and it was extremely quiet. We made our way through the various corridors, until we found the area where we would get tested. We let reception know we had arrived and sat in the waiting room.

I started tapping my foot on the floor to calm my nerves. Mitchell seemed a lot more at ease, but he was probably pretending to be calm so I wouldn't freak the fuck out.

'Mitchell Clarke?' a female doctor called from one of the rooms.

Mitchell stood up and I grabbed his hand.

'What?' he asked.

'Whatever happens, just know that I'll always be there for you,' I said.

He smiled at me and walked into the room with the doctor. I remained waiting, flicking through a magazine, when a guy sat next to me.

'Hi there,' he said.

I turned to him, unsure of whether he was talking to me, but I quickly realised there wasn't anyone else.

'Hi?'

'I'm sorry, I just hate being here and talking to people distracts me,' he said.

It was a guy in his thirties, with a bright smile and a friendly voice. We were wearing a very similar casual outfit, although he looked like he had actually had some rest.

'I'm Alex,' he said while tending his hand for me to shake.

'Teddy,' I said. 'Are you here to get tested as well?'

'I've already got my answer, I'm afraid.'

'Oh. I'm really sorry.'

'It took me a while, but I eventually realised I'd accomplished so much in life, already. You know? The happiest memories? I've already had them.'

'That's a nice way to see things.'

'I have to. I have to keep positive.'

'My mum was like that, at first.'

'Oh, so you're here for—'

'My brother and I may carry the gene. My mother recently passed, and he is about to have a baby, so we thought it was time.'

'I haven't met many people who've dealt with the disease.'

'It's a pretty rare one to come by. We...are actually trying to shoot a documentary on it. To raise awareness and all,' I said.

'That's great!'

'So, you're here...?'

'My child is getting tested. We figured we would rather know in advance.'

'How old are they?'

'Eight and a half; we'll keep the result sealed in an envelope for him to open it, if he ever wants to.'

'He may never do that,' I said, putting my hands together and looking at the floor.

'That's kind of what we're hoping for, but ultimately, it'll be his choice.'

I hesitated for a second and cleared my throat. 'Hey, can I ask you a question?'

'Sure.'

'Do you regret...knowing?'

'Well,' he smiled. 'Sometimes I do. I try to absorb every single memory I make now. And I'm aware my clock is ticking. I don't know. Maybe not knowing would allow me to live more freely.'

'I see.'

'You don't seem too sure. Would *you* like to know?'

'I...I found someone...'

'Okay...?'

'I think it would be unfair to start something that will end up in tragedy.'

'Look, I had some of my best memories in the last eight years. Best of my life. My wedding, the birth of my child...and we didn't know. We didn't know I had this disease. They are completely untainted memories.'

'So, you don't think it's selfish for me to—'

'It's your life, Teddy. You can live without the worry of it all ending soon, or you can be prepared. Have you lived enough to say you have already had your best memories?'

I hadn't. I had some of my worst memories behind me. I had just found Vincent again. I didn't know what to do.

Mitchell exited the room and walked towards me.

'Teddy Clarke?'

Mitchell looked at me and looked at the doctor. I shook my head at him. He nodded to let me know he understood.

'Best of luck, Alex. Thanks for the chat,' I said.

'Have a great life, Teddy,' he said, giving me the thumbs up.

I put my arm around Mitchell and left the hospital.

I wasn't ready to know, but I was ready to finally have my best memories.

It was a tiring early morning. I managed to sneak back into bed without Vincent knowing and finally fell asleep in his arms. Maybe I was a little too comfortable as we missed our check-out. We took much of the day to just stay in bed together, cuddling, joking around, some sex here and there...it was great.

We drove to the *Swan River* and found *Crawley Boatshed*. I was pleasantly surprised to see no one else there. We decided to have a picnic and a few drinks. Hazel bought a bunch of candles to make everything a lot prettier once the sun would set.

We parked the car and got out. The location was the perfect backdrop to any photo. The sky was coloured with streaks of pink, orange and purple, with the water perfectly mirroring it.

'Wow...' said Hazel.

'Holy fucking shit!' Mitchell shouted.

'Always classy, Mitch,' said Vincent.

Mitchell burped on his face.

'Great, thanks,' he said.

'That's what you get.'

I didn't have much to say. The place looked truly special. The peace, the colours and the scent of wildflowers around us made the entire landscape look like it came out of the pages of a fantasy book.

'Now, do we think it was really about this destination, or did mum trick us into driving for fifty hours to appreciate the journey?' asked Mitchell.

'I hate to be the one to remind you about the punching incident nearly two weeks ago,' said Hazel.

'Have we aged since?' asked Vincent.

'I certainly did. My demon is sucking my youth,' said Hazel.

'Alright,' I said. 'Shall we arrange our setup?'

Vincent smiled at me and started grabbing our supplies from the boot.

I took a deep breath and, for a second, I could swear I could feel my mother's touch on my shoulder.

We put a blanket down on the wooden bridge leading to the boathouse and poured champagne and strawberries into our flutes. Mum's favourite drink. Her urn was next to me, with the sky colours reflecting onto it. We were sitting at each corner of the blanket. I had my legs hanging over the bridge. Only the sound of the seagulls could be heard.

'Shall we say something?' Vincent asked.

'Like what?' said Mitchell.

'I don't know...a few stories? I'm sure you have a few.'

I looked at Mitchell to see who would speak first.

'I can go first,' said Hazel.

I looked at her and smiled with curiosity. I had no idea what kind of story she'd pull out.

'So...many moons ago, I was in Tasmania for my uni degree. I didn't know anyone except Vincent's little internet lover. We became really good friends, and the rest is history.'

'I already know this story. What does this have to do with my mum?' I asked.

'Jesus, calm down, boy. That same year I got to meet your glorious mother. I'd see her quite often coming and going out of my university, as she liked using the library there, and one time I saw her in the cafeteria eating a muffin by herself. I came by to say hi, and she told me 'you—little shit—' she said pointing at me. 'You had gone to Sydney to meet Laura.'

'Oh yeah, I remember that week,' I said.

'What you forgot, my dear, was Mother's Day.'

'Shit. I did forget.'

'I know. And...you know, it was a day where I was missing my own mum, so I was kind of like...why don't we go for a real drink?'

'Oh my god, where did you take my mother?' asked Mitchell.

'We had fun!' she said with a cheeky smile. 'You know the *Dirty Men Strip Club* in Hobart?'

'Stop,' I said.

'Oh yeah. It was so, so, so fun. We had so much to drink, so many naked men to watch, it was incredible!'

Vincent was laughing his head off. Mitchell and I were horrified.

'I cannot believe you took Veronica Clarke to a strip club. I can't even imagine it,' I exclaimed.

'It was really good and, funnily enough, she asked me a lot of questions about Vincent.'

'Me?'

'What?' I asked.

'She wanted to know who this mysterious English guy you kept talking about was. I showed her photos, told her stories...'

'What kind of photos?' asked Vincent, stroking the back of his neck and broadening his eyes in fear.

'Oh, would you just relax. She only heard the best things,' she turned to Vincent and held his chin. 'And just so you know, she would be very happy to know you're here with Teddy.'

I smiled at her and then looked at Vincent. She would indeed have been very happy to meet him. We cheered altogether and drank more champagne.

'Man, this sparkling apple bullshit drink really isn't the same thing,' Hazel muttered.

The orange sun started getting really close to the horizon, its light blinding us. I kept looking at Vincent and thinking how handsome he looked. I held his hand and kissed it, like some creepy Italian uncle.

'Sorry, was that weird?' I asked, almost immediately.

'No, not at all,' he giggled.

'Alright, alright. I feel like it's my turn. Before you two use this as an excuse to start foreplay,' said Mitchell.

'Jesus, mate. We are about to scatter our mother here. It's not exactly turn-on material!' I said.

'Sure, sure. Right! My story actually takes place years and years ago, when I was a young little wannabe actor auditioning for *Home and Away*...'

'You're joking...' said Vincent.

'Not at all! She drove me to the audition and there was a queue. A lot of people wanted to be Jarrod, the gnarly surfer.'

'Did you get into the fight with the other *bogans* in the queue, Mitchell?' I asked.

'That's exactly what happened! Except it wasn't me, love. It was your insane mother!'

'What?' I chuckled.

'Yeah, some woman named Chardonnay got her blonde weave pulled by Ms Clarke herself.'

'Why?!' I asked.

'She said I was ugly, and I needed to go home. It scarred me, you know.'

'Have you looked at yourself at seventeen? Your face looked like a pizza!' I said.

'I may or may not have had a brief affair with steroids during that time,' he whispered to Hazel.

'So you had a bunch of muscles and a face full of acne?' she asked.

'And my back, ugh. It was awful. But once it cleared, I became a model, so fuck Chardonnay and fuck you all for not siding with me.'

'We're all teasing. You're the best looking amongst us all,' said Vincent.

'Thank you, mate.'

I looked at Vincent and winced. 'Oh no.'

'You're the only one left, Teddy. Do you have a mum story to share?' asked Hazel.

I hesitated for a second and got a little emotional.

'You know...I can't remember her much, from before...my mind is riddled with memories of her being sick, of her falling, of her being unable to bathe herself. It's hard to get past those.'

'I know,' said Hazel. 'But I'm sure you can remember something else.'

'I remember when she took me to the airport, so I could start my exchange year in Italy. I hadn't travelled much before then, let alone by myself. She cried the whole way there. She told me that seeing the other side of the world would turn me into a better person and that she was so proud of me for being so brave,' I said smiling. 'She was truly a sobbing mess, and I was in such a rush to go as I was so excited. She gave me a big kiss on the cheek and told me she would miss taking care of her little baby.'

The sky turned a slightly darker shade of purple, and Hazel lit up a few candles.

'Is it time?' asked Mitchell.

'One second,' said Vincent.

He opened his bag and took out a few paper boats. 'I wanted to light up some lanterns and make them float into the sky, but I didn't think it would have been such a great idea. You know, bushfires and all.'

'So, what are those?' I asked.

'Well, these are biodegradable. You put a little candle on them and put them on water,' he said while giving one to each of us. 'Just a way to say goodbye.'

'That's really nice, Vincent,' said Mitchell. He grabbed one of the boats and lit it up. He placed it into water and watched it leave.

'Goodbye mum,' he said.

I opened the urn for him and he grabbed a handful of ashes. He sprinkled them onto the water, on his side of the pier. 'I hope you're well. Wherever you are.'

'Hazel?' I asked.

She did the same thing as Mitchell, except she blew the ashes away into the wind. 'Goodbye Veronica. You'll always be in my heart,' she said, with tears streaming down her face. 'I wish this baby got to meet you.'

'Teddy?' Vincent asked.

I put my boat onto the water and watched it sail in silence. I grabbed the last of the ashes and poured it over my side of the pier.

'I don't think I have much to say at this point...I'm just happy you're not suffering anymore. Goodbye mum...'

Vincent put his arm around me to comfort me and I sobbed for a bit. I looked over to my brother's side and realised I was lucky to have him in my life once again.

We remained in silence; watching the little boats burn and watching the sunset turn into night sky.

'I'm a little bit cold, do you guys want to head back?' asked Hazel.

I looked at Vincent and then back at Hazel and Mitchell. 'You guys go ahead, Vincent and I will get a cab to the hotel.'

'Alright, we'll see you guys later,' said Mitchell, grabbing his bag and heading back to the car with Hazel.

'More champagne?' I asked while pouring a glass for Vincent.

'Sure, what the heck,' he obliged.

'We need to talk, Vincent.'

'Sounds serious.'

'These last few weeks with you...have been some of the best in my entire life. I want to be with you all the time,' I said, holding his hand.

'I feel the same.'

'I was supposed to take a test today, to see if I have the gene for Huntington's...I couldn't go through with it.'

Vincent pressed his lips together; he didn't seem hugely surprised.

'I have lived the last ten years worrying about when my mother would lose her memories, her motor skills, or her life altogether. I don't want to live my life thinking the same things for myself. I'd like to live in the present for once, and I'd like to do so with you.

However, it's a hugely selfish thought. Your feelings matter and you shouldn't have to deal with it. So, I'm giving you an out.'

'What do you mean?'

'You can walk away now and go on with your life. Find someone who doesn't live so far away, someone without such a stupid accent or just someone who's better and that can make you truly happy.'

My heart was racing, and my breathing became shallow. I was more than ready to say goodbye to Vincent. Forever.

But he smiled.

'We have been through so much in the last...what? Twelve years? Teddy, I loved you then...and I love you now. There are no "outs". I want you and I want to have a life with you. Whatever the length or the difficulty of it.'

'You have no idea what that would be like, Vincent. You should really think—'

Vincent kneeled on both his legs and held my hand.

'What are you doing?' I asked.

'I'm making a promise to you. We'll live our lives to the fullest and make the best memories together. We'll do it all, Teddy.'

'You came to save me, my Romeo,' I said with a smile.

'I love you.'

We kissed passionately under the early stars of the evening and the candlelight gleamed in our eyes. Our lives had taken us to all sorts of dark places, split us apart, and eventually lead us to this perfect little moment.

Was it all worth it? Was the journey of it all worth the final prize of living my life together with the man I loved? The man I had always loved?

'Yes!' I said out loud.

'I haven't even asked anything yet,' he said with a smile.

'Whatever the question, whatever the case, just know my answer will always be yes for you.'

'Pinkie?' he asked.

I laughed, wrapped my finger around his and as I kissed my love once again, my life felt complete.

However long it may be.

ACKNOWLEDGEMENTS

This novel has been through a lot. What was once briefly titled *The Loving Kind*, featuring a much darker tone, has now turned into a special little story I'm truly proud of. But I didn't do this alone.

First and foremost, I'd like to thank my mum. Not just because she's the most supportive parent in the world, but also for exposing me to her work. The word carer doesn't really encompass all the ways she goes above and beyond to help the elderly, people with terminal diseases, and their families. It was through her work I got to hear about Huntington's and the way it operates. The way it destroys loved ones, before it even affects the patient. It's heart-breaking and not talked about enough.

I'd like to thank my group of friends, who always lend an ear to my story ideas and are always happy to listen to me rambling about them. Sara, Hannah, Bradley, Nic, Patrick, George, Jessica, Callum, Rob and Ash, your friendship means the world to me.

A huge shoutout to Lorrel and Joel, who have inspired the characters of Hazel and Daniel in *Out Of Touch*. Being together abroad at seventeen was one of the most incredible experiences of my life. I'll never forget all the memories we made as we navigated a new country, a new language and, really, a whole new life.

Laura and Martina, you're my oldest and most loyal friends. You read this story at its infancy and gave me tremendous feedback. You'll always get first dibs on my novels. Even those horrific first drafts.

A special thank you to the wonderful Alexis Hall, for not only writing incredible stories that are constantly changing the queer book industry for the better, but for also assuming the role of mentor. Your advice is so very precious, and I truly treasure all the times we get to catch up.

To Courtney, thanks for believing in this book and advocating for it so passionately.

Jack, you have adored this book since the very beginning and your love for it warms my heart. We've been through a whole lot, but we'll always be family.

Simone, thank you for your continued support and friendship. You're one of my biggest advocates and I couldn't be more grateful to have you in my life.

Thank you, Eric, for getting emotional while reading about these silly kids and their love for one another. And thank you for believing in me with all your might.

I wouldn't be here if it wasn't for the amazing book community I get to interact with. Charlie, Jacob, Shalev, Jordan, Jack, Dusty, Rosie, Brad, and many more, thank you for always taking a chance on me as an author. Even after traumatising you all with *All Of My Friends Are Rich* and all of Leo's shenanigans.

Amy Jane Lehan. I don't know what I'd do without you. You've been everything and more. There isn't a single aspect of our friendship I don't love. The chats, the times we brainstorm a new project, the terrible movies we watch. Not to mention all the ways you make my stories better in so many ways and how you always make time to listen to me. The biggest thank you goes to you. *tap tap*